THE LAST GUEST

Sue Gee was born in 1947 a............... early childhood
on a farm in Devon and in a Leicestershire village. She
was educated in Surrey and London and worked in book
and magazine publishing before going freelance as a
writer and editor in 1983. This is her third novel. She is
at work on a fourth, and lives with her family in London.

BY THE SAME AUTHOR

Keeping Secrets
Spring Will Be Ours

THE LAST GUESTS
OF THE SEASON

Sue Gee

ARROW

First published 1993

1 3 5 7 9 10 8 6 4 2

Copyright © Sue Gee 1993

Sue Gee has asserted her
right under the Copyright, Designs and Patents Act, 1988
to be identified as the author of this work

First published in Great Britain in 1993 by Century

Arrow edition 1993
Random House, 20 Vauxhall Bridge Road, London SW1V 2SA

Random House Australia (Pty) Limited
20 Alfred Street, Milsons Point, Sydney,
New South Wales 2061, Australia

Random House New Zealand Limited
18 Poland Road, Glenfield
Auckland 10, New Zealand

Random House South Africa (Pty) Limited
PO Box 337, Bergvlei, South Africa

Random House UK Limited Reg. No. 954009

A CIP catalogue record for this book
is available from the British Library

ISBN 0 09 925641 X

Printed and bound in Great Britain by
Cox & Wyman Ltd, Reading, Berkshire

1

In the afternoon heat the peeling blue shutters in the bedroom at
the back of the house had been swung to, their backs the colour of
dark honey, unvarnished, smooth. The metal bar hung down: the
shutters were not quite closed and sunlight came through the
chinks at the hinges and at the gap in the middle, falling upon
wooden floor and worn blue armchair, on the cotton dressing-
gown slipping off the arm and canvas shoes kicked off on to the
floorboards. A fly, which had found its way through the gap, was
trying now to find its way out again; it buzzed from lampshade to
shutter to the shadowy mirror on the wardrobe door.

Outside, a haze hung over the valley, the dark shapes of the
pines on the mountainside softened and indistinct, grey-green
clumps of eucalyptus dissolving into blue, the winding river pale as
the bleached sky. Above the clusters of terracotta rooftops the air
shimmered; above the village the church bell chimed twice, but
this indicated simply the passing of an hour, not a specific hour: it
sometimes chimed twice at midnight, three or four times at noon.

Below, the village slumbered, and here, in their double bed
pushed up against the wall, Frances and Oliver Swift, who had
risen in London just after daybreak, slept also, lying separately
against their pillows, dreaming: she small, pale, exhausted; he a
big man, dark, turned away from her, facing the bedside table, a
neat pile of books, a pair of glasses. Frances and Oliver, dreaming
deeply, and quite differently, did not hear the chime of the church
clock on the hillside, nor the buzz of the fly, nor the sound of a
door opening along the corridor. They did not hear the bare feet of
their son on the rag runner, nor the hiss of a steam iron on the
landing, where Guida, the little maid, stood in her flip-flops and
denim skirt, pressing good white sheets with drawn-thread hems.

It was warm on the landing, where the window opened on to a
peach tree. Dappled squares of brilliant sun fell from the window
on to the carpet, a faded green. Guida rested the steam iron for a

moment and pushed back her hair; she turned the long white train of sheet and heard footsteps behind her. The eyes of the English boy, a big boy, one of the new arrivals, regarded her blankly. She smiled at him, lifting the iron again.

'*Bo tar*'.'

He frowned, then smiled back, but did not speak; he moved past the ironing-board, bare feet crossing the brilliant squares of sun, and went down the slippery wooden stairs. There was a turning, treads broadening to accommodate it, a place to sit. He sat. Below him, on a half-landing, was another window, where the curtains were drawn, so that this warm quiet place on the stairs felt enclosed and set apart from the rest of the house, which felt enormous. Tom was used to a flat.

Here, there were three bedrooms opening off the passage from the landing, with its rag runner which slipped and buckled up on the boards every time you walked along. His parents were in the room at the far end, with the wonderful view, and he and Jack, from the other family, were on the left, in twin iron beds painted white, with blue and white covers.

Jack was eight, a year older than him, and seemed okay. Tom hadn't wanted to have a rest after lunch, but Jack didn't seem to mind, so he'd followed him up the stairs, expecting a pillow fight, or some kind of game, anyway, but Jack had climbed on to his bed, reached for a book and begun to read, just like that. Tom shifted about, sighing, scratching his arm, moving his feet on the cover, messing it up. After a while he took his own book from the chair beside the bed, *The Ship of Adventure*. Enid Blyton was wicked: they'd done *The Castle of Adventure* on Children's BBC last term, it was brilliant. He turned the pages, getting stuck in, smacking and pursing his lips.

'Stop it,' said Jack.

'What?'

'That noise.'

'What noise?'

'You're making a noise. With your mouth.'

'Oh.' He stretched his lips taut and yawned. 'D'you want to have a pillow fight?'

'I'm reading.'

2

'I mean after. When you've finished.'

'Perhaps.'

'Okay. Great.' Tom yawned again; he picked up his book and found his place. It was quite nice, really, reading up here with Jack. The pages rustled, the room was warm and the bed was okay, a bit hard. He yawned again, and the book felt very heavy. He closed his eyes.

Jack was still asleep when he woke up, so he'd left him. He'd gone along to his parents' door, remembering to knock, but there was no answer; he pushed it cautiously and looked inside. They were sleeping, too, dead asleep, he could tell. For a moment, in the quiet warmth of the room, he thought he might like to slip in beside them and just lie there, not disturb them or anything, just be there. But then he thought he might, by mistake, wake them up, and he carefully closed the door again and came along here; now he'd found this place.

He shifted his bottom in cotton shorts along the pleasing smooth surface of the wooden tread and listened, half listened, to the hiss and puff of the iron from the landing above him, and the buzz of a fly below, trapped between the half-landing window and the drawn curtains, patterned in orange and black. Guida's flip-flops moved intermittently along the carpet; the folded sheet was placed on a table by the wall, another taken from the basket beside her; there was a cloud of steam. It was lovely and peaceful: he shut his eyes, and as he did so he had the funny sort of feeling in his head which he'd had before – as if something inside it had moved, or as if, for a moment, he had gone somewhere else. Where?

He opened his eyes. He was still here. There was a dry dead fly on the stair: he flicked it with his finger and sat there making funny noises, absently. He thought he might go down in a bit and see if Jessica, Jack's sister, was awake: she was twelve, so she had the bedroom downstairs, off the big sitting-room, away from the grown-ups. Luck-y. She seemed all right, too, quite friendly, really. He hoped they weren't all going to go to sleep every afternoon like this.

Tom got up and made his way downstairs. At the bottom, a passage led off to the left to a bathroom; he went and had a pee, with the usual shiver at the end. The bathroom was cool and

3

shady, with a lot of green creeper at the window, and it smelt a bit. He pressed the handle, which was stiff, so he pressed it again, several times, getting impatient, until at last some water came, though not as much as at home. He wandered out, making clicking noises.

At the end of the passage he was about to turn down towards Jessica's room and the enormous sitting-room when he heard a sound, and stopped. It sounded like a cat, a rusty kind of cat: it was coming from the kitchen. He went in, and his bare feet stuck to the patches of old brown lino. It was dark in here, and felt like an olden-days kitchen, with a funny little gas stove and more of the creeper at the windows. He stood and listened, and the noise came again: it *was* a cat, outside the door, sounding weak. He hurried across, and tugged at the handle: this could be serious.

Sunlight poured through the cracks in the shutters in the other bedroom, too, the one across the landing, where Jack and Jessica's parents were waking up. Claire first, languorous and warm, stirring on the white cotton bedspread, stretching a long arm already browned from yesterday afternoon on the terrace and this morning by the river, flexing strong blunt fingers with pale unvarnished nails. Claire tanned easily: she was dark, with abundant hair and a skin which soaked up sun until by the end of the holiday she would be ripened to a sheen, the envy of the staffroom. She was wearing a sleeveless, soft white shirt with little, fabric-covered buttons, and a black and white unironed skirt, long and full, which no longer did up at the back; she lay with her head on her husband's chest and yawned like a sleepy cat, opening her eyes on to the golden strips of light at the far window, which overlooked the valley, and the one in the right-hand wall, which opened on to a little stone balcony above the terrace.

She had not finished unpacking and the room was strewn with clothes – clean ones, waiting for drawers, and grimy ones from the long drive across Spain, waiting for Guida. There were also jumbles of sandals and magazines, films and paperbacks and necklaces – on the floor, on the chest of drawers, on the little cane chair by the cupboard. After twenty-four hours the room looked, in truth, much as their bedroom at home looked – indeed, like

4

many of the rooms at home, for Claire, although a capable person, had never in her life been tidy and had no ambition to be. There were moments in the mornings during termtime when she cursed herself, searching frantically for socks, keys and something to write with, but by and large she preferred muddle. It was friendlier.

She yawned again, and rolled away from Robert, hearing, from down on the terrace, the quiet creak of the swing-seat. Somebody must be up, then. She herself had no desire at all to get up, although tea would be nice: she had spent the morning with the children while Robert drove dutifully out to the airport to collect the Swifts; she had prepared lunch and made them welcome and served it, and that felt like quite enough. And there was supper to come – hardly fair to expect them to cook on their first night. After this, they must come to some arrangement.

They didn't know the Swifts well, although Claire, at university, had once thought she knew Frances – Frances Horne, as she was then – as well as anyone. That was in Bristol, in the early seventies. They were both reading English, and in the first year they both lived in the same hall of residence, at opposite ends of the same corridor. They went to the same lectures but were in different seminar groups, and they went their separate ways for all other aspects of university life also, bumping into each other from time to time in the hall kitchen, making cups of coffee.

But where Claire would linger for conversation, with Frances, or with whoever else happened to be around, Frances never lingered. She was slender and neat, with fair hair cut in a bob; she wore jeans and T-shirts from Biba in muted blues and greys, and she had, it seemed, no time for conversation, although she smiled politely. She made her coffee and toast and carried it away down the long corridor to her room, her gym shoes light on the new flooring, and shut her door. Claire gathered, through passing remarks from people in the same group as Frances, that she was clever, and had once given a paper on Metaphysical conceits which their tutor, whom everyone fancied, had praised effusively; afterwards, someone had heard her throwing up in the loo. Claire, whose own essays and seminar papers tended to be written at the last minute, wondered briefly at such intensity, and on the whole gave her barely a thought.

5

At the end of the first year they all moved out into flats or bedsits.

On a rainy Sunday morning in November, Claire walked along the road in Bishopston to get the paper, wearing her purple Laura Ashley cloak with the hood up, and bumped into Frances in the newsagents. She was wearing a black gaberdine mac, and carried a black umbrella. Walking back up the hill they discovered they were living quite close to each other, and on impulse Claire, whose flatmates were away for the weekend, invited Frances for coffee, wondering almost immediately if she would regret it.

Claire's flat was on the second floor of a double-fronted Victorian house with a neglected garden. The kitchen was at the back. Frances sat at the table by the window, resting her elbows on a green-checked cloth covered in toast crumbs, and while Claire made coffee looked out at the rain, falling on rooftops and gardens, drifting, in sudden gusts, away towards the hills. She did not chat, as Claire's flatmates did, but neither, after the first few minutes, did she seem her usual stiff and awkward self: away from the vastness of lecture hall or canteen, or the crowded little kitchen in their old place of residence, she visibly relaxed, until she seemed at ease, as if she'd been here before, turning away from the window and taking the mug she was given – which in her thin white hands looked, Claire realised, not completely clean – and asking Claire about her course, her background, her plans. Claire had made no plans, she was too busy enjoying herself, but she felt flattered to be asked. Indeed, she found she could not remember anyone for a long time who had taken such an interest in her. Not in quite this way, drawing her out, attentive.

'You're a very good listener,' she said, getting up to answer the phone on the landing. 'That'll be home, they always ring on Sundays.' She sat leaning up against the wall and let her mother, on the cheap rate from Derbyshire, describe a contented week of WI meetings, parish council disagreements and supper with friends. Her father, an auctioneer, had taken the dogs out and sent his love, her brother had gone to the pub. Claire could almost smell the lunch they were all about to have; she said goodbye with

6

affection and returned to the kitchen feeling hungry. Frances was looking out of the window again.

'Would you like to stay for lunch?' Claire asked.

Frances turned to look at her, and smiled. 'Why not?' she said, as if she had known her for years. And over spaghetti with onions and tinned tomatoes, which was all there seemed to be, she described, in answer to Claire's polite return of questions, the house a few streets away where she had taken a room, and revealed something of her own background, eating little, while Claire had second helpings.

'I am the only child of elderly parents,' she said. 'They are dear, but it is a fate I should wish on no one. I grew up in a tidy little house in the suburbs of Middlesex, full of Dralon and air-freshener, and went to the local grammar school. I had a friend there called Rowan, who over the years prevented me from going crazy: she is now reading History at York, and I miss her. I find people a strain, in fact I am incapable of relating to more than one person at a time. I am still a virgin. Sometimes I feel my life is completely hopeless, but I am not without ambition and intend to let my work be my salvation.'

Claire laughed.

'Don't laugh,' said Frances gravely. 'I am clinging to the wreckage.'

The rain fell away; they had flapjacks and more coffee.

'Let's go to a movie,' said Claire.

They walked through the damp Sunday streets to the Scala, which was showing *The Garden of the Finzi-Continis*. A son lay dying; his father raised his hand and waved two fingers, almost imperceptibly, in farewell. Claire turned to look at Frances and saw tears in her eyes; by the end, they were both in tears, as the family of Jews was taken away, losing their garden for ever.

When they came out it was cold and almost dark, and beginning to drizzle. They put up their umbrellas and walked home in silence.

At Claire's house the second-floor windows were lit, the curtains undrawn. People had come home from the weekend, and she could see her friend Jo, ironing in the sitting-room, watching television.

7

'Well,' she said to Frances, 'that was great. D'you want to come up?'

Frances shook her head. 'No thanks.'

'We must do it again some time.'

'Yes. That would be very nice.'

'Your papers,' said Claire. 'They're still in the kitchen – don't you want to come and get them?'

'It's all right.' Frances looked suddenly as she usually looked, tense and shy, and Claire thought: she doesn't want to have to come up and be jolly. So she said, 'No, that's silly, hang on, I'll run up and get them.'

When she came down again, Frances was standing by the gate where she had left her, but turned away, and beneath the black umbrella her face looked drawn.

Claire handed her the *Observer*. 'Well,' she said kindly, 'see you soon.'

Frances tucked the paper under her arm. 'Yes,' she said stiffly, 'see you soon. Thanks for a lovely day.' In her gaberdine mac and good flat shoes she walked away down the wet street, and Claire, hearing the telephone, turned and ran up the path to the house.

In the weeks that followed she did not see much of Frances; indeed, for a time she seemed almost to have disappeared; other people pressed enjoyably upon Claire's days and she forgot all about her. But late one cloudy afternoon towards the end of term she came across her in the library. Frances wore a thick navy sweater and was wrapped in knitted scarves; bending over her books, she looked paler than usual, in a translucent, convalescent way. Claire touched her shoulder and she jumped. Claire smiled.

'It's only me. Where've you been?'

'I've had flu,' said Frances.

'Oh, dear, I'm sorry. Who looked after you?'

'Mr Beecham.' Frances put down her pen. 'How are you?'

'I'm fine, thanks. Do you want to come for tea in a bit?'

'That would be nice.'

Over in the refectory, they sat opposite each other beside the Gothic windows. The place was half empty, afternoon lectures over, those coming in for the evening not yet arrived. Across in Park Row, lights flicked on in the pub; people were getting up and wandering over. Claire said: 'Perhaps we should be going for a drink – you look as though you could do with a brandy or something.'

Frances shook her head. 'I don't really drink much, thanks.'

'That's a pity, I was going to ask you to our party. Last Saturday of term, if you can make it. Or would you find it unbearable?'

'Probably,' said Frances, 'but it's nice of you to ask me. What time?'

'Oh, any time after nine,' said Claire, and was pleased and surprised when Frances did indeed appear, looking rather good. Claire was wearing a voluminous smock, dyed coffee-colour, with lacy straps and floating Indian scarves; it wasn't until years later that she realised how dreadful she and most of her friends must have looked at that time. Frances, even then, stood out, in a straight black dress and black tights, with little buttoned shoes from Anello & Davide. Claire went over and kissed her.

'I didn't think you'd come.'

'No,' said Frances, 'neither did I.' She held out a bottle of wine and looked about her, at the filling room lit by candles in bottles, at the Indian bedspreads hung on the walls and the joss sticks on the mantelpiece, dropping threads of ash.

'Food and drink in the kitchen.' Claire took the bottle. 'Thanks for this – let me get you something.'

'What kind of something?' asked Frances. 'There is a smell not disguised by your strawberry incense.'

'Yes,' said Claire. 'I hope our landlady can't smell it, or she'll ring the police.' But she led her over to a little group sitting on floor cushions in a corner near the speakers, where Pink Floyd throbbed. 'Do you know any of these people?'

'By sight,' said Frances curtly.

'This is Frances, everyone,' said Claire, sitting down beside them, pulling Frances down to join her. Heads were raised, there were slow smiles. Claire made introductions, had a couple of puffs and passed the joint to Frances, leaving her to it as more people came. Surely they hadn't asked so many.

During the course of the evening she noticed that Frances seemed to know what was good for her: from time to time she caught sight of her smiling dreamily down in her corner and by

9

about midnight she was lying full-length upon the rug by the fireplace, wrapped round someone called David Blunden, with whom she eventually left, going down the steep stairs in her gaberdine mac very slowly, laughing.

'Happy Christmas,' called Claire from the top, leaning up against the wall with her arms around someone she had long liked the look of. 'See you next term.'

'Indeed,' said Frances, and laughed again as David Blunden opened the front door, panelled with yellow and violet glass, and let in a gust of cold air. It closed behind them, and Claire turned back to her interesting companion.

Frances reappeared the next term in the refectory queue for lunch.

'David?' asked Claire, after the pleasantries.

'Nice,' said Frances. 'Briefly fulfilled a need.'

'Why only briefly?'

Frances shrugged, and took a bowl of minestrone from the counter. 'Who can say? It doesn't matter anyway.' She put a roll on her plate and moved her tray along, blushing, Claire noticed. Ahead of them, steam rose diffusely and tin lids banged. 'Are you free for supper one evening?'

'Yes,' said Claire. 'Let's make a date.'

On a bright cold January night Frances cooked lamb chops with rosemary and garlic on her Belling ring and served them to Claire with mushrooms, broccoli and sauté potatoes. They sat at a varnished table with barley-sugar legs that doubled as desk in Frances's high-ceilinged bedsit, and the gas fire popped beneath a mantelpiece which doubled as a bookshelf. Pinned to the wall above the books was a film poster: Bergmann's *Persona*. On the table a wine-bottle lamp shone on to the tight buds of early daffodils which Claire had brought.

'This is delicious.' She picked up a forkful of mushrooms.

'Thank you,' said Frances. 'I enjoy cooking. Reading Elizabeth David has helped me to rise above Middlesex, where my mother makes food out of packets. How was your Christmas?'

'It was lovely,' said Claire, who had taken Marcus, the man from the party, home to Derbyshire and walked with him across snowy fields, returning to a lit-up house and tea by the fire with her family, who had liked him. At night, when they were all asleep, he had come to her room and slipped into bed with her. The moon had shone through the curtains of her childhood, and she had felt wonderful. She still did.

Frances listened to an edited version of all this with apparent interest.

'And your Christmas?' Claire asked.

'Different. The turkey did not, of course, come out of a packet, but the gravy did and the turkey might as well have done. My parents and my Aunt Myra, who is there every Christmas, watched the Queen's speech and fell asleep. I read, and went for walks in streets which felt like an old people's home, and vowed I would never return.' She picked up Claire's empty plate. 'I also took up smoking, I can't think why it's taken me so long. Do you mind if I smoke now?'

'Of course not. Do you mean smoking or smoking?'

'Not dope,' said Frances. 'I can't afford it. That's just for special occasions.'

Claire watched her cross the room with the plates and disappear into the kitchenette outside. She was wearing the black tights and little buttoned shoes again, and a long grey sweater; her fair hair shone. When she came back, Claire said: 'What about Rowan? Your friend.' Frances took a packet of cigarettes off one of the books on the mantelpiece; on the wall above her, Liv Ullmann and Bibi Andersson gazed across the room, pale and uncompromising. It all felt a very long way from Derbyshire.

Frances shook out her match and came over with an ashtray. 'Rowan's Christmas was more like yours,' she said. 'She has met someone nice at York and went home with him.'

'Oh.' Claire watched her, smoking intently. She wanted to ask again why David Blunden had not similarly rescued Frances, but didn't like to.

'I went up to see her at New Year,' Frances went on, 'but it was only partly enjoyable. People change. Never mind. There is always work. Work, as I have told you, is my salvation.'

And after that evening she dropped from view again. Claire saw her from time to time but only at a distance: smiling thinly across the lecture hall and disappearing afterwards, coming out of the

11

library with a pile of books, hurrying in a dark duffle-coat down the cold hill to the bus stop. Spring came, and by Easter Claire rarely gave her a thought; she spent most of her time with Marcus, and in the summer they went to Greece. There she discovered that you could have too much of a good thing: back in Bristol they drifted apart, and since no one came to take his place, Claire settled down at last to do some work.

Finals loomed. She became better acquainted with the library, and thus saw more of Frances, who seemed to live there, leaving now and then to have a coffee across the road in the Berkeley, or a cigarette on the square of grass. Claire watched her through a Gothic window-pane one warm June afternoon, sitting on a low wall, deep in thought. First-years drifted by, hand in hand, in shorts and platform shoes; Frances did not seem to notice any of them. Claire tapped on the glass and waved, but was not seen or heard; after a while, Frances stubbed out her cigarette and walked towards the doors again. On her way out Claire looked along the rows of bent heads and whispering pages, and found her, three seats in from the aisle, writing furiously.

'Frances?' she said softly.

Frances jumped, looked up, saw her, nodded briskly and returned to her writing. Claire went out, feeling obscurely rebuked.

The examinations came and were sat in a series of blazing days which in later years became indistinguishable, encapsulated in memory only as a blur of heat and nerves and silence. Afterwards, packing up the flat, saying goodbye at end-of-it-all parties, Claire found herself every now and then looking out for Frances, but she did not see her until the departmental lunch party ten days before the end of term.

It was held in a large sunny room on the first floor of the old buildings; Claire took a glass of wine from the table by the window, turned, and saw Frances coming in with Simon Blair, one of the senior tutors – the tutor, indeed, who had reputedly so admired her essay on the Metaphysicals. He was wearing a cotton jacket and narrow tie; she wore a straight grey dress and very good shoes; her hair was like silk. She nodded to Claire as if from a great distance, and laughed at something Simon said. And Claire thought: Well. Well, good for Frances. But again felt rebuked, rebuffed, cast aside, even.

Before the end of the party, when she'd had too many glasses of white wine and too much chicken tikka, she detached herself from Marcus, who was growing sentimental and nostalgic, and went across the room to the little group which contained Frances, poised and remote. Claire touched her elbow.

'I just came to say goodbye.'

Frances smiled graciously at her. 'Goodbye, Claire.'

'Do you know how you've done? What you're going to do?'

Frances said lightly, 'I think I did well enough to go on. I'm applying to do an MA. What about you?'

'I think I did well enough,' said Claire, 'but not well enough to go on. I expect I shall end up teaching, like everyone else. Anyway – I hope it all goes well for you.'

'Thank you,' said Frances. 'And you.' And she turned away, as if there were no more to be said, which, Claire felt, indeed, there wasn't.

'I have been put in my place,' she told Marcus, returning.

'And where is that?' he asked her, fingering her string of jet-black beads.

Claire looked at him.

'For old times' sake?' he wondered, and she thought: Well, why not?

And thus a chapter ended. In Derbyshire, in August, Claire learned that she had got the degree she both expected and felt she deserved, and later she read in the *Times* that Frances, as she had also expected, had done very well. And after that she really did, for years, completely forget about her. She went to live in London to do her teaching diploma, and then she began her career, in a comprehensive school near King's Cross which looked like a prison.

Little in Claire's life so far, except for a term's teaching practice, had prepared her for the baptism of sniggering and mockery she was given for three weeks, every day, in almost every class. She was unprepared for the adolescent boys who hung around on the stairs in rainy dinner hours and swore at her as she went past; for the fights which broke out in class when she turned to the blackboard; for the particular fight, out in the corridor, when a knife was drawn. She was unprepared for truancy, for fourteen-year-olds on drugs, for general apathy and specific misery, and in dealing with all this she changed. Where she thought she might go under, she found she had resources; where she thought she would leave teaching for ever, she found that she stayed on, at first for one or two particular children and then for herself. She changed jobs, moving to a mixed comprehensive in Kilburn where she eventually became head of department.

And then, at a supper party in Kentish Town, she met Robert, who was kind and reliable, when she was recovering from a man who was neither: the only person who had ever really hurt her, and who had made the Christmas term, always a long haul, with illness and absence and bad weather, even more difficult than usual. Robert Murray had been described by her friend Ruth, who was giving the party and who was usually rather critical, as a dear man, and when Claire met him she saw why. He was a few years older than she, ordinary in appearance – medium height, a bit overweight, thinning brown hair – but warm in manner, and so easy to talk to that long before the end of the evening she had stopped wanting to talk to anyone else.

He was an accountant, working for a housing association which provided sheltered accommodation for recently discharged psychiatric patients. He might have made heavy weather of it all, but he didn't. He made Claire laugh by describing a meeting of local residents near a run-down property being converted into one of the sheltered homes. The middle classes, naturally, had no objection at all to having ex-mental patients living nearby, they were just rather worried by the state of the building, which seemed to be not quite safe; one member of the audience knew of a rather good site some miles away. The working-class residents, on the other hand, couldn't care less about the state of the bloody building, they just weren't having a whole lot of lunatics wandering about the streets, and Robert and his architect and his bloody community liaison officer could take their bloody hostel somewhere else and be quick about it.

'And are you going to?' Claire asked, recovering.

'No,' said Robert, 'of course not.'

He asked her about her own work, and she made him laugh, describing one or two of the more colourful moments in the Christmas play. By the time Ruth was making coffee she had told him, too, about her unhappy love affair, and he had told her about a woman he had wanted to marry who had wanted to marry someone else who was already married. They sipped at the brandy Ruth passed round, and agreed they were cheering each other up no end.

'I knew you'd like him,' said Ruth, out in the hall.

'Why on earth didn't you produce him before?' Claire was pulling her coat on.

Ruth shrugged. 'I hardly see you, do I? You've been lying low.'

'Not any more.'

Robert rang her two days later, and took her out to dinner the following weekend. They met at a Malaysian restaurant in a narrow little passage off Wardour Street, and afterwards wandered hand in hand among the deserted stalls of Berwick Street market. By the end of the evening it seemed to Claire absurd that she might ever have wanted to stay with a man who had made her so miserable when Robert made her so happy; by Easter they were married, on a heavenly spring day in Derbyshire, where the wind shook the daffodils growing in joyous profusion against the grey stone walls of her parents' garden. And then she and Robert slipped into life together as easily as if they had known each other and already lived together for years and years.

They bought a flat in Hornsey, and after a while had Jessica; Claire left her head-of-department job in Kilburn and took one less demanding nearby. By the time they had Jack, who took longer to arrive than they might have wished – when they were, indeed, beginning to panic, neither of them being only children, and unable to imagine not having more – Robert had been made financial director of a different housing association. It had a higher profile, and was run by a man with charisma, whose name was often in the papers. They bought a very nice house in a leafy road in Crouch End, and Claire gave up teaching for a while and found life with a new baby exhausting. As the children grew older, and the mortgage rate went up, she went back to work again, at first

15

two days a week, then four. Gradually, life, which had had its moments of real stress when the children were small, began to reappear as something they could all enjoy, and the summer holidays in particular.

And Portugal, where they had come last year, was the best place: nowhere had ever been so beautiful, no house so easy to be in, with its space and airy rooms and wooden corridors, with the river close by and the weather, apart from a few wet days, quite perfect. Well, it had rained quite a bit, but that hadn't mattered. Last year was the first time they'd holidayed with other people, and it had worked: the other family friends from school, the children, on the whole, playing well together and the adults sharing domesticity quite equably. They would have come back with them this year but Geoffrey had broken his leg, falling off a ladder at the top of the stairs while changing a lightbulb. This was after they had booked the house and paid the deposit. Refunding Geoffrey and Linda their half with sympathetic noises, they cast about for other people to go with, and could not decide who to ask. It was quite a thing, sharing your precious two weeks with another family. They asked Robert's sister, Penny, but she, who had found life at home with small children intolerable, had just landed a wonderful job as production assistant with an independent television company and felt she couldn't get away so soon. Claire and Robert cast about further, but drew a blank.

And it was extraordinary, in the midst of all this indecision, that one Friday morning in the Crouch End supermarket, Claire, leafing through an article on school refusers, should look up to see how much longer she had in the queue and realise that the fair-haired woman two places ahead of her was Frances.

She was wearing jeans and a faded blue-grey sweatshirt over a white T-shirt, visible at the neck. Her sleeves were pulled up and her hair was tied back; she was leaning on the bar of her trolley reading a Virago paperback. She looked older, naturally, but not much, and seeing her now Claire felt the last eighteen years or so slip away as easily as if they had never passed: she was back in the library in Bristol again, finding Frances bent over her books, shrouded in thought, set apart. She still had that air of detachment, and for a moment Claire thought: I'll leave her to it. She remembered the patronising dismissal Frances had given her at the summer lunch party (remembered, too, the delicious afternoon she had spent with Marcus afterwards, something she had not thought about for years) and wondered if she really wanted to speak to her at all. But she found herself curious, despite all this, and said to the woman in front of her: 'Excuse me, I just want to – there's someone I know – ' and went up to Frances and touched her arm.

Frances jumped. She looked up, frowning, and then, when Claire said wryly, 'Remember me?' she gave a smile of pure, unaffected pleasure.

'Claire!'

'I knew you the minute I saw you. What are you doing here?'

'Much the same as you, I imagine.' Frances dropped the Virago paperback into her shoulderbag; Claire saw a thin silver wedding ring. 'God, I was miles away.'

'You were never exactly present,' said Claire, as the queue moved forward. 'It's very nice to see you.'

'And you.' Frances had reached the top of the queue; she leaned forward into the trolley, taking out boxes of cereal and eggs, loading them on to the belt behind Next Customer Please. Claire found herself being squeezed out of the aisle, and stepped back.

'Have you got time for a coffee?'

'Why not?' said Frances, smiling. She was neatly putting all the frozen stuff together. Late spring sunshine streamed through the plate-glass window and touched her hair. 'I'll wait for you outside.'

Outside, Claire found she had a parking ticket. She ripped it off the windscreen and flung it into the car. 'Damn.'

'You are on a double yellow line,' said Frances, her hand on her trolley.

'And where are you?'

'In the car park.'

'Of course.' Claire opened the boot and heaved in carrier bags. 'So am I, usually. I just thought I'd risk it for once. Well, what shall we do? Are you living round here? I can't believe it.'

'Muswell Hill. I've got the day off, and I had to come down here to pick up some papers from someone – to do with my son's school, not interesting.' She waved a hand dismissively; a passer-by banged into the trolley and rubbed her arm. 'Sorry,' said Frances, pulling it back. 'I'm usually working,' she said.

'Doing what?' Claire stuffed in the last carrier bag and closed the boot.

'I work for a publisher – it's a little company set up a few years ago. We're in Covent Garden. I run the editorial department.'

'Do you now? That sounds rather grand.'

'It does, but it isn't. The editorial department is me and an army of freelancers, some of whom are quietly efficient and many of whom are useless. I pick up the pieces.' She smiled. 'Actually, I like it, I've been there since Tom was two. The books are rather good on the whole, and I like small companies.' She was pulling the trolley away from the car. 'More of this later, perhaps.'

'Yes,' said Claire. 'Come back for coffee. Just tell me one thing – did you marry Simon Blair?'

'Who?'

'The tutor – don't you remember? You came to that party with him – '

'Oh, him. *Marry* him? Marry Simon Blair?' Someone else banged into her; she was beginning to sound impatient.

Claire said quickly: 'Okay, let's go, yes? We're only just off the hill.' She gave the address and directions. 'See you in a few minutes.'

'Fine.' And Frances turned, manoeuvring the trolley through the shoppers to the car park as Claire drove away.

At home, she pushed past the bikes in the hall and unpacked the shopping. She put the kettle on and stood at the back door, next to the crowded cork board where Jack's paintings and drawings were pinned up with school notices; she looked out over the garden, and waited for the doorbell. How extraordinary, after all this time, to bump into Frances again.

It was a beautiful morning, dewy and fresh: shadows from the trellis fell across the grass and a blackbird was singing its heart out in the pear tree. Claire, usually in a hurry, with people and children in and out of the house all the time, rarely had time for reflection. She thought now, in an unexpected rush of feeling, a moment of deep, domestic contentment: I have everything I ever wanted in my life, everything anyone could ever wish for. Unusually, a tiny sensation of doubt and uncertainty touched the moment like a stain: is it right for anyone to have so much? Isn't something bound to be taken away? And then the doorbell rang, and she hurried to answer it, finding Frances on the doorstep holding out a bunch of exquisite pink and white tulips, smiling again.

Claire took the tulips and kissed her. 'Come in,' she said. 'It's lovely to see you.'

The room was silent and still. Claire, her head on Robert's chest, lay listening to the lazy creak of the swing-seat from the terrace below, and from below that the enquiring voices of hens, scratching through the dry grass under the lemon trees. She could hear from the landing the sound of Guida, who must have let herself in, ironing the sheets from the previous visitors – bang of the iron on the metal stand, hiss and puff of steam, warm smell of cotton, dried in the open air. Heaven. There were two weeks ahead of this – the river, the mountains, the hot, unbroken sky – and then the house would be shut up for the autumn and winter, for they were the last guests of the season, and she was glad. They would close the doors on their two weeks and seal them, the house their house, undisturbed by strangers coming after. She closed her eyes again, feeling her hair warm on her cheek, not wanting to move.

Beside her, Robert stirred, lifting an arm, yawning. 'What's the time?'

Claire peered across at the travel clock. 'Nearly half-past four.'

'Wait for it,' he said, and they waited, and heard from across the valley the single chime of the half-hour. 'Very good. Nice sleep?'

'Very.' She stretched, and rolled away, on to her back. 'You?'

'Mmm.' He yawned again, and scratched his head. 'I suppose we ought to do something.'

Claire drew up bare feet beneath the black and white skirt. 'Go on then.'

'In a minute.'

They lay watching the sun stream through the gaps in the shutters.

'Glad to be back?' asked Robert.

'It's even better than I remembered.'

'Think it's going to be all right? With them?'

'Yes,' she said. 'I think so.'

'Not sure.'

'We can't be *sure*,' she said, 'can we? Going on holiday with people you've had supper with a couple of times and asked on impulse is hardly the same as going with lifelong friends, is it? Anyway, I think it's a challenge.'

Robert groaned. 'I told you – I don't want to be challenged on holiday. I want to have a nice time.'

'We will.' She turned to look up at him. 'We've done this one, Robert, we've discussed it all.'

'Good. In that case I'll get some tea, shall I?'

She patted his stomach. 'You're so good.'

'I know.' He swung his legs off the bed, moving stiffly across the room to the balcony window, opening the shutters, stepping outside on to the balcony for a look. Claire shut her eyes against the sudden brightness, listening.

'Hello, Jess.'

'Hi, Dad.'

'All right?'

'Fine.' The swing-seat swung back and forth, sandalled feet brushed the tiles.

'Anyone else about?'

'Dunno.'

'What's she doing?' Claire asked.

'Not a lot.' Robert came back inside; Claire shaded her eyes, looking at a dazzle of black window frames imprinted on his face. He swung the shutters to again, and bent to retrieve his shoes from one of the heaps on the floor. 'Right then.' He slipped them on, sitting on the edge of the bed, and stood up. 'I'll give you a shout.'

'Remember how long the kettle takes.' The stove was run on fitful Calor gas, stored below the house in enormous cylinders. 'Don't fill it too full.'

'I won't.' He moved towards the door; there was a creak from outside it. 'Ah. Noises off.'

Claire turned to see Jack in T-shirt and crumpled shorts, his face flushed from sleep. She stretched out a hand: he let the door click to behind him and padded across the floorboards, stepping over the mess.

'Had a good rest?'

He nodded, clambering on to the rumpled bed, and she put her arm round him. 'Tom still asleep?'

Jack shook his head.

'What's he doing?'

'Dunno, he's not there. I'm thirsty.'

'Tea and drinks coming up,' said Robert, his hand on the doorknob. 'I expect I'll find Tom on my travels.'

'I expect he's with Frances,' said Claire, as he went out. The door swung to, and she lay back against the pillows with Jack. They could hear Robert going down the corridor to the landing, stopping to have limited words with Guida in phrase-book Portuguese.

Jack picked at the bedspread, tugging at a loose white thread. 'I wish I was sleeping in here.'

Claire moved his hand. 'Don't, you'll make a hole. You're only just across the landing.'

'I know, but – '

'What? You're getting on all right with Tom, aren't you?'

'Yes, but – '

'But what?'

He frowned. 'This is *our* place.'

'It isn't, Jack, it belongs to a family in England. We're only renting it.'

'I know. But you know what I mean.'

'Yes,' she said, 'I do. But we're sharing it with very nice people, and we couldn't afford to come here without them, and I don't want any fuss.' His fingers wavered towards the loose thread again, and she dropped her hand on his in a pounce, making him laugh. '*Don't* pull it, please.'

He turned, and burrowed his face in her breasts, still laughing. 'Want a drink.'

'And stop that, too,' she said, kissing his dark hair. 'Shall I test you on your Portuguese? So you can talk to Guida?'

He raised his head, pulling dreadful faces.

'Come on, it's not that bad. What's hello?'

'*Olla.*'

'*Ola*, like Coca-Cola, remember? What about thank you?'

His hand lay across her breasts, casually intimate; he tapped his fingers, trying to remember.

22

'*Obrigado.*'

'Well done. That's if you can say it to a man, like the man in the village shop, yes? But if you say it to Guida, or any woman, it's *obrigad*a, remember?'

Jack shook his head; he was fingering one of the little buttons on her shirt.

'It changes depending if it's masculine or feminine,' explained Claire, wondering why she continually went on like this to the children, who were largely indifferent. No one had ever explained anything to her when she was little. 'If it's a boy or a girl. Remember in France, when you were six? *La fille* for Jessica, and *le garçon* for you.'

Jack had succeeded in undoing the button; his fingers slipped inside.

'I wish,' he said thoughtfully, 'that *I* was a girl.'

Robert found Tom sitting outside the kitchen door, at the top of the stone steps leading down to the garden. The whole house was raised above this circle of scrubby grass and bare earth, flowerless but full of fruit trees – peach, lemon, grapefruit, lime. There were one or two outbuildings, with greyed wooden doors half off their hinges; when they came here the first time, Jessica and Jack and the Hobbs children had spent rainy afternoons in the one next to the house, by the hen run. They'd kept caterpillars in there, furry and thick as fingers, and beetles, shining coppery-black, picked up on the upper path leading to the swimming pool, or rescued from the pool itself, more of a deep tank than anything, twelve by six or so and set in baking concrete.

'No one in the water without a grown-up nearby, okay?' Robert had said to the children this morning, showing round the new arrivals. 'Just to be on the safe side.' He led them away, past the concealing bushes, back along the path where table and chairs were set invitingly beneath cascading vines, and down to the garden again. Tom had looked into the outbuilding, last year's natural history museum, seen only broken furniture and dust and come out again, uninterested; he saw the hens in their run and hurried towards them, calling, 'Hello, sweeties, hello! Come on, come on!'

'Hens aren't *sweet*,' said Jack, who had followed them.

Tom ignored him, squatting down in the dusty earth in front of the netting. Behind him, the hens – pullets, Robert supposed – cocked their heads at him and stepped forward, murmuring. They had bare, featherless necks, and some of them had bare patches on their chests too; they were small and brown and scraggy, and when Tom put his fingers in through the netting they ran towards them eagerly, lifting grubby yellow legs.

He looked up at Robert. 'Have you got any food?'

'I expect we can find something,' he said. 'But Guida lets them out later – you'll see them scratching round for grubs and things.'

'Wick-ed!'

Oliver, watching with his hands in his pockets, said: 'I shouldn't put your fingers in too far, Tom.'

'It's all right, they're only hungry.' Tom wriggled his fingers in further. 'Poor things.'

From deep inside the house the bell rang, and then Jessica came out through the kitchen and stood calling them.

'Lunch!'

'Okay,' called Robert. 'We're coming.' He led the others back, and they climbed the steps. Above them, damp white sheets hung in the sun on long lines next to an enormous green-tiled water tank, whose copper tap was left on always, so that whenever you came out of the house you heard the sound of running water beneath the vines. The dazzling sheets were painted now with dense blue shadows: from the vines, and from the bushes at the top of the next flight of steps, leading up to the iron gate, and the hot mountain road.

Frances, coming up behind the others, last, stopped to look at this whiteness, this blueness, this miracle of light and shade and foreignness, which seemed for a dizzying moment to hold the promise of healing everything, and she shut her eyes. She could look at it for ever; it was almost too much to look upon. Then, from inside the house, came a yell, and running footsteps, and Tom, who had been first inside, came hurtling out from the darkness of the kitchen, bellowing.

'Hey . . .' She moved towards him, holding out her hand. 'What's happened?'

24

'I banged my *arm.*' He clutched it, just beneath the shoulder, hopping up and down.

'How?'

'On the bathroom door, on the catch.' Tears of pain and fury spurted as if from a geyser. '*Bloody* catch!'

'Stop that!' snapped Frances. 'Now let's have a look.' She moved to take his hand off his arm and he snatched it away.

'It's no use getting *angry*, it *hurts!*'

'Don't *shout!* I just want to see, that's all – '

Movement in the doorway: Robert, concerned and kind.

'Sorry, Tom, that catch is a bugger, isn't it? You okay?'

Tom, transfixed at being treated like one of Robert's mates, stopped crying immediately. 'Yes, thanks.'

'I was trying to have a look . . .' said Frances, as if she had to justify herself for something.

'Want to show us, Tom?'

Tom sniffed, wiping his eyes with the bad arm; Frances saw a long red weal.

'We'd better put something on that,' she said. 'No wonder you were crying.'

He shook his head. 'It's okay.'

'But – '

'I said it's *okay*, Frances.' He ran his nose along the other arm and stamped through to the kitchen. 'I'm starving. I'm starving!' They heard him running across the patched sticky lino and down the wooden passage. Frances looked at Robert and shook her head.

'He's tired.'

'Of course he is. You must be too.'

'Not too bad.' She followed him into the house, and along to the dining-room, where the others were waiting.

This first meal all together had been fractionally strained, after such a beginning, at least for the first few minutes, but a couple of glasses of wine had everyone unwinding; then they all went upstairs to collapse.

And Robert now, coming down to the kitchen, found that the door to the steps was open, with a patch of sun lying across the floor, and went to have a look outside. Tom was sitting next to a scrawny, dull-furred grey and white cat, talking to it quietly, encouragingly.

'There you are, you eat it all up. Is that better?' Beside him was a plate of chicken – remains from last night's supper: quite a few remains, which Robert had last seen in the fridge. The cat ate slowly, with difficulty; at the sound of his footsteps it stopped, and looked up, apprehensive, ears flat. Tom turned round.

'Isn't she beautiful?'

'I – yes,' said Robert, 'but I'm not really sure she should be having that chicken.'

'But she was starving, I could hear her, outside the door. She was crying.'

'Oh. Well . . . perhaps another time we'd better find some scraps. D'you think?'

'Okay.' He turned back to the cat again, and she resumed eating, cautiously, looking up with wary yellow eyes. Robert moved back inside and put the kettle on, dropping the spent match into a white saucer. Through the open door he could hear Tom making noises, a blend of back-of-the-throat Donald Duck and a pursing and smacking of the lips; he tried to remember if Jack used to be quite so audible all the time, and didn't think so. The room smelled faintly of Calor gas, and the kettle began to heat up; when he'd put everything on the tray, with a packet of biscuits from the village shop, he went to the door again, leaning on the frame. Tom was stroking the cat as she crunched on gristle, his hand running along her back to a thin, unhealthy tail.

'I've adopted her,' he told Robert.

'That's kind. Be a bit careful touching her, though, won't you?'

'Why?'

'Well . . . she looks as if she's got a lot of germs and fleas and things.'

'All cats get fleas sometimes.'

'Yes, but you know animals here aren't used to being petted – people don't feel quite the same about them as we do. She might scratch, or bite, and it could be a bit nasty.'

'She won't scratch me,' said Tom firmly.

'Well, just be a bit careful, that's all. How's the arm?'

'What? Oh, fine. Where's Jack?'

26

'He's upstairs with Claire – they're coming down for tea in a minute. Do you want to go and tell your parents? We're going to have it out on the terrace.'

'No, I want to stay here with the cat.'

'Well . . .' In the face of Tom's obduracy, which seemed to encompass many issues, Robert could hear himself begin a number of sentences with this hesitant, placatory 'Well'. The kettle was beginning to shake. 'Well . . . perhaps in a minute?' He went back inside to wreaths of steam. 'If you don't tell them,' he called out to Tom, turning off the gas, 'they won't know, will they?'

A heavy sigh. 'Oh, all right, then.' Robert heard him get to his feet, and then a sudden cry: 'The hens are out! The hens are out! Come on, hens, here I am!' He went running down the steps past the cat, racing towards them over the dry ground: Robert heard squawks, and beating wings.

He picked up the tray and carried it through the house and out on to the terrace, where Jessica, tawny-haired, white-skinned, lay beneath the canopy of the swing-seat in striped pink shorts, faded T-shirt and a string of beads. Beyond her, beyond the lemon trees, the valley's shimmering light was beginning to thicken and grow still, and the clock struck twice.

'Five o'clock,' said Robert, setting down the tray on the round marble table. 'Teatime.'

'Tea should be served at four,' said Jessica, stretching. 'In china cups,' she added, looking at the battered mugs and cheap, thick glasses. 'With egg and cress sandwiches.'

'I don't know where you get your ideas from.' Robert sank on to the swing-seat. 'Move up.'

'Not from you,' she said calmly, swinging her legs off. 'You never notice what things look like.'

There was the sound of panting and running feet: beneath the terrace Tom was in hot pursuit. Jessica got up and went to look, leaning gracefully on the parapet.

'If you chase them,' she called down, 'they'll just run faster, won't they?'

There was no answer. Robert called up to the balcony window. 'Tea! Claire?'

The shutters were opened, and Claire came out on to the balcony. Dark hair tumbled in unbrushed waves to her shoulders; she leaned on the stone ledge in her crumpled white shirt and smiled down.

'Will you tell the others?' he asked her.

'All right. Hello, Jess.'

'Hi, Mum,' said Jess, not turning from the parapet. 'Hey!' she called down suddenly. 'Hey, don't do that.'

There was a scuffle, and a furious flutter; Tom came up the steps, triumphant. 'Got one!'

'Poor thing,' said Jessica. 'Look at her, she's scared to death.'

'She's all right.' Tom carried the hen over to the swing-seat and plonked himself down. 'There you are, there you are,' he said to her soothingly, running his fingers over the scrubby brown feathers and balding neck. The hen sat motionless on his lap, her eyes bright and blank.

'Put her down,' said Jessica. 'She's filthy.'

'No she's not! Anyway, she can't help it, can she?'

'Tea,' said Robert. 'Put her down, Tom, there's a good chap.' He nodded towards the biscuits. 'Then you can have one of these.'

'Can she have one?' asked Tom.

'Well . . .'

'For heaven's sake,' said Jessica.

'Oh, go on,' said Claire, warm and amused above them. 'Stop being so snooty, Jess.' Beside her, Jack, who had emerged from the bedroom, said: 'Can I hold her?'

'Sure,' said Tom. 'Come on down.' He reached for the packet of biscuits with a large square hand. 'Do you want to feed her?' he asked Jessica, as her mother and Jack disappeared. 'You can if you want.'

'No, thanks.' She took a glass of squash and sat sipping disdainfully on the parapet, her legs drawn up, gazing into the distance.

Tom tugged at the top of the packet, still clasping the hen. 'You can change your mind if you want.'

There was no answer.

'Right,' said Robert firmly, reaching for the teapot, and as he did so Tom ripped the packet open with sudden, irritated force.

The hen struggled; half a dozen biscuits, with thick pink filling, flew from his hands and broke upon the terrace.

'Honestly!' said Jessica. She swung her legs off the parapet and stalked inside.

'Oh, come on,' said Robert. 'It's only a packet of biscuits.' There was no reply. 'We'd better clear them up,' he said to Tom.

'Sorry.' Tom struggled to get off the seat with the hen.

'These things happen.'

They bent to pick up the pieces, Tom with one hand, awkwardly, beginning to puff. Under his other arm the hen's head made little anxious darts. 'Keep *still*,' he said. 'You can have some in a minute.' He got up, dropping a handful of bits and crumbs on the table. 'Now . . . here you are.' He stood there, red-faced and hot, making offerings from the pile on his large, open palm: the hen pecked, and went on pecking. 'See?' said Tom happily. 'See? I knew she was hungry.'

Claire and Jack stepped out of the sitting-room on to the terracotta tiles. 'The others are just coming,' said Claire, and flopped down on to the swing-seat. 'Where's Jess?'

'Sulking,' said Robert. 'Do you want to – '

'No,' said Claire. 'I can't be doing with sulks. Do pour the tea, I'm gasping. What're all these biscuits doing everywhere?' She looked at Tom and the hen, pecking eagerly now. 'All right?'

'Fine,' said Tom.

Beside him, Jack said, 'Let me hold her.'

'In a minute. Come on, henny-penny, have some more.' He reached for fresh pieces, and then he stopped, looking suddenly blank; for a moment his hand hung in the air; when he moved it again he did so too fast, and a glass at the edge of the tray tipped over at once, obligingly, as if it had been waiting for this moment. Orange squash streamed steadily across the table and over the edge.

'Oh, God!' said Tom. 'Oh, God, what an idiot I am.'

He stepped back; Claire moved her own bare feet.

'You'd better get a cloth,' she said, not unkindly.

'I'll get it,' said Robert, moving towards the sitting-room, beginning to feel, now, a rising tide of exasperation. 'Tom, do for God's sake take that hen away.'

And Tom, defeated, took her, slowly descending the steps to the garden.

'But I haven't held her!' said Jack.

'You can come down here and hold her if you want,' said Tom's voice from below. 'I've still got her.'

'No, he can't,' said Claire. '*Do* let's settle down. Sit down, Jack, you can do it another time.'

Jack sat, grumpy. 'Why should *he* hold her?'

Claire passed him the last glass of squash, and reached for the teapot. Robert returned with a cloth and mopped all the mess away. Jessica came out asking: 'Can we have tea in peace now?'

And Frances and Oliver, looking refreshed, came out through the double doors after her, beholding the beauty of the terrace and the lemon trees, and tea awaiting them.

'How kind. Thank you so much.'

Dusk had fallen, the mountains were dark. Lights from distant villages twinkled here and there; here and there dim orange rectangles shone.

'Solar power,' Robert observed to Oliver, coming out of the sitting-room, nodding towards the ridge opposite the terrace, across the mountain road. 'There're only two or three houses up there.' He dropped a folder on the table and pulled back a chair. 'You might like to have a look at this,' he went on, indicating the folder. 'Notes about the area and stuff. Some of it's written by the owners, but it seems to have been added to by guests from time to time.' He leaned forward, and picked up the wine bottle, holding it questioningly above Oliver's glass.

Oliver nodded, moving the glass towards him. 'Thanks. Who are the owners?'

'He's an architect, I think. We've never met them, we just answered an ad in the *Independent*. They sound nice enough in their letters.' He put down the bottle. 'You must help yourself – it comes with the house. The cellar's packed; I should've taken you down there this morning. Still, plenty of time.' He raised his glass. 'Cheers.'

'Cheers.' Oliver reached for the folder and flipped it open. A

30

couple of postcards fell out, and landed on the tiles; he bent to retrieve them, cathedral interiors.

'That's an hour or so's drive from here,' said Robert, 'but it's rather good, worth a visit. We might do a trip one day, if you and Frances feel like it.'

'I'm sure we will.' Oliver slipped back the cards. He turned the pages, some typed, some handwritten, others with more postcards pasted on, and began to read.

Robert sipped his red wine, and watched him: a man with whom he was about to spend a fortnight, a man he barely knew – who, indeed, he had never even met until one Saturday evening a couple of months ago, when he and Claire had driven from leafy Crouch End to leafier Muswell Hill, invited for supper by Claire's old friend from Bristol.

They drew up outside a tall Victorian house in a quiet road off the hill. Early summer evening sunshine streamed through the trees; someone a few doors along was singing near an open window. They locked the car, feeling it almost unnecessary, and walked up to Frances, and Oliver's front door, painted a velvety green, with polished brass.

'All very nice,' said Robert, holding the Beaujolais, looking about him. 'A little too nice, perhaps?'

'Stop it.' Claire was ringing the upper bell. They waited, ready to smile.

Footsteps came running down the stairs, and the door was opened by Frances, in black linen trousers and cream silk sleeveless shirt. Claire kissed her, sensing that tense and edgy manner once again, and introduced Robert; they followed her up the stairs. Inside the flat, in a large, sash-windowed sitting-room, a tall man was standing at bookshelves with his back to them.

'Oliver?' said Frances.

He turned as they all came into the room, but not immediately. There was, for a perceptible moment or two, a silence which threatened a difficult evening, a silence in which Robert unhesitatingly transferred himself and Claire out into the car again and home, to a startled babysitter, supper in the garden and an early night for once. Or they could take advantage of the babysitter and go out for a meal, just the two of them. God, that would be a relief.

Frances was making introductions: he brought himself back in a hurry. Oliver was greeting them, shaking hands, offering drinks, taking the Beaujolais with thanks. He was almost as dark as Claire, with thick curly hair, and wore glasses, heavily rimmed. He towered over all of them, and as he poured drinks and handed them round he became, unequivocally, the perfect host, as if that perceptible silence had never been.

They sat down on comfortable sofas, their feet on lovely rugs; they admired the room, with its watercolours, its one or two oils, the windows with the trees beyond catching the evening sun, the shelves of art books, novels, poetry. They began to relax, drinks going down nicely and conversation taking off. Watching what began to seem now rather an interesting couple, in this beautiful room, Robert remembered, suddenly, that Frances and Oliver had a child.

Even as he thought it – so perhaps he had already heard the noises, quite out of place amongst the paintings, the little bronze figures on the mantelpiece, the low table piled with recent hardbacks – the door was pushed open and a boy appeared, a big, gap-toothed boy in pyjamas, tousle-haired. Frances and Oliver stiffened, only a little, barely noticeably, but Robert did notice: it was, somehow, more than the ordinary mild annoyance any parent might feel when an evening with grown-ups was interrupted.

'Frances? Mum? Can I have a drink?'

'You can get yourself a drink,' said Frances, and introduced him. 'This is Tom. He's supposed to be in bed.'

Robert and Claire made understanding murmurs – children, hopeless, theirs were just the same at this age. Still were. Tom hovered, looking at them, grinning hello; he made a little noise at the back of his throat and cleared it.

'Go on,' said Frances. 'Your beaker's in the bathroom.'

He shifted from one foot to the other. 'I felt a bit funny, just now.'

'Goodnight, Tom,' said Oliver.

He went. They heard him climb more stairs to a bathroom and run a tap; they heard him, making noises, go back to his bedroom, where he stayed. Oliver poured more drinks. Frances excused

32

herself, and went to the kitchen; she summoned them, not long afterwards, to a small, candlelit dining-room, hung with green-striped wallpaper. Robert looked at it all and marvelled. Perhaps it was different with only one, but even so. Where did the child keep his toys? Where did he play? Meanwhile, Claire, getting into her stride, was pressing for details. Oliver, pouring wine, and Frances, passing dishes, described Tom's school – not good enough – and his day: dropped off by each of them in turn, on alternate days, picked up by a child-minder, collected usually by Frances, at half-past six, or thereabouts, depending on work.

The conversation turned to work, and there, for quite a while it stayed, moving from Claire's school to Robert's office, and thence to the plight of both education and housing in the current climate. Publishing, Oliver assured them, refilling their glasses, was not immune, though so far he had been lucky. Frances, too. He became drily entertaining, describing his job as senior editor in an academic publishing house even Robert had heard of, where Frances had worked for a while, and where they had met.

'I saw her,' he told them, 'going through the manuscripts of scholars with a pencil like a blazing sword. She sliced their prose into pieces, and handed it back to them with the smile of an angel . . .'

'Please,' said Frances. Sitting away from the candles, at the opposite end of the dark polished table, she looked much more relaxed now, as though whatever had been wrong between them at the start of the evening had passed and could be forgotten. But she did not talk very much, and Robert from time to time felt, as she smiled, and served wild rice, red snapper, perfect salad, that she wasn't really listening very much, either. And although she and Oliver were unwaveringly polite to each other, although it was clear she admired him, that there were interests shared and tastes in common, their eyes did not often meet – not in the way his and Claire's met, all the time, without thinking about it. Every now and then Oliver asked her a question and had to ask it again: he made a joke of it, but he was obviously irritated.

Still. The food was as good as Robert could remember eating anywhere, though the helpings were much too small. Much. Ambrosial *crème brûlée* – made, it was disclosed, by Oliver –

arrived in tiny dishes, and he still had a gap when they said their goodbyes, after coffee and brandy on the comfortable sofas.

Frances and Oliver came down to see them off: they stood on the doorstep with the light behind them, and as Robert and Claire drove away down the road Frances and Oliver waved, then turned back into the house, his arm round her shoulders and she looking up at him, as if everything between them were perfect.

'Well,' said Claire immediately, 'what did you think?'

'About her? I liked her.'

'And him? And them together?'

'Who knows?' said Robert. 'Who ever knows?' He reached forward and turned on the radio: late-night Bach embraced them. 'Ah, that's better.'

'A man with a definite outline,' said Claire, after a while. 'A definite outline and a definite something. I found him a little alarming.'

'Mmm. I did like her though. At least I think I did.' They drove past the clock tower, and up to the brow of the hill. The evening had grown much cooler, and the trees on either side rustled in a rising wind. 'It's going to rain,' he said, and added, as they turned into their own road, 'Something a bit – '

'There was always something a bit about Frances.'

They were home. Thank God. 'I'm starving,' he said, pulling up.

'You can't be.' Claire found her key as they walked up the path and unlocked the door, whose red paint was kicked and scuffed from years of bikes and banging, calling out unnecessarily to the babysitter, 'Hello, Barbara, it's us, we're back.'

Robert, after greetings, went through to the kitchen, and while Claire and Barbara stood chatting in the hall he shook cornflakes into a bowl and sat enjoyably at the table, pouring on milk and sugar, reading the cricket again, while Bach, on the kitchen radio, continued to soar about him. The front door closed.

'I've had a thought,' said Claire, returning. She stopped, and looked at the cornflakes. 'Blasphemy.' She pulled out a chair and sat down. 'Heresy. How can you?'

'Sorry,' he said, folding back the sports pages. 'Can't help it. What was the thought?'

She reached for the cornflakes and took a dry handful. 'Portugal,' she said, munching. 'We could see if they're free.'

'Oh, no.' He stopped reading, and looked at her. 'No, I don't think so. I really can't see it.'

'We've got to find someone, haven't we? Who else is there? Anyway, it's years since we did anything with people we don't really know – it's a challenge.'

'It's supposed to be a holiday.'

'Let me just sound them out.'

Rain began to spatter at the window, the cat came shooting in through the cat flap. Portugal seemed unreal, and Bach made anything seem possible. Anyway, they were bound to be booked. 'Oh, go on, then,' he said, returning to the test match. 'She's your friend. All our friends are your friends. Go on, if it makes you happy.'

And now here they all were, and here was Robert, watching Oliver, long legs stretched out before him, long spare fingers turning a page. He had a strong face, almost a noble face – certainly it had qualities Robert knew were missing from his own undefined openness. A man with a definite outline, Claire had said. She had found him a little alarming. Why?

Robert was usually too busy for speculation. Also, he had been married to the same person for fifteen years and for almost eight had worked with more or less the same group of people. At home, Claire's friends drifted in and out, coming for lunch on Fridays, coming to pick up their children after school, coming for supper from time to time with their husbands, the only time he ever saw them. He could not think about many of these people, after all this time, with even a residual curiosity; neither did he, if the truth be told, feel much need for anyone, once he got home. He had always wanted a family, and now he had one it was enough.

At work, there were changes now and then, inevitably – people came and went in the office, sometimes in a flurry, and those who worked at the sharp end, running the sheltered homes, either left after six months or stayed for ever. On the whole, however, he did not have much to do with the sharp end, and on the whole life in the office went on much as usual: there were tensions, and sometimes rows, but they did not often involve him. That is to say, he did not allow them to.

Robert was by nature easygoing, a conciliator, a defuser of tension. He liked men, but preferred women, and the women in the office felt safe with him, and from time to time came and wept on his desk. Sometimes this was because of the frustration of work, and sometimes because of the frustration of living with difficult men. He listened, and took them out for consoling drinks in the lunch hour.

Across the table, a page in the folder was quietly turned. Robert, remembering the dinner party, the silences and irritations, thought that Oliver was probably difficult – and who knew about Frances? He also thought he was probably staring, drifting off in a steady gaze as he was apt to do on the tube, caught when the person opposite looked up and looked offended.

Up on the mountainside, the church clock struck once: half-past eight. He turned, and gazed out towards the village, catching sight of a bat flitting between the grapefruit trees. Dogs barked, and on the path from the main road that ran down past the garden he could hear conversation: two old men, walking slowly. He heard something else too, a sound remembered from last year: a motor bike, screeching up the steep unlit road. At night, to relieve the boredom of the village, with its single bar, those few young men remaining came up the side of the mountain on their bikes as if there were no tomorrow. Their engines had no silencers, and sliced through the darkness like chain saws, headlights careering wildly. There came now another, and then another, at intervals that led you to believe it had all gone quiet, until the next one split the air. Robert laughed, because if the noise was infuriating the timing was comical, like a cartoon fly, and Oliver looked up from his reading and smiled.

'Does this go on all night?'

'Intermittently.'

'Doesn't anyone get killed?'

'Probably.' He reached for the bottle again, and nodded towards the folder. 'Found anything interesting?'

'I've just been reading about the winter of 'seventy-six – it seems that half the village died of flu. Remember reading that?'

36

'Yes, I do. I should think winter here must be hell – it's getting cold in the evenings even now. You warm enough?'

'Yes, thanks.' Oliver put the folder back on the table. 'It also seems that all this eucalyptus planting is destroying the land, and that someone in 'eighty-seven sighted three solid pages of birds.'

'Creeps,' said Robert. 'We've seen wagtails and sparrows. You're supposed to see kingfishers down by the river, but we never have.' He drank, wondering when the women were going to come out.

They'd eaten out here early, *en famille* for this evening, and sent the children packing soon afterwards. Claire and Frances were supervising baths for the boys, Jessica had gone to her own room, with her Walkman and her book. He turned in his chair and saw her now through the open doors across the other side of the sitting-room, lying on her side, thick tawny hair hooked back behind her ear, wherein an earpiece nestled. Her fingers were drumming to the beat on the open book: how could she read and listen at the same time? Sometimes he came back in the evenings and found her doing her homework plugged in like this.

'All right, Jess?' he called, but she didn't hear him. There were footsteps along the wooden corridor, and someone went into the dining-room, switching on the lights. At once, there was a violent fizzing from the fuse-box above the terrace doors.

'Shit,' said Claire distinctly.

Robert pushed back his chair and got up. 'What's happened?' He went inside: the fuse-box sounded as if it were about to explode. Across the room, Jessica, oblivious, did not even look up. In the dining-room, Claire snapped off the lights and at once the fizzing and crackling faded.

'Phew.' She came out of the dining-room and she and Robert peered up at the box, whose noises were now muted. But still there.

'Everything all right?' asked Oliver, from the terrace.

'Think so,' said Claire. 'Must've overloaded it,' she said to Robert. 'We'll have to be careful. I suppose this means we can only eat indoors by candlelight.'

Robert looked cautiously up at the box. 'Did it make this noise last year? This sort of buzzing?'

'I don't know. I can't remember. I think so, don't you?'

'Yes,' he said doubtfully. 'Have we got any candles, by the way?'

'I think I saw one in a cupboard. Did you pack the torch?'

'Does that mean you didn't?'

'Yes. I mean no, I didn't.'

'Oh. Oh, well. I expect it's okay as long as we remember. How're the boys?'

'Fine. Frances is just saying goodnight – d'you want to go up? I'm going to make coffee.'

'Right.' He looked out on to the terrace again. 'Oliver? Coming up to say goodnight to Tom?'

Oliver shook his head. 'Frances is up there, isn't she? We usually take it in turns.'

'Oh. Okay.' Robert withdrew, a little taken aback. Turns? Even to say goodnight? He wandered off towards the corridor leading to the stairs, stopping at Jessica's open door. Her head was swaying from side to side; she looked up, saw him, and continued to sway. Might as well not be here at all, really, he thought, I'm just part of the furniture these days. He remembered, all of a sudden, Jessica at one and a bit, in a little blue sleeping suit with ducks on, staggering across the kitchen floor in their old flat, laughing, falling into his open arms to be scooped up and kissed all over, and he sighed. Oh well. He raised a hand, and she nodded almost imperceptibly; he left her to it, and went off to see the boys.

Frances was just approaching the top of the stairs as he rounded the corner; she was wearing the grey cotton trousers she'd worn at supper, but had pulled on a cardigan over her pale striped shirt. He saw, as she stood above him, that she was wearing earrings – perhaps she'd worn them at supper, but he hadn't noticed. They were silver, long and slender, and they swung in the light beneath her straight fair hair. She smiled down at him, waiting, and he smiled back, coming up the wooden treads, and forgot about Jess and the sudden pang.

'Boys all right?'

'Yes, they're just waiting for you.' She hesitated, her hand on a packet of cigarettes in her pocket. 'I think Tom's pretty tired still.'

'Don't worry,' said Robert; he had reached the landing, and

stood aside for her. 'I'm not about to stir them up. Goodnight, lights out, that's it.'

'Well – see you downstairs, then.'

'Claire's making coffee.'

'Lovely.' She went lightly down the stairs in her canvas shoes, and he walked along the corridor, feeling lingering doubts about the holiday begin to evaporate. He stopped at the boys' room and put his head round the door.

'Evening all.'

They were both lying on their pillows, Jack neatly on his side, facing the door, Tom on his back, his legs drawn up; he was looking at the ceiling, making little trilling sounds.

'Everything to your satisfaction so far?'

'Yes, thanks.' Jack was yawning, his eyes already beginning to close. Robert went over and kissed him. 'Night, Jack, sleep tight.' He crossed to Tom. 'Am I allowed to kiss you, too?'

Tom nodded, absently. 'There's a spider up there.'

'Is there?' Robert peered. 'So there is, just a little chap. You're a good spotter.' He bent down and kissed him on rather wild hair. 'I saw a bat just now.'

'A *bat*?' Tom shot upright, and his head met Robert's chin with a crack. 'Ouch! Ouch.' He rubbed his head; tears smarted in Robert's eyes. 'A bat? Where? Why didn't you call us?'

'Sorry.' Robert stepped back, his hand on his chin. 'It was out by the terrace – I expect he'll come back. Settle down now, see you in the morning.'

But Tom was already out of bed. 'Can I come down and see him? Please. Please?'

'Well, I . . .' Robert floundered; then, mindful of both Frances and his chin – who knew what part of the body might come next in Tom's orbit? – he said firmly: 'No. Not tonight. Stay up and look for him tomorrow – it's been a long day.'

'Oh.' Two long-drawn-out notes of dissatisfaction.

Robert gently moved him towards the bed again. 'Go on, in you go.' He switched off the light. 'Sleep well.'

'Leave the light on in the corridor, Dad,' said Jack.

'I will.' He pulled the door to a little, and left them, crossing the rag runner to fetch a sweater. The bedroom was shadowy, dimly lit

39

through the open shutters by the distant blueish-green of the village street lights and the stars. Quiet voices drifted up from the terrace. He rummaged on a chair, found and pulled on a sweater, and stepped out on to the balcony.

Behind the ridge of mountain facing him the moon had begun to rise. He leaned on the stone ledge and looked down. Claire, Frances and Oliver were drinking coffee companionably, Claire stretched out on the swing-seat in her full black and white skirt, bare feet crossed at the ankles. Oliver was reading again; he said to Frances, sitting opposite Claire at the marble table, 'Do you realise it's only twenty-five years since the last wolf was seen up here? In the mountain villages the dogs still wear spiked collars, just in case.'

He spoke in a tone which sounded to Robert as formal as if he were speaking to someone recently introduced, and he thought: it must be because they're with us, surely they can't go on like this all the time.

'Goodness,' said Frances. She was leaning on the table, her chin resting on one hand, smoking thoughtfully. She looked, in profile, neater than ever, smoke rising thinly into the air above her. And watching them all – not, for some reason, announcing his presence – Robert saw on her face, as she watched Claire, an expression which he found unfathomable.

3

'What's this?' called Tom.

'What's what?' Robert came out of the dining-room, where morning sunlight lit the cotton tablecloth, the packets of English cereal and glazed brown dish of crumbling yellow maize bread. They were breakfasting late, planning a morning by the river, all rather quiet this morning, feeling their way a little still; except for Tom, who had fidgeted, and kept leaning back in his chair despite repeated requests from Oliver not to do so.

'Well, can I get down, then?'

'We haven't finished. Sit still.'

'Please?'

'Oh, go on,' Robert had said easily, reaching for the honey jar. 'Don't you think? They can all get down.'

But Jack stayed where he was, next to Claire, slowly finishing his milk, and Jessica affected not to have heard, smiling loftily as Tom got off his chair, catching the edge of the tablecloth as he swung round. Claire reached out just in time to prevent his plate from falling, and Tom, oblivious, went out into the sitting-room. They could hear his bare feet on the wooden floorboards, and a series of clicking sounds. And Robert, coming out after a few minutes with a loaded tray, found him gazing up at the enormous straw cloak which hung on a wooden stand near the dining-room door. A hat surmounted it, a kind of vast straw sombrero; at the base, the ends of a pair of wide trousers were visible, thick and feathery, like shire horses' feet. On its stand, the outfit towered above them, taller than Robert by a good few inches, taller even than Oliver, who had brushed past it on his way to bed last night, going up first, earlier than the rest of them.

'That,' Robert said now, 'is a shepherd's cloak.'

Tom frowned, reaching out to touch it. Layers of dense combed straw were sewn in bands from shoulder to mid-calf on a coarse fabric backing; he ran his hand downwards, and again. The wooden stand rocked a little.

'Careful.'

'It feels nice. The hens would like it.'

Robert smiled. 'They would.' He thought how Jack, by now, would have been – had been, last year – asking questions: why was it made of straw? Did shepherds really used to wear things like this? Did they still? Tom asked nothing. He moved closer, and put his face against it, smelling it, his fingers rustling the layers. Again, the wooden stand began to rock.

'Tom, it's very heavy – come away from there. Do you want me to tell you about it?'

'All right.' Tom moved reluctantly, and Robert made for the kitchen, saying: 'It's made of all that thick straw to keep the rain out.'

'Oh.' Tom followed him, running his hands along the panelling in the passage.

'It must have been very uncomfortable, even so,' Robert went on, putting the tray on the table by the window shaded with creeper. 'Don't you think? Tramping about over the mountains with all that heavy wet straw hanging off you, and rain dripping off your hat brim.'

'A bit like a sheep,' said Tom, who had opened the fridge door.

Robert pictured wet Portuguese sheep in hats. 'True. What are you looking for?'

'Oh, just something for the cat.'

'I don't think you should encourage that cat, quite honestly.' Robert carried the breakfast things over to the sink. 'She'll become a bit of a pest.'

'Oh, please.' Tom turned round, leaving the fridge door open. 'She'll die if we don't feed her. She'll *die*.'

'All right, all right.' He reached out and shut the door. '*We'll* die if flies get in the fridge and crap all over the food.'

'Will we really?'

'No. But don't leave it open, there's a good chap.'

'Okay.' Tom leaned up against the draining-board, watching Robert squirt in violently coloured washing-up liquid and turn on the taps. The pipes banged and shook.

42

Through the open door to the passage Robert could hear the others wandering away from the breakfast table; he saw Jessica going into her room to get her swimming things, followed by her brother. 'Why don't you go and play with the others?' he suggested, rinsing cereal bowls.

Tom ignored him, twisting a worn tea towel on a hook. '*Please* can I feed the cat? Is there any milk?'

Robert looked at him. 'Are you always this persistent?'

'What?'

'Never mind.' He nodded towards the breakfast tray. 'I expect there's some milk left in the jug.'

Together they went to the back door and Robert pulled it open. Immediately there was a swift movement: the cat, who had been waiting, slunk down the stone steps and looked up at them.

'I told you she was hungry.' Tom made eating noises. 'Come on, puss, here you are, don't be frightened.'

Robert poured milk and stepped back into the doorway; he stood watching the cat's cautious approach up the steps again, and her eager lapping. Tom, squatting beside her, knocked the saucer and reached out to stroke the staring fur.

'I really wouldn't,' said Robert, automatically.

Footsteps came lightly along the passage: he turned to see Frances, in stone-coloured shorts and pale blue shirt, move towards the stairs. How had this woman, formal to the point of primness, produced this clumsy and eccentric child? He thought again of the curious expression on her face last night when she looked at Claire, and shook his head, musing, as she climbed the stairs.

More footsteps, brisker and heavier.

'How are we getting on?' Claire came into the kitchen, carrying a rucksack. 'We'll take fruit and crisps, shall we? And I'll make up a bottle of squash.' She looked at the unfinished bowl of washing-up, and the open door, and raised an eyebrow. Robert nodded towards Tom; she came to look.

'Oh, Tom – that mangy animal! I don't think you should touch her.'

'If you succeed in stopping him, you're a better man than I.' Robert returned to the sink, hearing Tom say fiercely: 'She's *not* mangy,' and Claire, as he had done, sigh and accept defeat.

'What about the dinghy?' she asked, pouring concentrated squash into an empty plastic bottle.

'Do we know where the foot pump is?'

'Not exactly, but I can look.'

'Leave it,' said Robert. He tipped up the bowl and let the water drain, with painful slowness, down the plughole. 'There's plenty of time. I haven't even seen the river yet, what with drives to the airport and all that. Let's just get down there, for God's sake.'

The path to the river led through maize fields, reached by walking down the hill and along the cobbled streets through the village. It was after half-past ten by the time they set out, the air hot and still, the sky without a cloud. They all wore sunhats; their sandals slapped on the stones. From the hillside the erratic church bell now rang steadily for mass; coming down the hill towards the intersection of streets they saw, ahead, one or two families walking slowly towards the main road in their Sunday best, the men and boys in open-necked white shirts and shiny flares, the women in brightly patterned frocks. Two old ladies in black, on sticks, followed slowly.

'Did you go to a service last year?' Oliver asked Claire.

'No, never. We went inside to have a look, of course, but not to an actual service.' She turned to look at him. He was wearing loose cotton trousers, a faded blue T-shirt and cream cotton jacket; with his Panama hat and glasses, carrying his book, he looked, she thought, like something out of Bloomsbury, the family bag of swimming things in his other hand almost as incongruous as it would have looked on Strachey, or Duncan Grant. She hadn't given much thought to Bloomsbury for a while. It was years since she'd taught *The Waves* at A level, and even then, she realised, she had connected it with life at university and the kind of intensity she used to associate with Frances, not life as it had since become: pleasurably ordinary, filled with children. Brilliant, neurotic Bloomsbury had produced, as far as she could remember, few children.

They walked past a stone wall covered in blackberry brambles.

'Why?' she asked Oliver. 'Would you like to go to a service?'

'Perhaps. Might be interesting, don't you think?'

44

'I suppose so – I imagine it's much like most rural Catholicism, though, don't you? Overblown, full of incense and ignorance – ' She stopped, suddenly embarrassed. 'You're not Catholic, are you?'

'Lapsed,' he said, looking at her in amusement. 'It's all right, please don't worry. You don't go to church in London?'

'No, never.' None of their friends went to church. 'Do you?'

'Sometimes. More out of nostalgia than anything else, I suppose. I take Tom occasionally – part of his education.'

They had reached the bottom of the hill, where the street divided: a great wooden barn stood at the corner, set on stilts in a spacious yard, and three small grubby children in oversized clothes were taking turns with a makeshift go-cart, rattling over the concrete. They stopped and waved, calling.

'*Bom dia, bom dia*!'

One of the children, a little boy, wore glasses; Claire remembered him from last year. She saw Robert and the others pause by the gate and smile; the children ran towards them and Tom began to climb the bars. Frances put out a restraining arm; he hung over the top bar, grinning, as Claire and Oliver came up.

Robert turned to them. 'Oliver – I was just telling Frances, this is a threshing barn, for the maize. When it's dry, they bring it in and beat it over a hollow manger: you'll hear them. Then they sweep up the grains from the floor. We went to watch them last year, didn't we, Jess?'

Jess nodded, running her sandalled foot up and down in the dust.

'And you wrote about it at school, didn't you?' Claire said encouragingly.

'Mmm.' She went on scuffing.

'Did you?' said Oliver. 'That sounds interesting.' She looked up at him, and they smiled at each other. 'It's rather magnificent,' he went on, turning to the barn again. 'Must be a good two hundred years old?'

'Easily,' said Robert. 'Most of the houses in the village are older than that.'

They stood gazing at it: the trailing vines overhanging the flight of worn stone steps to the doors, the weather-beaten wood, with

45

its peeling black paint. High on the rooftop, pigeons cooed. Frances put her hand on Tom's arm again as he made to clamber over; he shook her off.

'I want to have a go in that cart thing.'

'I want to go to the river,' said Jack. 'Come on. It's *hot*.'

'Yes, let's go,' said Claire. 'You'll like it down there, Tom. Are you a good swimmer?'

'I've done my ten metres.' He clambered down again, reluctantly.

'I've done my fifty,' said Jack.

'So?' Tom flushed. 'So? What's so great about doing fifty?'

'Well, it's better than ten, isn't it?'

'I'm sure,' said Robert, moving between them, 'that by the end of the fortnight you'll be both be doing a hundred. But the river's a bit deep in places, and it goes down quite suddenly, doesn't it, Jack, so you'd better be careful, okay?'

'You didn't mention that,' said Frances.

'Well, most of it's pretty shallow. Has he brought armbands?'

'I'm not wearing *arm*bands,' said Tom.

'Oh, yes you are,' said Oliver.

Frances said carefully, 'Let's discuss it when we get there.'

Jack said, 'I haven't worn armbands since I was in reception,' and Tom reached out and shoved at him.

'Shut up!'

'*You* shut up,' said Jack, recoiling, rubbing his arm.

'No, *you* shut up.' And Tom lunged towards him again, red in the face.

'Tom!' said Oliver and Frances together, and Oliver moved swiftly over and grabbed him. 'Stop that at once, do you hear?'

'Get off me.' Tom tried to wrench away, but he couldn't. He stood panting, like an enraged bull, fighting back tears.

'Baby,' said Jack.

'Okay, okay.' Clare moved towards him, brushing past Jess. 'Jack, will you stop teasing.' She held out her hand. 'Walk with me, please. Come on, we're all getting hot and bothered, we'll feel better as soon as we get to the river.' She was aware of the children in the yard behind them, hanging over the gate, fascinated. She gave them a cheery wave, and took Jack firmly by the hand. 'Let's go.'

'Sorry about that,' said Oliver.

'Please. It was Jack's fault.'

'No, it wasn't,' said Jack.

They went on their way, Claire and Jack in front, Robert and Jessica behind, Oliver, Frances and Tom bringing up the rear in silence, looking about them.

The front doors of the houses on either side of the narrow street were almost all raised up above ground level, entered, like the barn, by flights of stone steps. A few of them had roof terraces, or tiny gardens; most had balconies, shaded with vines, hung with washing above pots of geraniums. From hard straight chairs in doorways hung with plastic strip curtains, women smiled down at them. They wore print overalls, and showed gaps in their teeth when they answered Robert's greetings.

'*Bom dia*!'

Men in their fifties and early sixties leaned in doorways on frames, and walked stiffly over the cobbles on sticks.

'You see,' Robert said to Oliver, 'the effect of a lifetime's labour in the fields.' He winked at Tom, trying to cheer him up, but Tom, like Frances, it seemed, had long since stopped listening, and there was no returning wink.

'Indeed,' said Oliver. 'Did you write about that in your project, Jessica?'

'About what?'

'All these workers old before their time.' He nodded towards a man in a doorway, leaning on a frame as he surveyed the morning.

Jessica shook her head. 'I don't think so.'

'I shouldn't think she did,' said Robert, 'she was only eleven.'

'Dad . . .' said Jessica, flushing. He patted her arm affectionately. 'Only trying to help.'

They were passing the last few houses in the street: ahead, walled on one side, an earthen path, soft and broad, dappled with sunlight, ran towards the fields beneath a dense canopy of vines. Heavy clusters of milky green and cloudy purple grapes hung down; the air was warm, languid, caressing and seductive; from the fields beyond came the hot buzz of cicadas. And entering this shady, tranquil haven the group relaxed, walking slowly.

'I'd forgotten,' said Robert, stretching. 'I really had forgotten.'

'But this is perfect,' said Frances, smiling at him. 'How can we thank you for inviting us to such a place?'

'Wait till you see the river,' said Claire. She gave Jack's hand a squeeze. 'Be nice to Tom,' she said under her breath.

'Okay.' He let go of her, and went over to Tom, who had stopped and was working on the wall with a stick, digging out loose cement with slow concentration.

'There's grasshoppers in the fields.'

Tom looked up. 'Where?'

'Everywhere – there's masses. You can catch them in the fishing nets sometimes.' He turned, and began to move off again; Tom followed. Together, with upright nets, they walked towards the fields, and Claire lifted her camera and took them: two straight backs, one slender, one sturdy, two floppy sunhats, moving out of the shade and on to the hot open path.

'Why don't you join them?' she said to Jess, lowering the camera again.

Jess shook her head. 'They're better on their own. Anyway, I don't want to.'

Claire looked at her. This time last year Jess, at eleven, had been unquestionably still a child, almost a little girl. The Hobbs boys had been here, the elder the same age as she: the four of them had, on the whole, played companionably, and there had been little sense that Jess, as a girl, was set apart. This year was different, and changes which in everyday life at home Claire had been barely aware of seemed here, in a new summer, to be dramatic. Jess was taller, leaner – that is to say, she had lost most of her puppy fat – but there were already indications that her outline would change again, that she would gradually fill out, and have, like Claire, a noticeable bottom and heavy breasts. This time next year she would have begun to cross the threshold; now, with her clear soft skin and thick mane of hair she was still this side of it, but only just. And the distance between her and the boys was great. Of course – why should she want to walk with them? Yet she couldn't hang around the grown-ups all the time. I should have foreseen this, Claire thought, I should have arranged for a friend. But that would have introduced another element into what had already felt like quite enough: coming here with people they barely knew. She said nothing, but put her arm round her daughter's shoulders – briefly, because Jessica, so unlike Jack, was becoming undemonstrative.

Out of the canopy of vines the heat struck them again: that, and the dizzying whirr of the cicadas, the dance of butterflies in and out of the long straight rows of whiskery maize.

'We've got one!' came Tom's voice. 'Look!' He emerged from one of the rows, his hands cupped. 'It's tiny.' He came up to them slowly, stepping over the cracked and stony earth; he carefully opened his hands and they gathered round, admiring. The grasshopper, a bright, beautiful green, sat motionless.

'Oh, he's lovely,' said Jess.

'He came into my hands as easy as anything.' Tom carefully enclosed him once again. 'There's lots, come and see.'

They followed him across rough ground.

'He's just like Gerald Durrell,' said Claire to Frances, and even as she said it, thought: is Gerald Durrell who Frances and Oliver would have chosen?

Irrigation ditches criss-crossed the field, the thick red earth piled up alongside, caked hard, bordered by strings of vines. They found Jack squatting on his heels, looking intently into shallow water, the nets flung down on the earth; they went across to him, sandals crunching on last year's stubble between this year's crop.

'Sssh!' he said. 'There's another.'

They crept, like explorers, beginning to sweat, the air filled with cicadas. Little brown birds flitted in and out of the maize, and an enormous grasshopper leapt, suddenly, across their path.

'Wow!' said Tom. 'Did you see that? I'm going to get him.' He moved forward quickly, jerkily, his hands still cupped, tripped on a protruding stone and went flying. 'Ow, ow!'

The first grasshopper, released, leapt away, at once invisible, and Tom, bare limbs scratched by the sharp dry stalks, sat up rubbing his shin. 'Ow!'

Jack looked up, cross. 'You idiot – now he's gone.'

'Shut up!' said Tom. 'You wouldn't like it, there's *stones* here, how would you like it, having a great stone bang into you? Ow!'

'All right,' said Frances, bending over him. 'All right, never mind.' She tried to rub his leg, but he pulled it away.

'What do you mean, never mind?'

'Oh, for God's sake – ' She stood up, shaking her head. '*Please* can we go to the river?' And she set off, not looking back, a slender blue and stone figure against the browning maize.

'Oh, dear,' said Robert.

Oliver pulled Tom to his feet.

'Is there going to be any more fuss today?' he demanded.

'I – ' Tom faltered.

'Is there?'

'No.'

'Look at me.'

Robert and Claire exchanged glances; Tom, his face scarlet, looked at his father and then away, across the shimmering field.

'All right,' said Oliver. 'Now, you follow your mother and apologise, and I don't want to have another word of nonsense or cheek out of you for the rest of the day. Is that clear?'

'Yes.' Tom's voice was barely audible, thick with tears.

'Go on, then.'

He set off ahead of them, stumbling a little as he tried to catch up with Frances, rubbing his face, the fishing net abandoned. Robert bent to retrieve it; there was a silence.

'Well,' said Oliver stiffly, 'it seems I must spend the day apologising for Tom's behaviour.'

Robert shook his head; he and Claire, almost in the same breath, made noises: children . . . family life . . . just settling in . . .

Oliver shook his head, unsmiling. 'There are times . . .'

'There are always times,' said Claire. 'Come on, Jack, leave the ditch now.' She held out her hand. 'And bring your net, okay?'

He came, dragging it behind him, bumping over the stubble. They set off, she with the children, and Robert, in neutral male gear, explaining to Oliver that the ditches related not only to irrigation but to inheritance: as each parent died, the piece of land was redivided among the children, the family portions, over the generations, thus growing ever smaller. Oliver nodded, apparently listening, swinging the bag. In the middle of the field Tom had caught up with Frances; they were walking side by side.

And at last they came to a low stone wall, screened by trees and dusty blackberry bushes, with a gap. Their feet sank into warm grey sand, and before them was the river: broad, peaceful, cool. It flowed between this field and the one on the opposite bank, where thick stooks of hay stood drying; it flowed beneath a great outcrop of pine-clad cliff. In patches of gleaming light and deep shade it made a sweeping curve down from their right, and moved towards rocky shallows far down on their left, where shining dragonflies hovered and darted in the sun; it curled round the side of the mountain and disappeared.

'At last.'

'Thank God.'

'Hurray!'

Later, no doubt, teenagers and older children from the village would appear; for now, they had it all to themselves. The children raced to the water's edge, pulling their clothes off, and Jessica, quicker and more graceful than the boys, emerged from her shorts and T-shirt in a smooth green swimsuit, pushing back her hair.

'You look nice,' said Oliver.

She smiled at him, and waded in; stopped by the sudden cold, she stood there, the water just above her knees, and was taunted by the boys, who were ready now and raced in, shrieking.

Robert swam like a dog, steady and purposeful, making an effort; his round white shoulders and head of thinning hair pushed in a determined breaststroke towards the rocks beneath the cliff on the far side. Jess, a strong swimmer, kept pace beside him. For Tom's sake, the boys had been instructed to stay in their depth, Jack pulling faces which his parents affected not to notice. He and Tom were out of the water now, digging a trench.

Claire, who had had a brief, satisfying dip, and now wanted nothing so much as to feel off duty for a bit, sat dripping in ruched Liberty print, beneath her sunhat, her arms round her knees, absently watching them. Oliver had taken off his cotton jacket and said he'd swim in a little while; he had wandered off along the bank, downriver, taking his book, which Claire, squinting, saw was the *Collected Poems* of Larkin. How nice. How nice to be able to disappear to a shady spot with wry reflections on sexual and surburban loneliness, leaving your child to the care of others.

And meanwhile Frances, in a blue-grey swimsuit, had walked quickly into the water, struck out and begun to swim gracefully upriver, away from everyone. Claire followed the small fair head, the pale arms lifting and falling in a crawl, and then, after a while, the change to a smooth, unhurried breaststroke, moving into the broadest part of the river, shaded by the trees on the far side. Branches brought down in a winter gale had become lodged in the middle of the water, anchored by rocks beneath the surface, making an island: Frances swam towards it, further than Claire had ever reached, and then round, and beyond, following the curve of the river, until she was out of sight.

Claire raised a mental eyebrow. She had not known Frances to be such a strong swimmer; nor had she reckoned on being left in charge of Tom without so much as a by-your-leave. She contemplated the boys, amicably absorbed, as she was sure they would remain while close to water; she waved to Robert and Jess, who had clambered out on to the rocks beneath the cliff and were warming themselves in the sun, which beat upon their wet, hatless heads.

'Don't stay up there too long,' she called.

'We won't.'

'Did you put sun cream on?'

'No.'

'Well, be careful, then.'

'We will. Isn't it lovely?'

'Lovely,' said Claire. Tomorrow, when they brought the dinghy, they could run a ferry service for hats and other requirements. She lay down on her stomach, stretching out on the towel, reaching for P. D. James. Small striped beetles, chocolate and coffee, like humbugs, trundled over mountains of sand and boulders of dark twigs; she turned the pages, brushing off grains of sand, yawning a little. It was hot, even by the water, even beneath the trees; she closed her eyes for a moment and the voices of the boys and the distant sound of the church bell reverberated in sleepy ripples. She yawned again, resting her head on her arms.

And was woken by Frances, greeting the boys, dropping quietly down nearby, dripping wet, shivering. She wrapped herself in a towel and sat drying herself. Her hair clung to her head in damp strands; she looked not much older than Jessica. Claire, floating up from sleep, regarded her from beneath her sunhat, and patted the sand in greeting.

'You're frozen.'

Frances turned to look at her. 'I overdid it – it was wonderful, but I didn't realise how the cold seeps into you. I've never swum in a river before.'

'You did very well, then. How far did you go?'

'Oh, way beyond the island. It became quite hypnotic after a while, I really lost myself for a few minutes – I can't remember the last time that happened. Anyway, you're right, I'm frozen.' She drew the towel closer round her shoulders and looked down at Claire, smiling. 'Unlike you – you look warm as toast.'

'I am.' Claire stretched, raising her head, and her hat fell off. 'Too hot,' she said, retrieving it. 'Where is everyone?'

She made to sit up, but Frances lay down beside her and said quickly: 'Everyone's fine, they're all pottering about. Let's leave them to it while we can.'

'Okay.' Claire lay down again, feeling thirsty. There was a pause, in which a humbug beetle laboured over her outstretched fingers. Frances was silent, soaking up the sun. 'Well,' Claire said after a while, 'what do you think of it so far?'

'It's beautiful.'

'And it's perfect for the children, especially – the pool at the house, being able to walk down here . . . I can't bear having to drive somewhere every day on holiday, can you?'

'No.' There was another pause, in which Frances did not elaborate either on holidays or driving with children; Claire thought vaguely that perhaps, if it were not so hot, she might begin to find this one-sided conversation rather awkward, and remembered, simultaneously, Linda Hobbs, last year, chattering without pause, and Frances, at Bristol, quiet and remote. But the sun explained and excused all silences, dissolved all social barriers, thank God. Once they'd settled down, and Tom had unwound, they'd be fine. She made a little runnel in the sand for another approaching humbug, and watched it fall and bumble on, feeling herself grow fond of it. Beside her, Frances said quietly:

'I want to talk to you.'

53

'How nice,' said Claire. 'What about?'

Another silence. 'Various things.'

Claire thought: well, that can mean only one thing. The marriage. She's going to tell me about her and Oliver, and I'm not sure I want to know, just at the moment. We're on holiday, she could hear Robert say, and she agreed. And then she had a sudden insight: no, it's not that, or it's more than that. It's something about Tom. She's going to tell me . . . what? With a flash she knew: he's adopted. *That's* why he doesn't fit.

Footsteps came over the sand behind them; above them Robert announced: 'The kids say they're hungry.'

'Well, give them something to eat, then,' Claire said briskly. 'It's all in the rucksack.' She felt torn between wanting to hear what Frances wanted to tell her, and a desire for the morning, which had already had its unexpected moments of stress and distress, to be settled and ordinary now, undisturbed by problems.

'Right.' Robert paused. 'You all right?'

'Fine, thanks. You?'

'Hot.' He moved off again and she said: 'Sun cream. In the swimming bag.'

'Will do.'

Beside her, Frances said: 'Later. Not now.'

'All right.' Claire felt, with a shade of unease, as if she were being drawn into a conspiracy. She rolled over, and got up. 'I'm very thirsty. Would you like a drink?'

'Perhaps when I've thawed out.'

'Okay.' She got to her feet, her head swimming a little, the sun on the water dancing before her eyes. Not a good idea, falling asleep mid-morning; there'd be time enough in the house, this afternoon. Still, if you couldn't fall asleep mid-morning on holiday, when could you? Robert was doling out crisps; the children ripped open their packets and crunched contentedly. 'Squash,' she said, going over. 'I'm dying.'

'Me too. Here we go.' He withdrew the Thermos, unscrewing the top, and poured into the plastic cup: there was the delicious chink of ice cubes.

'Can I have some?' asked Tom, watching. 'Please?'

'Of course.' Claire drank quickly, observing pairs of shoulders turning scarlet. Why on earth hadn't she done them first thing, before they'd all dashed into the water? Why, come to that, hadn't Frances and Oliver, in some ways so overprotective, done Tom? Well, they'd all been seduced by the river after a difficult walk; never mind. She passed the cup back to Robert, and rummaged in the bag. 'Come here, Tom.'

He stood still obediently, like a rough pony waiting to be shod, as she rubbed cream into his shoulders and down his back. His skin was hot to the touch. I wonder, she thought, turning him round and rubbing his broad chest and stomach. Oliver was a big man, but he was spare, Frances not an inch over size twelve. Tom was built like a tank. 'Here,' she said, squeezing a snake of cream into his hand. 'You do your arms and legs.'

'Okay.' He wandered off to get his drink, rubbing his limbs abstractedly, leaving thick smears of white.

'Where's Oliver?' asked Jessica, munching on an apple.

'He's gone to have a bit of peace and quiet with his book,' said Claire. 'Come here and let me do you. Or would you rather do yourself?'

'It's all right.' Jess settled down on the sand, her arms round her knees; Claire knelt up behind her, smoothing in the cream. Jess's shoulders were firm, dusted with freckles from the sun. Like Claire, unlike her father, she tanned easily; the boys had gone scarlet but she was turning a rich honey-brown, and her hair had lightened. Last year's photographs showed, by the end of the holiday, a lovely child, a lion cub, tawny and gold, fit, clear-eyed. But last year she had been freer, more open, always laughing, hugging goodnight. Now she seemed from nowhere to have found this rather distant, standoffish air, which shrank from physical contact. Claire was surprised to be allowed such an intimate ritual now. But perhaps Jess wanted to talk.

'Did Oliver alarm you?' she asked, pushing the thick hair aside. 'I mean with Tom – getting so cross.'

Jess shook her head. 'Not really. Anyway, Tom was being a pain.'

'He'd hurt himself,' said Claire, taken aback. Had Jess really become so cool?

'You know what I mean. Have you got any sweat bands? For my hair?'

'I think so, up at the house. Can you manage for now?'

'I suppose so.'

Claire ran her fingers down the knobs of Jessica's spine, and across, covering the whole of her back, down to the curving line of swimsuit. 'There. You do the rest of you.' She looked over to Jack, who had picked up one of the humbugs and was scrutinising it closely. 'Next, please.'

He came over carefully, his palm upmost. 'Look.'

'I know. They're nice, aren't they?' Tiny feelers waved at the air. 'I think he's a bit frightened; put him down.'

'I want to see how he works.'

'And I want a hug,' said Claire.

Jack upturned his hand: the beetle fell like a stone.

'Poor chap.' Tom, she found herself thinking, would never have done that. His clumsiness was accidental, unconscious, a kind of affliction; he would, unless he had tripped on something, have put that little creature down with care, tenderness even. Still – the thought of living with Tom was daunting. She held out her arms, and Jack came into them, burying his face in her neck. Claire held him close, smelling his sun-warmed hair; she turned him round, so that he was sitting between her knees, and picked up the tube of cream again.

'Like monkeys,' he said, as she began to rub. 'It's like a grooming session.'

'Mother monkey and little monkey.' She kissed the back of his neck. 'I do love you.'

'I love you too,' said Jack simply. 'I'll always love you.'

Claire kissed him again. And turned for some reason, to see Frances, sitting up now, her hands clasped round her knees as Jessica's had been, watching them

'We must talk about food,' Claire said.

'Food?' She looked blank.

'For tonight. Are you and Oliver happy about this arrangement? Taking turns?'

'Oh. Oh, yes, that's fine.'

'There's not much in the larder, I'm afraid, we'll have to go and do a proper shop tomorrow in the market town. But there's enough bread and cheese and ham and salad stuff for a couple of meals. I don't really care what you put on the table, I just don't want to have to put it there myself.'

'Don't worry,' said Frances, 'I'm happy to do it. I enjoy cooking, remember.'

'Yes. That meal you and Oliver gave us was wonderful.' Claire ran creamy fingers along Jack's slender arms, and pushed away the memory of Robert and herself at home afterwards, munching cornflakes.

Frances was getting up, dropping her thick blue towel.

'Oliver likes cooking, too. It's one of the things we have in common.' And she walked across the sand to the edge of the glinting water and stood there, looking downriver in the direction he had taken; hesitating, as if undecided whether to stay or follow.

The rest of the morning passed agreeably. The sun rose, bleaching the cliff face and the comfortable flat rocks across the water where Robert and Jessica had been, but the rocky shallows were shaded by hillside and trees, and Robert suggested a wildlife expedition.

'Wicked,' said Tom. 'What's there?'

'Little fish, little frogs, butterflies, dragonflies. And sometimes you see water snakes.'

'*Water* snakes! Wow!'

'They're not dangerous, are they?' Frances asked, fastening on his sandals.

'Gentle as kittens.' They began to walk towards the shallows. 'Oh, look, here's Oliver.'

He came towards them smiling, raising his hand, heralded by an iridescent shimmer of turquoise dragonflies. They greeted each other and stood on the rocks, gazing down into sun-flecked brown pools of water. Little black butterflies, soft as velvet, fluttered amongst the reeds; the air was full of the sounds of birds and flowing water; far above them an aeroplane crossed the sky, leaving a long pale line of smoke.

'Well, this is very nice,' said Oliver, putting an arm round Frances. Her hands in the pockets of her shorts, she stood smiling up at him, fair hair light against his old blue T-shirt. A photograph taken then would have shown an undeniably appealing couple, happy and relaxed. Probably, thought Claire, observing them, all they need is a little sun and time to be together, like anyone else.

'Had a good swim?' he asked her, and Frances nodded.

'Very. Did you find somewhere pleasant?'

'I did. I've been lying with the scent of pines all around me, undisturbed by a soul.'

'Lucky you.'

'Fish!' said Tom suddenly from beneath them, kneeling on an overhang. 'There's lots!'

They all got down and peered. Dull grey, a couple of inches long, the fish flickered through the water, vanishing the instant his fingers touched the surface.

'Quick! Where's the nets?'

And thus the rest of the morning passed, tranquil and easy. They fished, and baked tiny finless bodies on the rocks; they captured butterflies and released them into the sun again; they admired the dragonflies, and hoped for kingfishers. Every now and then a car or a van made its way down the winding mountain road above them; apart from this they were quite alone. Oliver swam, in a strong slow crawl; the children went in again, and played.

Frances went on ahead to prepare the lunch: by the time they all gathered up their things and made their way back through the baking heat of the fields again, it felt as if they had, in the course of the morning, become something of a group, genuinely enjoying each other's company.

Back at the house they slowly climbed the steps to the terrace. Claire dumped all the swimming stuff inside the doors, and went into the dining-room to find the table freshly laid with bread and cheese and a big bowl of salad. Frances had closed the shutters and the shaded room looked fresh and inviting. Claire gave an inward sigh of relief: she might have known that Frances, once she had begun to unwind, could be relied upon to make an effort.

Behind her the children were coming into the room companionably, settling into their chairs, and here was Frances, her hair brushed and tied back, carrying a tray of glasses, welcoming them all home again. She put the tray down on the table and began to pour out squash for the children.

'There we are . . . All right, Tom? Careful with that.'

'I'm hot.' He took the glass and began to drink noisily. 'Can we swim in the pool after lunch?'

'After tea, perhaps,' said Robert, coming in with Oliver, and pulling out a chair. 'This afternoon all grown-ups are off duty and all children rest or amuse themselves quietly. Is that possible, do you think?' He drew the china jug of wine towards him. 'And don't forget what I said yesterday, will you? No one uses that pool without a grown-up nearby. Frances, this all looks wonderful. Thank you. Have a drink.'

In the deep and enveloping warmth of the late afternoon, the grown-ups, rested, sat beneath the overhanging vines at the round white table on the upper path. They were drinking tea, and Frances was smoking; from the far end of the path came the shouts and splashing of the children, leaping in and out of the pool, beyond the bushes. Beneath them, the half-starved cat slept on baked earth, stretched out, motionless. Robert yawned, and reached up to pull off a few more black grapes from the bunch above his head; he sat popping them into his mouth, one by one, flicking the pips on to the ground, where tiny insects scurried.

'You'll be ill,' said Claire.

'No I won't.' He popped in another one. 'One of the very nicest things about today,' he went on, reaching for Dick Francis, 'is the prospect of supper being presented to me by our companions. Now it begins to feel like a holiday. And now, if you'll excuse me . . .' He got up, scraping the white iron chair on the path. 'I am going to take my turn on the swing-seat. See you.' And he wandered away down the path.

The others smiled; Frances stubbed out her cigarette; there was a silence.

'Do you think the children need an eye?' she asked casually, looking at Oliver.

'I think they're all right, aren't they? So long as we're within earshot.'

Claire, who had begun to feel sleep and sun and wine soak into her bones, and thus no longer had the energy or inclination to care about anything very much, was nonetheless aware that Frances was willing Oliver to go, and that he was refusing. She couldn't begin to guess whether his refusal was simply because he, like herself, could not be bothered to move from this blissful spot, or because he would not be willed away. But he did not go, and the three of them sat listening to the children and watching the dissolving shimmer of heat over the valley as the sun slipped lower and the first pale streaks of grey appeared beyond the mountains.

We need Robert, thought Claire, seeing the swing-seat on the terrace begin to sway. Frances lit another cigarette and Oliver reached for his book again, something on Portugal he'd found in the house this time, not Larkin. Robert defuses, he makes everything easy and fun; I don't seem to be able to do that with these two, not on my own.

Oliver turned a page; Frances blew out smoke; wet feet came along the path.

'Hello, darling.'

'Hi.' Jess, with a towel round her shoulders, dropped into Robert's empty chair, pushing back damp hair.

'Boys all right?'

'Oh, yes.' She sat fiddling with little bits of grape stalk, left by Robert. 'Where's Dad?'

'Gone to have a read. Why don't you go and get your book and bring it up here with us?'

She shook her head. 'I don't feel like it at the moment.' She looked at Oliver, and at Frances, tapping ash into a saucer. 'What games do you play?'

'Games?' said Oliver, looking up. 'Well, Frances and I play chess occasionally . . .'

'I mean children's games. Do you know the Game Of Life? It's brilliant.'

He and Frances smiled resignedly. 'Tom's not a board games child,' said Frances. 'Perhaps he's still too young. Many have been tried and many hurled across the room in fury. We've given up.'

Jessica, coming from a family which customarily spent hours on wet afternoons in Crouch End playing everything from snakes and ladders to Monopoly, looked bemused.

'But chess isn't just a grown-up game, is it?' said Oliver. 'Haven't you ever played?'

60

'Actually, she hasn't,' said Claire. 'I think she and Jack would both be quite good, but somehow we've neglected it. Neither of us is very keen, to be honest. I'm not, anyway.'

'Well, there's a set in the house,' he said. 'I saw it in the sitting-room – would you like to learn, Jessica?'

She nodded. 'Yes, please.'

'Out here?'

'Oh, why don't you play down on the terrace?' said Frances. 'You won't disturb Robert, will you? Let Claire and me catch up on old times, go on.' She smiled at him, and he got up, pushing back his chair.

'Okay, then. We rendezvous in the kitchen in about an hour, yes? To organise supper?'

'Fine.' She and Claire watched the two of them walk away beneath the vines. 'Put on a sweatshirt,' Claire called to Jessica. 'It'll be cool quite soon.'

She didn't answer, following Oliver's long stride; they turned down the steps to the house and a few minutes later reappeared on the terrace, Oliver carrying a wooden box. They sat opposite each other at the white table, and he began to set up the board. Claire wondered if Robert did mind them being there, and decided he probably didn't. Let's face it, she thought, Robert doesn't really mind anything very much, thank God.

'That's kind of Oliver,' she said.

'He'll enjoy it,' said Frances. 'He loves teaching children – it disappoints him that Tom is so unreceptive.'

'Well, I'm sure it's just a matter of time. Tom's into other things, that's all. He's an outdoor child, isn't he?'

'Yes. Yes, he is.' Frances hesitated. 'Claire – '

Footsteps came flying down the path; Tom, shrieking with laughter, was chasing Jack, waving a soaking-wet towel.

'Careful . . .' said Frances, as they raced past. She covered her face. 'It'll end in tears or fury.'

'Don't worry,' Claire said kindly, as the boys disappeared down the steps and could be heard, having belted down the next flight to the garden, erupting into fresh gales of laughter. Squawks of alarm came from the scattering hens. 'Let them be – I was just going to call them out of the water anyway.'

61

'They've got no shoes on.' Frances lowered her hands. 'It's all scrubby and rough down there.'

'In that case, they can go and look for their shoes, can't they? And if they can't find them, no doubt their fathers will assist.'

Frances looked at her gratefully.

'You wanted to talk to me,' said Claire.

'Yes.' Frances visibly took a breath, but said nothing.

Claire waited. 'What a strange mixture you are,' she said, after a while. 'One minute you clearly can't bear having children around you, and the next you're all concerned about bare feet.'

Frances shook her head. She was looking out across the terracotta rooftops of the village beneath them, where the streets were filled with the sounds of activity again as the air grew cooler. Voices called, buckets clanked, children ran up and down. 'Don't most mothers feel like that?'

'I'm sure. But with you I sense that it's different.'

There was a pause. 'I'm different, certainly,' said Frances, and tapped out another cigarette from the packet. She lit it without turning, leaning back in her chair, her feet resting on a ledge in the stem of the table. She suddenly looked drawn, despite the day in the sun.

'How about a drink?' said Claire. 'Shall I go and – '

'No,' said Frances, 'please don't go. You'll get all tangled up with the children . . .'

'Well, what is it, then? Come on, Frances, it's okay, you can trust me. Is it about children? Tom? He's a nice boy, I like him. You and Oliver mustn't worry so much about things, it'll all be fine.' She could hear herself sounding brisk and dismissive and capable; perhaps that in itself was a threat to someone so apparently unsure of motherhood, someone who she had guessed was perhaps not, in any case, Tom's real mother. So she stopped, and Frances said abruptly:

'It's not about Tom, it's about me.'

'You mean – you and Oliver?' Claire asked, following this morning's train of thought.

'Indirectly, yes. Well – perhaps I should say directly.' She drew on the cigarette; smoke drifted up towards the overhanging vines and away towards the cloud of midges which had begun to dance above the path. She said: 'I thought everything would be all right, but it isn't. I thought I had changed, but I haven't.' There was another silence, and this time Claire did not attempt to break it. Frances said slowly, 'I've been in love with someone else for a long time.'

Claire waited; nothing more came; Frances still did not look at her.

'Well,' Claire said at last. 'That must be rather difficult. Does Oliver know?'

'I don't know. I don't think so. No one knows.'

'And are you actually having an affair?'

'No.' The hand which held the cigarette was shaking. 'I mean, I'd like to, but she's married.'

The running footsteps and laughter of the boys, the squawks of panic-stricken hens, had faded: they had moved right across to the other side of the garden, beneath the lemon trees. The sounds from the village seemed distant, too, as Claire let those last little words sink in. From the end of the path came the steady, unending flow of water pouring into the tank, a sound which was always with them, soothing and cool, but which now felt profoundly altered.

'Oh,' she said carefully. 'Oh.'

'Don't look so worried,' said Frances drily, turning at last to meet her eyes. 'It isn't you.'

'I – ' Claire swallowed. 'I didn't think it was.'

And then Frances smiled, warm and direct, and Claire felt suddenly as though she were seeing her properly for the first time. 'Didn't you?' she asked. 'Not even in Bristol?'

'What?'

'Didn't you realise what I felt for you then?'

'What?'

The house, the garden, Robert and the children were whirling away: Claire, frozen into this moment, sat looking at Frances in transfixed astonishment. With such clarity that the last eighteen years might never have passed, she saw her: jumping each time Claire came near her; hiding away; talking freely only when they were alone; hiding away again; finally disappearing, without so much as a goodbye. She saw her, pretty and self-assured, smiling at Simon Blair, the tutor everyone had dreamed about, distantly acknowledging Claire across a sunlit room, as if she cared nothing for her at all.

'I need a drink,' she said at last, and then, as Frances tipped forward on her chair and made to get up to fetch one, she added: 'No, wait, just a minute. You're right, we'll get all tangled up with the children.'

'What about a cigarette?' asked Frances, offering the packet. Claire took one, lit it, and coughed violently.

'Ugh.' She put it straight out again. 'You smoke far too much.'

'I know. I've tried to give it up, but I can't.' She gave a wry smile. 'Change is never so easy.'

Claire sat with her elbows on the table, looking at her. 'Go on. Who is this woman?'

Frances looked away. 'We work together – she was there when I arrived.'

Claire tried to remember what Frances had told her, the day they ran into each other again. 'You went there when Tom was two . . . That's a long time.'

'Yes.'

'And does she know?'

'No.' Frances was distant again. 'No, she hasn't a clue.'

'You're sure?'

'Certain. After all, you didn't guess, did you?'

'No. But perhaps this person is a little more astute.'

Frances touched her arm affectionately. 'You're astute enough, Claire.' She paused. 'And what would you have done if you had guessed? Or if I had told you?'

Claire considered. 'Probably run a mile.'

Frances gave a little laugh, and then she suddenly crumpled, and looked so stricken that Claire, in a wave of pity, found herself saying quickly: 'I'm sorry, I didn't mean – just because I said that, doesn't mean that she – your friend now – ' She broke off, feeling, although she had been invited, as if she were trespassing in unknown territory. And anyway, what was she thinking of, giving the slightest encouragement?

Footsteps from the far end of the path, and the chink of glasses: Robert, carrying a tray, with a blue-striped china jug.

'Oliver and Jessica are deeply engaged with the chessboard,' he

64

said, plonking it down on the table, 'So I thought I'd do the decent thing. Claire, move all this tea stuff out of the way, will you?' He sat down, and began to pour, handing them each a glass; he raised his own. 'Cheers.' He looked from one to the other. 'Oh. Sorry. I'm interrupting.'

'At last the penny drops,' said Claire, as much to herself as to Robert. She picked up her glass and drank quickly. Never had red wine hit the spot more accurately, or been more welcome.

'Shall I disappear?'

'No, of course not.' Frances was standing; she picked up her glass. 'This is very nice, thank you. I'll take it with me, if I may, and start the supper.'

'No rush . . .' Robert began, and stopped as she swept her cigarettes and lighter off the table and walked rapidly away.

'I'll do the children first,' she said, over her shoulder. 'In a little while, okay?'

'Fine,' said Claire, and watched her rapid progress between the vines, turning to run past the water tank, down the steps to the house.

'Well,' said Robert, drinking again. 'This looks promising. Drama on day two. Day one, really.'

'Shut up.'

'Sorry. Only joking.'

'I know.'

'Want to tell me about it?'

'Not at the moment. Just let me gather my thoughts, will you? And make sure the boys are all right.'

'I will,' he said kindly, patting her shoulder. 'See you in a bit.' And he took himself off again, up to the poolside to survey the view, then back again and past her, pulling off a few grapes on the way.

Claire sat at the round white table. A scooter puttered past, on the mountain road, going down towards the village. It was growing cooler, but she did not move. She thought: I am a woman of my time, I should surely be able to take all this in my stride. But she found that she could not, that she was unsettled and bewildered, feelings with which she had long been unfamiliar. If Frances had felt so much for her, all those years ago, did that say

65

something about herself, as well as everything about Frances? And what, anyway, was this 'everything' about someone who seemed to be neither one thing nor another? She refilled her glass, hearing, from down in the garden, Robert's voice, organising Tom and Jack, who had stayed too long in the pool, towards the idea of a bath and pyjamas.

'I don't want a bath with *him*,' said Jack.

Claire pulled on her sweater, and shivered.

Upstairs, in the bedroom at the back of the house, which still held the warmth of the day, Frances swung back the peeling wooden shutters and looked through the open window out across the valley. The sun was very low, and the sky's streaks of grey were thickening; she stood with her glass of wine and cigarette listening to domestic evening noises drift up from the village: clattering dishes, a tinny signature tune, a wailing baby. She could hear women talking.

She leaned on the narrow window-sill and tried to let these sounds distract and calm her, but they did not. She thought about secrecy and disclosure: about the distance, which she had just discovered to be infinitely greater than she had supposed, between knowing something about yourself and revealing it. There seemed to be, as she had always thought there to be, very good reasons for keeping up appearances.

She watched below her the children playing in the yard of the threshing barn, pulling their wooden cart up and down, laughing. Keeping up appearances helped keep everything as it should be – and I am not as I should be, she thought, seeing again the change in Claire's face as she listened, her expression of shock and retreat. No matter that she had quickly tried to cover it: it had been there.

Well. A lesson had been learned: there would be no more revelations. She drew on her cigarette, and closed her eyes, and Dora's calm and lovely face came floating up before her.

4

The road to the market town, some twenty miles away, wound high through the mountains, between forests of pine and eucalyptus which oozed milky gum into little cups like half coconuts, fastened to the bark. On the left the ground sloped steeply down to the river; clusters of red-roofed houses were sprinkled on the far hillside, beneath a cloudless sky.

They were all packed into the Murray car, an ageing blue Sierra estate whose upholstery bore the marks and stains of years of clambering feet, spilt drinks, wet knickers and burst packets of crisps. A jumble of cassettes lay between the two front seats; more were stuffed into the glove compartment. They had played endless tapes on the drive through Spain, letting rip, as you could do only when it was just the family. Sinatra for Claire, in moments of indulgence; Jason Donovan for Jessica, Roald Dahl and Chesney Hawkes for Jack. When he'd had enough of all this, and enough of driving, Robert got into the passenger seat, put on Bach or Satie, and let himself drift.

He was in the passenger seat now; in the end, he'd done most of the driving through Spain. He sat next to Claire, the window wound down but not so far as to blow out the others in the back. He wouldn't have minded a tape on now, but Oliver was asking about landmarks – a village within walking distance of the house, a radio transmitter set high on a bare and distant peak. He did his best to answer. Next to Oliver, Jess sat silent; the boys, bundled into the back like puppies, were playing on a pocket game that belonged to Jack.

Frances, on the other side of Jessica, was looking out of the window, miles away.

The car climbed higher; she gazed out at dry pines and sandy rock face, composing a letter.

Dear Dora,

*We arrived here two days ago, and find ourselves in a place of
great beauty: a spacious house, hens and fruit trees in the garden,
a broad, tranquil valley. Our friends are kind and generous, and
the children, after a little initial friction, seem to be getting on
well.*

*How is your summer? I imagine this letter will be amongst a
pile of post waiting for you on your return from Greece, which I
hope was enjoyable . . .*

Dora is walking up the path to the black front door of her house in
Barnes. She is suntanned and fit, if tired from a long journey; she
is carrying a heavy suitcase and the shoulder-bag she always
carries, in which, stopping now, she searches for her keys. Behind
her, outside the gate, her husband Adrian is paying the taxi-driver
and her daughter Sophie stands beside the pile of luggage on the
pavement: sixteen years old, faded jeans, loose T-shirt, tossing
back a stream of silken brown hair and allowing the taxi-driver to
admire her. Sophie's brother, Jason, has been dropped off to buy
milk and bread and pick up the papers from the newsagent on the
corner.

It is Sunday afternoon, and the sunlit street is quiet and still and
empty, looking, to all of them, somehow reinvented by their
absence and return. Adrian comes up the path with Jason's
suitcase and his own; Dora has found her keys. She goes inside
with a sigh of pleasure, stepping over the pile of letters on the
coconut mat, into the hall, with its tiled floor and dark banister.
She puts down her suitcase; she drops her keys and bag on the
table and bends down to pick up the post: brown bills, postcards, a
scattering of white, an airmail letter from Portugal. She carries
them through to the kitchen, where she puts on the kettle and
unbolts the door to the garden; she stands looking out on to uncut,
unwatered grass, fallen apples bruised, oozing, crawling with
wasps. Time to clear it all up. Not yet. She sits down at the garden
table and sorts through the post, putting it in piles for Adrian, for
Sophie, for Jason, whom she can hear putting milk cartons
down in the kitchen, and for herself.

And who is to say, or ever to know, whether or not it is the letter

68

from Frances that she is most pleased to come upon and open first, or save until last?

The road wound on and on: Frances continued, in dreamy conjunction, both this scene and her letter:

I look forward to hearing all about your holiday when I come back to work. In the meantime, I think of you at your desk, and wonder how you are . . .

To think of Dora had become, over the years, so much a part of Frances that it was almost like breathing, a natural function of being. It was a companionship, an internal tide of feeling which ebbed and flowed through her so continually that in times of practical necessity – a meeting with an author, a meeting with Tom's teacher, an unexpected ring at the door – to discover that time had passed without thinking of her was cause for remark. At such moments Frances would briefly wonder at her own absorption – behold, it is possible to live without it – and then she would return: to unwritten letters, unspoken conversations, dreams. Sometimes she relived the real encounters of their friendship, the meetings and discussions at work, and the times they shared outside it: lunch hours in Covent Garden cafés, evenings now and then at a concert or a play. Sometimes these encounters were rewritten, or new scenes invented, so that what had in reality been one conversation became, in imagination, quite another. And between the lines of the memos left on Dora's desk, mostly formal to the point of dullness, between the lines of occasional letters written over the years, was always something else, a continual reworking and rephrasing of the same, eternal letter:

Dora, I want to tell you something, but I am afraid to tell you . . .

'I feel sick,' said Tom.

The car climbed higher, and swayed round another bend.

'I feel sick.'

'Well, don't be sick on me,' said Jack.

'Frances . . .' Oliver was tapping her on the arm, across the back of the seat. She looked at him distantly, and he nodded behind him. 'Problems.'

She turned round to see Tom, white-faced, huddled up in the corner.

'Oh dear.'

'Everything all right back there?' asked Robert.

'I'm afraid Tom's feeling a bit sick.'

Robert looked in the mirror; the road began to descend, winding horribly.

'Want to stop for a minute?'

Tom nodded, ashen, mute.

'Pull in, Claire, okay? Go on, quick.'

But the road was very narrow, and another British car was approaching, climbing towards them.

'There's a passing place down there, let me get to it,' said Claire, also looking in the mirror. 'All right, Tom? Hold on, just for a minute . . .'

'You'd better not be sick on me,' said Jack again, edging away from him.

'Stop it.' Claire drove down the hill towards the passing place, the opening of a path leading high into the pines. 'Here we are, well done . . .' She drew in as the climbing red car came up alongside and went by, and pulled on the handbrake; Frances jumped out and ran round to the back, opening the door just in time to get Tom out on to the sandy path. He stood for a moment heaving, then threw up violently.

'Ugh,' said Jack, watching in fascination. 'Yuk.'

Frances drew Tom away from the car in mid-heave. Tears leapt from his eyes; he continued to throw up convulsively, then stood there shaking. A long line of drool hung down from his open mouth.

'Here,' said Claire, approaching. 'Tissues. Poor old Tom.'

Frances took the pack of tissues gratefully and wiped the trembling mouth. 'Blow your nose, Tom, that'll help. Do you want a drink?'

He nodded, still very white.

'Mineral water,' said Claire. 'There's some in the box – hang on.'

Frances watched her walk back to the car, where doors were opening, everyone getting out, Jack making an exaggerated detour round the pool of sick. Claire, returning with the plastic bottle of water and a mug, looked, in unironed scarlet skirt and sleeveless white top, like a beacon of competence and good sense.

'You're wonderful,' said Frances.

'Why don't you two sit down for a bit and have a rest,' Claire suggested. 'We can stretch our legs.' Tom, still standing there, waiting for his drink, looked like someone surrounded by far too much space: she wanted to take him on her lap and smooth down his hair. 'I'm afraid these roads are rather a nightmare,' she said, as Frances passed him the mug of water, and he sat down. 'But he was all right on the drive from the airport, wasn't he?'

'Yes, but we'd given him a travel pill for the plane,' said Frances. 'It probably hadn't worn off.'

'Ah. You haven't got any with you now, have you? Never mind, I expect we can get something from the chemist in town. For the journey back.'

Tom looked up, half a degree less white. 'I'm not going in the car again.'

'Just to the town . . .' said Frances.

'No.'

'All right, don't worry about it now.' Claire smiled at him. 'You sit there till you feel better, and then we'll see.'

'I'm not going.'

'Tom . . .'

'I'll leave you to it.' Claire, seeing Oliver approach them, went back to the car and reversed it over the pool of sick, and then went on sitting there, tapping her fingers thoughtfully on the steering-wheel, watching in the mirror the rest of her family wandering rather aimlessly up the path in the heat, and, through the window, Oliver and Frances, standing over Tom.

'Feeling better?' Oliver was asking.

Tom nodded. 'A bit.'

'You didn't bring the pills,' he said to Frances.

'No. But Claire says we can get some in town.'

'I'm not going – ' Tom began.

Frances looked at Oliver. 'What are we going to do?'

'Leave him,' said Oliver. 'Let him get over it.' He bent down to Tom, who had picked up a bit of stick and was twiddling it between

71

his fingers. 'Frances and I will go and explore,' he said. 'You stay here, there's no rush.'

'Where're you going?'

'Just up the path – see? Where the others are?'

'Okay.' Tom sounded flat and resigned. He lowered his head again and began to run the stick up and down the sand as his parents walked away.

'Oh dear,' said Frances. 'Poor Tom.'

'He'll be all right.' Ahead, on the mountain path, Robert and the children had stopped and were waiting for them to catch up. 'What about you?' Oliver asked her, as they walked on.

'What?'

'I thought you seemed rather quiet in the car. Anything wrong?'

She shook her head. 'Why should there be?'

He gave a small, exasperated sigh.

'How's the patient?' Robert enquired as they drew near.

'Recovering,' said Oliver, and they all stood looking, from this height, at the harsh, unforested line of mountain peaks that stretched along the distant horizon on the far side of the valley. Below, uncultivated terraces tumbled towards the river.

'Have you done much walking up here?' Oliver asked.

'Me?' said Robert, and Jessica laughed, prodding the soft overhang of flesh above his trousers.

'Can you see Dad walking up a mountain?'

'Do you mind?' He wiped trickling sweat from his forehead. 'What about you, Oliver? Are you keen?'

He nodded. 'I enjoy walking, certainly, so does Frances.'

'But not in this heat,' she said. 'Still, why don't you go off one day, you'd enjoy it. I'm sure there must be maps in the house.'

'There are. I was looking at them last night, after you'd gone to bed.'

Oliver spoke as if to say: I don't need you to tell me about maps, or anything else, and Frances said, 'Oh. Good,' and looked away.

'Where's Mum?' Jack demanded suddenly. 'What's she doing?'

'I don't know.' Robert, taking in the unspoken sharpness between the Swifts, a little wounded by Jessica and very hot, was beginning to feel somewhat out of sorts. Below them he could see

Tom, on his feet again, looking round, and he said abruptly: 'Come on, let's go,' and set off back down the path.

'I'm not going in the car,' Tom announced as soon as they reached the bottom, and as Frances and Oliver both made to protest Robert said quickly:

'Now, look, Tom, I'll tell you what. You can sit in the front, if Mum and Dad agree, next to Claire, like a grown-up, and we'll have all the windows down and play a game. And in no time we'll be there, all right?'

He was shepherding Tom towards the car in a manner, kind but firm, which did not allow for disagreement.

'What sort of game?'

'Animal, vegetable, mineral. If you don't know it we'll teach you.' Almost before Oliver and Frances had made their murmurs of assent, he had opened the front passenger door and presented Tom to Claire with a flourish. 'Your guide.'

'Oh,' said Claire, smiling in welcome. 'That's nice.'

Robert helped Tom with the seat belt and closed the door. 'Jess, you go in the back with Jack, please.'

'But I want to sit next to – ' She broke off, seeing his face, and went round. Everyone got in, doors were pulled shut.

'Mum?' asked Jack, as Claire eased out on to the road again. 'Why didn't you come with us? What were you doing, all by yourself?'

'Thinking,' said Claire, turning the wheel.

'Fatal,' said Robert, as they drove away.

The town was clogged with traffic, a crawling line of little local vans, beat-up cars and motor bikes, with a few tourists in larger, sleeker vehicles like theirs. Baking heat hung over unfinished concrete apartment blocks and the narrow streets leading steeply off the main through road. Petrol and exhaust fumes shimmered; they crawled past a draper's and an ironmonger's on one side and a piazza with a news-stand on the other, where fountains sparkled between dusty trees. Up on the hill to their right, the covered food market and open stalls of pottery and clothes stood below another building site.

73

'Christmas,' said Robert, wiping his forehead again as the car inched forward. 'I don't remember it being like this.'

Claire was changing into second gear. She glanced at Tom, sitting beside her. 'You okay?'

'A bit hot,' he muttered, 'and thirsty.'

They had finished the mineral water a mile or two back. 'Won't be long now,' she said. 'You keep your eyes out for a parking place.'

He didn't answer.

'Animal with vegetable connections,' said Robert gamely from the back.

'A donkey after a carrot,' said Jessica. 'God, Dad, you've done that one millions of times.'

They eventually found somewhere to park on the other side of the town, squeezing in between a trailer and a Fiat outside some offices. Jack and Jessica, released from the back, stretched themselves and groaned.

'It's *awful* in there.' They stepped into the road as a motor bike sputtered fiercely past.

'Careful,' said Oliver, putting an arm across.

Jessica gave him a dazzling smile. 'Thanks.'

'Hats on,' said Claire, emerging from the front with her shoulder-bag. 'So. How shall we organise ourselves?'

'I thought you were going to organise us,' said Oliver drily.

'Did you? In that case I suggest drinks all round, and then whoever wants to come to the market can do so, and whoever doesn't can explore. There's the church' – the children groaned – 'and various cafés,' she went on, ignoring them. 'We can all meet up for lunch.'

'Can I come with you?' Tom asked.

'Of course. I expect Mum's coming anyway, aren't you, Frances?'

'What? Oh, yes, yes, that's fine.'

Oliver wanted to look at the fish stall, and so did Jessica. Neither Jack nor Robert, seeing the crowds, wanted to go near the place, but Jack wanted to be with Claire. So in the end, after bottles of fizzy orange from a stall, they all set off up the steep, half-made road to the market. Motor bikes bumped unsteadily up and down over the potholes, weaving in and out of shuffling old women in black with baskets and plastic shopping bags; children darted. 'Careful,' said all the grown-ups together, taking hands. They passed endless pairs of shoes, set out on the ground on tablecloths, and stalls of glazed brown and yellow pottery.

'A good place for presents,' said Claire.

'Not now,' said Robert.

Dora, wrote Frances, *I wish you were here. I wish we were drinking from cool tall glasses in an empty café shaded with slatted blinds, listening to the whirr of a fan . . .*

Tall iron gates, fastened back, stood at the entrance to the covered market. They could smell fish and cheese and sausages as they stepped into the welcome cooler air, passing a fat old woman in a headscarf: she sat on a low wooden chair beside baskets of herbs, a basket of eggs, and three plump brown hens. They lay on a piece of sacking, their feet stretched out and their beaks open.

'Look,' said Tom, quite recovered now from the sickness.

'Come on,' said Claire.

'*Look!* They're alive.' Glossy brown wings lifted feebly, feathery chests rose and fell. 'They're tied up, their feet are tied up!'

Claire looked. Orange wool bound scaly yellow legs; the hens were gasping. The fat old woman smiled. '*Mil escudos.*'

'What did she say?' Tom demanded. 'What did she say?'

'She said they were a thousand escudos.'

'A thousand *what*?'

'Escudos,' said Jack, from the other side of Claire. 'Don't you know what escudos are?'

'It's the Portuguese money,' said Claire, wondering if Jack were sickening for something. 'Come on, Tom.' She turned to the others behind her. 'Perhaps we should split up, and one lot do fruit and veg and the others meat and fish. We should have worked out a budget, I suppose.' She moved aside as another, Portuguese family pushed past.

'Does that mean they're for sale?' Tom asked. 'Does it?'

'Of course they're for sale,' said Jack. 'What else would she be doing with them?'

'But how much? How much is a thousand thingummy in English money?'

'How should I know?'

'Jack . . .' said Claire. 'Please. What is the matter with you?'

'I'm hot.'

'We're all hot. Come on, buck up, the sooner we do the shopping the sooner we can go home.'

'How *much* is it?' Tom persisted.

'Oh, Tom.' She checked a sigh of impatience. 'It's about four pounds.'

'Four pounds . . .' She could see him struggling to add up weekly sums. He turned to Frances, his broad face passionate with longing. 'Mum? Frances? How much pocket money do I get?'

'Surely you know how much pocket money you get,' said Jack.

Claire said, 'I'm going to get cross with you in a minute.'

'Seventy pence,' said Frances. 'Because you're seven. Next year it'll be eighty.'

'And how much have I got in my money box?'

'I can't remember.' She stepped aside in the throng. 'I think we'd better move on, hadn't we, Claire?'

'I'm trying to.'

'What's the hold-up?' Robert asked.

'How many seventy pences are in four pounds?' asked Tom. 'Mum? Frances? Please can I buy them?'

'Buy what?'

'The *hens*. Look at them.'

'No,' said Frances, looking.

'Please. If I haven't got enough saved up, you can stop giving me pocket money for the rest of the holidays, I don't mind, honestly. Please.'

'Tom, don't be silly, what on earth would you *do* with them?'

'I'd have them as pets, of course. We could take them in the back of the car . . .'

'No.'

Claire left them to get on with it, seeing that Oliver, Jessica and Robert had long since decided to do the same and were well ahead in the crowd, stopping at a stall of shining sardines on a marble slab. She took Jack's hand and they made their way towards them.

'Tom's bonkers.'

'Stop it.'

'Fish tonight?' Robert suggested, as they came up.

'I should think so.' She gazed at rows of sunken eyes. 'We'd better make a plan for the week.'

'I thought you'd have a list.'

'Well I haven't. I was going to make one last night, but somehow –' She took a breath, and released Jack's hot hand. 'Fish tonight, whatever Oliver and Frances want for tomorrow, what about cold meat on Wednesday? I suppose someone had better do groceries, too; we'll have to go to the supermarket after this . . .'

'May I suggest,' said Oliver, 'that Frances and I take over for today? We can work out and buy, and you can just cook on your days from whatever we've got. I should think between us we could manage to stock up sensibly.'

'Now you're talking,' said Claire, and he smiled at her, charming and considerate. She smiled back, relieved that for once she did not have to plan and be practical, but also thinking: he's okay, he's nice, he just needs getting to know.

Beside him, Jessica was saying: 'Can I come with you?'

'All right. You can help choose things.' He looked at Robert and Claire enquiringly. 'Is that permissible?'

'Of course.' Claire's eyes searched the throng near the entrance for Frances and Tom, but she could not see them. 'Well, we'll do the supermarket, anyway. And we'll meet you back at the car in about an hour. Yes?'

And she and Robert, with Jack between them, left Oliver and Jessica buying a kilo of fat sardines and moved towards the aisle on the left, where the cheeses were.

'Hurray,' said Jack. 'Just us.'

Claire put her arm round him. 'Is that why you're in such a grump?'

'It's nice being just us sometimes.'

'Yes.' She stood watching Robert exchange halting pleasantries with a pretty girl behind one of the stalls, trying a bit of rubbery cheese, and wondered what their lives would have been like if they had had only Jack, just the three of them, like Oliver and Frances and Tom. Looking down into Jack's adoring eyes, she

77

thought it would probably be rather nice: no quarrels, no need to balance the needs of one against the other. But the Swifts? Despite her new found liking for Oliver, on the evidence so far it was hard to decide which might be more difficult: to have Tom as child, or Oliver and Frances as parents.

Robert had finished flirting with the girl behind the cheese stall; he took Jack's other hand and the three of them wandered off. They passed stalls of old grey socks, which they recalled were dried fish, and a butcher where fresh-cut pork oozed blood on to the chopping block and stiff white rabbits hung upside down on hooks.

'Tom would have something to say about them,' said Robert.

'He's got animals on the *brain*,' said Jack.

'I thought you liked animals.'

'I do, but not like he does.'

'Yes. Well . . .' Claire searched the crowd, wondering if Tom and Frances had met up with the others yet – and, indeed, if Frances would mind having the whole week's shopping devolved upon her. Ah. There she was, looking fresh and cool in her striped blue shirt and cotton skirt, with her hair tied back and her hands in her pockets; she was walking unhurriedly along the stalls on the far aisle, lost in thought. And where was Tom? Well, where was he? Hard to pick out children in this throng unless they were close by; easy for one to get lost.

'Robert? Can you see Tom anywhere?'

He looked around. 'No. Where's Jess?'

Jess was in a queue at a fruit stall right up at the end – they could see her because they could see Oliver, head and shoulders taller than almost everyone, making a list in a small black notebook. Tom, it seemed, had disappeared, and his mother seemed not to have noticed. Well – Claire checked reproach by thinking how easily that happened, how she'd nearly lost Jack in Sainsbury's once, bumping into someone from school and gossiping, taking her eyes off him for five minutes. Still. In a foreign country, in a place you'd never been to before . . . She remembered the sudden lurch of sickness and fear when she'd realised Jack had vanished, the rush of relief at finding him, moments later, prising open a tube of Smarties at the checkout. And she felt a tingle of fear and panic now, beginning to rise. If she were Frances she wouldn't let Tom out of her sight in this place for a minute.

'Where is he?' she said to Robert. 'Where on earth is he?'

'Could be anywhere, couldn't he? Give her a shout.'

'Frances! Frances!'

She turned, frowning, caught sight of them and gave a little wave.

'Where's Tom?' Claire called.

Frances frowned again and looked round, clearly expecting to see him beside her. They pushed through the crowd.

'He was here,' she said, as they reached her. 'He was right here. Where's Oliver?' Claire pointed. 'I'd better tell him . . .' Frances sounded as if it were the last thing she wanted to do. 'How on earth can this have happened?'

'Do you think he's been kidnapped?' Jack asked hopefully. 'Are there kidnappers in Portugal?'

'Stop it,' said Claire, still looking. People around them jostled and shoved. 'Where was he when you last saw him?'

Frances spread her hands. 'I can't remember – '

They searched among half a dozen stalls of knobbly potatoes and onions the size of grapefruit.

'Tom!' Robert shouted, cupping his hands. 'Tom!' One or two people in the queues turned, curious.

'Oh, dear God,' said Claire, and then she became aware of a ripple of laughter and exclamation, and Jack suddenly tugging at her hand, saying:

'Look! Look at that hen . . .'

On a nearby stall, feathers fluffed out, head cocked, a fat brown hen was perched on the top of a pile of potatoes, clucking quietly. As they watched, she began to pick her way along open sacks of other vegetables, pecking here and there at broad beans and carrots, dropping messes. The stallholder made to grab her, and she retreated, flapping her wings, unsteady feet clinging to potatoes; messes splattered everywhere. There was more laughter.

'Lay an egg,' Robert murmured. 'Please lay an egg.'

And here was Tom, a hen under each arm, grinning from ear to ear, triumphant.

79

'I untied them when she wasn't looking – it was *easy*. I tried to get them all together, but that one, she's called Mary, she made a dash for it.' He looked down proudly at the birds on either side of him, darting their heads. 'This one's called Beaky, and the other one hasn't got a name yet, but she's really nice. They're terribly thirsty, what can we give them?'

'Oh, Tom . . .' Claire and Robert burst out laughing; even Frances, clearly embarrassed, was smiling. Jack reached out to stroke sleek brown wings.

'Careful,' said Tom. 'They're still a bit nervous.'

'*Pare, pare! As minhas galinhas!*' With a stream of excited Portuguese, the owner of the hens was bearing down upon them, the crowd parting like the Red Sea to accommodate her. At the same moment, the stallholder's dives for Mary were finally successful: he grabbed her, turned, and presented her at arm's length with a bow.

'*Obrigado.*' The old woman reached out an enormous bare arm and took possession: in moments the hen was hanging upside down by her grubby feet, struggling ineffectually to raise her head.

'Stop it!' said Tom. 'They hate being held like that.'

The old woman turned to him with a smile. '*Obrigado*,' she said again, and put a plump brown hand on his shoulder, making to shepherd him back towards her place at the entrance. Tom looked at her stonily.

'If this were Spain,' said Claire to the others, 'we could be in trouble by now. Come on,' she added to Tom. 'Give them back, there's a good boy.'

'No.' A dark flush spread across his face.

Claire looked at Frances. Frances said warningly: 'Tom . . .'

'I'm not giving them back. She's cruel, she's keeping them cruelly. I want to save them from death.'

Claire and Robert looked at each other. Robert said gently: 'Listen, mate, give them back for now, all right, and then we'll go and have a talk about it.'

'*Toma là.*' The old woman was smiling broadly, showing three teeth. She reached in the pocket of a vast green apron and produced a plump purple fig streaked with yellow; she held it out to Tom, and he turned his head away.

'Tell her I don't want it.'

'Frances,' said Claire, more sharply than she intended, 'has this child got any pets at home?'

Frances looked at her. 'We can't have pets in a flat.'

'You could have a mouse or something,' said Jack helpfully. 'They don't take up much space.'

Tom looked at Frances, shifting the hens beneath his arms. 'Could I have a mouse?'

'I – '

'Please. Please.'

Frances said: 'Give those hens back, Tom, and we'll discuss it. We'll have to see what Oliver says.'

'Okay,' said Robert, moving forward. 'Okay, now, Tom, you heard what Mum said.' He ran a finger over the head and neck of one of the hens, making clucking sounds. 'Come on, old girl.' Sweat dripped from Tom's arm on to the feathers. Robert carefully prised the hen off, talking soothingly. 'Laid any eggs today? Come on, there's a good hen, chook, chook, chook . . .' He had her in his hands; Tom flexed his arm, then wrapped it round the other bird, bringing her up close to his chest. Robert passed Beaky over to the old woman, who in a single practised movement had her swinging by her feet, like Mary, who had given up the struggle. There was a round of applause from interested onlookers; he reached for the third hen, cradled in Tom's arms.

Tom looked at him pleadingly. 'Can't we just keep this one?'

'Think of the possible mouse,' said Robert, easing the bird away. 'Good girl, clever girl . . .'

'Can *I* have a mouse?' asked Jack.

The nameless third bird was swinging next; there were whistles and cheers. The fat old woman, nodding and smiling, made her exit as they stood aside for her. Within moments the crowd had returned to its shopping; stray pats landed on Tom's and Jack's heads.

Tom stood by himself, and his eyes followed the waddling old woman and the gasping hens. He scratched one arm, absently; there was chicken shit all down his shorts.

'Here you are,' said Oliver to Frances, appearing with Jessica and a bagful of fruit and vegetables. 'I was wondering what – ' He

81

saw all the others, still there, and raised an eyebrow as Tom ran up
to him.

'Oliver! Oliver, can I have a mouse?'

'A mouse?' He frowned. 'What on earth are you talking about?'

'Right,' said Robert, taking Claire's arm. 'I think we'll be off
now – see you all later.' And he moved his family firmly towards
the exit.

'Hey – ' said Jessica.

'You were great,' said Claire to Robert.

He mopped his brow. 'Get me out of here.'

They had lunch in a café full of flies, and bought Portuguese sick
pills just as the chemist was closing. Shutters were put to, blinds
descended, the sputtering motor bikes disappeared; a pall of heat
and quietness enveloped the town as they drove away.

And the house, when they returned to it, felt like a haven:
familiar, shady and cool, a place they knew and where they were
known – by the creeping cat, and by Guida, who had washed up
supper and breakfast, swept the wooden floors and made the beds,
leaving the shutters closed and a cotton bag of fresh bread on the
kitchen table.

Dora, wrote Frances, carrying shopping, following Claire down
the stone steps beneath the vines, *I could sit and talk to you for
ever . . . Please don't be too shocked, please don't be afraid . . .*

Water, steady and calm, poured into the green-tiled tank above
her; shouts and laughter came from the pool, where the children
had raced the moment they were let out of the car, Oliver keeping
an eye. Up on the blinding hot road Robert was slamming the
boot shut; he came down the steps with the last box of groceries,
and Frances turned to smile at him.

'Thanks so much for helping with Tom.'

'That's all right. What did you decide about the mouse?'

'The mouse . . . Oh, Oliver's told Tom he'll think about it, if his
behaviour improves. Do you think that's reasonable?'

Robert opened his mouth and closed it. He shrugged, shifting
the box on his arms. 'It's not for me to say, is it?' A tin of flageolet
beans, perched on top of a box of crackers, rolled off and banged
down on the steps, bouncing on to Frances's neat canvas foot; she

winced, and bent to retrieve it. Ahead of them, Claire had opened the door and was carrying bags inside; they followed her into the kitchen, shaded by creeper, smelling faintly of gas.

Robert dumped his box on the table and poured a long glass of mineral water from the fridge; without another word, he went out of the room, leaving Claire and Frances to unpack the shopping, hearing his heavy tread going up the stairs and along the landing. The bedroom door opened and closed; the house was silent. In silence, Claire and Frances put tins and boxes in cupboards, meat and fish in the freezer, fruit in a bowl.

Dora, said Frances, bending down, putting potatoes into the vegetable rack beneath the sink, *Dora, Dora, please don't go . . .*

Behind her, Claire said, 'Do you want to talk to me?'

'No.' She straightened up, and stood with her back against the wooden draining-board. 'Where are my cigarettes? Where's my bag?' She saw it, lying on the table next to the empty cardboard box, and went quickly over; she took out the packet, and lit a cigarette with a match from the box by the stove, shaking it out with exaggerated care, inhaling as if her life depended on it.

Claire stood watching this performance. 'Frances – '

On the wall above the stove was a cheap electric clock, its plastic face covered in a film of grease. It ticked into the silence; Frances glanced up at it.

'It's after two,' she said, her voice brittle. 'I think the children should have a rest, don't you?' She was moving towards the door, talking into the air. 'Certainly Tom should . . .' And she was gone, climbing the steps towards the water tank, walking at speed along the path to the pool.

Claire stood watching her go. 'Tell Jack and Jessica to come in too,' she called, and Frances waved a hand in acknowledgement and was hidden by the vines. And Claire felt suddenly overcome with heat and sleepiness, and a longing for Robert, and normality. She would try to deal with Frances later. She went out and up the worn wooden stairs, shadowy and warm, along the rag runner, shaken out by Guida. Distant voices came from the pool. She pushed open their bedroom door. Robert was lying on his back with his eyes closed, snoring gently. She pulled off her sandals and in bare feet went quietly across the untidy floor to wake him.

The path to the pool was shaded with vines, but the poolside itself was exposed to the blazing afternoon sun, which beat upon the rusting fence by the road and the concrete surround where Oliver, his feet in the water, sat watching Jessica swim up and down. The pool had been roughly painted in pale green; the water, unchanged all summer, having received the muddy feet of all the previous guests at the house, was a cloudy brown, although the surface sparkled. Oliver, in his swimming trunks and old straw hat, felt the sun on his shoulders beginning to be uncomfortable, even though, unlike Frances, he enjoyed the heat.

'I think we should move,' he said to Jessica, as she reached his end.

'In a minute.' She touched the side, turned and pushed off again, moving through the water in her sleek green swimsuit like a seal: firm, well-covered, strong. 'I want to do fifty lengths,' she said, her mouth above the water. 'That's about twenty at home, I should think.'

'And how many metres is that?' He moved his feet, swishing gently.

'Four hundred.' She was beginning to pant. 'How many have I done so far?'

'I don't know.'

'You're supposed to be *counting*.' She had reached the far end, was already turning back towards him.

'It's too hot. Come on.'

'Three more. I think that'll be thirty. I can't do it when the boys are here, mucking about.'

'No.' The boys, bidden by Frances, had gone inside to rest; Frances had gone for a walk, charging Oliver to look after Jessica, who said she didn't want a rest.

'When will you be back?' he had asked her.

'Oh – teatime. Fiveish.' Frances stood on the steps leading from the bushes to the pool, impatiently ushering the boys away. They looked at each other through their sunglasses. 'I need some time to myself – is that all right?'

'Of course.' It was built into their agreement. 'Enjoy yourself.'

'Thank you.' She went down the steps and along the path to the

84

water tank, up the next flight to the road; there was the creak of the iron gate, and footsteps, going away.

There were footsteps on the road now, slow and quiet. Frances had gone up, towards the bend; these were coming down, passing the house, approaching the pool. Oliver turned to see a wiry old woman in black, her lined face beneath a towering heap of ferns piled on her head, held by one hand.

'*Bo tar*'.' Her voice was a croak, distant and dry; she did not smile.

'*Bo tar*'.' He watched her steady progress beneath her load, down towards the village, to the line of empty cottages waiting, surely, for some British developer. After a few moments, a scrawny brown dog came slinking out of a gap in the mountainside and began to follow her. He was more than scrawny: he was half starved, ribs and haunches sticking up through a dull, flea-bitten coat. His claws clicked on the hot surface: the old woman turned and he shrank back, but a low growl came from him, and as soon as she walked on he followed her, and the growl of hunger came again.

'*Cao danado!*' The old woman stopped suddenly and swung round; ferns dropped on to the road, and she raised her fist. '*Vai – te embora!*'

The dog snarled; strings of saliva shone. She took two steps towards him, and he retreated, still facing her, hunched down, haunches high above a skeletal spine. '*Cao danado!*' Still she advanced, and he suddenly gave in and leapt up, turning, running weakly from side to side, back up the road to a clump of bushes, where he disappeared. The old woman waited a few moments, and then she walked on, swaying a little beneath the ferns.

'What was all that shouting?' Jessica had done her three laps; she rested her arms on the poolside, looking up at him.

'Just an old woman.' He told her about the dog.

'Do they get rabies?' Jessica's hair clung to her head in thick, wet strands but on the top it was still dry, burnished with lights from the sun.

'I don't know,' he said. 'Yes, I expect it's possible. We'd better be careful.'

She sniffed, wiping water from her face with a suntanned hand, and smiled up at him.

'Come on,' he said, 'we'll get sunstroke if we stay out here.'

'What shall we do, then?' She pulled herself out of the water and sat beside him, dripping on to the hot concrete. She shifted her bottom. 'It's *boiling*.'

He got to his feet, and held out his hand. 'Get up. Let's go and sit in the shade.'

'And play chess?'

'If you like.'

'Out here,' said Jessica, taking his hand. 'Away from the boys.'

'All right.'

They walked down the path to the round table set beneath the vines. Even here, in the shade, it was so hot that the air felt breathless, motionless, the sky above the valley drained to white. From somewhere down in the village came the sound of a saw; then it was quiet again.

Jessica sat down on an iron seat with care; she rested her chin in her hands and waited while Oliver went down to the house for the chess set. After a while, she took away her right hand, the one he had held, and looked at it; she pressed it to her cheek again.

'Here we are.' He was back, with the chess and also, balanced on the wooden box, two tall glasses of squash, with ice cubes. Glistening drops of condensation clung to the sides.

'Brilliant.' She drank thirstily, watching him set up the pieces. 'You can be black.'

'All right. Can you remember all the moves?'

'I think so.' She leaned forward, her hair brushing the board; she pushed it back impatiently. 'The knight is the difficult one, it goes . . .' She picked up the white knight and moved him, two forward and one across, biting her lip. 'Is that it?'

'Yes, that's exactly right.'

'And the queen . . .'

'The queen can go anywhere,' he said. 'She is omnipotent.'

'What?'

'It means she is all-powerful, she can do anything. Like God.'

'I don't believe in God,' said Jessica. 'None of our family do. Well, Jack might, he's a bit soppy sometimes.'

He gave a laugh. 'But you are never soppy.'

She shrugged, finishing her drink. 'Mum and Dad still treat me

86

like a baby, sometimes.' She looked at the board, all set up and waiting. 'Come on, let's play.' Her fingers hovered above the line of pawns.

'You seem rather grown-up to me,' said Oliver.

Beneath her rucked-up cotton skirt, Robert's fingers slid into Claire: practised, affectionate, sure. She gave a long sigh of pleasure.

'More. More.'

Sun poured through the gaps in the shutters: up here, in the heavy fullness of the afternoon heat, the tension of the morning ebbed away: it was possible, in this tender and erotic rhythm, to feel the quiet house and the beginning of the holiday reclaimed, just for themselves. Claire lifted her legs and spread them wide, moving her head upon the pillow; she stretched out her arms to Robert, kneeling above her, moving in deeper, his other hand beneath her; she heard his breathing, aroused but unhurried. They had plenty of time: the rest of the afternoon, the rest of their lives. He lifted her higher, withdrew from her, lowered his head.

'Yes. Yes.'

Waves of desire came up to meet him; his mouth and his tongue were everywhere, over her, inside her, searching and discovering, knowing and still wanting to know more.

'And you,' said Claire, rising, rising. 'And you . . .'

In an old embrace they moved, the warm bed creaking beneath them, and devoured each other with infinite and exquisite slowness, until Robert, the most generous of lovers, at last brought her round and beneath him, and slipped inside her and withdrew, and inside her again, and on and on and on and on, mouths locked and bodies pounding, until at last they came, hard up against each other, crying out, rocking, murmuring, falling asleep.

The mountain road Frances had taken was steep and winding, but there were places, on the long slope down towards the river, where the ground levelled out and it was possible to walk for some distance among the trees without too much exertion. The heat was intense, the air was still, rich with the smell of the pines; she walked on a carpet of long sharp needles, stepping over drifts of dry, grey-brown fir cones, larger than fists. At this height, upon this plateau, the river far below and the road above were both invisible: Frances felt suspended, secluded, unreachable.

There were no birds. Occasionally the far away sound of a car or motor bike droned through the afternoon, going up, going down, going away; then it was quiet again. Frances walked on, continuing her letter.

In all the years we have known each other I have been sustained simply by knowing that every day, when you come through the doors to the office and walk down the room I shall be able to look up, and see your face. Dora, forgive me – I have never seen anyone so beautiful . . .

The publishers where Frances worked as editor and Dora as designer had offices on the top floor of a long-since converted warehouse in a narrow street not far from Long Acre. There was no lift, and no reception area. You came in from the street and climbed narrow stairs; you passed, on each floor, swing-doors and corridors leading to other offices, then came, at last, to the fourth floor, the top, where swing-doors painted midnight blue led into a large, open-plan space running the width of the building. Prints and posters hung on the walls, plants trailed from shelves and window-sills, broad desks stood on either side of the room, flanked by metal bookshelves. On the right-hand side the ceiling sloped, and skylight windows had been set into it at intervals: Frances had her desk beneath one of these, a bookshelf at right angles making a secluded corner.

At other desks sat other people. Nearest the doors, ready to welcome visitors, was Elaine, secretary and production assistant, young, cheerful, living with somebody nice. Opposite sat Derek, the production manager, not quite so cheerful since the divorce, liable to bark at printers, liable to drink. Like Kate, rights and contracts manager, overworked, overweight from too many lunches, single, witty, lonely. Down at the far end was Jocelyn, who had set up the company with money from the city and his redundancy money from another, much larger publishers; who had vision and drive and believed in good books and was nice to everybody. Sometimes Kate made caustic remarks about perfect Jocelyn and his 2.1 family in East Horsley, but Frances, who also tried to be perfect, had a certain admiration for him, when she gave him thought. Most of her thoughts went in a rather different direction.

Opposite her, by a casement window overlooking the street, were Dora's desk and drawing-board. Dora, standing before the board in her sweater and jeans and tortoiseshell glasses – clipping on layout sheets, sketching in headings, illustrations, text, pausing, frowning, stepping back to think – was lit, as was her work, not only by a lamp but also by the light above the rooftops of the buildings opposite. From down in the street came voices and footsteps and irritably braking taxis; up here, huddles of pigeons considered the world from rooftop and window-ledge, and up here, from her desk across the room, Frances considered Dora.

She was a little taller than Frances, a little older: in her forties, on the brink of change, she looked like someone about to enter the next stage of her life with grace and beauty. Dark hair was cropped very short; she wore, for close work, expensive tortoiseshell glasses, and make-up so rarely that its effect was extraordinary, a lamp illuminating a painting already full of interest. For this subtlety, this understated plainness, served not to diminish but to enhance her. Her skin was clear, her features well set; even so, at first glance, among more immediately striking and colourful women, she might go unnoticed. Dora had thus what Frances had discovered to be the most potent of all attractions: that you look, and do not remark; that you look again and cannot imagine how you missed the first time. Her face was not simply well made, but full of intelligence, lit in repose by an air of calm self-sufficiency and in communication by her smile and by what seemed, at least, to be a complete concentration upon her companion.

Like Frances, she was reserved, but where Frances was often taut with tension Dora was simply still. She appeared relaxed, contented. She was on the threshold of an age that could precipitate a crisis, but she had no crisis: she had created a home which felt interesting and welcoming; she had a job she found satisfying, children who had not yet done anything terrible and a husband in whom, if they did, she seemed to have confidence would help to see them through.

In all this, Dora was not unlike Claire, but Frances felt her to be much more than Claire: cleverer, more complex, more complete. Dora, it seemed, wherever she went, was herself. Frances had spent much of her life asking herself who she was.

On her desk, the manuscripts and proofs awaiting her stood in a row, secured by rubber bands. Those she was working on lay in front of her, in two distinct piles – pages read, pages about to be read – beside a jar of pencils and pens and a lined pad of notes and queries. Publication and production schedules were pinned to the board on the wall beside her; all her reference books were on the shelves. Everything in this corner of the room conveyed order, purpose and accomplishment: authors, coming in for meetings, looked and were reassured, both by the corner and by Frances herself, rising to greet them with a handshake, well dressed, professional. The only jarring note on the well-kept desk was an ashtray: somehow Frances did not look like a smoker, but then she did not smoke much in the office, and never if people objected. And the ashtray was redeemed: by the well-kept plants in the corner, by the framed photographs of her husband and son, and by the sense she gave her authors that theirs was the book she most cared about, that it had her undivided attention.

Nor did she disappoint them. If anything went wrong – a crisis at the printers in Madrid – or right – the sale of foreign editions at Frankfurt – they were telephoned, calmed or congratulated. On publication day each one received a card and flowers. And if they never, as some authors and editors do, grew close, they respected her, and thanked their lucky stars. And Frances, dealing with them all so well, albeit at a distance, genuinely enjoying her job, sat in her corner when they had left and stacked up the pages of the manuscript they had gone through, line by line, and looked up, and across the room.

Dora, it is friendship and it is more than friendship . . .

As well as the illuminated drawing-board, there stood on Dora's desk sheets of Letraset, tins of cowgum, fine cartographer's pens. Pinned up haphazardly on the board beside her were book jackets, postcards, photographs of her teenage children and middle-aged husband, newspaper cuttings and cartoons. In the midst of all this, Dora moved with no less efficiency than Frances, but with more grace. She stood at the drawing-board thinking, tapping a pencil against her teeth; she picked out a colour transparency, put on her glasses and held it up to the window: thoughtful, preoccupied, working things out. She reached to answer the telephone, discussing in the same unhurried tones where her daughter might have left her trainers and what Jocelyn might take to Frankfurt.

This air of serenity was part of what had drawn Frances to her. Part, but not all: after years of thinking of her, she still did not feel she knew the whole, and no longer tried to. For what seemed at times infinitely complex felt essentially, as always in love, perfectly simple: she wanted to be with her, that was all.

Dora, she wrote now, hearing, far above her, an aeroplane climb the hot white sky, *I wish you were with me, you would so like it here . . .*

Her feet crunched on twigs in the carpet of needles; she could smell resin from the eucalyptus trees, as well as pine. She walked on, heading downwards, towards the river. *Last night I sat out on the terrace, after everyone else had gone to bed, looking at the stars above the mountains. I wanted to hear a footstep, to turn to see you coming gravely out through the tall white doors to sit beside me. I miss you. I miss you . . .*

So many unwritten words, so many unspoken declarations.

She had come to the end of the level ground; beneath her she could see the river, lit by the slowly sinking sun. The air was no longer baking, as it had been when she left Oliver and Jessica down by the pool, but balmy, warm, the light as clear as honey, slanting through the trees. She sat down, suddenly overcome with exhaustion, and the pain of absence; she leaned against the peeling trunk of a eucalyptus, beneath motionless blue-grey leaves, and wrapped her arms around her in a trance of longing.

Tom woke first, and lay for a while without moving, looking up at the ceiling, where a brown patch of damp made two islands and a giraffe. Well, a sort of giraffe. Only three legs. A lot of spots, though. He went on gazing at it, wondering how long it would take a three-legged giraffe to swim between the two islands, and how it had come to lose the leg in the first place. Engrossed, he forgot where he was, in the same way he forgot when Oliver read the *Just So Stories* to him: he did that, sometimes, when he came back from work. The giraffe was a kind of *Just So* animal – perhaps Oliver would like to come and look at it later. Or perhaps he would be too busy. He gave an enormous yawn, coming to, and rolled over, towards Jack's bed.

Jack lay sleeping peacefully, head on one side, arms flung out on the pillow. Tom pushed back the blue and white bedcover and slid on to the floor; he crossed the room and stood looking down at him, shifting from one foot to the other, clearing his throat. Jack's eyelids fluttered, but he did not wake. He had fantastic eyelashes, furry as caterpillars – well, perhaps more silky than furry. With one large finger Tom reached down to touch them, just to see what they felt like: Jack stirred, and the finger slipped, poking into the corner.

'Oi!'

'Sorry.' Tom backed away.

'What are you *doing*?' Jack, flushed, furious, rubbed at his eye. '*Ow*.'

'Sorry,' said Tom again, and reached for the door handle. He'd better get out of here, before there was really a fuss. The door swung towards him and he went out quickly, but the catch caught his side, as the one on the bathroom door had done the other day, scraping all along his waist at the gap between shrunken T-shirt and outgrown shorts. He fought back tears, clutching his side, and went along the landing to his parents' room. Outside the door, he knocked; no one answered. He turned the handle and pushed.

The room was empty. The shutters were closed, the bed made, clothes folded in piles on the chest of drawers, waiting to be put away. He flung himself down on the bed, and wrapped his arms round a pillow, pressing hard. He wasn't here. Not in Portugal, not anywhere. He wasn't, any more, he simply wasn't: it was like being dead.

After a while he lifted his head, listening. Jack wouldn't dare come in here, but he might be waiting. He wiped his face on the pillow and crept to the door, opening it just a little crack, just to see. And the corridor stretching ahead was empty and sunny and quiet. It looked lovely, as if everything was quite all right, with people doing things downstairs, like sewing or something.

Jack must have gone in to his parents: where were Frances and Oliver?

Tom crept out of the room, softly closing the door. He went along the loose rag runner in the corridor very carefully, and over the brilliant patches of light on the landing carpet, down into the large and airy sitting-room. This was empty, too, and so was Jessica's room, the door wide open, a muddle of clothes on an unmade bed.

He went out on to the terrace: no one was there. From a long way down in the village he could hear a saw, rather a nice sound, but he couldn't hear voices, or anyone doing anything. The swing-seat was still: the cushions looked smooth and cool, and he thought he might like to lie in it, while he had the chance. It was a bit like Goldilocks, trying things out: he moved towards the seat and lay down, pushing himself back and forth with his hand against the table, hearing the creak, and then the church clock, striking two.

His hand slid down inside his shorts. He wasn't supposed to do this, Oliver and Frances were always frowning about it, but he hadn't done it for a long time, in fact he'd forgotten all about it since they came on holiday. Anyway, it was nice; anyway, they weren't here. The swing-seat moved gently to and fro; leafy shadows from the lemon trees played on the canopy; he closed his eyes and his fingers rubbed slowly up and down. It felt lovely; you could forget about everything, doing this.

From the bottom of the steps leading down to the garden came the gentle murmur of the hens, the scratch of their feet on dry grass, dry earth. They were free here, not like the poor gasping ones in the market this morning, who were going to die. He rubbed harder, trying to get rid of the sight of their open beaks and the doom in their eyes: it had all gone away with the sick pill and the sleep, he didn't want to have to think about them now, he was feeling comforted, and nothing mattered any more; not being sick, not the hens, not people getting angry. He'd never get angry again, either: everything was going to be all right.

From far above him, a voice. 'Hey, look at Tom! He's playing with himself!' Jack, in joyful mockery, was looking down from the balcony.

Tom whipped out his hand and went scarlet. 'I wasn't.'

'Yes you were, I saw you.'

The canopy . . . The gap. Jack could see through the end, through the treacherous gap. Tom swung his legs round, and sat up; he put his hands on either side of him.

'Okay, Jack, that's enough.'

From beside Jack came Robert's voice, steady and kind. He was leaning on the parapet, calling down. 'All right, Tom? Had a good rest?'

He felt himself go redder still, mumbling a reply. And then footsteps came up from the garden, and Oliver appeared, followed by Jessica.

'Hello, Tom. What've you been up to?'

'He's been playing with himself.' Jack's clear voice came floating down through the warm still air.

'Jack . . .' said Robert, but it was too late. Jessica burst into giggles, and Oliver, who he thought was going to get angry, seemed to think it was funny too, and then they were all laughing, as if they couldn't help it, as if he was on television or something. He sprang up, and tears of rage and humiliation spurted from him as he made for the other flight of steps.

'Tom . . .' Oliver was reaching out for him, trying to take his arm: he snatched it away and began to run, stumbling across the orange tiles of the terrace, down the stone steps and round through the scrubby garden, up the next steps to the water tank. The water running into the tank sounded wonderful: he wanted to plunge into it, or race along the path into the pool, but he could hear Oliver calling him: 'Tom, Tom!' and he ran up to the iron gate, panting, yanking at it, bursting out on to the road.

'Tom!'

He stood undecided, breathing hard: should he go down, to the village? No, more people would see him – anyway, he'd be going past the garden again. He'd go up, away from everyone, away from them all. He swung round and went pounding up, panting even harder, terribly hot, the road beneath him swimming

94

through the hateful blur of tears. How could he have done that, how *could* he? All out of doors, where anyone could see him, he must have been mad.

Someone was coming down the road towards him: he looked up, heaving. And there was Frances! He flung himself upon her.

'Oh, Tom,' she said wearily, holding his hot, sweating body away from her. '*Now* what's the matter?'

Night, the house in darkness. The shutters, opened in the late afternoon and evening, were closed again now, against air which began, as the sun sank behind the mountains, to grow chilly, and then, as the evening wore on, to grow cold. Jessica, the last of the children to come in from the terrace after supper, complained it was still too early; nonetheless she seemed glad to be in bed, suddenly tired, asking for another blanket. Claire found one in the cupboard, and tucked her in. 'You really have caught the sun today.' She kissed her, and Jessica turned away, yawning.

Now, the whole house was asleep: Jessica, in her room by herself downstairs, her door open on to the sitting-room, where the moon shone through the pane of clear glass above the terrace doors; everyone else upstairs, soundless. The church clock struck three, but it could have been two o'clock, or four; after a while, a door on the corridor opened, quietly, and was closed again. Slow footsteps moved along the rag runner, hands felt along walls.

Tom, deeply asleep, was making for the stairs.

He came down them carefully, holding the banister, stopping at the turn; his lips moved and his eyelids flickered; he came on down, moving steadily, carefully, reaching the bottom, feeling for a step that wasn't there, standing very still, waiting. Then he moved again, along the wooden passage into the sitting-room, feeling the panelling, stopping when it stopped, feeling the air. He turned, and made for the doors to the terrace, across the moonlit expanse of floorboards, with nothing to stop him, everything airy and open and free.

But Jessica, dreaming uneasily, turned over and cried out something, and he came to a halt, and waited. Silence.

He moved on, reaching out again. His hands met something enormous and hairy, which rocked: his eyes flew open. The room

95

was bright with the moon, but the figure towering above him was huge and dark, headless, with a hat. It swayed towards him, and he pushed at it, shouting. It fell with a dreadful crash, like thunder; somebody screamed. He felt hot pee pour everywhere.

Lights on, doors opening, Jessica's scream. A horrible fizzing sound, which grew louder. Bare feet raced down the stairs, voices were calling.

Someone was holding him close.

5

Jessica, shivering and tearful, was taken upstairs and tucked into her parents' bed: Robert, turning off lights to quieten the fuse-box, dispensing brandy to shaken grown-ups, said he would sleep down in her room. Jack, undisturbed by any of the uproar, slept on, breathing steadily, as Frances, by the light from the landing, helped Tom in to clean dry pyjamas.

'There,' she said, buttoning him up, guiding him towards his bed, smoothing the pillows. 'In you get.'

He was ashen, clammy, his hair sticking up in thick dark tufts. He clambered heavily on to the mattress and sank down.

'Stay with me.' His eyes were blank.

'Of course I'll stay.' She sat on the edge of the bed, holding his hand.

'What happened?' he asked her. 'What did I do?'

'You – ' she hesitated. Were you supposed to tell children they walked in their sleep? She knew you were never supposed to wake them: they never had woken him. Tonight – what should she say?

'You went downstairs to the loo,' she said slowly. 'You must have been half asleep and gone the wrong way, I suppose. So you banged into – that thing.' Well – it might have been the truth. 'Poor Tom. Never mind, it's all right now.'

'Mmm.' His breathing slowed. She realised suddenly, as he began to relax, that she had been dreaming of Dora when the crash came from downstairs, but that since then had not thought of her once. Let it go, then, she said to herself, summoning sense and reason, and an ordered future swam up before her, in which Dora had disappeared and Frances and Oliver were reunited, their child between them. Let it go, let it go.

Tom yawned, falling asleep with his hand in hers. Frances knew that Dora, who loved her children dearly, and was always talking about them, would have been the first to fly downstairs at the sound of that terrible crash and the scream; that it would have

97

been she, no one else, not a woman he barely knew, who would have cradled her son in her arms, rocking, reassuring, holding him. *Dora,* she wrote, looking into the darkness, loving her more than ever with this vision, *I was dreaming of you tonight when Tom went sleepwalking . . .* What was the dream? She closed her eyes, feeling sleep heavy upon her, trying to recapture it. *Let me sink into sleep again, let me find you . . .*

The floorboards on the landing creaked.

'Frances?' Claire whispered.

Frances opened her eyes to see her standing in the doorway in her nightdress, holding two cups of hot milk on a tray.

'How is he?' Claire indicated the cups. 'Would he like some?'

'He's almost asleep – look.'

Claire looked. 'You're not taking him in with you?'

'Oh, no, we never do that. He's much better off in his own bed.'

'But if he does it again – '

'He won't, he never does. Usually we just take him back to bed still asleep, and he doesn't know anything about it.' She yawned, carefully releasing her hand from his. 'Where's Oliver?'

'Down in the sitting-room with Robert. They're finishing off the brandy.'

'Oh. Right.' Frances yawned again, 'Claire? Thank you – I'm sorry about all this . . .' She smiled wanly. 'You must be wishing you'd never asked us.'

'Nonsense. We'll talk in the morning. Goodnight.'

'Goodnight.' Frances turned away, smoothing the bedclothes over Tom, looking down into his pale, heavy face.

Claire crossed the landing, and pushed open the door. There was a light on the chest of drawers, a bulb stuck into a wine bottle, with a shade made of raffia: the room looked comforting and warm. Jessica, propped up on the pillows, looked crumpled and tear-stained, not much more than six.

'Here we are.' Claire sat down beside her, passing her milk. 'You'll feel better when you've had this.'

Jessica took it mutely, cupping it between her hands. 'It's got skin on it,' she said after a while.

'Because you're not drinking it.' Claire reached out and lifted the skin with her finger, draping it over the side of the mug.

98

'Remember Dr Dolittle? Gub-Gub the pig had a clothes-line for the skin on hot chocolate.'

'Dr Dolittle's racist,' said Jessica. 'They said so at school.'

'Are you sure?'

'Yes. The parrot wants to change the black prince to white in one of the books. She keeps on about it.'

Claire shook her head. 'I don't remember. Anyway, drink it.'

They sipped in silence. Across the landing she could hear Frances, coming out of the boys' room, going quietly along the landing to her own. She had looked like a nurse, sitting there beside Tom, as if she were taking his pulse. No, she thought, reflecting, actually she looked like a patient: frail, in crumpled white pyjamas, dark beneath the eyes, sitting in silence.

'Mum?'

'Yes?'

'Is it normal to sleepwalk?'

'It's unusual.'

'Did Jack and me ever do it?'

'No, never.'

'So why – '

'I don't know why,' said Claire. 'These things happen, children grow out of them. I'm sorry you had such a fright. Are you feeling better now?'

Jess put the cup on the floor and lay down, yawning. 'A bit. Where's Dad?'

'Having a drink with Oliver. I expect they'll go to bed in a minute.' Claire finished the milk, tepid now, and went to switch off the light.

'Leave it,' said Jess from the pillows. 'Please.'

'Okay.' She came back to bed, and pulled down the duvet, climbing in beside her. 'Isn't this nice?' She put out an arm and stroked Jess's thick heavy hair. 'We haven't slept together for a long time.'

'Don't start getting soppy.'

Claire smiled. 'You are feeling better.'

Jess yawned again. 'Goodnight. Thanks for the milk.'

'Goodnight, sleep tight. No rush in the morning.' Claire lay in the warm, contented light of the lamp across the room, hearing, from downstairs, Robert and Oliver's low voices and then, from somewhere far away in the mountains, a dog, yowling. Then everything was quiet again, and she closed her eyes, uncertain in those last, drifting moments before sleep whether it were Jess or Jack or Tom who lay so close beside her.

'I'm sorry about all this,' Oliver was saying.

Robert shook his head. 'Please don't be. We're just glad he's not hurt.'

'Yes.' Oliver looked into his brandy, thoughtful.

'It's happened before?'

'From time to time. Perhaps every three months or so. Occasionally there's a run of it, two or three nights together, but that's rare. I shouldn't think, after tonight, he'll do it again while we're here.'

'And he doesn't wake up? This is the first time?'

'Yes. Unfamiliar house, I suppose. Normally he finds his way around, quite often we've heard him and found him making his own way back to bed. It's more of a problem for us than for him – he's quite all right the next morning. Straight off to school.'

Robert was moved to ask, he didn't quite know why, about the holidays. In the holidays, said Oliver, Tom went to his child-minder. This was the first time, it seemed, that they'd spent more than a day or two all together since – well, it was probably Easter.

He shrugged. 'I expect we're all still needing to settle down a bit, that might have something to do with it. But we've discussed it with our GP – she says he'll grow out of it. All the literature confirms that view.'

The literature, thought Robert. It was a word that sat ill with a child, somehow.

They were in the far corner of the sitting-room, Robert low in an unsprung armchair, Oliver opposite on the worn sofa, brandy on the coffee table between them. Placed thus for direct conversation, they did not meet each other's eyes, looking down into their glasses, or round the room. A single low-watt lamp stood on the desk in the other corner, which was lined with bookshelves, the foot of the L in what Claire and Robert always spoke of as a lovely room, broad and spacious, beautifully proportioned. Now, shadowy beyond that dim pool of light, Robert felt it threatening and unfamiliar. Jessica's screaming rang in his ears; across by the dining-room door the dark shape of the shepherd's straw cloak was back on its stand, where it always stood: righted again, waiting to topple again.

Oliver was silent, drinking. He wore a long, deep blue Paisley dressing-gown, a good one, which looked as though it might have been inherited from a father who had bought things to last. Robert didn't know anything about Oliver's father, or, indeed, anything about Oliver, and sitting there waiting for him to continue, distant and unemotional, he felt that he did not very much want to know. However, he did want to learn more about Tom, and he said now, keeping it light, 'Children . . .', as if in the kind of complicity he imagined Claire shared with her women friends, other mothers: coping, raising their eyes to the heavens.

Oliver did not answer. Moths bumped against the parchment shade of the lamp; Robert cleared his throat in the silence. Oliver said suddenly: 'We never wanted children, they never came into it.' He drained his glass, made a gesture of resignation. 'But these things happen.'

Robert reached for the brandy bottle. Refilling their glasses he thought: yes, but I don't want to know how they happen – not in this case, not now. Long used to confidences from women friends at work, long used to an easy, unquestioning intimacy with his wife, he surprised himself by thinking: this is women's talk, it's private. It was the kind of information he expected to be fed to him by Claire – perhaps this was what Frances had disclosed to her the other evening, up by the pool, although he couldn't imagine why Claire should have seemed so thrown by it. But it was, surely, a conversation much more appropriate to them: he didn't want to be the recipient of Oliver's slow and heavy unburdening, even though, concerned for his child, he had invited it. Indeed, when he tried to think of one man with whom he had ever had, or wished to have, such a conversation, he found he couldn't. Not one. Nor had he ever missed it. Still –

'So a son is born,' he said, striving for the right note.

'When we wanted a daughter,' said Oliver. 'If there had to be a

101

baby, we wanted a girl. A girl would have been easier for both of us, I'm sure of that.'

Robert, thinking of Jessica these days – offhand, dismissive, hurtful – wasn't convinced, but said nothing. Anyway, such behaviour was recent, and, it was to be hoped, temporary. At this moment, recalling her tears, it was impossible, in any case, to think of her with anything but love and protectiveness. And perhaps Oliver was right, perhaps a daughter would have been better for them. Certainly a different kind of boy.

'And instead,' he said, almost without thinking, 'instead you have a changeling.'

They looked at each other directly, for the first time.

'Yes,' said Oliver, acknowledging his accuracy. 'Yes, exactly that. Our only child, and we don't know what to do with him. Certainly I don't. Frances has a little more patience, but – ' He broke off, with a deep, involuntary sigh. 'As I said, we didn't want children. We wanted each other – God, that seems a hell of a long time ago.' He stood up abruptly. 'What a mess. What an unholy mess. I'd better go and see if they're all right.' He put down his glass, but he did not go, he stood there frowning and thoughtful, very tall, naked beneath the Paisley dressing-gown, long feet thrust into flat black espadrilles. Despite his height, his physical presence, something of the power which Robert and Claire had both sensed in him seemed to have gone: he looked weary and defeated, years older. It might have been the shock, the wrenching out of sleep, the disclosures made in the middle of the night to someone who was almost a stranger. It was, Robert knew, more than all this, though what he could only guess at.

He said: 'We'd better get that thing out of the way in the morning,' and nodded towards the shepherd's cloak.

Oliver looked at it. 'Yes. Well – ' He gave a wry smile. 'Let us hope that the rest of the night passes without incident.'

'Indeed.' Robert poured out the last of the brandy. 'I'll finish this off, I think. Sleep well.'

'And you.' Oliver crossed to the darkened corridor, making his way to the stairs; he climbed them slowly, and Robert heard his footsteps creak on the landing, a pause as he checked the boys' room, and then the door of his bedroom with Frances open and close. The house was silent again.

He went on sitting there for a while, finishing the brandy, thinking, beginning to yawn. The memory of Jessica's scream receded: she was safe, they were all safe. He heaved himself out of the armchair and in Jessica's room lay down on the creaking bed, pulling up the blankets. But he found himself tossing and turning, rearranging thin pillows. In spite of his tiredness, in spite of the brandy, it was a long time before he fell asleep, seeing over and over again before him in the darkness the figure of Tom by the fallen cloak stand: white-faced, staring, clutching at himself in terror.

Next morning, everyone slept late, the sun already brilliant when Jack opened his eyes, reached for his book and smelt something. A pair of pyjamas lay on the floor; what were they doing there? He knew: Tom must have wet the bed, like a great big baby. He looked across at him, lying asleep with his mouth open: perhaps he should go and poke *him* in the eye, let him see what it felt like. No – he didn't want to go near him. He picked up his book and found his place, read a few pages and realised he was hungry. The digital watch he'd been given for his birthday in March showed 9:01, no wonder he was hungry. But the house was very quiet, not a sound from downstairs. He pushed back the bedclothes and got out, going across to his parents' room, where he found a light still burning, and Jessica lying next to Claire, her hair spread out on the pillow, both of them fast asleep.

He shook Claire's shoulder. 'Hey! What's going on?' He climbed in beside her, shoving her with his feet. What was Jessica doing in here? 'Move up.'

Claire frowned, moving her legs away. 'Gently, Jack, stop it, please.'

'But what's going on? Where's Dad?'

'Sssh. He's down in Jessie's room, we had a bad night . . .' She opened her eyes, and pulled him towards her. 'Don't be so grumpy, everything's okay. There, that's better. Settle down now.'

'What do you mean, a bad night? Tom's wet the bed, it *smells* in there.'

'Sssh! I don't want to wake Jess.'

But Jess was already stirring, disturbed and disgruntled. Even with the shutters closed you could tell from the light streaming through the gaps how bright it was outside. She pulled a pillow down over her head, and turned away. Claire sighed.

'What *sort* of bad night?' Jack persisted.

'Tom sleepwalked,' said Jess, from beneath the pillow.

'What? What did you say?'

Footsteps along the corridor. They heard Robert putting mugs down outside the door at the end, calling discreetly: 'Oliver? Frances? Tea.' He came back again, into their room.

'Thank God,' said Claire. 'Just what we need.'

'How are we all this morning?' Tousled and puffy in his old pyjamas, Robert pushed the door to with his elbow and put down the tray on the chest of drawers, moving along a muddle of suntan cream and hairbrushes. He switched off the light and began to pour. 'Sleep well?' He stepped over kicked-off sandals and yesterday's clothes, holding out mugs.

'You are an angel,' said Claire, taking one.

'I am a bearer of trays,' said Robert, easing himself down by Jack's feet. 'This bed is too low. Move up a bit.'

Jack drew up his feet, Jess took the pillow off. They all regarded each other.

'Phew,' said Claire.

'Quite. Any sounds this morning?'

She shook her head. 'Tom wasn't awake when you got up, was he?' she asked Jack.

'No. What *happened*?'

'I told you,' said Jessica, reaching for Claire's tea. 'Tom sleepwalked. He knocked over the shepherd's cloak . . . you slept through *everything*.'

He was furious.

'Listen,' said Robert, a little less puffy with the tea. 'I'll explain. But no more teasing, Jack, got it? Give Tom a break for a bit.'

Jack looked mulish.

'I mean it.'

'Perhaps,' said Claire, 'we should all have a break for a bit.

104

Perhaps we should go off for the day and leave them all to calm down – do you think?'

'Yes!' said Jack. 'Just us. Oh, yes, let's. Where shall we go?'

The landing floorboards creaked, the door swung open.

'Hello, Tom,' said Robert.

'You're supposed to knock,' Jack muttered.

Tom looked rumpled, greyish, as if he might be sickening for something – no, thought Claire, stretching out a hand towards him, more as though he were getting over something, which of course he was. He stood in the doorway gazing at them all, and she patted the bedclothes.

'Come and sit down. How are you feeling this morning?'

'All right.' He sounded puzzled by the question; he came towards the bed slowly, with a faraway, anaesthetised air. 'Can we go swimming today?'

Jack glowered at him. 'This is *our* room. You're supposed to knock.'

'Jack . . .' said Claire, warningly.

'Sorry,' said Tom. He sat down heavily on the bed, and Jack moved irritably away.

'You're on my feet, get off.' And then suddenly, in an outburst, as Tom clumsily shifted his large frame, 'Get *off!* This is *our* room! Go away!'

'Jack!' said Claire and Robert sharply, in unison.

'Tom,' said Robert, 'it's all right, come back . . .'

But he had gone.

Dora and Frances are walking by a river. It has been raining, and the fields on the further side of the water are lush and shining. Willow trees overhang the bank; beyond them they can hear cows, munching summer grass. Behind them is the house where they are staying, empty, peaceful, awaiting their return; in its tranquil garden, established, well tended, is a table where they sit and have breakfast when it is fine. Here, to their left, old men are moving among tall bamboo canes in a sprawl of allotments; runner beans clamber towards the clear rinsed sky, green and scarlet against smoke from a damp bonfire. The air smells fresh and earthy; ahead, a fisherman reels in his line, and flings it out again: ripples spread wider, wider. Frances puts her head on Dora's shoulder; Dora's arm goes round her. They walk on.

'I love you,' says Frances. 'I have always loved you.'

'I know,' says Dora. 'It's okay – I've always known.' And she gives Frances a smile of such acceptance and affection that Frances is overcome, light with happiness. I have come home, she thinks. I am where I belong.

And suddenly is alone again, the river and the afternoon's tranquility vanished. She is walking through dark streets, somewhere in a city she has never visited, looking at names she does not recognise, knocking on doors. Behind her, a girl is calling.

'Frances! Frances! Remember me?'

'No,' says Frances. 'No, not now. I'm looking for someone, leave me alone.' The streets grow narrower, darker; she breaks into a run, calling out: 'Dora! Dora!' A long way away from her, someone is crying, a door bangs open and shut, as if a wind is rising . . .

'Frances, Frances . . .'

She opened her eyes on a room full of fierce sunshine: Oliver had flung open the shutters, and was standing over her, dressed, ready for the day.

'You were dreaming,' he said.

She covered her eyes.

'It's late, you were dreaming badly, I thought I should wake you.'

'Close the shutters. Please. Please – it's too much.'

He crossed the room again, pushing them to. 'Robert's brought us some tea – do you want it?'

'In a minute.' She went on lying there, her eyes still covered.

'What were you dreaming about?'

'Nothing,' she said. 'I can't remember.'

'You looked troubled.'

'Did I?' She uncovered her eyes, her limbs like lead. Then: 'Tom!' she said suddenly. 'Is he all right?'

'I've just been to look – he's playing outside. Everyone else is getting up for breakfast. Here – ' He passed her a mug from the pile of books by the bed. She sat up and took it, sipping lukewarm tea.

106

'What did you and Robert talk about last night?'

'Nothing,' he said. 'I can't remember.'

They looked at each other.

Frances said: 'Oliver . . .' But Dora's arm went round her again, lovingly holding her, and she turned back to her mug of cold tea and left his name hanging in the air.

And Oliver said, 'I'll leave you in peace,' and went out, closing the door with unexpected gentleness.

Guida was downstairs, waiting to wash up the breakfast she had laid but which no one had eaten. Robert, smelling coffee, made efforts to explain, standing in the sitting-room with the doors to the terrace wide open and the sun pouring on to the floorboards, on to the yellow straw shepherd's cloak and hat, which hung askew.

'Bad . . . *noite*,' he said, thumbing the dictionary. 'Everyone has slept late.' He folded his hands and laid his cheek upon them, closing his eyes, and Guida smiled.

'Party,' she said. 'Drinking.'

'Drinking, yes,' said Robert, noticing that the brandy bottles and empty glasses had gone. 'Party, no.' He moved to adjust the hat. 'Never mind. Perhaps you can . . .' What could she do?

'Washing,' said Guida, and moved her arms up and down, as though she were riding a horse.

Robert laughed. 'Yes, washing,' he said. 'Well done.'

She went into the shady bathroom, humming, gathering piles of discarded clothes from the basket, and carried them slowly down the corridor and out through the kitchen, flip-flops flapping, climbing the steps to the water tank. Robert stood for a moment, looking up at the huge heavy cloak on its stand, which looked so solid and fell so easily. They must put it down in the cellar; he and Oliver could do it after breakfast.

He turned back into the room, which since they all arrived had been used more as a thoroughfare than anything else: a place to pass through on the way out to the terrace, or to dump swimming things, coming indoors. He recalled from last year, when it had rained and been cooler, endless afternoons in here of Monopoly and the Game of Life with the lively Hobbs boys, and evenings of

107

bridge with their undemanding parents. This year, it seemed, the game of life was of a different order.

But the room this morning felt restored to its original airy calm: he looked at the tall windows, hung with loosely woven curtains, at the wooden ceiling, the white walls above the panelling hung with old farm implements – a scythe, a wooden yoke, a saw – and gave an inward sigh of relief.

However. There was still Tom. Where was he?

Robert went out on to the hot, empty terrace; he leaned on the parapet, shading his eyes, and looked down. Cicadas scraped and sawed; Tom was standing beneath a peach tree, gesturing, murmuring, in a perpetual, unconscious river of sound, clearly lost in a game. Robert was about to call to him, to ask if he was all right, but there was something unapproachable about that air of complete and private absorption, and he found himself remembering long distant summer days from his own childhood, when he, too, had needed time to himself. Perhaps Tom should be left to find his own way through his troubles; and perhaps Oliver was right – they were less of a problem for him than for those around him. So long as they kept an eye on Jack it would all blow over. In the clear – well, dazzling – light of day, he didn't want to think about it any more, he really didn't.

It was much too hot out here. He stepped back indoors and, waiting for the others to come down to breakfast, he wandered over to the library in the foot of the L, looking along the shelves where they had done much browsing last year on those rainy September afternoons, finding something for everyone: biographies, novels and journals, travel books. Holiday paperbacks, some of them no doubt left by other guests in other seasons, occupied, with worn copies of the Reader's Digest, two or three shelves: Agatha Christie, Dick Francis, Barbara Cartland, Barbara Pym.

'I *adore* Barbara Pym,' he heard Linda Hobbs saying earnestly, standing there in her Laura Ashley dress, feet in the Dr Scholl sandals which had clumped across the wooden floors all fortnight.

'Who is she again?' asked Geoffrey, wrinkling his nose.

After last night, Robert thought he could do with a bit of Geoffrey.

On the marble-topped desk in the middle of this L lay a guest-book, and the folder of local information Robert had shown to Oliver on the evening he and Frances had arrived. That evening, he remembered now, he had stood unseen on the balcony overlooking the terrace, watching them, so formal with one another, so polite. He had speculated on them then, and on the intensity he had seen in Frances's face, as she looked at Claire, and he continued, despite himself and his desire to let things be, to speculate, although some of his questions were now answered.

Noises came from the terrace: he found Tom squatting down on the orange tiles, watching something. Robert shielded his eyes again. Christ, it was hot.

'What've you found there?'

'Just some ants. They're really interesting, ants, aren't they? Really strong.'

'Yes.' He stood looking down at scurrying legs, enormous breadcrumbs. He squatted down beside Tom, putting out a finger, and the ants, undaunted, turned to left and right. 'You mustn't worry about Jack,' he said casually.

'What?'

'I mean teasing, being grumpy. Don't let it bother you.'

Tom didn't answer. His face had a better colour now; he put out a finger of his own, and laughed. 'Look at them, all in a muddle.'

From behind them they could hear voices, people gathering. The smell of coffee, being brought through from the kitchen, wafted through the open doors. About time.

'Come on,' he said, patting Tom's shoulder, getting stiffly up again. Perhaps he should start doing morning exercises. Oh, to hell with it. Life was too short for morning exercises. 'Breakfast.'

Tom got to his feet. 'Can I sit next to you?'

There were two entrances to the cellar. One was inside the house, a narrow door almost opposite the bathroom, the other a padlocked door in the house wall beneath the terrace, a place where, when unlocked, deliveries of Calor gas could be made from the lower road running down past the garden to the village. Unpacking the car on the afternoon of their arrival, Robert and

109

Claire, as last year, had put the deflated dinghy there, in its bag, out of the way but easy to get at and blow up again. The football and cricket stuff was there too. But it was, naturally, the upstairs door through which, after breakfast, Robert and Oliver manoeuvred the heavy wooden stand, up-ended, lying on its side like a corpse. Behind them came Claire and Frances, bearing the garments themselves, and behind them the children, excited. Tom, it seemed, was quite recovered now; Jessica, after some disagreement and adult negotiation, was wearing the hat.

The light – a single bulb, a single grimy window in the corner – was dim, the narrow stairs steep. Oliver, going first, had the head and shoulders, Robert the crosspiece of the base, a little more awkward, banging against the walls. Behind him the straw cloak and trousers rustled.

'Don't push,' said Claire.

'We're not,' said the children.

Oliver reached the stone floor, and moved away from the foot of the stairs rather too quickly. Robert, bent over, carrying most of the weight at their point, was for an unnerving moment almost dragged down after him.

'Steady on.'

'Sorry.' Oliver stopped, looking over his shoulder, then inched forward until Robert, step by step, had come to the bottom. They moved out into the middle of the floor; the women and children followed.

'Where should it go?'

Robert grunted. 'Anywhere. Over in that corner.'

They carried it across, past a table of empty wine bottles, thick with dust, and set it down beneath the window. Robert felt his arms trembling; he wiped his forehead.

'Well done. Right, let's have the cloak.'

Claire and Frances brought it between them – like hand-maidens, he thought suddenly, and as they reached up to ease it on to the wooden shoulders, smoothing down the layers of straw, Jessica said: 'It's like dressing a bride, or something.' She stretched her arms wide. 'I feel pretty, oh so pretty . . .'

'Not much wrong with you this morning,' said Robert.

'And you look very nice in that hat,' said Oliver.

110

'That's because you can't see her face,' said Jack, but half-heartedly, looking around. 'It's wicked down here.'

The cellar was large, with a passage, walk-in cupboards, a pleasantly woody, musty smell. A half-filled wine rack ran from floor to low ceiling; there were large Calor gas bottles, paint tins, a paraffin stove, a couple of deck-chair frames, the accumulated bits and pieces of years of getting things out of the way. There was a box, for younger visitors, full of old toys kept from when the children of the house were small – bricks, a push-cart, a pull-along duck.

'Cars!' said Jack, digging into it. 'I'd forgotten all about this box.' He knelt on the floor, running a blue pick-up truck up and down. Across the room, Jessica was taking off the hat, shaking her hair. She passed it to Oliver, who took it with a bow, then carefully replaced it on the stand, barely taller than he was.

'Well, that's that done,' said Robert. 'Good. Now, what does the day hold in store? What does everyone feel like?'

Sitting at the breakfast table, neither he nor Claire had, in the end, mooted the idea of a day apart. Somehow, when it came to it, it seemed rude and unfriendly – particularly looking at Frances, who came down late, and sat eating maize bread and honey in silence; particularly after Jack's outburst upstairs.

'I mean it,' Claire had said to him, coming down. 'One more piece of behaviour like that and there'll be trouble.' What sort of trouble? She couldn't imagine, she didn't want to have to think about threats and discipline.

'All right, all right,' said Jack, leaping the last two stairs to the bottom.

'Well,' she said now, seeing Oliver and Frances havering, not quite sure of the options, 'we could take the dinghy out, couldn't we?'

'Yes!' said Jessica. 'Yes, brilliant. The dinghy's really nice,' she told them, and Oliver smiled at her. 'You can drift downriver in it like a queen.'

'White or black?' he asked her gravely.

'Is that all right then?' Claire asked, pleased to have Jess so enthusiastic. 'Jack? Happy with that?'

He was digging around in the box again. 'Can I pump it up?'

111

'We'll take it in turns. Tom? Where've you got to? Would you like to go for a row?'

'Okay,' he called. He had found something, too, an old wooden doll's house, pushed to the back of one of the walk-in cupboards along the passage. He drew it forward on its shelf and ran his fingers down the dusty rooftop; it left a trail, and he blew at the dust and sneezed.

'Come on, then,' said Robert, to whom the prospect of drifting downriver in the dinghy felt all at once quite perfect, just the thing to put everyone right, but who knew very well who would be the one to pump it up properly and carry it, and wanted to get it over with. 'Jack? Leave that stuff now, you can come down here another time.'

'If it rains,' said Claire, and they all laughed at such improbability – seizing, after the night's events, on anything to laugh at – and began to make their way up the stairs again. Already the morning's dense heat had begun to soak into the house.

'Come on, Tom,' said Frances, over her shoulder.

'Coming.'

The doll's house roof had dull orange tiles, but the rest of it, the walls, were unpainted, and the windows, most of them, anyway, were staring squares, without frames or glass, though one on the upper floor had shutters on tiny hinges. Downstairs there was an entrance at the side, also unfinished and doorless, but at the front were double doors, half closed. Tom picked at the gap and got them open; he peered inside but could see nothing. Then the whole front must come off – yes, there was a catch at the side. He fumbled with it, hating little fiddly things, and as it came up, and the front swung away in a yawn, he suddenly saw, in the way you saw things in a dream, a human head, with a hinged lid lifting off it and a hollow of darkness inside. Horrible. For a moment he went blank. Then he slammed it down again in his mind.

The double doors would lead you, if you were a doll, into what was now revealed as an enormous downstairs room, with smaller ones leading off it, and a corridor to wooden stairs with a turn in them. On the upper floor was a broad landing, another long corridor, three bedrooms. Somehow it felt as if he had seen all this before, and again he had the disturbing sensation of being in a

112

waking dream, not quite real, until he realised that he *had* seen it before, that it was this house, somebody's model of this house. Wow.

He stood back, to check, and saw the tools he hadn't noticed before on the shelf below: chisels and a little saw, boxes of wooden bits and pieces and screws. And realising that it was, indeed, a model, he felt better, sort of back in the world, though there remained a strange sensation: as if he, seeing a small version of the house, was also shrunken, like Alice in Wonderland, which he'd seen the cartoon of. As if one of him had gone upstairs with the others, a normal-sized boy, and another one of him had got left down here, much smaller. More than that. More as if he were both inside himself, very small, looking out, and at the same time watching himself, from a long way away.

A rhythmical puffing sound was coming from somewhere, like a distant train. Or someone gasping for breath. He was beginning to feel peculiar now, he didn't like it. Then he heard voices, and someone asking: 'Where's Tom?' That was Frances.

'I'm in here,' he called. He shut up the front of the house, and the lid in his head went click, though he'd shut it already. The huffing and puffing continued, from quite close, he realised now, from just the other side of the door across the cellar. He went over quickly, pressing his face to the gap: he could see Robert's back, and bits of the others. 'Here!' he called. 'Let me out.'

'It's locked,' Robert said to Frances, who came to the door, putting her eye to the gap. She and Tom looked at each other: he saw her pupil grow dark and enormous.

'What are you doing in there?' she said. 'You'll have to go back up the stairs, go on.'

'Can't I come out here?'

'Tom, it's locked, Robert's just said so. Go on, off you go – you can help us with the dinghy, can't he, Robert?'

'More the merrier,' said Robert. Frances moved away from the gap and Tom caught a glimpse of blue and yellow, Robert's foot going up and down.

'Coming!' He turned and made for the stairs. In the far corner, in the shadows, the shepherd's cloak stood watching: he felt himself, realising this, turn, as sharply as if a wire were pulling

113

him, into a wide, sweeping circle away from it. He ran up the stairs, slamming the door behind him at the top, and dashed through the kitchen, where Claire was doing things.

'You okay?' she asked, as he went past.

'Fine, I'm going to help Robert.' He pushed open the door and Guida, ringing out clothes up at the water tank at the top of the steps, waved down to him.

'*Bom dia.*'

'*Bom dia!*' he called. '*Bom dia!* We're going out in a boat.'

She smiled and nodded, uncomprehending, and he raced down the steps to the garden, disturbing the crouching cat beneath them: she leapt towards the bushes.

'Hello, puss!' Running round the side of the house, he meant to tell Frances about the model house down in the cellar, but then he saw the dinghy, the white nylon ropes round the side, its beautiful colours swelling and growing with the steady puff puff of the foot pump, coming alive, and he forgot about everything else.

Deep reflections of the towering cliff face and the pines sank into the shining water on the far side of the river, and broke, rippling, steady and slow, over the slippery rocks as Robert rowed the dinghy down towards the bend. Out here, in the middle of the river, the water was deep, the current lazy: they were away from the rocks, away from the pebbled shallows on the near side where they had spent the other morning watching dragonflies and fishing with the nets. It was very hot, but the boys were wearing their sunhats and trailing their hands over the sides; birdsong and the gentle plash of the oars were the only sounds to break the silence.

Claire and Frances, sitting on the shady grey sand of the bank, waved as they went past, and the boys waved back, smiling, clearly soothed.

'Perfect,' said Frances, watching them. 'You're very clever.' She felt in the family beach bag for the last packet of cigarettes. 'Do you mind. . . ?'

'Go ahead,' said Claire. 'It keeps the flies off.'

Frances lit and inhaled deeply, shaking out the match. Robert and the boys were rounding the bend, the mass of cliff to their right, and on their left the gentle slope of the mountainside where she had gone walking yesterday afternoon, writing to Dora. She blew out smoke in a slow cloud, feeling this, the first cigarette of the day, make her light-headed.

'Tom seems fine now, doesn't he?' said Claire.

'Yes, yes, he does – I told you, he always is the next day. Last night was different, but I think he's forgotten all about it now, thank God.' She inhaled again, coming down a little as nicotine and bloodstream renewed their acquaintance. 'I'm just sorry it gave you all such a bad night.'

'It didn't, not in the end. It was rather nice having Jess in with me again, we haven't done it for ages. What about you – did you sleep all right afterwards?'

'Oh, yes, fine, thanks.'

I should have *Fine, thanks*, stamped on a badge and pinned to me, thought Frances, in whom last night's dreams still lingered, and she shut her eyes, at once seeing herself in the office, on a stream of Monday mornings, waiting for Dora's step on the stairs.

In the separation of the weekends, the intensity of the inner life Frances led was sometimes overwhelming. She and Oliver had people for supper, or went out for supper. Frances smiled at everyone, and thought about Dora. Adrian and Dora had themselves been to supper with them once or twice; Frances and Oliver had been to their house, once with Tom. Oliver liked Adrian, as did most people, as, indeed, did Frances: a kindly, musical man with an administrative job in the Open University. Occasionally Oliver had suggested they saw more of them: Frances had reacted vaguely.

At weekends, she and Oliver were on duty for Tom – every other Saturday in turn, and Sundays together. Dutifully they met other families from school; they took Tom, and assorted children, on outings. Walking across Hampstead Heath, watching the kites fly on Parliament Hill, wandering from snake-house to ape-house at the Zoo, Frances thought about Dora. She set scenes, she replayed conversations, she wrote and rewrote her eternal letter.

'Wake up,' said Oliver, as they reached the top of the queue in the Science Museum, or as he saw her, hands in her pockets, pacing about while the children gazed up at specks of blue and red amongst the clouds.

'Sorry. I was miles away.'

'You're always miles away.'

'Sorry. I'm here now.'

On Monday morning, as every morning, Frances was one of the first in the office, and Dora, with the much longer journey to make across London from Barnes, was one of the last.

Frances put the coffee on and sat at her desk beneath the skylight window. Up at her desk near the blue swing-doors Elaine was sorting the post, greeting Derek, who came in looking the worse for wear, and Jocelyn, who looked fresh and fit and ready for anything, beaming at Frances as he went past. Kate came in swearing, dumping a bulging briefcase of books on her desk, and Dora, a few minutes later, arrived looking like none of the others, neither flustered nor out of sorts nor needing to ingratiate herself, although she greeted everyone. She looked as if she had just been thinking something over and was now collecting herself, ready for what came next; she looked, taking off her navy jacket and hanging it by the doors, pouring a coffee, walking down the office with her easy, graceful stride, like someone perfectly approachable, receptive and warm, but whose life was already interesting enough for her to need few new approaches. And Frances, as always, watched her coming, returned her smile, and thought: you know how to be and you outshine all the rest. You're the one. It's as simple as that.

'And how was your weekend?' Dora asked her, putting down her shoulder-bag, picking up her post.

'Fine, thanks.' Frances got up to get herself a coffee, and collect from Elaine her own post. She came back with a pile of letters and manuscripts in Jiffy bags, carefully balancing the mug in her other hand.

'Can you manage?' Dora asked, looking up, tugging open a packet of transparencies.

'Yes, thanks.' She put it all down on her desk. 'What about your weekend?

'Dreadful,' said Dora calmly. She put the packet aside, and sipped at her coffee. 'Oh, that's better. Sophie is one long mood

116

these days: I suppose we shall live to see the end of it, but sometimes I wonder. She has a New Boyfriend.' She looked at Frances with comic meaningfulness, and Frances laughed.

'What's he like?'

'Mute. Never mind, more of him another time, perhaps. Now, what have we here?' She slit open a cardboard-backed envelope, plastered with Please Do Not Bend. 'Aha, the Scottish islands. At last. They're rather good . . .' She put on her glasses and slipped glossy photographs one by one off the pile, spreading them on her desk, carefully moving the coffee. 'They're very good, in fact, come and have a look . . .'

Frances went over. She stood beside Dora looking at black and white islands drowning in mist, wild seas and storm clouds, a rowing boat left on an empty shore. Together they discarded one that was overdramatic, another which verged upon the sweet.

'Brilliant,' said Frances. 'Do you want to show them to Jocelyn? And I'll go and give Philip a ring, shall I, to say they've come? He's supposed to be delivering final copy this week.'

'Okay.' Dora was putting the photographs carefully back in a pile. She turned and touched Frances on the shoulder with affection. 'How about lunch? Are you free? Then I can tell you about the boyfriend.'

'Lovely,' said Frances steadily. 'Yes, let's,' and went back across the room to her desk, walking on air.

'Tom all right?' Dora continued in passing, taking all the photos down to Jocelyn.

Frances sat down in her swivel chair and reached for a cigarette. 'He's fine,' she said, lighting it. 'He's fine, thanks.'

'Frances?' said Claire, beside her. 'Do you want to talk?'

'No.' She opened her eyes. The dinghy was out of sight, and the water smooth and unbroken again.

'Are you sure?'

'Yes.' She wrapped her arms round her knees, letting the cigarette burn on itself, and a thin tendril of smoke rose from between her fingers. 'I'm sorry,' she said. 'I shouldn't have told you anything, it isn't fair to involve you – and anyway I don't want to. Please let's just forget about it.'

'Can *you* forget about it?' Claire said, after a pause.

Frances was silent; she started to smoke again. 'No, of course not. But I've lived with it for a long time, I've come to terms with it.'

That is clearly a lie, thought Claire, but she said only, 'Well, if you change your mind, I'm here.' She looked round. 'I wonder where Jessica and Oliver have got to.'

'Yes.'

They had left them up in the village: at the point where the two roads met, Frances, remembering she was almost out of cigarettes, had asked where the shop was. Claire and Robert hesitated, wanting to get down to the river and leave the shop for later, when it was cool.

'I'll show you,' said Jessica. She stood on the cobbled slope with her hands in the pockets of orange shorts, which suited her deepening tan. Long thick hair beneath her straw hat fell on to her shoulders, bare arms honey-coloured against white top. She's beautiful, Frances realised, watching her smile. 'It's just down there, you follow the road round to the right. I'll take you, if you want.'

'All right, thank you,' said Frances, but Tom, holding an end of the dinghy, said impatiently:

'I want to go to the *river*!'

'I know, Tom, it's all right, we're going. I just need some cigarettes, that's all. Wouldn't you like to come and see the shop?'

'No.'

'Well, he can come with us,' said Claire, but Frances, aware that there had already been enough of this kind of thing, wanting to make a fresh start today, refused.

They all stood for a moment, undecided in the heat, a detectable irritation beginning to rise.

'Oh, I'll go,' said Oliver. 'Come on, Jess, you can show me, all right?'

And they set off down the hill.

'Don't expect Rothmans,' said Robert to Frances, as they made their way down the other street, past staring children. 'Who knows what Portuguese fags are like?'

'They'll do,' said Frances. 'Anything'll do, so long as it's tobacco.'

'Thank God I've given up.'

And now, waiting for Oliver and Jess to reappear, she stubbed out her cigarette in the sand, and said to Claire: 'I'm sure they'll be here soon. Shall we go for a swim?'

They got to their feet and waded out into the water, which despite the morning's heat was still cool, a shock to the skin.

'I think,' said Frances, as they stood together, preparing for the plunge, 'it's time you talked to me about *your* life.'

'There's not much to tell,' said Claire, feeling, indeed, that there wasn't. I have everything I ever wanted, she said to herself, remembering the last time she'd thought that, looking out on the garden in London, waiting for Frances, rediscovered, to ring at the door. She had thought then: is it right for anyone to have so much? Isn't something bound to be taken away?

'I've done it!' Frances, lithe in the water, lay on her back, looking at her. 'It's wonderful – come on.'

Claire took a deep breath and followed, gasping. And striking out, gradually growing accustomed to the chill, she wondered: well, what should I say about my life? Behold, here it is. When I was young – in the days when I knew Frances – I tried to imagine what the future would be, and I tried to shape it: moving to London, teaching, getting about, getting my heart broken. Then I met Robert, and forgot about shaping – everything fell into place, and I was too busy just being alive. And here I am, and here is everything: work, family, friends.

Then why, she asked herself, swimming steadily upriver, should I feel now, when Frances asks me to tell her about myself, as if there is still something missing? Why should I feel as if there is still something waiting to happen, waiting for me?

She was passing the hayfield on the left, bordered by trees: stooks like witches' hats stood drying in the sun. Frances, a stronger swimmer, was far ahead of her now. I suppose, Claire thought, pushing unhurriedly through the cool brown water, that if I did not think that, I might feel that my life was over.

'Actually, there are two shops,' said Jessica, as they came out of the dark interior of the first. She stood at the doorway, a pile of plastic washing-up bowls on one side, soft rush brooms propped up on the other, trying to remember. 'The other one's a post office as well.'

'That's useful,' said Oliver. 'Shall we try and find it? I need to get some stamps anyway.'

'I think it's on the other side of the village . . . on the other road, you know, the one that comes up past the house. But it's not anywhere near the house, it's sort of going the other way . . .'

'I hope you never have to lead an expedition,' he said drily, dropping the cigarettes into his pocket, and Jessica smiled.

'I'm hopeless with directions.'

'Come, come. Well, if it's on the other side of the village, I think we just carry on along here, don't we? This must cut through.' An old man, leaning on a stick, was coming up to the shop, behind Jess; Oliver put out an arm and moved her away from the entrance, so that he could get past. 'Let's have a look,' he said. 'I'm sure we'll find it. Or are you desperate to get in the water?'

'No.'

They walked along the cobbled street, past grubby little girls in polyester frocks, sitting in doorways with broken dolls. Plastic strip curtains hung in the doorways; they could hear women's voices behind them, and a radio coming from somewhere, fuzzily tuned to pop. Further down the street was a gap between two houses, roofed with vines: beneath it, two or three young mothers were washing clothes in a stone sink fed by a single cold tap in the wall. Like Guida, they used a thick yellow bar of soap; the water in the sink was grey and scummy. This was where the radio was playing, propped on a window-sill. Children with unbrushed hair ran sticks idly up and down the wall or sat with their heads bobbing to the beat; grey speckled hens with scarlet combs and luxuriant feather trousers, quite different from the scrawny birds up at the house, picked their way over the cobblestones. As Oliver and Jessica walked deeper into the village they passed more hens, penned behind chicken wire in tiny gardens or in rotting sheds, and hutches of brown rabbits, feeding on limp greens.

'I remember all this now,' said Jessica, as the street divided again, leading steeply ahead of them uphill and branching off to the right to pass a little barnyard. 'It's up there, the post office, up on the main road. And there's a café-bar next door, I think.

Dad and Geoffrey used to go there in the evenings, sometimes.'

'Did they?' The air was scorching; Oliver, though a strong walker, felt sweat drip down the back of his neck as they climbed. 'Tell me about last year,' he said, more to engage Jessica's attention than out of real curiosity. Since they left the shop she had barely spoken, and he wondered if she was bored, if she would have much preferred to join the others at the river straight away. But after last night, he felt the need to explore, the need for distraction and a change of scene, and he wanted, in any case, to set the house in context, to begin to understand the village and the area more fully.

'What were the other family like?'

Jessica shrugged. 'Okay. We've known them for years – Jack and Neil are in the same class.'

'And your parents are good friends of theirs?'

'Linda and Mum are. Well, Mum's got millions of friends.'

'Yes,' said Oliver. 'I can imagine.' A little brown bird in a wooden cage nailed to a wall was chirruping listlessly overhead, as if it, too, were finding the heat exhausting. But it wasn't only the heat which was slowing him down; it was the aftermath of the broken night, a sleepless hour afterwards. That might account for Jessica's silence, too, although at breakfast and ever since she had seemed quite recovered.

'And what about you?' he asked. 'Do you have millions of friends?'

She pondered. 'I think I'm a bit fussy.'

He nodded. 'The chosen few.'

Jessica didn't answer; perhaps she didn't quite understand. Not for the first time, he found himself wondering if Claire's invitation to join the family holiday here had more to do with lack of discrimination than a genuine desire for their company in particular. Of course, their friends had had to cancel, but still. He could imagine neither Frances nor himself making that kind of move towards someone they hadn't seen for so long. If anyone was discriminating, it was Frances.

They were nearing the top of the street, passing small detached houses with shady gardens. The mountain road ahead was, he realised, the road they had taken yesterday out of the village to the market town, and he could hear the steady clip-clop and tinkle of a bullock cart climbing the hill. Hearing that sound recalled their reasons for coming and drove away much of the night's disturbance: here, in a foreign country, the growing silence between them in their ordered life in London might be broken. But he didn't want to think about it now. Far more pleasant, after last night, to push away the sight of her, sitting wanly up against the pillows this morning, and focus on the pleasant company of Jessica, who interested him.

'So what sort of things did you do last year?' he asked her.

'Oh, I don't know. Swam and mucked about, I can't remember. The dinghy was the best, it's really nice.'

'Can your row?'

'Of course.'

'Perhaps you can take me out in it later, then.'

'All right.'

They were out on the road.

She nodded down towards a letter-box in a wall, a metal ice-cream sign on a stand. 'That's it. Do you want to get your stamps?'

'First I want to buy you an ice-cream,' said Oliver. The bullock cart, piled high with timber, swayed towards them, the animals yoked by a leather harness stained with sweat. Their eyes were gentle and dark and enormous; their mouths foamed.

He touched Jessica lightly on the shoulder. 'Lead on.' Inside the little post office, hung about with pots and pans and toys, a doorway on the left led straight into a tiny café-bar: a jukebox, three spindle-legged tables, a dozen cheap chairs and a counter. More chairs and tables stood outside, beneath an awning of vines. Using his phrase book Oliver purchased his stamps from a diminutive woman in a print overall and spectacles. He flicked through the book for ice cream, but Jessica knew it already. '*Gelado*,' she said to the little woman, who smilingly lifted the counter and led them through the doorway to the café. They bought cylinders of strawberry and vanilla wrapped in paper.

'We used to have ices a little like this when I was a child,' he told Jessica as they came out into the sun.

'Was that before the Flood?' she asked innocently, licking round the top of hers.

122

He looked at her, and laughed. 'What a nerve.' A car was coming up the road behind them: he shepherded her on to the verge. 'Now. To the river. Yes?'

'Yes,' she said, peeling away a little of the paper at the edge. The bullock cart was out of sight; they turned down the cobbled street, retracing their steps with less effort, though the sun had risen high.

'Your father was saying it rained quite a bit last year.'

'Yes,' she said again, 'but it was okay. We played lots of games.'

'But not chess.'

'No.' They walked on. 'Actually,' she said, as they came to the fork in the road again, 'this year's better than last.'

'Is it really?' He turned to her, surprised. 'Why's that?'

She looked down at her ice cream.

'I don't know,' she said. 'It just is.'

'Here you are,' said Claire, looking up from her book. 'I was beginning to wonder. God, you look hot.'

'It's *boiling*,' said Jessica. 'Where's the dinghy?'

'Dad's taken the boys out – don't look so cross, I'm sure they'll be back soon. Come and have a drink.' She unscrewed the Thermos. 'Oliver?'

'Please.' He lowered himself on to the sand. 'Where's Frances?'

'Still swimming – she went on past the island. She's good, isn't she?'

He nodded, taking the cup. 'Stronger than I am.' He drank thirstily, brushing an insect off his bare arm. 'That's better. I think I'll have a swim while we're waiting. Jessica has kindly offered to take me out in the dinghy.'

'Have you, Jess?'

'Unless,' he added quickly, 'you and Robert – '

'No, no, you go ahead, there's plenty of time.' But how interesting, she thought, pouring Jess more squash, that she should be the one to get through to Oliver, so formal, so withdrawn. So dangerous, she thought suddenly, recalling his explosion at Tom in the blinding heat of the maize fields, on their first walk down here – and then she dismissed it. Everyone had been a little on edge then, their first full day together, Tom overtired and overwrought, and everyone, after all, shouted at their children sometimes.

'I'll swim, too.' Jess was pulling her shirt off over her head to reveal the shiny green swimsuit. She shook out her hair, in a gesture long habitual, but which was, Claire realised, beginning to look different: she was not just older, but more self-aware.

Beside her, Oliver, too, had peeled off to his swimming trunks; he and Jessica were treading the warm sand down to the water's edge. And here was Frances, returning, swimming across from the hayfield on the far side towards them.

Oliver raised his hand in greeting. 'I've got your cigarettes. And stamps.'

'Well done.' Frances came into the shallows; she stood up, dripping, panting a little from the exertion. 'Are the others still out in the dinghy? They must have gone for miles.'

'So must you,' said Claire.

Frances wiped the water from her face. 'I feel much better.' She came out, smiling at Oliver and Jessica. 'You two look hot. I like that swimsuit.'

'Thanks.' Jessica moved past, wrapping her arms round herself as the chill of the water rose around her knees.

'We saw a kingfisher!' A cry came from the bend downriver, and there was the dinghy, with Robert rowing much more slowly now, and the boys shouting and waving.

'You didn't.'

'We *did* – it was brilliant!'

Claire stood up to greet them, ready to help pull the dinghy ashore, but Oliver and Jess were already plunging in, swimming towards it.

'Our turn!' called Jess. 'Our turn now.'

Robert rested the oars and let the dinghy drift, blue and yellow reflections dancing brokenly at their approach. Claire and Frances stood next to each other, watching.

'I've changed my mind,' Frances said quietly.

Claire turned to look at her. 'What?'

'I mean I want to talk. I think. If you don't mind. I don't mean now, I mean sometime.'

'Of course. Yes, of course. Whenever.' Claire turned back to

124

the river, shading her eyes. Robert was laughing, trying to fend off Jessica, scrambling in, no mean feat from the water. 'You'll have us over!'

'Good,' said Jessica, laughing too.

'Careful!' called Claire. 'Don't be silly, Jess, let them come ashore.'

But the boys were loving it. 'We're being attacked! Pirates – abandon ship!'

Oliver held on to the rocking side. They heard him say, 'Come on, Tom, out you get,' and Frances said suddenly:

'He can't swim that far. It's too deep for him there.'

Claire cupped her hands. 'Robert!' she shouted. 'Robert! Stop mucking about – bring it ashore!'

She was too late. With four people lurching about inside and a big man pulling at it, the dinghy reared up, slow but unstoppable, tipping everyone into the water with a splash that seemed to go on for ever.

For a moment Frances and Claire just stood there, unable to move. Then, as they raced down over the sand, they saw that no one was trapped beneath it, that they all had hold of it, and that everyone was laughing still, Tom clinging on to Robert's shoulders and Jack shrieking with excitement: 'Wicked! Wicked! Do it again!'

By evening the village, after the long hot afternoon, was cool again, coming to life. Carrying the dinghy, carrying bags and baskets, the two families, minus Claire, who had gone on ahead, made their way out of the maize fields. They walked along the soft earth path beneath the vines and up through the cobbled streets again, greeting familiar faces.

'*Bo tar*'.'

'*Bo tar*'.' The women in their flowery overalls, the toothless old men in shirtsleeves, nodded as they passed, leaning on sticks, tearing off bits of bread as they ate out on balconies, amongst the geraniums.

'There's Guida,' said Robert, suddenly recognising, in a group of young people ahead, the girl in jeans and broderie anglaise blouse. She was wearing lipstick, something he didn't remember noticing before, and her hair was tied back in a ponytail.

125

'*Bo tar*', Guida,' they chorused, as they drew near, and Guida nodded, turning from her conversation with a boy with slicked-back hair, flickering a smile at Robert and turning back again, clearly not wishing to prolong the encounter.

'Seems funny, seeing her here,' said Jack.

'Yes.' Robert eased the weight of the paddles on to the other arm and promised himself a long drink out on the terrace when they got home. Claire was up there already, doing something about supper; they had picnicked down by the river today, no one inclined to make the trek up to the house in the heat, everyone in a good mood, relaxing, falling asleep beneath the trees at select points along the river-bank. Even the boys had slept, something he'd thought impossible out of doors. But now, despite the rest, he was tired from too much fresh air, beginning to yawn.

They were approaching the intersection with the threshing barn high on their right, where the children were playing out in the yard, and the street to their left, running downhill again, curving round to the shop. Crisps, Robert thought idly; lunch felt a long time ago, and they'd need something to go with the drink. Crisps, as usual, were disappearing out of the cupboard by the sackful. He stopped, and turned to the others.

'I'm just nipping down to the shop. Anyone want anything?'

'Crisps,' said Jack. He had one end of the dinghy, and Tom the other. They looked sunburned and tousled, as if they'd sleep well tonight.

'Apart from crisps.'

'What else is there?' said Tom. 'Can I come with you?'

'Sure.' He glanced at Oliver and Frances, walking with Jess between them. They looked contained, well-matched, the kind of well-educated family of three you might see walking through an art gallery, at ease, talking companionably. A daughter did suit them, it was true.

'Help Jack with the dinghy then,' he said to Jess. 'Go on, it's only two steps up the hill, it won't kill you. Right, Tom, off we go.'

The evening sunshine mellowed the cobbles; they walked hand in hand down the hill, past dogs waking up, scratching themselves, past toddlers with pushcarts, bumping up and down. There was a sudden, extraordinary noise by their feet.

126

'Hey!' said Tom, laughing. 'What was *that*?'

They stopped, seeing what looked like a stable door set in the wall beneath the house beside them. Grunts and snuffles came from behind it.

'It's a pig!'

'Well, well. I'd forgotten about him.'

They approached the door, seeing, at the base, a gap of some several inches above the step; Tom crouched down, peering. Beside him, Robert saw a moist pink snout, and bristles. The grunting grew louder and more encouraging.

'It's pitch *dark* in there.' Tom pressed his face to the gap.

'Careful.'

'Why?'

'He might bite.' Did pigs bite?

'He's sweet. Can we give him something?'

'Well . . .'

'Just an apple or something.'

'Perhaps. On the way back.'

The shop was quite full, doing a brisk trade in tinned vegetables and washing-powder. As last year, Robert noted that he was the only English person there. They might flock down to the Algarve, but here, praise be, they had not discovered. The shopkeeper made broken pleasantries of recognition; they shook hands. Robert bought enormous red bags of crisps and, for the pig, a bag of wrinkled yellow apples no bigger than eggs. They walked back up the street through lengthening shadows.

'Here we are!' Tom called, as they approached the stable door and the grunting began again. He knelt on the step and pushed through an apple: it disappeared in a flurry of snorts. 'Another one? Here you are.'

'Not too many, he might get tummy-ache.' Robert nodded to one or two passers-by, who smiled indulgently at the English boy, and yawned again.

'Come on, Tom,' he said. 'We'll see him again another day.'

Tom got up reluctantly. 'Do you think he's always lived in there?' he asked, as they climbed the hill.

'Probably. I think he belongs to Guida's uncle. I seem to remember something about pigs from last year.' Ahead, through the fruit trees, Robert could see Oliver and Frances out on the terrace; he could hear the clink of bottle and glass. Thank God. They reached the big gates and walked past the car just inside, through the garden.

'Hello.' Frances, changed into a summery green skirt, her hair freshly washed, was leaning over the parapet, cool and relaxed.

'Mum! Frances! There's a pig! We found a pig!' Tom broke away from Robert and dashed across to the steps, racing up towards her, completely happy.

Dusk fell; the children were sent to bed. Frances, after supper, sat in the library corner of the sitting-room, deep in an armchair, deep in a book. So much swimming had left her susceptible to the sudden chill of the evening. The others were still out on the terrace, where they had lit a candle, but she, coming indoors for a sweater, had felt cold even with it on, and stopped to browse along the shelves.

Letters and journals and biographies: for old times' sake, she pulled out Quentin Bell on Virginia Woolf, dipping here and there into a prose as clear, direct and intimate as if he were addressing her alone, as if he had known her for years. Well, she and Virginia had known each other quite well in Bristol, they'd spent hours together in the library. She turned the pages, she sat down. She came upon a relationship she hadn't known about at all then, concentrating as she had – as you were supposed to in those days – upon the works. Frances began to read these particular pages, their speculations on the nature of a particular friendship.

Virginia was fond of Vita. She enjoyed her interest and admiration, she found what she could to admire in Vita's own writing, though 'In brain and insight she is not as highly organised as I am.' The prospect of her coming to lunch was 'a great amusement and pleasure'. But more?

'Her being "in love" (it must be comma'd thus) with me, excites and flatters and interests . . .' That was all? So it seemed, close as the two women became. 'What is this "love"?' Virginia had demanded of her journal, marbled pen in febrile fingers racing across the page.

From up on the hillside came the chime of the church clock, five

128

wavering strokes. Frances stopped reading and looked at her watch: it was just after ten. She sat with her hand on the open pages, listening to the crickets whirr and the low voices of the others outside, engaged in conversation: they sounded at ease, interested in one another, recovered from the effects of the night before. Perhaps the very events of the night before had helped to break the ice. They were beginning to settle – into the place and each other – and England was beginning to feel an immeasurably long way away, as if their lives there were no longer of any importance, no longer, even, quite real.

Dora, wrote Frances, uneasy with this feeling, *I think of you, and wonder what you are doing now* . . .

There were times when the letter, the long internal conversation, brought Dora so close that Frances could spend whole hours engaged in it – making the journey home from work, collecting Tom from the child-minder, walking back with him to the house and preparing supper all in a daze. Now, she could neither continue writing nor summon Dora's calming presence to her side. Virginia had loved Vita – had been, it seemed, in some ways devoted to her – but not as Vita loved her. Not in that way.

Dora, wrote Frances, *I am losing you, come back, come back –*

It was no use. Dora, an unwilling spirit in a seance, would not, tonight, be summoned. Frances slowly closed the book and got up to replace it on the shelves, feeling flat and bereft.

She walked back towards the doors to the terrace; she heard the rustle of other pages, and she turned to see Jessica, falling asleep, propped up in bed with her Walkman on, her book sliding down to the floor. What was she reading? What had Frances been reading at twelve, going on thirteen? Long empty summer evenings came back to her as she crossed the wooden floor to Jessica's doorway. She saw herself, up in her bedroom, hearing lawnmowers pushed up and down suburban gardens by men in shirtsleeves, hearing birds call, beginning to settle, and the bus on the main road changing gear, driving off and away. Tomorrow's school uniform lay on the chair at her desk by the window; in her pyjamas, Frances sat propped up against the pillows, lost in *Anne of Green Gables*, *Anne of Avonlea*, *Anne of the Island* . . .

Did I know then? she asked herself, entering Jessica's room.

No. Anne of Green Gables fell in love with Gilbert, in her class at school, who grew up to become a fine doctor, and marry her, and I fell in love with him, too. It was later, when Rowan came to live near us and came to the grammar school late: that's when I knew. That's when I tried not to know. I used to comfort myself: when you grow up, all this will be behind you, you'll grow out of it, fall in love and get married – like Anne of Green Gables, like everyone else. And I did. And then I met Dora.

She bent down to retrieve Jessica's fallen paperback. Judy Blume: *Are you there, God? It's me, Margaret*. She smiled, and closed it, and put it on the chest of drawers by the bed.

Music came faintly from the Walkman, slipping down. *So we gotta say goodbye for the summer . . . I'll send you all my love, every day in a letter . . .* Jess wasn't listening now, she was fast asleep, head lolling, skin flushed from the sun. Frances leaned forward and carefully slipped off the headphones: drifts of thick soft hair clung to the little foam pads. She lifted the cassette player and wires away from the sheets, and put it all down by the books on the chest of drawers, and then she leaned forward and kissed her, as she might have kissed her own daughter, surprising herself, because until now she had not really taken Jessica in at all.

Goodnight, she said silently. Jessica did not stir, and Frances switched off the light by the bed and went out, thinking, as she walked towards the terrace doors, of Dora's daughter, Sophie, coming into the kitchen one evening as she and Dora sat talking over their coffee. Adrian had gone to Milton Keynes for a couple of nights.

Sophie, smiling distantly at Frances, and ignoring her mother, was looking for something in one of the cupboards, swishing back long glossy hair, different from Jessica's mane, but in a gesture not dissimilar.

'Can I help?' asked Dora.

'No, thanks, it's all right.' Sophie went on searching, opening each door in turn, and at last went out again – whatever could she have been looking for? – and up to her room with her silent boyfriend.

'I must go,' said Frances, wondering about Sophie and her search through the cupboards as she and her mother sat together.

She spooned up crystals of brown sugar in the bowl on the table between them, watching them fall. A concert came to its end on the radio – the radio was always on in Dora's kitchen – and the applause began, fading as the announcer returned his listeners to the studio. Getting late. Time for Frances to return to her family.

'One more coffee,' said Dora, getting up to put the kettle on. 'Stay a bit longer, it's so nice having you here.'

And Frances smiled, lighting a last cigarette, watching the crystals tumble slowly down the sides of the sugar bowl, and settle there.

She stepped out on to the terrace.

'Hello.' Claire, from the swing-seat, stretched out a hand. 'We were wondering where you had got to.'

'I switched off Jessica's light,' said Frances obliquely, picking up her cigarettes from the table. 'She's fast asleep.' She crossed to the chair next to Oliver, and lit a cigarette. 'So,' she said, wanting to show an interest, to make up for so clearly having chosen solitude. 'What have you all been talking about?'

Robert reached for the wine jug. 'Your husband has been trying to raise the tone.'

'Not at all,' said Oliver. 'It had no need of raising, and I should hardly count myself qualified to do so in any case.'

It was the kind of overcourteous, verging on the pompous, disclaiming and meaningless remark of which Oliver was master, distancing himself from any real engagement, and Frances, who had heard it too many times over too many dinner tables, said, more sharply than she intended: 'Well, what heights did you reach, anyway?' and felt at once his rise of irritation at her tone. She blew out smoke. 'Sorry. I've interrupted everything.'

Robert was refilling glasses. 'We were talking,' he said, 'prompted by the ring of church bells, about religion.' He sat down again, rather heavily. 'So there.'

'Were you, now?' Frances could not think that either he or Claire had introduced this one: she looked at Oliver enquiringly. 'Has this been particularly exercising you recently, for some reason?'

He shrugged, still irritated. 'It interests me as a general question, as you know.'

'As far as I'm concerned,' said Robert, who seemed to have drunk rather more than usual, 'there are only two questions when it comes down to it. Do you love me? Is there a God? What else is important, after all?'

Frances regarded him with a hitherto unquickened curiosity. 'That's a rather interesting remark.'

'Isn't it?' said Oliver. 'But I think there are other questions.'

'Do you?' she asked him. 'Can't things be simple for once?'

He looked at her. 'You are not simple, Frances.'

'Nor are you. All the more reason to crave simplicity.'

There was a silence, an exclusion of others that was impolite. It was broken by the fierce whine of a motor bike, racing up the hillside towards them. When it had passed, Claire said: 'At least three questions, surely. Do I love you? That's just as important.'

'Well,' Oliver said drily to Robert, 'I should not presume to ask you about affairs of the heart, but I should like to know about God. Is there one? Jessica gave me to understand that you were a family of atheists.'

'Jessica?' Robert looked at him in astonishment. 'Since when has Jessica gone in for discussion? About anything.'

'As I recall, it was more in the nature of a passing remark. Anyway,' he waved cigarette smoke away, 'was she right?'

'I suppose so. About me, anyway,' said Robert. 'I believed when I was little – '

'When you're little you'll believe anything,' said Claire.

'Quite. Adolescence put paid to all that, as it usually does – well, either that or you go overboard about religion, don't you? I gave it all up with a sigh of relief, as far as I can remember. More than that – there were things about it I deeply disliked.' He stopped and drank. 'And yet – '

'There's usually an "And yet",' said Frances. 'About most things.'

'Mmm. And yet: I suppose I still try to behave as if I believe.'

'And what does that mean?' She tapped ash into the saucer. 'As if you are to be judged?'

He thought about it. 'Not judged, exactly. But as if there were some kinds of absolutes.' He finished his glass and poured another. 'It's easier to talk about absolutes than specifics, isn't it –

132

you can get carried away with the sound of your own voice, if you're not careful. I can, anyway. When it comes down to it, living by absolutes can mean being kind, that's all. What more do you want?' He picked up the wine jug and waved it. 'Who wants more out of this?'

'I'm surprised there's any left,' said Claire, rocking.

He looked. 'There isn't much. Oliver? Want to finish it? Want to tell us what you believe in? Are you a fucked-up Catholic?'

'Robert . . .' Claire stopped rocking.

But Oliver was smiling, pouring the last of the wine. 'I don't know. Possibly. I don't know if I believe any more. But I do believe in the search, I think. That does seem important, still.'

'The search for – '

'Meaning. For salvation, too, I think.' He was tapping on the table, concentrating. 'Anachronistic though it may sound.'

'And strangely enough,' said Robert, 'anachronistic though it may sound, I think one of the things I believe in is sin.'

'Mighty and magnificent words.' Frances drew on her cigarette. 'Milton words. The Fall. Salvation. Sin. Do they still mean anything?'

'Well?' said Robert. 'Do they? What do you believe in, Frances?'

'I used to believe that work was my salvation.' She gave Claire a smile. 'Remember?'

'Yes,' said Claire, looking away. 'I do.'

'You two must have a lot to catch up on,' said Robert.

'This and that.'

There was no elaboration.

'Go on,' he said to Frances. 'Be serious. Just for fun.'

She put out her cigarette. 'Like the man said: I don't know what I believe in, but I know what I want.'

'And what is that?'

'The moon,' she said, and fell silent, sensing Oliver's eyes upon her.

There was a pause.

'Well,' said Claire helpfully, rocking again, 'if anyone wants to know what I think, I find it irritating that people should feel you have to have religion in order to have a moral code. It requires

133

much more of people to go through the world without the prop of faith.'

'Exactly,' said Robert. 'We are as one.'

'Shut up.'

'But we are. On this, anyway.' There was a brown dish of fruit on the table, mostly finished by the children, one or two soft pears left and a lot of pips and grape stalks. He picked at the few remaining grapes. 'Anyway, doubt is surely far more interesting than faith. As you said, Oliver, it's the search that counts.'

'But meanwhile one has to live,' said Claire. 'And you don't keep the show on the road with quests and questions, not as far as I'm concerned. Life is sustained by the ordinary, the everyday.'

'Oh, no,' said Frances. 'Life is sustained by dreams.' Robert looked at her. She picked up her packet of cigarettes, tapped out another one, and lit it.

Oliver apparently ignored this. 'I still think there are quite a few questions left. I still think humanism has its shortcomings. Enduring pain, for instance. Christianity has all sorts of explanations for suffering – '

'Far too many,' said Robert.

'I don't know. How you cope with illness? With death? In moments of crisis everyone prays.'

'Do you?' Claire asked him.

'I used to.'

Robert flicked grape pips over the parapet. 'Well, I neither pray nor expect to look for something outside myself when something dreadful happens. But then, so far, nothing dreadful has. Perhaps, if it does, I shall change.' He drained his glass, and stretched, yawning.

Oliver waved more smoke away. 'You said you believed in sin – what, in the last gasp of the century, might constitute sin, do you suppose?'

Robert tugged off the last grape and swallowed it. 'As the man said, I think I might know if I saw it. Betrayal? Screwing up people's lives? That gives quite a bit of scope, wouldn't you say?' He got up, the iron chair scraping on the tiles. 'On which note, I think I might hit the hay.' He looked across at Frances, still smoking. 'You've gone rather quiet.'

134

She gave her little laugh. 'Am I usually rowdy?'

'Not exactly. Are you all right?'

Her eyes met his, wary, surprised. 'Of course. Why?'

'Just wondering.'

'Don't quiz her,' said Claire, and swung her legs off the swing-seat. 'She's tired, and so am I. I think I'll join you.' She held out her hand towards Robert. 'Help me off here, I can't move.'

He pulled her to her feet and they stood holding hands, saying goodnight to the others.

'Sleep well.'

'Thank you. You too.'

'And I hope Tom sleeps well,' said Claire, as they went towards the doors.

'I'm sure he will,' said Frances. 'Please don't worry. He's had a lovely day, thanks to you both.'

'Well, we've enjoyed it as well. Goodnight.'

Frances watched them cross to Jessica's room and check her for the night. She heard them walk along the wooden corridor, and Robert go into the bathroom and Claire, yawning, climb the stairs. 'Shan't be long,' said Robert, closing the bathroom door.

Beside her, Oliver had picked up her cigarettes and was turning the packet over and over, tapping it on the table, where the candle had almost burned down. Above her, the moon and the stars were brighter than she had ever seen anywhere.

'Tom will be all right, won't he?' she asked.

Oliver went on turning the packet of cigarettes, over and over, between long, beautiful fingers. 'I expect so.' There was a pause. 'What about us? Are we going to be all right?'

She did not know how to answer.

'Frances?'

There came, with that enquiry, the memory of endless evenings in London, supper over, Tom long since in bed, the television news switched on.

'I must do some work,' said Frances, when it had finished.

'Yes,' said Oliver, getting up, turning off famine and war and desolation. 'I've got quite a bit, too.' He moved towards his desk in the corner, piled high, like hers, with other people's writing. He

135

put on the lamp she had bought for him one Christmas, thought for a moment, turned.

'Frances?'

'Yes?'

'You seem a bit – is everything all right? I mean, at the office?'

'It's fine,' said Frances. 'Busy, that's all. What about you?'

He shrugged. 'I've been in meetings all day, I told you. I just get the feeling – never mind.'

He pulled out his chair and sat down. Frances went to her own desk. Pages were turned.

'Frances?' he said again now.

'Yes?'

'The thing about going on holiday . . .' He put down the cigarettes. 'The thing about going on holiday is that people have to talk to each other.'

'Oliver . . .'

'Is that what you were trying to avoid, staying in the house this evening?'

'No, not directly.'

'Were you thinking about all this? About us?'

She thought: I could get up now and put my arms round him and say to him, Oliver, I am torn in pieces, help me, help me, forgive me –

She said, 'No, not exactly.'

'No,' he said. 'No, I didn't suppose you were.'

He got up and went into the house.

Frances lit a cigarette. Dora came out and sat beside her. She had her own views on God, as on most things.

6

Days passed, each hotter than the last. They fell into a pattern of activities: swimming, boating and walking when it was cool enough, reading and resting in the heat. Oliver, who often woke early, as he did at home, took a map and walked through the village before it was fully awake, making preliminary excursions into the mountains, returning as the others were just getting up or having breakfast. He and Jessica took to playing chess at odd moments in the day: after lunch; after tea; in the library corner of the sitting-room, or on the upper path when the boys were in the pool. She was getting rather good. The families made plans to visit the cathedral town, and posters appeared on the telegraph poles along the mountain road announcing a fiesta in a neighbouring village. For the moment they stayed local, exploring all along the river, Robert and Claire rediscovering and describing to the others a particularly pleasant stretch about half a mile east of the village.

Its banks there were broad and marshy, the way to it a long shady path below the village, bordered on the right by the gates and gardens of houses at the bottom of the sloping streets, and on the left by a cool damp ditch and little fields, where unyoked oxen wandered in the evenings, grazing, sounding bells.

In Indian file, one morning after breakfast – and after a detour to see Tom's pig – the two families made their way along this path, wearing sunhats, carrying fishing nets, swimming things, a picnic. Robert and Claire were up in front, followed by Tom and Jack, Jessica and Oliver; Frances brought up the rear, walking slowly.

The foliage brimming over the garden walls was lush. Down here, the shimmering dry heat of the mountains and the pines, even of their own house, set high above the valley, felt distant as another country: this was a place where the climate became manageable, where it was possible to imagine working for much of the day. They had reached the path by cutting through a gap between two houses up in the village, discovering a winding, surprising descent of steps, flanked by stone walls, generously shaded by trees. At the bottom, a wicket garden gate was set in the curve of the wall, and beside it a ceramic plate, stencilled with the number four.

The others went on ahead, the children excited by the secret feeling of the steps, the anticipation of a new, or partly forgotten place to spend the day. Frances, seeing the wicket gate, lingered, and looked over the mossy wall, feeling like an intruder.

But there was, it seemed, no one to intrude upon. Within the small, stone-flagged garden, a low house with tiled roof and dark green paintwork was shut up and silent, as if long unvisited. It did not, however, look neglected: the closed shutters and unarguably bolted door were in good condition, and the geraniums which stood in tubs beneath the windows were fresh, as if someone came in from time to time and watered them.

So. A house for a summer let which had not been let, a house well cared for, awaiting occupation. Frances saw a table, like the table in the garden of the house she had dreamed of: weather-beaten, warped, but still solid. It needed a couple of chairs with old, sun-warmed cushions, a pile of books, plates put out for lunch. It needed Dora to come with her calm grave air from the house and arrange these things, or it needed Frances to arrange them for her, to sit half asleep at the table with her head on her arms in the still and unbroken warmth of the afternoon, and wait for Dora to join her.

Who lived here? Who might be approached and enquiries made of, for a long summer let in some timeless future where such things might be possible?

'Frances!' The others were calling her. 'Where has she got to?'

'Coming!'

She moved away from the gate and waved, calling, going slowly along the path to catch them up.

And now, the last in the procession, she walked alongside Dora, who had returned. *Last night*, said Frances, *I dreamed I came upon you sitting in a square in a foreign city. It was the afternoon, and I was walking down a cobbled street – I suppose that must come from the streets in the village here, but it wasn't here – and I saw you,*

sitting on a low wall with your back to me. You were wearing a
white shirt and a dark soft skirt, and you were writing, working.
And as I approached you, you turned round, and took off your
glasses, and smiled as if you had been waiting for me . . .

They had reached a point in the path where it was joined on the
left by another; broader, more open and very sunny, scattered
with drifts of straw.

'This way,' said Robert, up at the front.

Within a hundred yards or so they had come to two buildings.
On their left was the ruin of a house that had once been grand, at
least by the standards of the village: substantial, with mellow brick
and large double doors still remaining beneath the ornate façade
of an upper storey whose lines at once struck Frances as familiar
from her dream, so that, not for the first time, she felt as though
she were living on a blurred line between dream and reality, where
one might at any time spill into and re-create the other. Opposite
this house, on the other side of the path, stood the ruins of a small
barn, or outbuilding, where vines had been strung across the
gaping roof. This was where the straw was coming from: bales of it
were piled up in the sun and a brown-painted handcart stood
nearby.

'It smells like a farm,' said Tom, wandering over, and he began
to climb up on the bales, which were loosely made, tearing out
handfuls to get himself a grip. 'It's very scratchy.' Straw and chaff
floated out into the air, the upper bales began to shift a little.

'Steady,' said Robert.

'Get down,' said Oliver.

'I'm coming up too,' said Jack.

'I shouldn't,' said Claire.

'Why? Why not? Tom's up there.'

'No, he's not.' Robert reached out an arm and scooped Tom off
the tottering pile. 'Come on, Worzel.' Tom giggled, bits of straw
clinging to his shirt, and put his arm round Robert's neck. 'Crikey,
you weigh a ton.'

'No, I don't. Gee up.' His legs were wrapped round Robert's
waist, he felt down his shirt front for straying straw. 'It's all itchy.'

'*I* want a ride,' said Jack.

'Can't have both of you,' said Robert, beginning to sweat. 'Go on, Tom, down you get, we're almost there.' He prised away large hot hands and clinging feet in sandals.

'My turn,' said Jack, as Tom dropped to the ground.

'Give me a break,' said Robert.

Jack scowled; Claire took his hand. 'Do you remember any of this?'

'A bit,' he said, crossly.

The path widened again, was bordered by dense bushes, and they had come to the edge of a meadow. Bees and butterflies buzzed and fluttered through tall grass and wild flowers, peat-brown patches of water shone, the air was full of the sound of crickets. Beyond was the slow calm river, much broader here than on the stretch they had grown used to. And –

'Frogs!' said Jack and Tom together.

The grass was alive with them: thumb-sized, mossy-green and speckled yellow, leaping at approaching footsteps, disappearing, reappearing, visible, invisible, everywhere.

'Got one!' said Tom, leaping forward with his net. But when he lifted it, peering beneath, there was only flattened grass. 'Where did it go?'

'I've got one!' said Jack.

'Where? Let me see.'

The grown-ups and Jessica left them to it after a while, walking on towards a clump of trees some distance from the water's edge, finding a good place to settle. It felt refreshingly different to spread out their towels on grass instead of grey sand.

'Who's for a swim?' asked Oliver.

'Me,' said Jessica.

'And me,' said Robert, wiping his forehead. 'Claire?'

'In a bit.' She had parked the picnic bag in the coolest and shadiest patch and was leaning up against a tree trunk, opening the flask. 'I'll keep an eye on the boys,' she said, getting comfortable. 'I'm not feeling energetic enough yet.'

'Nor me,' said Frances, sitting down beside her.

'Coffee?'

'Why not?'

'Look at them,' said Robert, pulling off his shirt as they drank. 'Dear things.'

'Buzz off,' said Claire.

When they had gone, Oliver and Jessica holding hands in a sudden dash into the water, Robert following more slowly, splashing himself before he took the plunge, Claire said firmly: 'Okay. Now talk.'

Frances pulled out her cigarettes, looking round for the boys.

'The boys are perfectly all right,' said Claire. 'They're enjoying themselves. Talk to me.' She put a hand on Frances's hand. 'Please,' she said. 'I think you should, don't you?'

A packet was turned over, a lighter fiddled with. 'I don't know where to start.'

'There is this person,' said Claire gently. 'Do you want to tell me her name?'

Frances was silent. 'Dora,' she said at last.

'This Dora, who you care so much for. Yes? Or is she fading a little, while you're here?'

Frances looked up. Iridescent dragonflies darted above the reeds along the river; beyond them, Robert, Oliver and Jessica were swimming away. 'Oh, no,' she said. 'She isn't fading.'

'Well. Tell me about her. Why is she so special?'

And why was I? Claire found herself wondering, as she waited for an answer, recalling jumpy encounters in distant Bristol days. I wasn't, I was just me.

Frances was smoking. Frances was always smoking. 'Who knows?' she said at last. 'Do you know why you fell for Robert?'

Claire thought about it, trying to remember. 'I'm not sure if "fell for" is quite the term I'd use,' she said. 'We felt right. We fitted.'

'And you still do?'

'Yes. Yes, on the whole.'

'Then you're very lucky.'

'Yes,' Claire said again. 'I know. I think,' she added, 'that perhaps what you're going through is more like what I went through with someone before Robert.'

'Marcus?'

'Who? No, no, not Marcus. Oh, I wonder what happened to Marcus? No, not him. A man in London, whom I was mad about and who made me unhappy.'

141

'Dora doesn't make me unhappy,' said Frances. 'She makes me complete.'

This time Claire was silent. 'How?' she said, after a while. 'How, if you will forgive me asking this in the 1990s, can another woman possibly do that?'

Frances blew out smoke and looked at her. 'Shall I tell you something? You may not believe this, but it is quite irrelevant to me that Dora is a woman. It might matter to other people, and it might matter to her, but it doesn't matter to me one iota. It isn't the point.'

'What is the point?'

'Who she is. I care for her because of who she is, the kind of person she is. I don't feel like this *because* she's a woman – it isn't even that I prefer women. It might be much easier if that were the case, don't you think?'

'I don't know. Possibly.' Claire waited. 'Go on. Do you want to? The kind of person she is – what kind of person is she?'

Frances had her arms round her knees; she was looking out over the meadow, to the reeds at the edge of the river. 'She's my type,' she said at last. 'It sounds so simple, and it goes so deep. I said she made me complete – perhaps it's more to do with my feeling that she is complete. She has a quality, she has an air: she's beautiful, but it's more than that. She seems sufficient unto herself. If you saw her out walking alone you would never think she wanted company: it would be clear that her own thoughts are quite enough, that she is walking alone because she chooses to. I suppose that sounds like such a small thing, but it seems to say everything, somehow.'

'But that's always how I thought of you,' said Claire. 'You always had an air of distance and preoccupation – '

'But Dora's different. With me it was retreat, and defence and protection. It still is. With her it's simply because she's engaged in her thoughts – but she's also engaged with people. When she's with you she gives you everything.'

'Does she?' Claire wondered. 'Does she really?'

Frances flicked ash on the grass. 'She seems to,' she conceded. 'Actually, I think she does. And I feel when I'm with her as if I'm in the right place, at the right time, with the right person, it's as simple as that. I don't feel churned up in the way I'm sure you think I do. I feel at peace.' She buried her face in her hands. 'It's when I'm not with her that's the problem.'

Claire put down her empty coffee cup and sat thinking. Far along the river Oliver and Jessica were laughing, swimming well. For a moment or two she couldn't see Robert, but then he appeared from beyond the reeds, panting a little as he came out, waving. She made a gesture – not now, leave us alone – and he nodded, and began to investigate the shining pools of water in the grass, looking for frogs.

'And you've never told her any of this,' she said to Frances.

'No.' She raised her head, and ground the cigarette out in the grass beside her.

'Because you don't want to drive her away . . .'

'Obviously.'

'Are you sure it would? You don't . . .' Claire hesitated. 'You don't think she might feel the same.'

Frances looked at her with affection. 'Did you?'

'No, but . . .'

'There aren't any buts.'

'How can you know?'

'I just do know. I just do.'

'And what about Oliver?' said Claire, seeing him and Jessica begin to swim towards the bank, ready to come out. With any luck Robert would interest them in frog-spotting. The boys, she could see, had abandoned each other, but each was still intent on his own pursuit.

'I love him, too,' said Frances sadly. 'When I met him, I thought he was God.'

Claire looked at her. 'You met at work, didn't you? I remember when we came to dinner – he described you slicing through manuscripts.'

Frances smiled. 'I didn't slice, I was terrified, I just didn't dare show it. Especially not to Oliver – everyone there was in awe of him, they still are, I think. He seemed to know everyone, to have read everything. I couldn't believe it when he – ' She drew a long breath. 'I couldn't imagine ever wanting anyone else.'

'But – '

143

'But things change. Babies are born, and everything changes. Oliver retreated, I was hurt, then I changed jobs, and then – then I met Dora. And discovered that some things don't change. You think you have put things behind you, and then you find – ' She tugged at a wild flower, picking the petals off, one by one.

'And now? You and Oliver now?'

'He is on one side of the river, and I on the other.' Frances threw the petals away. 'As it were. Neither of us knows how to get across.'

'But you still want him.'

'I still want him. I want him, I want Dora – I told you: I want the moon.'

Claire shook her head.

'How can you bear to live with all this?'

Frances went quiet again, watching Oliver and Jessica wading out towards them through the shallows. 'Let me tell you something.' She turned to her. 'It was you, for a while. Dear Claire. It was Rowan at school, for a while. It's been Dora for years and years. No one else. I can't imagine anyone else now. And I don't know how else to live. I simply don't know how to, not after all this time.'

'You don't think perhaps you should have some kind of therapy . . .' Claire said tentatively.

And Frances was suddenly sharp, as only Frances could be, in quite that way. 'Will you tell me,' she said coldly, 'why I should have to have "therapy" for something which thousands of enlightened women up and down the bloody country are not only enjoying but declaring to be a political act? Will you tell me that?'

'Because,' said Claire, stung into sharpness herself, 'you are not making that declaration, are you? You're living a secret life, you're living a lie, and I can't believe it isn't tearing you apart. And anyway – '

Frances got to her feet. 'I knew I shouldn't have told you, I knew.' Her voice was shaking. 'I don't want to say another word about it, and please, whatever you do, don't tell Robert. Please. I can't bear the thought of you both discussing me.'

'I – ' Claire found that she was shaking, too. 'Listen – '

'Frances! Mum! I've got one!'

144

Tom was stumbling through the tall grass towards them, his hands cupped. Frances stepped out of the shade.

'Have you?' she said, her voice quite without emotion. 'Let's have a look.'

He came up to her, red in the face, very hot, and carefully opened his hands, just a crack. She bent down and saw within them the little frog, emerald bright, absolutely still, save for the small frantic throb of a pulse in its throat.

'Poor thing,' she said quietly. 'Poor little thing. Let him go, Tom.'

'No. I want to show Robert and everyone.' And he moved away from her, closing his hands again, calling out. Frances stood watching him, her hands in the pockets of her shorts, and then she went down to the river, speaking to no one.

'That was my frog,' said Jack.

'No, it wasn't.'

'It was, actually. I saw it first.'

'Yes, but I caught it.'

'I was just *going* to catch it, wasn't I? I was just *going* to. And you pushed.'

'No, I didn't.'

'Yes, you did.'

Their feet squelched over the marshy ground; soft mud oozed through their sandals as they walked side by side with their fishing nets. The sun was climbing higher. It beat upon their hats, and their rising voices were carried on the air to where Robert, beneath the trees, was dozing after his swim.

'Do put a sock in it,' he said, as they drew near.

'It was my frog,' said Jack, stepping into the shade, and he dropped down on his knees beside his father, letting his fishing net fall. 'What shall we do now?'

Robert groaned. 'I was just dropping off.' His head was resting on the empty nylon swimming bag, folded over; he opened a reluctant eye, seeing Tom standing on the edge of the shade, his square shape dark against the brightness of the sun. 'Mum still swimming?' he asked Jack.

'Yes.' Jack tugged at blades of grass. 'Why didn't you bring the dinghy?'

'Too far,' said Robert, closing his eyes again. 'Too hot.'

Jack found a long and succulent stem and broke it. He leaned forward and carefully inserted a wavering tip into Robert's right nostril, amongst the hairs.

'Stop it!' Robert pushed his hand away and gave a violent sneeze. Jack burst into giggles. 'You sneeze like a *whale!*' He clambered on to Robert's chest, sitting astride him, patting his face. 'Wake up, whale.'

'I'm going to do something to you in a minute.'

'What? What are you going to do?'

Robert sneezed again; Jack shrieked. 'Whoosh!'

Robert sat up and felt in the pocket of his shorts for a handkerchief. He blew his nose and wiped his streaming eyes with Jack still on his lap, and then looked at him crossly, stuffing the handkerchief back in his pocket.

'Was that kind?'

'Sorry, Dad.' Jack put his arms round his neck, and Robert gave a sigh.

'Can't a chap ever have forty winks in peace?'

'Sorry,' said Jack again, and kissed him.

Over his shoulder, Robert saw Tom, watching them.

'What did you do with the frog, anyway, Tom? I thought he was rather nice.'

'I let him go,' said Tom. 'Frances wanted me to.'

'Well, perhaps that was kindest.' Jack's head was buried in his neck, his sunhat fallen to the grass, his dark hair sleek and warm. 'Where is Frances, anyway?'

Tom shrugged. 'Dunno.'

Robert held out an arm. 'Come here.'

Tom came, dropping his fishing net.

'Want a drink?'

He nodded.

'Get off, then,' Robert told Jack.

'No.'

'Yes. Come on, that's enough now. Let me get at the drinks.'

Jack rolled off, on to the other side; Robert, reaching for the

146

picnic bag, saw beyond the trees Oliver and Jessica, still down by the shallows, where dragonflies darted and the water sparkled. They were exploring the pools, Jessica in her floppy straw hat, shorts pulled on over the green swimsuit, Oliver with binoculars slung round his neck against his faded T-shirt. They moved at some distance from each other, but looked companionable and relaxed, pointing things out like a couple of naturalists on holiday. Like the perfect father and daughter. I don't know, thought Robert, pouring out squash from the larger flask, trying not to feel hurt. It seemed light years since he and Jessica had spent time together in quite that way, happy and unquestioning. Still, here was Jack. And here was Tom, hot and thirsty, making noises at the back of his throat, flexing his jaw.

'There you go, then,' he said, passing them both their drinks. Ice clinked in the flask; he poured himself a cup, making a mental note to replenish the beer next time they went to the market town. 'If you two want a swim, I should have it soon, don't you think? Before lunch. You both look as if you could do with it.'

'Will you come in with us?' asked Tom.

'No, I've just had mine, but I'll watch.' He scanned the water, looking for Frances and Claire, who had both gone off without a word, separately and, it seemed, rather abruptly. I don't know, he thought again, and gave up on that one, seeing, beside him, Tom's hand straying absently down his shorts. Probably not a good idea, with Jack here.

'Not now,' he said quietly, and gave Tom a wink, man to man.

Tom flushed, pulling his hand out.

'Not what?' said Jack on the other side. 'What's he doing?'

'Nothing,' said Robert, getting up. 'Right, who's for a dip? Have you got your trunks on?' He held his arm out high before him, trumpeting. 'All young elephants at the ready – quick, march!'

They fell in behind him, laughing, moving in procession out of the shade and down to the river, where Claire was just coming out, waving.

'You lot look happy,' she said, as they drew near.

'Just off for a mud bath,' said Robert, and then, as the boys stripped off, dropping their clothes on the grassy bank, 'Everything okay? Where's Frances?'

147

'I've no idea.' She shaded her eyes, looking towards Oliver and Jessica, wading through pools of water, blue as the sky. 'Those two look happy as well,' she said.

'Yes,' said Robert, still thinking about Frances. 'What did you two talk about?'

'What? Oh – ' Claire made a gesture of dismissal. 'Nothing much. I'm going to dry off, and then I'll put lunch out, shall I? Don't let the boys stay in too long, it's after midday.'

And she was gone, walking away as if she had nothing more to say to him, though he somehow felt sure that wasn't true.

Jessica, after lunch, prevailed upon her father to walk all the way back to the house for the dinghy.

'Please,' she said. 'Please. It's so beautiful here, it seems such a waste . . .'

'I can go,' said Oliver, finishing a fig.

'All right, and I'll come with you.' Her head bare, Jessica sat with her arms round drawn-up knees on the edge of a towel, shoulders patched by the sunlight through the leaves.

'Why don't you come with me?' said Robert, casually. 'How about that for a change?'

She shook her head. 'I can see you any old time.'

'You're not very kind to Dad these days,' said Claire mildly, leaning, at her son's request, back to back against his knobbly spine.

'Oh . . .' Jessica frowned, beginning to look uncomfortable and cross. 'I just want the dinghy, that's all.'

'Okay, okay.' The last thing Robert wanted was to make a big deal out of her withdrawal, it could only make things worse. These thing happened; they passed, surely. He got to his feet, throwing an apple core into the grass. 'Anyone want anything else while I'm there?'

'Will you see Frances?' asked Tom.

'I might.' Robert looked down at him, sitting between Oliver and Jessica. 'Is that where you think she might be?'

Tom shrugged. 'Dunno.'

'Well even if she isn't, I'm sure she'll be back soon.'

'She's been gone for *ages*,' said Jack.

'Sometimes people like to be by themselves for a bit,' said Claire.

'I don't.'

'I know you don't. You just want love and cuddles all day, you're just a soppy old puss cat.' She shifted against the knobbly spine as he giggled. 'Do we *have* to sit like this?'

'God, you two,' said Jessica. She looked over to Oliver, raising her eyes to the heavens, and he laughed.

'Right, then,' said Robert. 'I'll see you all in a bit.' And he bent to pick up his sunglasses and walked off, cutting a path through the tall grass and meadow flowers, dry and still in the heat.

'And when you come back you must have a rest,' Claire called, watching him flick at butterflies with his hat.

'A nice thought,' he called over his shoulder. 'See you.'

When he had gone a silence fell on the group, which was perhaps accounted for by full stomachs and sleepiness and sun, but not, thought Claire, completely. Had she and Oliver been left alone with the children before? She didn't think so. What could they talk about? And where had Frances got to?

'Move up,' she said to Jack, and then: 'Actually, Jack, I've had enough of this, it's too hot. Go on, let me lie down for a bit.'

He moved, unprotesting, his own back damp with sweat, and she put her head on a rolled-up towel and he put his head on her stomach, settling down.

'I can hear your lunch,' he said, with interest.

'Sssh.'

And he was quiet, his dark head rising and falling as her stomach rose and fell, soon asleep, and she lay listening to the crickets all around them in the grass, and the buzz of bees, watching Oliver and Jessica clearing away the remains of the picnic, brushing off crumbs, stacking up the plastic cups. Jessica was being much more helpful than at home; perhaps she and Robert, in their easygoing muddle, had made her lazy, perhaps she needed someone like Oliver, who had and expected high standards, to help her grow up. He was organising Tom, now, to put all the leftovers in a bag.

'Thank you,' she said sleepily.

Oliver smiled at her. 'Not at all.' His face, which could look so

149

sombre and withdrawn, was altered utterly by that smile: she thought so every time she saw it, remembering now the outing to the market, and the charm with which he had offered to do the shopping. She remembered, also, the moments of coldness or irritation which threatened to become fury – with Frances, with Tom.

Tom had done as he was asked, and was clumsily stuffing the bag of crusts and orange peel back in the picnic bag.

'Well done.' Oliver shook out his towel, spread it out on the grass, and lay down, reaching for his book. Larkin again, Claire saw. Larkin had come and gone intermittently ever since their arrival, interspersed with books on Portugal borrowed from the house. Tom hovered, watching, making noises. Oliver looked at him. 'Where's your book?'

'What?'

'Your book. Have you brought it?'

'Dunno.'

Oliver gave a sigh.

'Perhaps it's with mine,' said Jessica kindly, rummaging in Claire's cotton shoulder-bag, bought on a long ago childless holiday in Greece. 'Mum? Did you pack our books?'

'Possibly,' said Claire, who had gathered up a pile from the table as usual, just as they left the house.

But Tom's Enid Blyton was not with her Nina Bawden and Jessica's Judy Blume, not that he seemed to care. It's Oliver who wants to see him reading, thought Claire, watching all this; Tom himself looks in need of a rest. He stood beside Oliver looking down at him.

'Can I do what Jack's doing?'

'What's Jack doing?' Oliver looked up from his book and across to where Jack lay, his head on Claire's full stomach, fast asleep.

'It's not so bad,' said Claire. 'Quite nice, really.'

'It depends,' said Oliver, 'on the level of fidget.' He looked up at Tom. 'Promise not to wriggle or fidget or twitch?'

Tom nodded.

'Come on, then.'

And that, thought Claire, watching Tom drop down beside his father and carefully settle his rough thatched head on his stomach,

150

must be the first time I've ever seen them in any kind of intimacy at all. It can't be, but I think it is. Well. The holiday must be doing some good to someone, then. And she yawned, as Jessica lay down too, on her front with her feet in the air, opening her book.

And what about Frances, Claire wondered, seeing her sitting beside her here this morning, smoking, talking at last.

She makes me complete . . . When I met him I thought he was God . . .

No doubt a few disappointments there.

Tom was making noises.

'Stop it,' said Oliver.

'Sorry.'

Silence fell, pages were turned, the noises began again.

'I said stop it. What's the matter with you?'

Tom rolled over.

'Tom . . .'

'Sorry.'

More noises, more wriggling about.

'Oh, get off,' said Oliver. 'Go on, please. I can't take it, not in this heat.'

Tom sat up, picking off stray bits of grass.

'Find a place to settle.'

Jess turned another page, yawning.

'Do you want to come here?' asked Claire.

Tom stood, hot and undecided. Then: 'I'm going for a pee.'

'Go on, then,' said Oliver. 'Perhaps that's what's wrong with you. And then come back and rest.'

'All right.'

He wandered away from them, out of the shade, into the dense heat of the meadow, taking the direction Robert had taken, through the long grass towards the bushes where the path began.

'Don't get lost,' called Claire. 'Come straight back.'

'Don't worry,' said Oliver. 'I'll keep an eye.'

And Claire, by now almost overcome with the effort of keeping awake, closed her eyes, thinking: well, of course he will, it's his child, after all.

Jessica looked at him. 'Can I do what Jack's doing?' she said, mimicking.

'What?' Oliver lowered his sunglasses, making her laugh.

'Can I?'

'No.'

'Why?'

'Because I say so. Get on with your book.'

'Please.'

'Don't be silly.'

'Oh, go on, don't be so stuffy.'

'Jessica,' said Claire. 'Stop pestering.'

'I thought you were asleep.'

'I am. Mothers sleep with their eyes open, didn't you know?'

Jessica made faces, and went back to her book.

Claire looked towards Oliver, for a brief adult exchange of glances, but he was already reading again, and she sank back on to the towel. Tom was out of sight, the air was full of the sounds of crickets, bees, birdsong down by the river. Where was Frances, who had gone down there such a long time ago? Was Oliver so used to her wandering off that he no longer noticed?

I want him, I want Dora, I want the moon . . .

She wants a good smack bottom, she could hear her father say in his comfortable Derbyshire tones, and she smiled to herself and fell asleep, just as Robert, halfway along the shady path beneath the village, came upon Frances, walking towards him, weeping.

'Hey . . .'

She stopped, rigid with embarrassment.

'What is it?' he asked her. 'What's happened?'

'Nothing. Nothing.' A cloud of midges danced in the sun in front of her; she waved them away. 'I was just coming back.'

'Yes, so I see. And I've come back for the dinghy . . .' He smiled at her, feeling she needed a smile. 'I'm sorry to have disturbed you.'

'You haven't.' She was looking away from him, wiping her eyes.

'Women weep on me all the time for some reason,' he said, keeping it light. 'At the office, I mean. You can tell me if you want.'

But she didn't smile back, and moved to pass him. 'It's nothing,' she said. 'I was just thinking, that's all . . . I expect it's the heat.'

'Yes. Yes, it's very hot, isn't it?' He drew to the side, pressing

152

into the thick hedge and tall lush weeds, to let her pass. 'Frances –' he said, on impulse, and touched her arm. 'I'm not going to interfere. But I'm here if you need me, okay?'

'Thank you,' she said, but she did not meet his eyes. They walked past each other and away, in opposite directions, and neither of them saw Tom, who, looking for Robert, had taken a detour through some bushes alongside the broad, straw-littered path which led to this one, and then heard voices, and stopped, seeing his mother in tears and Jack's father touch her, as if he were her husband or something.

Frances found a tissue in the pocket of her shorts and blew her nose; she lit a cigarette and walked on, the cool damp ditch on one side, the luxuriant growth of hedge and weed on the other. Above her, the village was silent, sleeping; she came to the turning, the ruined house and the sweet-smelling piles of straw beneath the vines and, sitting on the low wall in the cobbled square, Dora turned towards her, smiling in welcome.

'No,' said Frances aloud, and started to cry again. The path was yellow with sun and straw, her footsteps slowed in the heat. She came to the bushes, the opening into the meadow, the stillness of the long grass and the quivering butterflies, pale blue, pale brown, creamy yellow; she saw ahead the clump of trees, and everyone flat out beneath them, though from here, through her tears and in the dazzling brightness, she couldn't tell which child lay on Claire's lap, nor see Jessica's head on Oliver's chest, her glorious hair spread out like a faery queen as she slept contentedly upon him.

After that, he didn't feel like following Robert any more, and he waited until he was out of sight and then came out of the bushes, stepping over the wicked dark ditch and squatting down beside it, looking for creatures. Water-boatmen darted, midges hovered round his head. He tried, over and over, to catch a boatman, but they were too quick; he lifted the weeds hanging down at the side of the ditch and peered beneath, to see if there were any more frogs or anything, but there weren't. He lay down on his stomach, reaching across, raising the dangling weed on the other side; he imagined a particular creature waiting in there, a bit like a chameleon, or a watery lizard, something with legs, anyway, hunched and still, green within the murky green of the ditch's edge, with a bright yellow eye and enormous black pupil, watching him. And as he imagined it, the lid in his head unhinged itself, swinging up and open, and for a moment, once again, he wasn't there at all, it was as if his brain had done a kind of blink. Then he came back, and the lid closed up again, fitting nicely.

Tom got to his feet, and went wandering along the path. He found a stick and swished at the tall weeds, breaking tops off, breaking stems. The air was full of midges, but everything else was still; he walked past gardens and houses all quiet, with the shutters closed. He rounded the corner of the last garden wall, finding himself at the foot of the long flight of steps they had come down this morning. He stood looking at it, winding up and away in the shade above him, like the beanstalk that led to the giant's castle in the clouds, and the lid in his head went click, just once.

Long-legged insects in the grass crawled over the bare limbs of those at rest beneath the trees, leaving little hot pinpricks, like a rash. Jessica, feeling something ticklish make its way over her face, stirred, brushed it away, and woke; she lay for a moment or two and sat up, scratching her legs. Beside her, Oliver was still asleep, as she was almost sure he had been when she crept alongside and put her head on his chest. A few feet away Claire and Jack were beginning to waken; beyond them, she could see Frances, coming across the meadow. She was wearing her sunglasses, walking slowly. Jessica waved.

'Hello.' Frances moved into the shade and stood looking down at them all. 'Where's Tom?'

'Didn't you see him?' said Claire, moving Jack off her, lifting her shirt up and down to cool her skin. 'He just went off to have a pee.'

'Where?'

'Well . . . over there in the bushes, I think. He can't have been far behind Robert – he's gone back to the house for the dinghy.'

'Yes, I know. We met on the path.' Frances spoke distantly, as if to someone with whom she had only recently become acquainted and with whom she had no intention of spending longer than she had to. 'Well . . . how strange. I wonder where he's got to.'

Oliver, hearing their voices, woke, and stretched. He rubbed his forehead, sitting up, taking in Frances's arrival with a nod.

'We're wondering where Tom is,' she said.

He frowned.

'Claire says he went for a pee – he hasn't come back.'

'In that case,' said Oliver, 'I imagine he's looking for you. What have you been doing?'

'Walking.' Frances addressed him, too, as if she barely knew him. 'I left Tom with you.'

You didn't, actually, leave him with anyone, thought Claire. You just left him. 'Well,' she said soothingly, 'perhaps he's with Robert, do you think? Let's hang on for a few minutes until he gets back. Would you like a drink?'

'No, thanks.' Frances stood looking across to where the bushes grew and the path began. 'I suppose he's all right,' she said uncertainly. 'Perhaps I should go and – '

'Please don't go and do anything,' said Oliver. 'He's probably with Robert and if he isn't I don't want to have to look for you too. For God's sake stay in one place for a minute.'

Frances flushed, and felt for her cigarettes.

'Perhaps he's been kidnapped,' said Jack.

'Oh, do stop saying that.' Claire was scanning the meadow.

'I don't keep saying it.'

'I wish Dad would hurry up.' Jessica, hot and prickly, pushed back her hair. 'It's boiling.'

'Why don't you go and have another dip while we're waiting?' She shook her head. 'I just want to go out in the dinghy.'

'Well you might not be able to.' Claire was suddenly impatient. 'We might have to look for Tom. And please take that sulky expression off your face.'

Jessica turned away, and a silence it felt quite impossible to break with a light remark fell on the group and stayed there.

'There he is!' said Jack. 'There's Dad!'

And they all looked across in relief to where Robert, the dinghy carried by a nylon rope in one hand, the paddles slung over his shoulder with the other, had emerged from the bushes and was walking towards them.

'Is Tom with you?' called Claire, getting to her feet.

'No.' He sounded puzzled. 'He was with you lot when I left.'

'Oh, God.' Claire stood beside Frances, waiting for him. 'We'd better go and have a search,' she said. 'I don't want Robert wandering about in this heat any more.'

'No. No, of course not. But there's no reason why you – ' Frances broke off, and turned to Oliver. 'Will you come and help me look?'

'No,' said Oliver. 'I've been in charge of him all morning. I'm pretty sure he's hiding quite close, and I'm sure it's you he wants to find him, don't you think? He's been fidgeting about ever since you disappeared.' His tone was casual, his words not entirely unreasonable, but Claire, shading her eyes as Robert came up to them all, felt chilled.

'I'll come with you,' she said to Frances, and wanting to lighten the atmosphere for Jack's sake she held out her hand to him. 'Come on, you can help.'

Robert dropped the dinghy and paddles and wiped his forehead. 'We're in Portugal,' he said. 'Don't flap. He's safer here on his own than in London, wouldn't you say? Somebody give me a drink.'

'You don't have to come,' Frances said to Claire, her voice tight, as they set out.

Claire held Jack's hand. 'Of course I'll come.'

He'd just go and see how the pig was getting on, then he'd go back to the others. He began to climb, counting, panting: eleven steps, twelve, thirteen . . . rounding the bend . . . twenty-one, twenty-two . . . they went on for ever. Twenty-nine, thirty . . . thirty-four. He had reached the top, and come to the gap between the houses: he rattled his stick along the wall and came out into the silent cobbled street, frowning, trying to work out where he was. It was boiling up here, much hotter than down on the path, and he was sweating and thirsty from the climb. But he couldn't see a tap anywhere and after a moment or two he remembered where the pig was, somewhere near the shop, off to the left, and set off slowly, passing curled up brown dogs asleep in the sun, and mangy cats.

'Pig!' he called. 'Pi-ig!'

Someone moved on a balcony above him: a fat old woman with rotten teeth, staring down at him.

'I'm looking for the pig,' said Tom, and walked on.

But when he came to the rough wooden door set in the wall, with its peeling black paint and gap at the bottom, he couldn't hear a sound. He knelt on the worn step, peering in, screwing up his eyes to see through the smelly darkness. He saw churned-up wet straw, and then, right at the back, the huge pale hairy shape of the pig, on its side, not moving a muscle, as if it was dead.

Tom rattled his stick all along under the door. 'Pi-ig!'

There was a snort, and the animal raised its head. He could just make out a whitish-pink eye and white lashes; then it moved, awkwardly, grunting, heaving its enormous bulk, getting up on small, filthy feet, coming towards him.

'Hello.' Tom pressed his face to the gap, looking up at dirty pink chest and swaying belly, and the pig, reaching the door, lowered its head and began to nose about, hopeful, grunting again. 'Oh, dear. Sorry.' He should've thought. You couldn't just come and visit without bringing anything, that was mean.

'I'll go and get the apples,' he told it. 'I shan't be long. You stay there, all right?' The pig snorted, moving its wet bristly nose all along the gap: you couldn't help laughing, even though you felt sorry for it. Poor thing. Poor thing, all shut away. How could they shut it away down here? It should be out in the sun, out in a nice sunny field, with turnips. He scrambled to his feet and hurried up the hill to the house, wondering if Robert was there, hoping he wasn't.

He wasn't. The house was shut up, the double doors on the terrace locked, the door to the kitchen locked. Tom stood outside it wondering what to do. People would start looking for him and getting cross.

Behind him, water poured into the green-tiled tank. He didn't know if it was drinking water, but no one had said it wasn't, and anyway he didn't care. He climbed the steps and stood beneath the line of clean clothes drying in the sun, and dunked his face in the

157

water, getting his hair wet, splashing his neck and arms. He cupped his hands beneath the brass tap in the wall and drank and drank, and then, feeling much better, he went down the steps to the garden and up the next steps to the terrace again.

Out across the valley grey smoke rose from the pines. Beneath, the faraway river looked like a river in a dream. He turned away, sinking on to the swing-seat, feeling it sway, stretching out, yawning. Shadows of the leaves of the lemon trees played on the canopy as he swung; after a while his hand went down inside his shorts again, finding it waiting for him, stiff and smooth. There was no one to see him, no one to know, and he did it and did it and did it, as much as he wanted, until he stopped wanting, and fell asleep.

Jessica lay back, one hand trailing in the water, her straw hat slipping down a little on to the broad rim of the dinghy, warm in the afternoon sun. The water was like greeny-brown silk, deep and still beneath the cliffs on the far side, holding the shady reflections of the trees, breaking in a rippling rise and fall against the silver paddles as Oliver rowed slowly upriver, leaving the flowery meadow behind. Robert was resting now, flat out in the shade with a drink and his book, beginning to drop off.

'It's like a film,' she said, as they drew further away from him and rounded a bend. Tall reeds grew at the water's edge; soundless fish broke the surface and disappeared.

'Yes.' Oliver looked at her and smiled, and then he lowered the paddles and they drifted for a while, carried by the sleepy current, listening to the birds.

'We're going backwards,' said Jessica.

'*You're* going backwards. I'm going the right way.' He reached for the paddles again, looked up for a moment and frowned.

'What?'

'There's a fire, can you see? Almost at the top of the mountain – it's spreading quite fast.'

Jessica turned, craning her neck. Dark clouds billowed angrily from pines along the ridge of a mountain she recognised as one they could see from their house; the smoke rose towards the pale haze of the sky, became diffuse, disappeared, was followed by more.

'What's going to happen?'

Oliver shook his head. 'I don't know. I expect it'll go on spreading and ruin half the plantation. They'll probably send beaters up when they can, but there's not much they can do really, is there?'

'Try water, dear Henry.' Jessica began to giggle.

'What?'

'Don't you know that? We're always singing it in the car – "There's a hole in my bucket, dear Liza, dear Liza . . ." '

'Oh, yes. Yes, of course. "Then mend it, dear Henry, dear Henry . . ." '

'You be Henry,' said Jessica, as they rowed on, approaching more maize fields, leaving the fire behind. 'Go on, you start, and I'll be Liza.'

'No.'

'Please.'

'God, you're a pest.'

'Go *on*.'

Oliver cleared his throat, began and stopped. 'I can't sing.'

'Of course you can. Anyway, who's going to hear?'

'Oh, all right.' He cleared his throat again. 'There's a hole in my bucket, dear Liza, dear Liza . . .'

His voice grew stronger; Jessica took up the next verse, and the song, after a couple more, rang out over the water so that anyone passing, though no one passed, would have smiled to see a father and daughter so clearly enjoying themselves.

'With what shall I fetch it, dear Liza, dear Liza . . .'

Jessica left a long pause.

'With a bucket, dear Henry . . .' She burst out laughing.

Oliver looked at her solemnly. 'There's a hole in my bucket, dear Liza, dear Liza . . .'

'That's much better,' said Jessica, when he had finished. 'You don't look half as cross.'

'Did I look cross?'

'With Tom.'

'Don't your parents ever get cross with you?'

She thought about it. 'Not quite like that.'

He didn't answer.

159

'And Frances, sometimes,' she said. 'Why are you cross with her?'

He didn't answer that, either, but rowed on, the air a little cooler now, a breath of wind beginning to rustle through the maize.

'Are you going to have any more children?'

'I – no, I don't think so.'

'Why?'

'That's quite enough questions.' He turned the dinghy round in a slow circle; she looked at him in consternation.

'Where are we going? I don't want to go back yet.'

'I think we should, it's getting on.' They rowed in silence; every now and then a fish came up. He offered her the paddles. 'Want to?'

'No.' She shook her head, gazing down into the water. 'I like it when you row.'

'Well I will then. It's all right. Don't look so stricken.'

Jessica didn't answer, her mood changed, subdued. After a few moments she said: 'Are we going back because of the questions? I didn't mean to be rude.'

'You weren't. I want to find out about Tom, that's all.' He nudged her with his foot. 'Come on, what's the matter? Am I such an ogre?'

'You can look terribly fierce sometimes.'

'Well,' he said, lifting the silver paddles high, letting the water fall in shining waves, 'I can assure you I'm not feeling fierce with you – ' He broke off. 'Look! Look – there's a kingfisher!'

'Where?' She sat up quickly, rocking the boat. 'Oh, yes!'

They gazed after it. A bright and glorious flash of blue streaked past the cliffs on the far side, followed by another, swift as light, vanishing, gone.

'That was amazing!' Jessica turned back to him, radiant, all smiles again.

'Wasn't it?' He lowered the paddles and reached out suddenly, touching her sunburnt face. 'Happy now?'

'Yes,' she said, and watched him lean back again and take the oars, rowing with the current now, but still going slowly. They still had plenty of time.

160

'He's here,' said Claire, climbing the steps to the terrace. 'I told you he'd be all right.'

'Oh, thank God.' Frances, following, came up beside her; they looked at Tom fast asleep beneath the gentle shadows of the canopy of the swing-seat, sprawled out, relaxed. 'Well – let me get you a drink.' She felt beneath the stone by the double doors for the key and went into the cool dark sitting-room.

Claire sank down on to one of the chairs at the marble table; below, in the garden, Jack had picked up a cricket bat and ball left outside the door to the cellar, and was swiping into the vines.

'Don't knock the grapes off,' she called.

'I'm not knocking them off.'

'Good.'

She stretched, running her hands through her hair, feeling, despite the rest earlier on, like lying down beside Tom and going to sleep again. They had been looking and calling for over half an hour, along the paths, through bushes, up the steps to the village, barely talking to each other apart from that, restraining Jack from over-enthusiastic shouting. Now she just wanted to be left alone: no children, no difficult marriages, no problems. She leaned back on the hard white chair, looking out across the valley, noticing another forest fire raging along the mountain. I've had enough of this heat, she thought, for the first time since they arrived, and remembered the rain last year, sweeping over the rooftops in the village, falling steadily on the garden and the terrace, dripping from the lemon trees on warm damp afternoons while they all played games indoors with the windows open. I wouldn't mind if the weather changed, she thought, and rested her arms on the table and put her head upon them, wishing, suddenly, for tranquil rain and tranquil companions, too.

And Frances, inside the creeper-shaded kitchen, which smelled, as always, faintly of gas, made tea and squash for the boys, found biscuits, put everything on a tray and carried it out to the terrace. Where she stopped, seeing Claire in that restful and picturesque position, reminded at once of the morning's reverie, of herself at the weather-beaten table in the quiet secluded garden, her head on her arms, waiting in the warmth of early

161

afternoon for Dora to come out from the house and join her. For a moment she stood there, pierced by feelings so powerful she thought she might drop the tray, and then Claire looked up, with her lazy smile, and said: 'Oh, how lovely,' and Frances stepped calmly towards the table, and put everything down, saying, as if it were nothing at all, light and remote:

'I'm sorry about this morning – can we just draw a veil?'

The next day felt easier. They spent the morning down in the village, buying provisions from the shop, calling on the pig as they went past, visiting the butcher, who once a week opened a little shop eight feet square, white-tiled, the floor sprinkled with sawdust. Slabs of cheap meat lay in the window, hens hung from hooks above them. Claire glanced at Tom, gazing up at the limp bodies, but he, like Jack, was soon distracted by two wiry and bare-chested men over the road, who began sawing piles of pine logs, the branches brought in a wheelbarrow out along a path from the mountain. The activity and the sound felt soothing, and the air through the open door of the shop smelled sweet and fresh. The two boys wandered across and stood watching, joined in a little while by Jess and the grown-ups. Smiles and greetings were exchanged; the boys squatted down and ran streams of sawdust through their fingers, watching it fall.

'We'll need a lot of sawdust for my mouse,' said Tom.

They walked on, round the outskirts of the village, taking the road which became a bridge over a dried-up tributary of the river, where children were playing among bricks and weeds. The road broadened to run towards the main road and the market town. The post office was on this road, and the little café next to it; they sat beneath the awning of vines, having coffee and ice cream, watching their corner of the world go by.

It felt easier, but Claire, from time to time observing Oliver and Frances, wondered at how little they spoke to each other, how much time they spent apart.

Back at the house they made lunch for everyone. Coming into the kitchen to fetch drinks for the children, who were up at the pool, she found Oliver chopping cucumber and tomato for salad, sprinkling in herbs she knew the children would pick out bit by

162

little bit, and Frances laying a tray of plates and cutlery, in a silence that felt heavy with words unspoken.

'That looks wonderful,' she said brightly, as Oliver laid out pieces of fish, and he smiled at her, but she felt like a fool, and went out quickly, spilling squash on the floor.

After lunch, they all retired to rest. Claire felt grateful to be indoors in a shady room after yesterday's heat and the long search for Tom, who seemed all right today, making his noises as usual but enjoying the pool, happy to go up with Jack after lunch and lie down. She settled them into their beds and crossed the rag runner to her own room, closing the door.

'Come here,' she said to Robert, taking off her shoes.

He turned from the window above the terrace, and swung the shutters to.

'What has got into you?' he said, as she lay down and held out her arms. 'It must be the heat.' He came across to the bed, and sat down beside her, laying his hand on her stomach.

'It isn't the heat,' she said, reaching up to him, hearing Oliver's heavy footsteps go past along the corridor, the door at the far end open and close. 'It isn't the heat, it's you.'

Frances did not go upstairs with the others. She lay on the sitting-room sofa, with the long cotton curtains drawn, reading and thinking as Jessica slept in her room. In mid-afternoon, before anyone else was awake, she took her swimsuit and towel and walked down through the village and along the soft earth path beneath vines to the maize fields, where the heat was spread out like a blanket beneath the sky.

There was nobody down by the river: she swam and swam. The water was silken, yellow and green; it parted before her in a shining and gentle rise and fall, holding tree and rock and sky, broken, rippling, smooth again. She swam for perhaps half an hour, perhaps longer, and when she came out she felt calm.

It was cooler now. She walked along the paths of caked earth through the tall dry maize, crossing the little irrigation ditches, hearing water fall. She looked up to see a fine spray ahead of her, gleaming, pattering on to the papery leaves and the ground, and at the end of the row came upon an old sunburned man in a dark cloth cap and shirtsleeves, hosing his patch. He nodded to her; she

163

murmured a good afternoon, although it was almost evening now, the sun beginning to sink towards the mountains.

In another place, she thought, walking on, in another country or even in England, I might be afraid to find myself alone in a stretch of field with a strange man, even an old one. Here, although the rows of maize made endless hiding places, she felt perfectly safe, the warm dry air all around her, no one to disturb her thoughts. And anyway, she was not alone; she was never alone: she was walking, as always, with Dora.

Frances left the field and returned along the soft earth path to the village, and the feeling of peace remained with her, until she reached the house again, and climbed the stone steps to the terrace, where Claire and Robert were sitting together on the swing-seat, reading, rocking slowly to and fro. She stopped, and the sight of such real and unquestioning companionship almost undid her.

They looked up and greeted her, and she smiled and said she had had a good swim, and asked about the children, who were up at the pool with Oliver. And then she went slowly into the house and leaned up against the first wall she came to, willing herself not to sink to the floor and weep.

That evening, they all ate early outside with the children, watching a tiny bat flit through the lemon trees as the light began to fade.

'We saw a shooting star last year,' said Jessica suddenly.

'So we did.' Robert was finishing a creamy vanilla pudding from the shop. He leaned back, scanning the sky. 'Perhaps there'll be one tonight,' he said, but there wasn't.

It grew dark; the children had baths and were read to; the grown-ups went to their rooms one by one. And when Oliver had gone, taking his book and his glasses, and the house was quiet, Frances, who had busied herself in the kitchen, tidying away every last cup and plate, came back to the empty sitting-room, sat down at the generous desk in the corner with its parchment-shaded lamp, and wrote her letter.

More posters appeared in the village for the fiesta, and on Sunday morning Guida presented Robert with a roughly printed handbill, which he perused with the aid of the dictionary. There was, he told the others over breakfast, to be a procession, bearing the Virgin Mary and assorted saints, as well as stalls and a band, the arrival of whose sound equipment at three o'clock was billed as an attraction in itself. It was generally agreed that they could give this a miss, but at five that evening they locked up the house and set out, walking up the mountain road towards the next village, some half a mile away.

The heat of the day was fading, though it was still warm. They walked slowly, in single file, over dry heaps of pine needles at the edge of the road, grown-ups putting arms towards the children at the hectic approach of motor bikes and, less often, cars.

'I'm *okay*,' said Jessica, irritably shaking off Robert. 'Don't fuss.'

'Don't be silly,' said Oliver, from behind. 'We have to keep you safe.'

She flushed, and walked on, looking down, her face invisible behind a falling screen of hair.

'Look!' said Jack. 'They've done decorations in the trees.'

They looked up to see trailing loops of pink and white in the lower branches. 'It's toilet paper!'

'So it is,' said Claire. It grew thicker and more elaborate, although here and there single sheets clung roughly to twigs, or had fallen to the earth. They began to hear pop music, vastly amplified, and the boys began to jig.

'Careful!' said Oliver, as Tom danced out from the verge, and as a car approached from the opposite direction, coming towards them, he grabbed his arm. '*Will* you keep in!'

They passed a small concrete chapel, set back in a clearing, and rounded a bend, and then the music faded and stopped. Ahead they saw a line of parked cars and vans, propped-up bikes, and a throng of people, pressing back on either side at the approach of a bright procession. Children in cotton frocks and embroidered waistcoats followed the priest at the head, carrying flowers, teenage girls had ribbons in their hair, and embarrassed-looking boys walked with decorated crooks and sticks. Behind them all swayed a gaudy litter, borne by small men in hats. The crowd began to sing, there was a percussion of bells.

'Come on,' said Robert, 'find places,' and they hurried towards the edge of the crowd, reaching for the boys' hands.

The procession drew closer, the singing of the hymn grew louder; from the litter, piled high with dozens of plastic flowers, a large and tinselled plaster doll in blue and white smiled with crimson lips and gazed at the air with blank brown eyes.

'Who's that?' asked Tom.

'The Virgin Mary,' said Oliver. 'Our Lady, they say here.'

He frowned. 'I thought she was in London. In church.'

'She's supposed to be in heaven,' said Jack.

'It's just a *model*.' Jessica was scathing.

'It's just a model,' said Oliver, 'but it means something to these people – you shouldn't mock.'

'I wasn't . . .' Jessica's voice trailed away, and Claire, glancing at her from the other side, saw her eyes fill with tears. She put out a hand.

'Jess . . . what is it?'

'Nothing,' said Jessica angrily. 'Nothing!'

'Oh, dear.' Claire turned to Robert, then thought better of it: this was hardly the place. She saw one or two other English faces in the crowd across the road, people she had never seen down in their village, who must be renting somewhere up here: a tall fair man with a beard, a woman with cropped dark hair and glasses. Then the Virgin Mary drew alongside, and they were lost to view. Behind Mary were two more saintly plaster dolls, and she saw Tom bend down as they went past, picking up a fallen plastic flower and moving quickly to replace it on the litter in a gesture that surprised her – she'd have expected him to pull it apart and be reproached by his parents, but he looked awed and excited, clearly caught up in the atmosphere and the sonorous singing of the hymn.

Families moved to follow the retreating figures down the hill towards the chapel, and as they disappeared round the broad curve there was an agonising, amplified squeal from loudspeakers and they saw what had been mostly obscured before: a beer stall and then, set up next to a café, a raised platform, painted black and festooned with toilet paper. Three or four men in shirtsleeves were wielding electric guitars. There was another squeal and they all covered their ears, and with a violent twang the music began again, so loudly that they could not hear one another speak.

'Wick-ed!' Tom, in wild responsive excitement, leaped out into the road and began to dance, his whole body moving, clumsily enraptured. Jack took Claire's hand.

'He's gone mad.'

'What?' She bent down, and he yelled it at her.

'I said he's gone mad!'

'Ssh,' she said, absurdly, and began to enjoy herself. People were moving out into the street in couples, dancing sedately; on the other side of the café a bar billiards table was almost invisible, surrounded by adolescent boys. Robert touched her arm.

'Ice cream?' he mouthed. 'Drink?'

'Drink,' she mouthed back, and they began to move through the couples, beckoning to Jessica to follow them.

But Jessica was hovering, and seemed not to see them. She was standing near Oliver, who was looking at Frances. And Frances, it was apparent, was miles away. Claire tried to follow her gaze, to work out who or what she was watching, but gave up as Jack pulled at her hand. She followed Robert towards the packed café, leaving Tom whirling and leaping, Jessica, with exaggerated concentration, moving up and down on the spot, Oliver watching Frances and Frances lost in a dream, gazing across the street to where Dora, as if summoned here at last by an unposted letter, stood watching the dancers, smiling.

Of course, it was not Dora – but the hair, the glasses, that particular smile . . . That particular air, sufficient unto herself. Frances, whose heart had turned over when she first caught sight of this unknown woman, stood looking at her now, suffused with emotion, with longing. *Turn again*, she said to her silently, for there was something, too, of the way Dora moved in the way this woman moved, turning – yes, now – to the tall, fair-haired, bearded man beside her, saying something, taking his hand. They moved out on to the street with the other couples and began to dance, slowly, their arms around each other's waists, casually intimate.

Of course, it was not Dora. Frances, able to observe her more closely, saw that this woman was younger, her face not as fine; the glasses, which Dora wore only when she was working, were not ones she would have chosen. There was only one Dora, there was no one else to touch her. And yet to see someone here who so resembled her, who both was and was not her . . . Frances closed her eyes, searching for the real, the original. And Dora came towards her, greeted her with a smile.

'*Hello, Frances.*'

'*Dora . . .*'

'Frances!' She was being shaken; she opened her eyes to see Oliver looking at her with bemused impatience. The music was deafening, vibrating through her; it had taken her over like a lover.

'What?'

He mouthed at her, made gestures. 'Do you want to dance?'

She shook her head, about to add, Later, in a little while. Oliver looked at her, his face darkening. 'Please . . .' she said. 'I was . . .' But he had left her, marching across the street, seizing Tom's hand as he passed, dragging him, astonished and afraid, towards the café. Frances, shaken, felt Dora also – the real Dora, not her likeness, who went on dancing – abandon her and disappear; she was left with Jessica, who looked distressed.

'What's the matter?' she asked, struggling to regain a sense of herself as someone capable of looking after a child.

Jessica shook her head, not meeting her eyes, trying, clearly, to indicate that nothing was the matter at all.

With a sound like a nail being dragged across glass, the song came to an end; there was a burst of clapping and cheers, and the bandleader stepped forward, taking the microphone, which shrieked.

'*Obrigado, obrigado . . .*' He began to talk rapidly, greeted with laughter and more applause.

'Come on,' said Frances, taking Jessica in charge. 'Let me buy you an ice or something.' They moved through the dancers, and she cast one last look at the woman who was not Dora, seeing, ahead in the queue, Oliver and Tom, next to each other in a silence that she could sense from here was grim; then the music began again, louder than ever.

'Oliver . . .' She went up to him, trying to smile, to defuse. 'You misunderstood – '

168

'Did I? I don't think so.'

'But you did. I was thinking about something else, that was all – you didn't give me a chance – ' She could hear herself trying to absolve her own part, to make light of her abstraction, and he said coldly:

'Please don't try to tell me what I did or didn't do,' and turned away from her.

Between them, Tom was clutching at himself.

'Do you need a pee?' she asked him. He shook his head. 'I think you do.' She took his hand.

'I want an ice cream.'

'You can have one when we get back. Come on.' She led him through the crowd, looking bleakly about her. Apart from the single café there seemed nowhere which might house a lavatory, and anyway, who cared? There were gaps between the houses, leading straight to the mountainside on earthen paths bordered by ferns. She ushered Tom through one of these and waited, trying to recover herself, while he peed into the ground; he finished, giving a shiver, and pulled up his shorts again.

'Oliver's angry,' he said, as they made their way back.

'Not with you.' The singer on the stage was wailing; the air throbbed. 'Did you like the dancing?' she asked, and Tom nodded, but said no more as he walked beside her. They moved to rejoin the queue, seeing Claire, Jack and Robert, who had reached their goal and were out in the street again with ice creams and cans of beer, wave and beckon to them. Frances waved back –in so far as she ever waved – and looked along the line leading into the café for Oliver, who wasn't there.

'Can you see Oliver anywhere?' she asked Tom.

'He's dancing.'

'Dancing?' she repeated blankly, and then she saw him, with Jessica, on the far side of the bandstand near the beer stall. Jessica had her back to the café queue; she was swaying to the beat, her hair swishing across her shoulders, her hands at her side. Oliver, opposite her, was studiedly looking at the ground, a tall, beautiful man moving little, shifting on his feet.

In a long ago time when Frances and Oliver had gone dancing –a time which felt so distant it might never have happened – she had

169

found that control and restraint, and the sense of power which lay beneath it, overwhelming, full of excitement, a match for her own reserve, a challenge.

Now, in what had become a marriage of silence and withdrawal, she saw only repression, withholding, coldness. She wondered that he was dancing at all, and particularly with Jessica, guessing that it was she, a pretty and determined child whom Oliver clearly found a relief from Tom – and probably herself – who had dragged him out there.

Perhaps forty people were dancing now, and Oliver and Jessica, adult and child, looked not at all out of place: there was an old woman in black with her granddaughter, a mother and baby, laughing, a group of little girls, teenagers returned from the procession, holding hands. And where was Dora? Dora was nowhere to be seen. Searching through the watchers and the dancers for that particular and graceful turn of the head, waiting for the lift of the heart, Frances saw only strangers.

'What about my ice cream?' Tom was asking. 'What about my *ice cream*?'

'Yes,' she said, distantly, filled with disappointment – for if there were not to be Dora, Dora's likeness had helped – and she turned back to the queue and stood, waiting, as Tom went to join the Murrays and a bar football table rattled and banged beside her to whoops of excitement from the boys pressed all around it. The queue moved slowly, the air filled with the smell of sweat, bacon, spiced sausage, coffee and beer; the few spindly tables in the hot little room were packed solid with noisy families. Frances stood watching a girl in apron and ponytail scooping out ice cream from a box, pressed on all sides by people coming out, people pouring in to replace them. And here, as she neared the top of the queue at last, was Dora, leaving with her bearded companion, coming towards her. She drew closer, holding herself in a little, keeping herself apart from the throng as both Frances and the real Dora would choose to do, and as she drew near, Frances, who rarely initiated any social encounter, looked her full in the face, and smiled at her. The woman looked back, puzzled by a stranger's friendliness; she did not smile, and Frances said unsteadily, 'I'm sorry – I thought you were someone else.'

170

The woman turned to her companion. '*Was sagt mir diese Frau*?'

Smiling smoothly – blandly, thought Frances, finding him of no interest – the man said to her in halting English, 'Can we help you?'

'No,' she said shortly. 'I made a mistake.' She had reached the counter. She opened her purse, indicating strawberry-flavour cornets to the girl with the ponytail, knowing she had been rude and intrusive to a couple who would probably speculate before they forgot about her, and she felt, as she counted out worn escudos notes, a complete exhaustion with herself. Outside again, carrying her ices, she saw the German couple walking away from the dancers, leaving, going back through the village.

Enough, she said. Enough, enough.

Tom was standing with Claire, Jack on her other side; they were watching the dancing and, in particular, not Oliver and Jessica, but Robert and Guida, who were much enjoying themselves, arms linked, turning each other about.

Frances, glad of the distraction, gave Tom his ice and then Jack, who looked at it longingly, her own.

'And how did this come to be?' she asked Claire, who was observing the scene with amusement. There was a break in the song; Robert and Guida drew apart, laughing.

'I hadn't realised Guida was here,' she added more quietly.

'Nor we,' said Claire. 'I think she came up after the procession, with her friends. Anyway, she's managed to lure Robert out there, which is more than I could do.' Another song began, and she covered her ears. 'I'm not sure I can take too much more of this,' and she waved an elaborate goodbye to Robert, who was dancing again.

'Shall we go?' Frances mouthed at her, and Claire nodded.

They began to move through the bystanders and the stalls of pottery and leather bags, the boys following, dripping melted ice cream. They passed the bandstand, deafened, and came up behind Jessica and Oliver, who were no longer dancing but queueing at the beer stall. Claire tapped Jess on the shoulder.

'We're off,' she said.

Jessica looked at her, all smiles. 'Bye.' She saw Jack's ice cream and moved towards him. 'Let's have a lick.'

Oliver looked at Frances. 'Will you dance with me now?' he asked her, and it was clear that he was angry still, his invitation made in that tone impossible to accept.

Frances hesitated. 'I – ' she began, and then she realised, and sensed that Claire was realising it also, that Oliver, who rarely drank more than a couple of glasses of wine with a meal, had been drinking now for some time.

'No,' he said, beads of sweat all along his forehead beneath the line of thick hair. 'Of course you won't. Why should you dance with me?'

Beside Frances, Tom was looking at the ground; licking Jack's ice cream, a few feet away, Jessica heard none of this exchange.

'Jessica,' said Claire, going over to her, 'I think you'd better come with us now.'

'What?' She looked at her mother and her face fell. 'I don't want to,' she said. 'It's lovely here.'

'I know, but – ' Claire floundered. It wasn't getting late, it wasn't getting cold, there was no obvious and familiar reason she could give a twelve-year-old for leaving. 'It's nearly suppertime,' she said weakly.

'I'm not hungry.'

'Jess . . . I'm sorry, I don't want to have an argument, I just want you to come.'

'Why?'

'Because I say so,' said Claire, clutching at parental authority. '*Why?*'

'Because Oliver's drunk,' she said at last, exasperated.

'*Is* he?' asked Jack, fascinated. 'He doesn't *look* drunk.'

'Oh, God.' Claire turned, seeing Oliver at the top of the beer queue now, buying cans. She beckoned to Frances. 'Will you keep an eye on these two for me?' she asked as Frances came up with Tom, dragging his feet, making noises. 'I just want to have a word with Robert.' And she pushed through the crowd, waving and calling, finding Robert and Guida still, as she thought crossly, jigging about.

Robert looked at her enquiringly.

'I thought you'd gone,' he shouted.

Claire cupped her hands to her mouth.

172

'We had. I need you.'

Robert sighed. He made ruefully apologetic gestures to Guida, who smiled and nodded and returned to her companions, a group of teenagers whom Claire recognised from their own village.

'What's up?' he asked, when she had gone, and Claire explained, leading him back to where Frances and the three children stood in an awkwardly disconsolate group, the boys scuffing at the ground, Jessica chewing at a nail, something she hadn't done for years. Claire looked around.

'Where's Oliver?'

'He's gone.' Frances was white-faced. 'He's stormed off.'

'Oh. Oh, dear. Well . . .' Claire's voice died away.

'Right,' said Robert, marshalling them all. 'Let's go home and have something to eat.' He took Jack and Tom by the hand, one on either side of him, swinging their arms to the music as they walked away. 'Had a good time? Jolly little do?'

'Idiot,' said Jessica, under her breath.

Robert stopped swinging, and looked at her. 'What did you say?'

'Nothing.' Her hair fell over her face; she buried her hands in her pockets.

'I hope it was nothing,' said Robert, in a tone none of them was used to hearing. 'Because I've had just about enough of your rudeness to me on this holiday. Got it?'

Jessica didn't answer. She stood waiting for him and the boys to move on, and as Claire, approaching with Frances, put out a hand towards her, she pushed it away.

'What is it?' Claire asked. 'Come on, Jess, please don't be like this . . .'

'Stop it,' said Jessica. 'Stop it!'

Claire shook her head, and gave up. They had come to the end of the line of cars leading out from the village; ahead, a few people were walking down towards their own village, on a road littered with pieces of toilet paper fallen from the trees; drink cans and paper bags lay beneath the blackberry brambles. Robert and the boys stopped to pick a few of the berries and Claire, searching for neutrality, a way to make things better, said to Frances:

'We could come up here tomorrow, perhaps, with a bowl . . .'

173

Frances didn't answer, looking straight ahead. They walked on down the road, rope-soled summer shoes quiet on the tarmac, the light and the music beginning to fade. Behind them, Jessica followed, slowly, wanting nothing to do with any of them, looking around at every footstep on the road behind for Oliver, who had left without even saying goodbye.

The children, after a game of Scrabble, had been put to bed; Frances, too, had gone up early, pale, with a headache, leaving Robert and Claire out on the terrace with the last of the jug of red wine. Every now and then the air was pierced by a speeding motor bike, and the road past the house lit by a wildly swaying headlamp; then it was quiet again, except for the half-hearted fizz of the fuse-box from inside the house, and the crickets from down in the darkened garden. They sat, Claire on the swing-seat and Robert leaning back in his chair, watching the moths bump against the outside lamp above the double doors.

'Where do you think he's got to?' asked Claire.

'No idea,' said Robert. 'Do stop worrying.'

'I can't help it.' The candle in its saucer was burning low; she leaned forward and fiddled with a matchstick, poking it into the wax. 'Aren't you worried?'

'I think he's all right,' said Robert, reaching for the jug. 'As much as he's ever all right. He and Frances, perhaps I should say. It's quite clear they're not.' He refilled their glasses. 'Do you want to tell me about it?'

'No.'

'Breaking confidences?'

'Yes.'

Robert shook his head. 'Which leaves me to speculate,' he said, and slowly turned his glass in his hands. 'What am I going to do?' he said, after a while. 'What am I going to do about Jess?'

'Nothing. It'll pass.'

'That's what I keep telling myself.' The glass in his hands went round and round. 'Were you like this with your father?'

She tried to remember. 'I don't think so. Perhaps, a bit. What about Penny? What was she like?'

Robert thought of his sister, so different from him, liable to fly off the handle, frustrated by her children, desperate to get back to work. 'Mmm,' he said slowly. 'Perhaps that's where it comes from. Oh, well.' He drank, finishing the glass. 'Shall we go in?'

'How can we?' Another motor bike raced past, and she covered her mouth at an inward vision of horror: Oliver weaving drunkenly down the road, unseen in a thin and wavering headlight, hearing a screech of brakes too late, too late . . .

'Stop it,' said Robert, watching her. 'He's okay. Hey – what was that?'

Above them the outside lamp was flickering, and the line of the street lights coming up from the village flickered too. Then, beyond them, the lights of the whole village went dim: street lamps, televisions, neon strips in kitchens and low-watt bulbs in upstairs bedrooms. They flickered, faded again, and then came on and stayed on, as though nothing had happened.

'Well, well, I wonder what all that was about.' Robert got to his feet. 'I'd better have a look at the fuse-box, I suppose.' They could hear it fizzing softly still.

'You can look at it,' said Claire, 'but there's not a damn thing you can do with it, is there?'

'We seem to be powerless all round,' he said, going inside.

Claire went on sitting there, rocking the seat to and fro, her feet on the ground, vaguely comforted by the rhythm, still straining her ears for Oliver's footsteps approaching the house from the road above, for the creak of the gate by the water tank. But there were no footsteps, there was no creak, and in a few moments Robert returned, standing in the open doorway.

'Well, I don't know,' he said. 'It's just buzzing away, I don't think it's anything to worry about. Come on, let's go to bed.'

She sighed, and got up. 'What shall we do about the door? Just leave the key as usual?'

'Yes, what else?' And Robert went inside again, leaving her to blow out the stump of candle.

In the sitting-room she took the key from her purse and went out to put it under the stone at the top of the steps; then she closed the double doors and went to check on Jessica, who had, as usual, fallen asleep with the light on. Claire stood looking down at her, trying to see, in sleep, her daughter's steps towards adolescence

175

and independence fall away, leaving a child again. She tried, but it was difficult. Bending to kiss her, switching out the light, Claire felt a mixture of sadness and apprehension that went deep, and she went slowly out of the room and along the panelled corridor to the bathroom with her heart full, forgetting, for a while, all about Oliver, wandering in a drunken fury out on the mountainside.

They fell asleep soon after eleven, and were woken at who knew what hour, hearing from somewhere a violent banging on a door, and shouts.

'Christ.' Robert, who had been dreaming deeply, sat up in bed. He put out a hand for the light on the table, fumbling for the switch. Nothing happened. He tried again. 'Bugger.'

'What is it?' Claire sat up beside him. 'My God, is that Oliver?'

'Must be. Hang on, the bulb's gone.'

From downstairs the banging grew louder; they heard a door on the corridor opening. Robert got out of bed.

'It's so *dark*,' said Claire.

'Of course it's dark, it's the middle of the night . . .' He was stumbling across the room, stepping over dropped clothes and jumbled-up sandals, still half asleep. He felt for the switch by the door and flicked it on. Nothing happened. Again. Nothing.

'Power cut,' said Claire shakily. 'No torch. Oh, God . . .' She pushed back the duvet and then pulled it up again as the pounding from downstairs grew fiercer. And then came Jessica's voice: 'Mummy! Mummy!' She sprang out of bed.

'Okay, okay, keep calm.' Robert, opening the door on to the passage, waited for her to get to him; they reached for each other's hands, moving out into the darkness of the corridor.

'Claire?' Frances, invisible, was standing in her own open doorway, sounding horribly calm.

'Yes,' said Claire, then jumped as Jessica's voice came again. 'Quick!' she said to Robert. 'Quick!'

'It's everywhere,' said Frances, from behind them. 'Not just the house. I looked out of our window – the whole village is dark.'

'Mummy!'

'Coming!' called Claire, and her stomach gave a lurch of fear as they felt their way along the corridor, moving past Jack and Tom's room to the terrifying open landing. The moon was hidden by cloud: not a glimmer of light shone through the window overlooking the peach tree.

'Stay with the boys,' said Robert to Frances.

'Yes, all right.' A thin, distant voice, like a ghost.

They left her, moving carefully towards the stairs, treading the slippery wood in their bare feet, coming to the turn, passing the black square of window.

'Open-this-door! Open-this-fucking-door!'

Oliver was kicking now; it felt as if the whole house were being picked up and shaken.

'That's the kitchen door – must be too drunk to go round the house,' said Robert.

'*Mummy*!'

'I'm here!' called Claire, and broke away from him as they reached the bottom of the stairs, stumbling down the corridor, feeling along the panelling, coming up, suddenly, against Jessica's cold and trembling body, standing in her nightshirt by her open door, her hair soft, comforting, as she fell into Claire's arms to be comforted.

'It's all right, it's all right . . .'

Behind them she could hear Robert, banging against things in the kitchen, swearing.

And then the lights came soundlessly on, shining from the upper landing so that she was able, in the reassuring gleam on the stairs, to find the switch here, and fill the corridor with light. 'Here we are, come on, come up with me . . .' Across the wide expanse of the sitting-room floor the fuse-box began to fizz again, but she ignored it, leading Jess upstairs, hugging her.

'What's happening?' asked Jessica miserably. 'Did Tom do something?'

'No, no . . . I think Tom's slept through it all, so's Jack.' She could hear the kitchen door being unbolted, unlocked, and Oliver come crashing into the room. Should she – no. Robert could cope with anything. They had reached the turn in the stairs, and climbed to the landing, where Frances, in her pale pyjamas, stood leaning up against the wall like someone about to faint. Claire

177

reached for her hand. She led both of them, Frances and Jessica, along the corridor, leaving Jess in her own room, taking Frances back to hers, putting her back into bed as if she, too, were a child.

'Stay there,' she said. 'I'll get you a brandy.'

'Oliver . . .' said Frances, reaching for her cigarettes.

'Robert will deal with Oliver. And don't set the house on fire, that's all we need.'

Frances put the cigarettes down and lay back against the pillows. 'I'm sorry. I'm sorry.'

'Sssh. Thank God the boys haven't woken.' Claire went out, back to Jess, who had buried her head beneath the bedclothes, then crept to the top of the stairs, where she stood listening to the voices of the men below.

Oliver was sitting slumped on the edge of the sofa, his head in his hands, shivering. For the second time in a week Robert was sitting with him in the middle of the night, though he felt only like going back to bed. He stayed out of duty: towards Oliver, in a mess; towards Frances, who needed protection from all this, even if she had somehow caused it.

Oliver, however, did not want to talk. Too drunk to think about keys and ways into the house in darkness, he was shaken by his own fury, exhausted.

'I'll sleep down here,' he said.

'All right.' Robert cast about, wondering where. The sofa was much too small, but there was nowhere else, since he, presumably, would be sleeping in Jessica's room again. He sighed, and went off to look for blankets, meeting Claire coming quietly down.

'What's going on?' she whispered.

'Not a lot – he's going to sleep down here. Is Jess okay?'

'More or less.'

'Frances?'

'In a state. Where's the brandy?'

'On the kitchen table. Have we got any extra blankets?'

'In the cupboard in Jess's room. We sound like a couple of school matrons.' Claire began to giggle, and then she began to cry.

'Sssh,' said Robert. 'Sssh. It's all right, we're still here.'

'It's *not* all right – this is appalling. How are we going to get through this holiday?'

'Tomorrow is another day.'

Claire looked at him. 'Sometimes,' she said, 'you are a complacent fool.'

'Thanks. It was, if I may say so, you who wanted to ask these people. I did say – '

'Oh, shut up!'

From the sitting-room they could hear Oliver, starting to pace.

'Oh, help me – ' said Claire, and sat down on the stairs very suddenly, very white.

Robert went for the brandy. She drank, and he took her upstairs and put her to bed with Jessica.

'Frances – ' she said, sinking on to the pillows.

'All right, all right.'

He went along the corridor, and knocked at the door.

'Yes?'

She was hunched up in bed like a child, her arms round her knees.

'Oliver's going to sleep downstairs.' He held out the brandy enquiringly. 'Want some?'

She shook her head. 'No, thanks. I'm so sorry – '

'These things happen.'

She looked at him gratefully. 'But they shouldn't.'

'Never mind. See you in the morning.'

Frances nodded, and buried her face in her knees. He left her, and went downstairs again; he put Oliver to bed on the sitting-room floor, laying out sofa cushions, covering him with blankets. And then he went into Jessica's room and crawled into bed, falling almost at once into a deep sleep, though not before he suddenly remembered that when they were woken by that frenzied banging on the kitchen door he had been dreaming of Frances, weeping.

Upstairs, Tom lay wide awake in soaking-wet bedclothes. He shifted about, cold and uncomfortable, but he did not dare to get out of bed and in the end, feeling his legs give a funny sort of twitch and jerk, he fell asleep again, like Jack, who on the other side of the room looked completely ordinary, just as usual, as though nothing could ever happen to him.

179

In her room at the end of the corridor, Frances smoked a cigarette and waited until everything was quiet; and then, as the church clock chimed twice, indicating what could be any hour, she put her arms round her pillow and began to drift towards the longed-for embrace of sleep, searching for Dora.

In bed with Jessica, with the light still burning, Claire put her arms round her daughter and shut her eyes, trying to forget the fear she had felt, moving about in the darkness, listening to all that rage. She tried, but she could not. She lay awake for a long time, fighting not only the fear she had felt then but a feeling that grew out of it, which not so long ago she would have dismissed as hysterical and neurotic: that it was possible, in the tension rising all around her, that something truly terrible might happen on this holiday.

7

'I owe you all an apology.' Oliver, at the dining-room door, looked and sounded well in control again, observing them all as they had breakfast late, tired and dishevelled. They had come down in ones and twos, Claire first, taking tea through to Robert in Jessica's room, opening the shutters on to the dense greenery outside the window.

'How's Oliver?' he muttered, rolling over.

'I wouldn't know – he's not about.'

The bed on the floor had been taken up, cushions replaced on the sofa, the blankets folded and put on a chair. The doors to the terrace were open.

'Probably gone for a swim,' said Robert.

And he obviously had: standing in the doorway now he looked fresher than any of them, his hair damp, his skin clear, a towel flung round his shoulders. Jessica, spooning sugar on to her cornflakes, looked up at him and looked away; sugar fell on the tablecloth.

'Careful,' said Claire, beside her. 'Well,' she said to him, feeling her way, aiming for ordinariness, for the children's sake, 'how is the river this morning?'

'I haven't been to the river, only up to the pool.' Oliver did not come in any further, and he did not meet her eyes; he did not look directly at any of them, and most particularly not at Frances, who sat next to Tom, sipping coffee as though there were nothing else she might ever want to do.

'And I do apologise,' he went on, addressing the air above their heads. 'I must have frightened you all, especially the children.'

'We're all in one piece,' said Robert. 'Come and sit down.'

But Oliver said, 'I'll join you in a minute,' in a tone which to Claire announced clearly that he was still in no mood to be told what to do by anyone, and he went out again: they could hear him going through the kitchen and outside, to hang up his towel on the line by the water tank.

'What happens when you're drunk?' asked Jack.

'I'll tell you another time.' Robert reached for the coffeepot, finding it empty.

Frances pushed back her chair. 'I'll make some more.'

'Are you sure? I don't mind . . .'

'You've done more than enough, already,' she said, coming round the table to pick it up, and she slowly left the room.

Robert and Claire exchanged glances. Beside Jessica, Tom began to make noises, fiddling with his cereal spoon. Across the table, Jack began to imitate him, clearing his throat, clicking his tongue.

'Jack . . .' said Claire, but Tom seemed not to notice, and watching him she felt there was something which could not be accounted for only by fatigue and wet beds: despite the intrusive noises he seemed distant and withdrawn – she realised that she wanted to click her fingers at him, to check he was all there.

'Tom? Are you okay?' He stopped fiddling with his spoon, but didn't answer. 'Tom?'

'What?'

'Are you feeling all right?'

'Yes.' He sounded surprised. Rising voices came from the kitchen; he slid off his chair.

Robert said quickly: 'Shall we go and let the hens out, Tom?'

'I want to let them out,' said Jack. 'Why should he do it?'

But Tom, stumbling and then regaining his balance, was already out of the door, making his way towards the kitchen, and the voices.

Claire made to follow him.

'Leave it,' said Robert. 'What can we do?'

'Answer me,' said Oliver. 'Answer!'

He was standing with his back to the entrance from the corridor, his arms outstretched across the door, blocking escape, so that Tom, coming up from behind, could see only this towering back view of his father, and nothing at all of his mother, who stood in the middle of the room, clasping the coffeepot, absolutely still.

'Answer!'

'I can't. I can't talk to you when you're like this . . .'

'And how do you expect me to be?'

The room, as always, smelled faintly, sourly, of Calor gas. I shall come down here when everyone is asleep, thought Frances, locking herself away from this voice, this fury. I shall come down and turn on every switch on that stove and seal up every crack.

Oliver made a move towards her. She stepped away and put down the coffeepot, next to the stove; she lifted the thin aluminium kettle and went to the sink to fill it; she put it back on the stove, and picked up the box of matches and pushed it open and they all fell on to the floor.

'Leave them. Leave them! Look at me.'

'No.' She bent down, her hands shaking, trying to scoop them up. 'Go away,' she said, straightening up again, the box half full, the matches all at angles, sticking out like little bones. 'I'll talk to you, but not now. Please.' She turned to the stove and lit the burner beneath the kettle, shook out the match, dropping it into the saucer, and shut her eyes, willing him to leave her. Footsteps came swiftly and heavily towards her: she saw herself lie broken, and her hands flew up to her mouth, but the footsteps went past her, and the door to the sunlit steps beneath the vines was flung open, battered from where it had been beaten upon last night and now slammed shut so hard that pieces of paint flew off it, on to the floor.

Frances stood quite still until she could no longer hear him, running away down the steps to the garden, and then she opened her eyes. She waited for the kettle to boil, rinsing out the coffeepot, swirling the grounds away, and then she made fresh coffee, and carried it out and down the corridor, by which time Tom, who had pressed back into the shadows at the bottom of the stairs, had carefully opened the door to the cellar, and gone down.

The towering shape in the corner did not move, and the head was hidden beneath the hat, but he knew that it had grown a face and was watching him, and he breathed fast, his heart banging and his knees trembling as he crossed the dusty floor, well away from it. The slam of the kitchen door was still in his head, mixing up with the banging last night and the shouting: it was like the tuning fork they'd been shown when he was still in the reception class, that went on and on. The girl sitting next to him in the circle on the floor had wanted to hear it again, and they'd heard it again, and then again, and everyone thought it was wicked, but he, as it hummed above him, had covered his ears. He hadn't thought about that for a long time, funny to think of it now, in a foreign country. Twaaaang, baaaang, twaaaang. Something was happening in his head again – nothing to do with the lid, which was helping, actually, keeping the noises down, but he didn't like it.

Still, he was safe down here, all shut away, like the pig. That made a funny noise, too, grunting and snorting in the dark. Twang, bang; not quite so loud now. Good. Now – where was the house?

He found the passage, and the cupboard. He stepped inside and drew the house towards him. Dust had settled since the last time and he blew it softly away, surprising himself – he hadn't known he could be so quiet. Then he opened the front, and the lid in his head opened too, but not much, and he forgot about it, anyway, looking through all the rooms again. It was clever, making something like this, he wished he was good at making things. Perhaps he could make some people to live here, and some furniture or something. It was sad seeing such a beautiful place all empty.

Tom bent down, and looked on the shelf below. There was the box of chisels and screwdrivers, and the nice little saw, and there was a box of left-over bits of wood. He looked through them, sorting out sizes. A big piece, a medium-size piece, and a little piece. He held them all in his hand.

Now then, what about furniture? A thick square shape for a table, that was easy. He put down the family: they lay there as if they were dead. He put the table in the middle of the great big room, and found some little round bits for chairs, and arranged them nicely. They'd need some food, but he could bring that down later, pieces of bread and stuff. Of course, he didn't have to feed them, not if he didn't want to. He could do anything he liked with them, starve them to death if he wanted. Now then, where were they going to sleep?

He picked them up again, and walked them up the stairs, one by

184

one. Tap tap tap of wood on wood. Tap tap tap along the corridor. Where should they go?

Above him floorboards were creaking, and he could hear footsteps, then voices. 'Tom? Tom! Now where's he got to?' He went absolutely still and invisible. You could do anything you wanted if you were invisible, take all the food off people's plates or kill someone, and no one would ever know who it was. The footsteps went away, and the voices went quieter. Good.

Now, then. Three bedrooms. Three people in the family, so they could have one each. He walked them in, one by one, and laid each of them down. How did that look? Lonely and sad. Put them all together, but that wasn't right, families didn't ever all sleep together. Put them as they were now, then: the little piece in one room, and the big piece and the medium-size piece in another, and why didn't that feel right? He picked up the big piece, and began to feel afraid. How could you be afraid of a bit of wood, a stick, almost? Things like this, dead things, hadn't got power, had they?

'Tom!' That was Frances. He wanted to call out, to tell her where he was, but he didn't want anyone to know he was here, not even her. So he waited until she had gone away, guessing she was outside now, and then he put down the big piece of wood, just left it on the landing, not with anyone, and shut up the house at the front and went out of the cupboard, shutting that up, too. Click, click, click. Doors and lids on everything.

And across the cellar, panting with fear as he passed the shape, because that was real, he couldn't make that be nothing, it was too big, and then up the stairs to the door, flicking the light off, going out quietly, as if he'd just been to the toilet or something.

Somehow they got through the day.

Guida came: that helped. She arrived soon after Tom re-appeared, saying he'd been outside with the hens. No one believed him, but no one had the energy for questions, and anyway, what did it matter? He was here. And here was Guida, visibly hungover but full of smiles, shrugging about the power cut, indicating it had happened before, bringing luridly coloured little cards for the children.

'*Nossa Senhora*,' she said, presenting them. 'From the fiesta.'

They stared at swirling bright blue robes, uplifted faces, crimson hearts in a sunburst of bleeding rays.

'*Obrigada*, Guida.'

They took them away.

'What do we do with them?' asked Jack, out on the terrace.

'Go and put them somewhere,' said Claire feebly. 'Where's Frances?'

No one knew.

'Are they stickers?' Jack turned them over. 'They've got glue on.' He licked, cautiously. 'Ugh.'

'I shouldn't,' said Robert, watching. 'It's probably made of Third World chemicals and will kill you. Go on, put it down. Now then, who's for a swim?'

They ran to fetch their things from the line, leaving the cards to curl in the sun.

Claire said to Robert, 'I'm sorry I was foul last night.'

'You weren't foul. Anyway, let's forget it now.'

She gave him a look, as last night. 'Robert – you can't always just skate over everything, you know.'

He looked back at her. 'That's enough. Stop telling me how to behave.'

'But – '

'For now. Please.'

She took a breath. 'All right. Let's deal with today, then. Do you think we should try and go somewhere? On an outing, or something.'

'Where?'

'Well . . .' She cast about. 'We could go to the cathedral . . .' She tailed off, seeing his face.

'A carload of over-emotional people in the heat. Tom throwing up. Jessica sulking. Oliver and Frances – '

'No. You're right. Not today.'

'Thank you,' he said. 'Keep it simple. For Christ's sake keep it simple. Let them unwind. Let us all unwind.'

'Where's Oliver?' asked Jessica, returning, her towel round her shoulders.

'Gone for a walk.' Claire stretched out her hand. 'We're going to have a quiet day, after – well, after the fiesta, and everything.'

'Okay.' She sounded indifferent.

'Right.' Robert got to his feet as the boys appeared. 'See you all up at the pool.'

'Where're you going?' asked Jack.

'I'm going to see a man about a dog.'

'What?' He turned to Claire. 'What's he talking about?'

'It's just an expression.' Claire looked at Robert. 'Where *are* you going?'

'Just checking,' he said. 'Go on, off you go.'

'Stop bossing *me* about,' she said; but they went, down the steps to the garden, freckled with sunlight, where the hens, let out by Guida on her arrival, were wandering hopefully, scratching the earth. Robert stood watching as Claire and Jack, Tom trailing behind, slowly crossed to the other flight of steps, climbing to the upper path to the pool. Glimpses of bare shoulder moved along the vines, voices grew fainter; after a few moments he heard the first splash. He went back into the house.

Guida had washed up the breakfast things and was sweeping the sitting-room. The coarse yellow broom went back and forth, crossing enormous slabs of sun from the open doors, moving into the shadows; dust and sand and breadcumbs lay in soft heaps on the boards. She looked up at Robert and smiled; they both began to laugh.

'Good dancing,' she said.

'Very good.'

The door to the dining-room was half open; he could see Frances, sitting at the table, smoking. A Dutch interior, he thought, remembering a print in the hall of his mother's house in Maidenhead. Give or take a cigarette, give or take a mood. The little servant girl in a broad cool room, a woman glimpsed deeper, through a further door, tranquil, alone. But this woman wasn't tranquil.

He knocked on the door. Guida, behind him, moved out on to the terrace and began to sweep there. Swish swish swish in the sun over the tiles.

'Frances?'

'Yes?' She looked up, elbows on the check cotton tablecloth, coffee and cigarettes beside her. This early in the day the shutters

187

were open, and the window, too, at the top; smoke rose into the air and went drifting out through the gap.

'How are you?'

'All right.' She looked away again, sitting more still than any painting.

'Do you want to talk?'

'No.' There was a pause, then she began to smoke again. 'Where's Tom?'

'Up at the pool with the others. With Claire.'

'Okay.' Another pause. 'Oliver?'

'Oliver isn't back yet,' he said. 'Well . . . See you later.'

'See you,' said Frances, and did not move.

Tom who had returned, and was listening by the coat-stand, heard Robert coming towards the door again. He went quickly out to the terrace.

Jessica sat on the edge of the pool, watching the mountain road. The bullock cart creaked past, carrying pine logs; a bike went up and a van came down, and apart from that there was no traffic at all. It grew hotter; Claire went indoors for drinks, telling her to watch the boys; she came out again with a tray and called them all down to the table on the path beneath the vines for lemonade with ice in it, but Jessica stayed where she was, with her sunhat on.

And at last she saw him, coming out of the gap between the bushes a bit further down the road, where there was a path leading up to the mountain. That was where the hungry stray dog had come from, chasing after the old woman the afternoon soon after they'd arrived. They'd had the whole pool to themselves then, the whole afternoon.

He was walking up the road towards her: she waved and called. He looked at her, and she knew he could see her, but he didn't wave back, he just came on, with his lovely walk. She waved again, and this time he moved his hand, but that wasn't a wave, it was more as if he was flicking something away. She swallowed. Surely he couldn't mean to wave like that, surely he couldn't. She didn't know what to do; her hand dropped to the hot surface of the poolside and she sat picking at loose crumbs of concrete, her feet in the water, the sun beating down upon her legs.

He drew nearer, coming on towards her, still on the other side of the road, the shady side.

'Hello.' She turned her face towards him, trying to smile as she usually smiled, but it felt stiff, and her stomach was full of butterflies.

'Hello,' he replied, as if he was talking to a stranger, just someone he happened to pass. He walked on, along to the upper gate, pushing it open. She heard him come down the first flight of steps, past the water tank, and then stop, as if he wasn't quite sure what to do next, and then he must have seen her mother and the boys; she could hear his footsteps along the path between the vines, and she willed him to come on, to nod curtly to the others and come to her, the one he was looking for, but he didn't, he stopped at the table. She heard him pull out a chair and sit down; she could hear the boring rise and fall of adult voices, his and her mother's, who surely had nothing to say to him, and she wanted to get up and go there, just to be with him, but she wouldn't, she wouldn't, she'd wait and see.

Somehow they got through the day.

Guida stayed: that helped. She swept and dusted, and washed the kitchen floor and cleaned the cooker; she piled up books and papers, put clothes to soak in the water tank and went home for lunch, leaving the house looking fresh and cared for. The families had their lunch in the dining-room, with the shutters closed. No one talked much, but everyone made an effort, solicitously passing bread and cheese and wine, making sure the children had what they wanted, rallying when Robert suggested memory games.

'I went on holiday and packed my bag, and in my bag I put . . .'

'A toothbrush,' said Claire.

'A toothbrush and a pair of pyjamas,' said Robert.

'A toothbrush, a pair of pyjamas and a chess set,' said Jessica, looking at Oliver.

'A toothbrush, a pair of pyjamas, a chess set and a book,' said Oliver, slicing more bread.

'A toothbrush, a pair of pyjamas, a chess set, a . . . a book? A book, and a bucket and spade,' said Jack.

'Frances?'

'What?'

'Your turn.'

'Sorry. I went on holiday and packed my bag, and in my bag I put . . . a toothbrush, a pair of pyjamas, a chess set, a bucket and spade – no, a book, and a bucket and spade, and a letter.'

'A letter,' said Robert, wondering.

She picked up her cigarettes.

'Tom?'

'What?'

'What did you pack in your bag?' asked Claire.

'What bag?'

Afterwards, clearing away, Jessica said to Oliver: 'Will you play chess with me later?'

'I'll see,' said Oliver, and her heart lifted: he hadn't said no, he'd said he'd see. She carried the tray to the kitchen and started the washing-up, to save Guida, because she thought it was the kind of thing he'd approve of. The door was open; afternoon sun fell on to the freshly washed floor, the bubbles in the sink shone in the light. She put clean plates in the wooden rack, feeling like her mother, trying to feel like herself. Had Oliver seen her, helping? Where had he gone?

Guida returned, and climbed the stairs to the landing. She set up the ironing-board and plugged in the iron; the house was filled with the smell of clean clothes being pressed, with the hiss and cloudy puffs of steam. Everyone went to rest, in an atmosphere which felt calmer, soothed: Claire and Robert in their room, the boys in theirs, Frances in hers, where she lay on top of the freshly made bed and went through her letter, line by line. Jessica, down in her own room, did not close the shutters, because the creeper at the window made the room shady and dark already. She lay watching the shadows of the leaves on the wall, listening to her tape, wondering how long she could leave it before she went out to the terrace, where Oliver was on the swing-seat, looking at maps, rocking, lying stretched out. She had set up the chessboard on the desk in the corner of the sitting-room because that was a cool place, near the tall window, away from everyone, so they could concentrate. Every piece was in its right place, all ready to play.

I'll send you all my dreams, every day in a le-etter . . .

She yawned. Perhaps, when the holiday was over, they would write to each other. Perhaps it was easier to write things than say them. *Dear Oliver . . .* What should she say?

I don't want to say goodbye for the summer/but I'll fill the emptiness . . .

She closed her eyes, and began to go through every moment they had spent together, starting at the beginning, with the first day, when she had come up the steps to the terrace and seen them all standing there, just arrived, with their luggage everywhere, and he smiling at her as Claire introduced them all, holding out his hand as if meeting a grown-up, saying 'How do you do' in his beautiful voice. Had she known, even then? It felt as if she had always known, though she didn't understand how someone who could be so nice could be so frightening, too. What had happened yesterday? Why had he been like that?

Darling, I promise you this . . .

The song was growing louder, as music sometimes did before you fell asleep, as the voices of her parents used to in the car, when she was small and going to sleep in the back. She yawned again, pulling her hair, which felt all warm, across her face, and fell asleep, as Oliver, out on the terrace, traced with his fingers the outline of contours on the map, and worked out where he should go.

Guida went home, leaving piles of neatly pressed and sorted clothes on the deep landing window-sill.

'Tomorrow,' said Claire, over tea on the upper path, 'Robert and I thought we'd go into town again – we're getting rather low in the larder.' She handed out mugs and glasses. 'Anyone else like to come?'

'I'd planned to go walking,' said Oliver, 'if no one objects.'

'Where?' asked Jessica, fiddling with her beads.

'As far as the eye can see,' he said, sounding more friendly again. He indicated the ridge beyond the village. 'There are other villages, there's another valley. I need to see a bit more, I need the exercise . . .'

'Do you need to be by yourself?' asked Jack. 'Mum says people do, sometimes.'

191

'All right, Jack.' Claire looked at Frances, lighting a cigarette. 'Would you look after the children?' she asked her. 'If they don't want to come into town.'

'Of course.'

'I don't want to come,' said Jessica. 'Oliver? After tea will you play chess with me?'

'I'll see.'

But he didn't, though she sat by the board and waited, pretending to work out moves.

'How do you play?' asked Jack.

'Go away. Please, Jack. Please.'

She sat there after tea, and she sat there after supper, hoping and hoping, but he didn't come, he stayed out talking to her father, looking at the boring boring map, while Frances and Claire put the boys to bed and she was left all by herself.

Oliver left next morning at eight, wanting to get going before the heat. Trying to feel like a proper group, almost succeeding, they all went to see him off at the garden gate, watching and waving as he walked away down the road. He was going to make a circle, crossing the river at a bridge a mile or so further on, climbing the first ridge of mountains on the far side, down into the next valley, then up again and round, walking along the top of the ridge that ran to the right of the house. He would come home through the pine woods and down by the path from where Jessica had seen him emerge yesterday morning.

He was going to walk for miles and miles, about twenty, he said. She couldn't imagine anyone walking so far, or even wanting to, when it was so hot. Why did he have to go? She didn't know what to say, except goodbye.

'Goodbye, then,' he said to them all, not to anyone in particular, not to her. He was wearing his straw hat, old cotton trousers and a T-shirt, carrying a canvas shoulder-bag with drink and map and apples. He looked wonderful, tall and fit, and she wanted to run after him, ask if she could come too, to have them all watch her going away with him, jealous because it was she whom he had chosen, but instead it wasn't at all like that, it was miserable, going back into the garden with everyone else and a pointless empty day ahead.

'Are you sure you wouldn't like to come with us?' Claire asked, as they went up into the house for breakfast, and Robert and Jack went to let out the hens. For a moment Jessica hesitated, thinking perhaps that would fill up the time, and be better than hanging around with the boys, but then she thought Oliver might change his mind, or get tired, and come back early, and she didn't want to be stuck with her parents doing boring shopping when he might want to talk to her, so she shook her head.

'No thanks.' Beside them, Tom was making his noises. 'Oh, do stop it,' she said crossly.

'Jess . . .' Claire looked at her reproachfully. Whatever else this holiday, Jess had not been bothered by Tom, it was only Jack who needed watching. Well – Jess had hardly been around the boys anyway, had she?

'It gets on my nerves,' she said now, as Tom went wandering into the dining-room, where Frances was putting out cereal bowls. '*Why* does he make those noises?'

'I don't know,' said Claire, 'but if it really gets on your nerves do come with us – we'd love to have you.'

'I've *said*.' Jessica looked stubborn. 'I've said I don't want to.'

'Okay, okay.'

Through the open dining-room door Claire could see Tom following Frances round the table, putting out a handful of spoons she had given him, one by one. How nice. How nice and companionable and ordinary for him, and how rare. Well – perhaps it would be a good day for them all, Frances clearly more at ease now Oliver had gone. And now there were hours for her and Robert to be by themselves for once, to take their time in the market, to have lunch together and make it up. All the anxiety she had grown used to feeling fell away at the prospect: what a treat.

'I want to come with you,' said Jack, coming in from the terrace.

'Oh, Jack . . .'

He pulled at her, whispering. 'I don't want to stay here with her.'

'Oh, Jack . . .' Oh, dear. 'Where's Dad?'

'Here,' said Robert, coming in too.

'I want to talk to you.'

In the end they persuaded Jack to stay, feeling a mixture of guilt and relief as they drove away, waving, soon after ten.

'After all,' said Claire, turning from the window, 'it really won't do him any harm to be away from Mummy's side for a little while. Sometimes I do worry that he's too attached.' She turned for a last look through the back as they rounded the bend by the butcher's shop, seeing the little group up by the gate in the beating sun, still waving, Tom holding his mother's hand, Jessica standing well apart, Jack visibly saddened. Well, it was only a few hours.

'Can you see Oliver anywhere?' Robert asked, as they came out of the village and crossed the bridge. They scanned the view, but could not see him, only the great stretch of valley and mountain beneath the burning sky.

Already the river – not their river, but a tributary – was a long way below him, a gently winding thread of blue, intermittently obscured by trees. This valley was of a different nature to the one they had grown familiar with: he was looking down now not on pine and eucalyptus woods but upon a sweeping corrugation of terraces, bordered with drystone walls. The mountain road had been cut a few hundred yards above the lowest terrace; clumps of oak trees had been planted at intervals all the way down the slope below. This, he knew from one of the books he had found in the house, was cork oak, functional, like the eucalyptus, but less erosive. The terraces themselves were mostly bare and uncultivated: where once crops had grown there was now only grazing down near the river and here, halfway up the ridge, parched earth. A few were still planted, with pumpkins and damson trees, but mostly what he was looking at was evidence of a retreat from the land.

He thought of the young couples who appeared now and then in the village, coming to visit the place of their childhood in their shiny suits and shiny cars, driving all the way back to Oporto, even as far south as Lisbon. Whereas in Ireland they would have gone across the water, here they were emigrants in their own country, working as chemists, lawyers, teachers, anything but farmers. It was only the old who remained on the land, working

194

on their tiny squares of maize and on the vines, fattening a pig, subsisting.

It was growing very hot; the map showed a stream near here, and a path. He was making for a hamlet, perched beneath the summit, powered, he had read, like most of the dwellings high up the mountain, by solar panels. He wanted to have a look at them; was curious to see what it might be like to live up here. More than either of these reasons for coming, he wanted distraction.

The heat, in itself, was that: already he had taken off his shirt, and hung it across his shoulders as protection. Sweat ran into his eyes; he wiped his face every few yards, searching for the stream, and here at last it was, bubbling from rocks above, coursing down towards him. He stopped gratefully, splashing himself, drinking, letting it run over his face and head, standing up again, dripping and refreshed. A baptism. He ran his hands through his soaking hair. Baptism cleansed and washed away sin, which Robert had so curiously said he believed in. And so do I, thought Oliver, but that is less curious: a fucked-up Catholic would.

He could see the path now, a baked cart track running from one of the upper terraces to the hamlet, and down again to the distant road; he could see, too, the shining solar panels set alongside: large rectangles, criss-crossed with mesh, upturned to the open sky. It was hard not to expect to hear a humming as he approached them, but there was no hum, and the hamlet, when he entered it, was silent.

On its threshold stood a little shrine: a cave of piled-up rocks, with a plaster Virgin, much smaller than the one used in the fiesta, set within, plastic roses laid at her feet. He didn't want to think about the fiesta, or the events which had followed it, and he looked beyond the shrine to a ragged cluster of stone houses, roofed in weather-beaten tiles, set along a narrow cobbled street. It was barely mid-morning, but already the shutters were closed: except for a few trees, blown out to the side by winter gales, there was otherwise no protection from the sun. There were no geraniums on balconies, no little brown bird in a cage. This place, perhaps two thousand feet above the river, felt deserted, abandoned: who could bear to live up here?

Oliver walked slowly over the cobbles, seeing with relief at the far end of the street a stiff old man loading a cart with cabbages. Between the rails a drooling bullock blinked away flies. Well. If there were cabbages there must be gardens, brave and exposed, with crops for market, watered from the pump he could see near the cart, fed by the stream. Life, somehow, went on. The shutters were closed, but some of the doors stood open, hung with plastic strip curtains; outside one of them a dog was curled up asleep, flea-bitten, dull-coated, thin. There were dogs like this everywhere in their own village, but this one seemed somehow different, though until he drew closer he couldn't work out why. Then, at his approach, it raised its head and he saw: its neck was ringed in spikes.

They were there for the animal's protection – but against what? There were no wolves any longer; what might come prowling along here at night, ready to kill? Whatever it might be, the effect of the spikes was threatening and disturbing, and meeting the eyes in that long mongrel face, with its cruel-looking frame, he hesitated, and stopped.

Slowly, the dog rose to its feet, seeing a stranger; he growled. Oliver felt the sweat on his back grow cold and he looked away. The old man at the end of the street had his back to them: if he called out – and what should he call? – it might provoke more than growling. He could hold out his fist for the animal to smell, but that gesture, too, might be misinterpreted. So he stood, without moving a muscle, looking about him, and then the plastic curtain in the doorway was pushed aside, and an old bent woman came out, carrying a basket. She looked at the dog – '*O que éque tens*?' – and then at Oliver. He moved forward, raising his straw hat.

'*Bom dia.*'

'*Bom dia.*' She looked at him with a sharp inquisitiveness much as the dog had done; at her command he retreated to the step, still watchful. She and Oliver regarded each other; he pulled out his map and gestured at its folded pages, and at the mountains beyond; he smiled in reassurance, and the old woman nodded. Side by side they went along the street, she in cracked and flattened shoes, in widow's black, with eggs in her basket, calling to the old fellow loading the cart. He looked at Oliver with slow-witted curiosity, took the basket of eggs from the woman and put it

196

carefully into the cart, then stood staring after Oliver as he walked out of the village.

The cart track wound away towards the mountain road below; he was crossing stony ground now, broken by tufts of coarse grass. Up ahead was the ridge he was making for, strewn with boulders. On the other side was his own valley: a long, exposed climb lay before him, but then he would come down among trees again, the familiar dense plantations giving shade. He put the map back in his bag and began the ascent, turning every now and then to look down upon the diminishing village and the bullock cart making its slow way down along the track between the terraces, towards the road.

Like his gesture with the hat, the scene was something from another age; there might be twentieth-century solar panels up here, but everything else felt medieval: a remote mountain village where travel was by cart, where hungry wolves once roamed and where a scrawny dog still wore a vicious-looking collar.

It was a long time since Oliver had felt afraid, as he had done at the sight of those spikes, hearing that growl. He had forgotten what fear felt like. He wanted to forget it now, among many other things, not least the fact that in the last forty-eight hours what had most frightened him had been himself. He had come on this walk for distraction; he began to climb higher, panting, pouring with sweat.

The ground was stony and hard. Beetles and little clambering creatures moved through occasional clumps of fern and leggy heather, but there were no birds, no cicadas, no trees. The sun beat down from a sky of cloudless blue; his legs were beginning to tremble, but he climbed on, forcing himself not to give in, to reach the top of the ridge without stopping, thinking of nothing but the next few steps, the next scattering of rocks or boulders. There was only the climb, the summit.

He reached it at last. A rough plain of barren earth and sun-browned grass, criss-crossed with low stone walls, stretched out before him as he stood there gasping. Good walking land, harsh and unyielding farmland, though people had, clearly, once farmed up here in these little fields, as they had cultivated the terraces below. He drew out his bottle of water and drank and drank, walked on a little, looking around. He was higher than he had ever been: stretched out on either side was a panorama of mountain and valley, of bare rock, tumbling terraces, clumps of woodland, isolated villages. Here and there the river gleamed, here and there a speck of traffic crept along the winding road; he was far above all of it, with this bare and lonely place, this view, this moment.

He looked at his watch: just after one, he'd done well, and from now on the going was easy. He would sit down in the pine woods and have a rest and something to eat, before he began the long walk home.

Not home. Back. Beautiful as it was, he could not see the house as anything more than a place where people were staying, and at present he felt not so much as a thread of connection with any of them. Frances and Tom he could not bear to think about, although he knew he must; the Murrays, virtual strangers until this holiday, pleasant and kind as they were, he could contemplate since the other night only with embarrassment. As for the children: Jack was too painful a contrast to Tom; it was Jessica, alone among the whole group, whose company he had found enjoyable: bright, pretty, easy, while his own child so distressed him.

No, don't think about it. Keep walking. Walking was better than drinking, better than thinking. But thinking was what he was used to, books and thought were his work, his life, and as he stepped over one of the low stone walls an elegant little sentence came up from nowhere, again from another, but more recent age: *Forgive me – I am not myself*. It spoke of courtesy and formality, qualities he had always valued; it indicated a self that was used to being in control, running things smoothly; it reassured: this state of affairs is only temporary. He had not been himself the other night – furious, murderous, beating on the door in the dark. That was not a self he recognised.

Forgive me – I am not . . . It also implicitly asked for comfort, that little phrase. It looked for someone else to run things smoothly for a while while the door of the sickroom was gently closed, and the patient rested. He was used neither to behaving as he had done nor to asking for such things. He was used to – what was he used to? He wasn't used to anything any more: in the last

198

few years everything in his life had changed. *Forgive me – I am . . .* Who was he? Where did he belong?

He had come to the end of the level ground; almost without noticing he had reached a depression from where he could look down again upon the valley he knew. He could see – just – the tiny white spire of the church, and the village below; he could see – just – the house, far up on the climbing road.

He did not want to see the house. He did not want to go back. Not only because he was relishing the physical challenge of the walk itself, as he had known he would; not only because there was no one there he wanted to talk to. It was because, in this free and wandering solitude, he was beginning to feel able to discard things in himself recently discovered and much disliked, as though, like Peter Pan, he had peeled off his dark shadow and left it behind. The house contained that shadow now: irritation, frustration, anger, violence. Here he might try to rediscover the person he had once thought himself to be: formal and reticent, yes, but capable of warmth and generosity, capable of love. Might he do that? Might that be possible? He felt, and had felt for a long time, a very long way from any impulse which might be graced by the name of love. *Neither the love of man, nor the love of God . . .* And where did those words come from? Somewhere in a youth or childhood where faith, or loss of faith, had seemed to be everything.

He had left the bare and rocky mountaintop behind; he was walking amongst the pines. I am trying to cast out demons, he thought, looking down at the sharp needles beneath his feet; that is a biblical phrase, and is, surely, an impulse which must be called religious – to cast out demons, to look for the goodness within. Where is the goodness left in me?

The needles abruptly came to an end. He could smell charred wood, and he looked up to see that he had come to burnt-out land, a place where a forest fire had raged. Blackened tree trunks stood skeletal and bare above others which had fallen; the ground itself was black, heaped here and there with grey ash, brown branches. It stretched silently for perhaps a quarter of a mile, bleak and devastated, and walking through it, trying to get out of it, Oliver thought, perhaps this is how I am, or how I shall become – burnt-out, godless, lifeless.

199

It came to an end at last. At some point the fire had consumed itself and died; he was back amongst living trees again, the smell of resin and sun-warmed earth.

But he was still a long way up the mountain, the ground scattered here and there with small rocks and stones, a long way from the path which would lead him down again. It was still very quiet, and deep in the forest there was no longer a view to distract him, or erase a rising despair. I am unloved and unloving, he thought . . . *and there is no health in me*. That is from the Confession. Of whom, if there is such a thing as sin, should I ask forgiveness? Who might ask forgiveness of me?

A faint, animal sound disturbed the quietness: he stopped, and looked round, but could see nothing. I said to Robert that I believed in the search, he thought, walking on again. I was talking about God, but let us forget about God for a while. I can continue to pursue abstractions or I can search for real answers to these questions. I can search my child, who does not seem to be my child; I can search my wife, who no longer seems to be my wife, who is remote, distracted. I can try again to confront her, search out her own demons – but when I do, mine threaten to destroy us both. What am I to do? How should I be?

The sound came again; he stopped again. Something was padding over the pine needles, sniffing about, growing closer. As in the hamlet, seeing the dog with its collar of spikes get to its feet and growl, Oliver felt a ripple of fear run through him, and then the sounds grew louder as whatever it was caught his scent and increased its speed, and he suddenly saw what it was: not one, but several, not wolves but starving dogs, barking and snarling now, as they raced through the trees towards him.

Dora, wrote Frances, following the children back from the river through the maize fields, *everyone else is away today. Oliver has gone walking, Claire and Robert have gone to the market town, so I am in charge of the children. We have spent the morning swimming, as usual, and now we are going back to the house for lunch. It is another hot, beautiful day – we have all forgotten what rain looks like, although I think of you, in London, where perhaps it is pouring now.*

I think of you all the time . . . No. This was not that kind of letter. That kind of letter lay with the envelope sealed, zipped up in her writing case, tucked right at the back of the bottom drawer of the desk. She would post it tomorrow. Perhaps. One more night to sleep on it, and then perhaps. This, now, was an ordinary letter, such as she might send to almost anyone.

The children are all brown and fit. We had one difficult night with Tom, early on, but since then he has been fine . . .

Dora was concerned about Tom. She listened sympathetically to compressed accounts of broken nights and difficult behaviour, was inclined, in fact, to press further, seeking for explanations, while Frances herself made light of it all.

'Our GP says it's a phase . . .'

'Yes, but even so. Living through phases can be hell, can't it?'

'I suppose so.'

They were sitting at a table out in the Covent Garden piazza, just a few minutes' walk from the office. A Friday, people in a good mood, taking long lunches, so that the tables were crowded, but they had managed to find one for two, up at the end near the open space near the buskers. A young couple, he in collarless shirt and waistcoat, she with long, unbrushed hair, were playing the violin and cello: thin, high-speed Mozart spun in and out of clattering dishes and scraped-back chairs and conversation. Dora moved her own chair in a little, to let new arrivals pass, and put out her hand to protect the shrub she'd bought from a stall on the way there to plant in the garden at the weekend. Dora cherished her garden; she cherished her husband and her children, too.

'Did Sophie and Jason go through bad patches?' Frances asked.

'You know they did. When Jason was three I thought I should murder him. I thought I should murder Sophie only yesterday.'

They laughed, but Frances knew that people who really felt like murdering their children did not talk like that, open and easy, making a joke of it. She knew that Dora and kindly Adrian would see their children through anything, and when Dora said now, serious again, 'It must be hard on you both at the moment – must be a struggle for Tom, too, poor chap,' Frances said quickly:

'I'm sure we shall all survive.'

For everything must be seen to be under control, and she, holding back so much, must be seen to be ordinary, capable, coping.

Since no one else in the office had children, and since Frances, dropping off and picking up Tom from the child-minder each day, had little contact with other parents in his class, it was natural that she should spend more time discussing him with Dora than with anyone. She did not want to discuss him. Faced with Dora's directness, with the central place her children had in her life, Frances could feel only a heightened awareness of her own shortcomings and inadequacy as a mother. And anyway –

'Dora?'

'Yes?'

It's not the children I want to talk about, it's you. It's us. What would you say if I told you that I . . .

'Yes?' Dora asked again. She put down her knife and fork and looked at Frances. Her lovely face was receptive, attentive; she stretched out a hand across the table. 'You can tell me,' she said. 'Don't lock it all away. Children can get under your skin like nothing else, it's painful, I know.'

'You make it seem so easy, you're so calm . . .'

'Frances – we all try to seem calm. Please don't be under any illusions. Come on, what is it?'

Frances swallowed. 'It's not – '

They were looking at each other directly. For a moment, just for a flicker, it might have been not as their eyes usually met, with the ordinary warmth of friendship. That was, as usual, all to be seen in Dora's eyes, but Frances nearly – oh, so nearly – allowed into her own an expression which would say everything.

'Nothing,' she said, and looked away. 'Perhaps another time.'

Dora shook her head, smiling in affectionate exasperation. 'You're hopeless. Never mind – you know I'm always here.'

'Yes,' said Frances. 'I know. Coffee?'

'Lovely. I'll get it.' Dora got up, and made her way through the noisy tables to the counter.

In love and fear Frances sat watching her, standing in the queue in her navy jacket with the collar turned up, bag slung on her shoulder, stepping aside for a waiter to pass, smiling at him as she smiled at everyone, sure of herself, relaxed. She watched her taking the two white cups, coming back towards their table, graceful, concentrating, looking at Frances as if to say: I'm here, it's okay, stop worrying, and behind them the thin sounds of Mozart came to an end, and everyone clapped.

The children are all brown and fit . . . It's not the children I want to write about, it's you . . .

The sun beat down upon the field, upon the bare backs of the children, wandering ahead in shorts and sunhats, not talking, wanting their lunch. I shall blow it all apart if I'm not careful, Frances thought, and felt in her bag for her cigarettes, stopping to light one, walking on. Blow it all apart, then – go on, do it, post it, see what happens. No no no.

'Frances?' Jessica had stopped, and was waiting for her. 'D'you think Oliver will be there when we get back?'

She looked at her watch. 'No, I'm sure he won't. It's not even half-past one, he won't be much more than halfway.'

'Oh.' Jessica was silent, walking alongside. Cicadas rasped in the stubble by the ditches, the air was dry, burning.

'I'm thirsty,' said Tom, turning towards them. 'I'm *thirsty!*'

'So am I,' said Jack, but subduedly, as if he felt he shouldn't say it, mustn't complain.

'We've finished the drinks,' said Frances. 'Never mind – we're almost there.'

The field stretching ahead of them looked endless, the path beneath the vines unreachable.

'I feel funny,' said Tom, and stood there, waving at the air as if brushing insects away.

'You'll be better when you've got some food inside you.' She came up beside him, moving him on.

'I'm hungry too,' said Jack.

'And me,' said Jessica, with a little laugh, as if it didn't matter.

'Sorry,' said Frances. 'I should have brought something – well, we should have left the river earlier, shouldn't we?'

None of the children answered; they walked on, their hands straying towards grapes on vines strung between the rows of maize.

'They don't belong to us,' said Frances automatically, as Oliver, also, would have said, and their hands fell back to their sides.

Oh, surely, said Dora, whose children were always provided for. *Surely just a few . . .*

'Oh, go on,' said Frances. 'No one's looking.'

'Thanks.' They tugged off little bunches, and crammed them into their mouths.

'Will Mum and Dad be there when we get back?' asked Jack, as they came at last to the soft and shady path.

She shook her head. 'I shouldn't think so.'

'What time do you think they will be?' His voice sounded high.

'Teatime at the latest,' she said, and put a hand on his shoulder, trying to be kind, but he moved away.

'What time do you think Oliver will get back?' asked Jessica lightly.

Frances sighed. 'About the same time,' she said, dropping her cigarette to the ground, and grinding it out with her heel. 'I'm afraid it's only me for now, you'll just have to put up with it.' The children fell into an uncomfortable silence, broken by Tom making noises. 'It's all right,' she said, more warmly, making an effort, seeing the other two frowning. 'We'll have a nice lunch, and then we can rest. Come on, let's speed up a bit.'

The path came to an end; they walked up through the village, shuttered for the afternoon; they reached the house at last, and Frances took out the key from beneath its stone on the terrace, and opened the big double doors. The children followed her and she tried to make everything nice for them, quickly cutting easy children's tuna sandwiches, nothing elaborate, nothing unfamiliar; but when they all sat down to eat in the shady dining-room she knew they felt strange and uneasy, in a quiet house suddenly much too large and much too empty without the other grown-ups, and she no substitute at all for any of them.

He stood without moving a muscle, and the dogs stopped suddenly, too, in a half-circle just a few feet away from him, heaving, waiting. There were four, no, five of them, and one he recognised: the skeletal creature he had seen on the road one afternoon, following the old woman with her pile of ferns, snarling with hunger. His eyes gleamed yellow, his jaw hung open, drooling; he was small, no bigger than a whippet, but the others around him were huge, great black and tan mongrels whose bones stuck out beneath rough and matted coats. Their skin hung loose, their jaws were heavy; they growled low, tensed and ready to spring.

Oliver did not move, but his heart was pounding, his body flooded with terror. He was liquid, powerless. Then one of the dogs, the largest, took a step forward.

'No!'

The dog growled, horribly, from the depths. Oliver, drenched in cold sweat, looked round, took in properly the scattered stones all round him, and edged towards the nearest. The dog growled again, and his lips drew back; they were all snarling and slobbering now, and then, as he bent down and grabbed a handful of stones, they began to bay, the sound echoing through the pines, and as he stood up and raised his arm they made for him, as a pack.

'Grrrrr!' He leapt into the air, roaring at them like an animal himself. 'Grrrrr!' He flung his handful of stones in a fury. Some of them landed on the ground and pine needles flew into the air, but one or two hit the dogs hard, striking jawbones or bony haunches, and one of them yelped, and skidded aside. He bent down again, scrabbling, grabbing more, bellowing at them.

'Grrrrr! Go on, go away, to hell with you! Grrrrr!'

He hurled the stones, moving towards them, daring them; more stones, more. He hit the big black one hard on the side of the face and it turned, and they all turned then, looking over their shoulders but racing away now, streaming back through the trees and up to the top of the mountain.

When the sound of them had died away, Oliver sank to the ground. His legs were shaking – he was shaking all over, soaking. His throat rasped, and he fumbled with the strap of his bag, pulled out the water bottle and drank as if he were dying. Then he sat with his head between his knees, still trembling, still listening in case they came back.

But they did not come back, and after a few minutes he checked the map and got up to his feet again, beginning the long walk home. The prospect of the house, and his return, did feel now more as though he were, indeed, going home. His heartbeat slowed, his breathing grew steadier, he pulled out an apple from the bag and ate it, chucking away the core. He did not feel plagued by questions, he did not feel as though he had to find answers; he felt as though, in that terrible encounter – with the dogs, with fear itself – he had, indeed, cast out demons. I have been saved from death, he thought – no, I have saved myself. I have found my own salvation.

The children didn't want to rest after lunch, they wanted to play a game, but Frances had had enough, and sent them to their rooms. They went off, subdued, while she took coffee and cigarettes out to the terrace and lay on the swing-seat, dreaming.

Time passed. The water poured ceaselessly into the water tank, a lizard ran along the parapet and disappeared into a hole beneath it. On the upper path the hungry cat lay in her warm safe place in the bushes, and down in the garden the hens went scratch, scratch, scratch, over bare dusty ground. Frances finished her coffee and cigarette and swung gently back and forth. *Dora*, she wrote, *I have written you another letter, another kind of letter, but I don't know if* . . . It was very hot, and very comfortable here; soon she was fast asleep.

Time passed. Jack heard Tom making noises. He followed them.

'What are you doing down here?'

'Nothing.' Tom jumped. He came out of the walk-in cupboard backwards, closing the door with his foot, leaning against it.

'What's in there?'

'Nothing.'

'Why are you standing there like that, then? Why don't you open the door?'

He didn't answer.

'There must be something in there.'

Tom scuffed at the floor, making a line through the dust. 'It's private.'

'Private? How can it be private? This isn't your house.'

'It isn't yours, either,' he muttered.

'What? What did you say?'

206

'Nothing.' It was stuffy down here, not hot but stuffy, shut in, shut away. He didn't like being trapped like this – this was his place, his secret place, how had Jack known he was here? Last time he saw him he had been asleep, like everyone else.

'Open that door.'

'No.'

'Go on – I dare you.'

'No.'

'Coward.'

Tom didn't answer.

'You wet the bed,' said Jack. 'You make funny noises.'

'So?'

'You play with yourself.'

He felt a trickle of sweat run down the back of his neck, like a thin cold animal. 'Shut up.'

'You sleepwalk.'

'What?'

'Why do you keep saying "What?" all the time? Didn't you know? You walk in your sleep, that's how you knocked over that thing.' He nodded back towards the figure in the corner; it was watching them angrily: whose side was it on? Tom could hear himself begin to breathe faster, as if he were panicking or something, as if he couldn't control it.

'You're pe*culi*ar,' said Jack, and at the sound of that bit of the word, that sound like a twisting knife going into something, opening something, the lid in his head lifted open and banged shut again so hard that he felt himself reeling, and he reached out, clutching the air. He had gone. No, he was back again. He sank to the floor.

'Now what's the matter?'

He couldn't answer.

'What are you doing down there?'

'Nothing.' He was going to wet himself, no, please no. He pulled himself to his feet and made for the stairs, leaving the cupboard door to swing open, leaving Jack to go in, and find his secret house and the people all starving to death inside it.

*

Time passed. Jessica went out on the terrace.

'Where are the boys?'

'Upstairs, I expect. I haven't heard them.' Frances, still sleepy, smiled at her, wanting to make amends for an unsatisfactory morning. 'Had a good rest?'

'Yes, thanks.' Jessica pulled out a chair and sat down at the round white table, her chin in her hands, her hair tousled. It wasn't so hot now, but she felt thirsty. 'What's the time?'

Frances looked at her watch. 'Just after half-past four,' – and as she spoke the church clock struck six, and they both smiled. 'Your parents will be back any minute, I should think.'

'Mmm.' Jessica got up again. 'I think I'll go and look for them.' She went back to the open doors, then stopped on the threshold, asking politely, as Oliver would like her to ask: 'Can I get you anything?'

Frances shook her head. 'That's kind. But I'm all right, thanks, I'll wait for the boys.'

'Okay.' And she went inside, walking towards the kitchen for a drink, hearing the flush of the loo from the bathroom and then Tom making squelching sounds with his tongue. Yuk. He came out and almost bumped into her.

'Where's Mum, I mean Frances?'

'On the swing-seat.'

He went off, clicking. God, he was peculiar, no wonder Oliver got cross. Oliver would be back any minute, she could hardly bear to wait any longer, perhaps she should brush her hair, and put on a necklace or something – no, never mind, leave it. She hurried through the kitchen and tugged at the stiff door, seeing that mangy half-starved cat leap away as it opened and then come crawling back again, yowling. 'Go away,' said Jessica. 'Shoo!' She climbed up the steps to the iron gate, two at a time, and stopped to drink from the tap at the green-tiled tank. Dark trails of ivy hung from the wall above it, the sound of the pouring water beneath was beautiful, romantic. Perhaps this evening they could come and sit out here, in the dusk. She would listen as he described his walk, and the water would pour on and on as a beautiful background and then she would tell him.

*

'I don't feel well,' said Tom, out on the terrace.

Frances frowned. 'Do you think you've got a temperature? Does it hurt anywhere?'

'I don't know. I just feel sort of funny.'

She swung her legs off the swing-seat. 'Let's have a look at you.'

He came and stood before her, and she felt his forehead. It was cool, perhaps a bit clammy, but nothing dramatic. He looked a bit tired, but then he often looked tired.

'You'll live,' she said. 'I expect it's the heat. Where's Jack?'

'Down in the – I don't know. I don't know where he is.'

'Well, I expect he's somewhere. And Claire and Robert will be back soon – do you want to help me get tea ready?'

He nodded, and followed her into the house. Oliver will be back soon, too, thought Frances in the kitchen, filling the kettle, lighting the gas. She blew out the match and stood for a moment watching Tom put biscuits on a flowery plate, carefully, one by one. He tried, he did try, though she knew that at any moment the packet was likely to drop to the floor and he, bending to pick it up, would probably tread on it and crush all the biscuits to pieces. She thought of herself in here yesterday morning, dropping the matches, scrabbling on the floor to pick them up again as Oliver raged above her. No more of that. Please, no more of that. Perhaps the walk would have done him good, perhaps they could draw a veil.

Jessica pulled open the gate, and went out on to the road. Any minute now. Twenty miles! She could hear a car, climbing up from the village. Oh God, it was probably them. She wanted Oliver to come back before them, before all the fuss. It was them. The long blue car rounded the bend and came up towards her, hooting. Well, it was quite nice, she supposed, and they might have brought something. She raised her hand and waved, and then Jack came racing up the steps behind her, shouting.

'Is that them? Is it?'

'Keep your hair on.'

'It *is* them!' He burst out through the gate, bellowing. 'Mummy!' The car drew up with a crunch on the loose stones at the roadside, and he dashed round to the passenger door and flung himself into Claire's arms. 'Mummy!'

'Well, well. Have you been waiting there all day?' She hugged him, pulling him on to her lap. 'Miss me?'

'*Miss* you?' He covered her with kisses.

'I don't suppose anyone missed me,' said Robert drily, switching off the engine. He looked at Jess through the open window as she came slowly down towards them.

'Hi, Dad.'

'Hi. Had a good day?'

'Yes, thanks.'

'It was awful,' said Jack. 'It was *awful*.'

'Why? What happened?'

'Oh, we went to the river, and came back late, and it was boiling, and I *missed* you – '

Claire smoothed his hair. 'Okay, that's enough, let me go, Jack. Where are the others?'

'Oliver's not back,' said Jessica casually. 'I was just going to look for him, actually.'

'Were you now?' Robert climbed out of the car and went round to the boot for the shopping.

'Yes. I'll just go down to the path, okay?' She was already leaving them, walking down the road with her hands in her pockets. 'Frances and Tom are out on the terrace,' she said over her shoulder, as if it were really important, as if in telling them that she was excused from further conversation for the rest of the day, and then she quickened her step, and it was clearly too late to suggest that perhaps she might help with the shopping, or indeed have anything more to do with them. Whereas to go and meet Oliver, of course . . . Robert sighed, and drew the cardboard box of tins towards him.

For a moment, as he carried it down to the house, he caught himself wondering. Was it really just a better or more desirable father that Jessica saw in Oliver? What was it Oliver saw in her?

'Claire,' he said questioningly, as she came into the kitchen behind him, with the box of fruit and veg. 'Do you think – '

But Jack had followed her, and then there was Frances, coming in to greet them and say that tea was ready, and then there was

210

Tom, saying that he had helped get it and where was the cat. Somehow the moment passed.

Jessica went hurrying on down the road – quick, before they could stop her, before she got asked lots of boring questions, and had to be nice. She'd be the first to see him, she would greet him casually, very ordinarily, as if she just happened to be passing, and they would go back to the house together, joining the others then but sitting a little apart, making it clear they were different, not exactly better or anything, just different. She went through it all again. She would wait at the entrance to the path, she would greet him casually . . .

Hello, Oliver. Did you have a good walk?
Very good, thanks. How nice to see you.

Oh, he had such a beautiful, beautiful voice. Then what would they say? She began to worry – she never used to think about what they might talk about, they just talked, it was easy, that was what was so nice. But since he'd gone so strange and funny, after that terrible night she didn't want to remember, it felt all difficult, and awkward, and she was scared of saying the wrong thing, of making it all worse.

Hello, Oliver. Did you have a good walk? Surely there was nothing wrong with that. Surely it was okay to come down to meet him. It was, wasn't it? *Hello, Oliver . . .*

'Hello, Jessica.'

She jumped six feet in the air and went scarlet. He was here! She'd been walking along looking at the ground, muttering probably – God, how stupid – when all the time he was walking up towards her, watching her make a fool of herself.

'Hello.' She raised her head diffidently, feeling her heart racing. He looked exhausted, absolutely exhausted, hot and sweaty and much much older than she remembered, but still it was so wonderful to see him again, to have him here again, as if everything was falling back into place.

'What are you doing here?' he asked her, smiling.

'I – I came to look for you.' Well, she had, hadn't she, why not say so? Why not say everything, why not, when all she wanted to do was fling herself into his arms, like Jack had done with Claire, only different.

'Did you?' he said, and they began to walk up the hill together. 'That's nice.'

It was nice! He said it was nice! He hadn't gone off her, everything was going to be all right.

'Did you have a good walk?' she asked him, just as she'd planned.

'Very good, thanks. But guess what happened?'

'What?'

'I met a pack of wolves.'

'*Wolves*?'

'Well, almost wolves.' He told her about it, walking slowly because he was so tired, and she slowed down to keep in step with him, listening in absolute and utter silence. 'So,' he said, finishing. 'That was my day. How was yours? Any wolves?'

'No.' They had come to the gate, which stood open from where the others had gone trooping in with the shopping. The kitchen door at the bottom of the steps was open too, and they were all doing things and talking; this might be her last chance to be alone with him for the rest of the day. She said, not looking at him: 'I'm glad you're all right.'

'Thank you. So am I.' He gestured towards the gate for her to go through, but she didn't move. She wanted to say: 'I'd die if anything happened to you,' but she didn't, she couldn't, she just stood there.

'Go on,' he said kindly, and put his hand on her shoulder, ushering her through, down the first steps to the upper path. 'I'm going to get straight in the pool. Will you tell the others? I shan't be long.'

'All right,' she said, and stood watching him walk away between the trailing vines, tall and tired and wonderful, and she shut her eyes, seeing him up in those distant woods all alone, conquering wild dogs, hurling stones, a hero. And he had told her first.

'Jessica? Jess?' Claire was calling her from the kitchen doorway; she opened her eyes. 'Are you joining us for tea?'

She nodded without speaking; she didn't want to speak to

212

anyone, she only wanted to think of him, and his voice, as he told her. Told *her*.

'Oliver back?' Claire asked, as she reached the bottom of the steps, and she nodded again.

'Lost your voice?' Robert asked breezily, but she didn't bother to answer, it simply wasn't worth bothering. What did it matter, what did anything matter? Nothing mattered at all except that he was safe, he was back, and they were all right again.

All through tea she kept quiet, waiting for him to come down from the pool and join them, hugging all her feelings to herself, deep inside, where no one even knew they existed, waiting for his special smile, just to her; and then she heard his footsteps.

'Hello there,' said Robert, when Oliver stepped out on to the terrace at last, cool and changed. 'How was it?'

'Good,' said Oliver. 'Very long and very good.' He didn't particularly smile at her, but it didn't matter; she knew he couldn't really. She watched him go over to Frances and put his hand on her shoulder, a bit as he had done to her, but of course it wasn't the same; she watched them smile at each other, and she watched him go over to Tom, and greet him, and saw Tom gaze at the air in that funny way, and Oliver give the flicker of a frown, and then he sank down into a chair and Claire passed him a big mug of tea and he drank and drank.

'So,' said Frances, 'tell us all about it.'

And he told them, describing it all, boring stuff about solar panels and agriculture, and then, casually: 'I was telling Jessica – I had a bit of an adventure towards the end.'

She listened to it all again, she could see they were all impressed with how brave he had been, not that he was boasting or anything, just describing it. It did feel a bit funny, having him tell everyone else, but still, he had made it clear to them: he had told her first, there was something special about her.

And she held that close, all through the evening, through helping her mother get supper, though she wasn't sure if he'd noticed her doing that, through eating all together, catching his eye, just once, and being given a beautiful tired smile. Twenty miles! He went to bed early, so of course there was no chance to suggest a game of chess so that they could be alone together, but tomorrow there might be. Tomorrow was Wednesday: three days left of the holiday. Seventy-two hours before they had to say goodbye. She looked at her watch. That was four thousand, three hundred and twenty-two minutes. Twenty-one. She would tell him, and then, at last, he'd tell her. She went off to bed without a murmur, hardly noticing when her mother came in to say goodnight and switch off the light. She just lay there, going over it all again, planning it all.

'Dora,' says Frances, 'I wrote you a letter . . .'

'Yes.' Dora is standing at her desk, busying herself with a pile of transparencies in plastic envelopes. She turns away, holding them up to the light, one by one, scanning the sheets, searching for something. Frances, from her desk across the room, can see nothing of what she is looking at, only Dora's back, straight and beautiful, as she stands at the window overlooking the street. She is wearing her navy jacket and a straight dark skirt; it feels as though thorns surround her.

'Dora . . .' says Frances again. There is no one else in the office, but from downstairs she can hear a door bang, and footsteps on the stairs. She must be quick. 'Did you get it?' she asks, trying to sound matter-of-fact, as though it were any letter, and this were any day.

The telephone rings on Dora's desk; she moves to answer it. 'Please,' says Frances, 'leave it.' But Dora does not leave it, and Frances waits, taking a cigarette out of the packet. She has lost her lighter, and uses a box of matches; she opens it the wrong way and all the matches fall to the floor. She gets down to pick them up, scrabbling frantically, as if it is very important, so that when the telephone is put down again, and Dora is free to be addressed, she is kneeling like a supplicant, trying to get to her feet again, but with feet and legs filled with lead, so that she cannot move.

'Did you get it?' she asks again, looking up. Dora has her back to the light now, so that Frances cannot properly see her face, cannot tell what expression is there.

'Yes,' says Dora, 'I got it,' and then the door swings open, and the room is full of people, people they both know, who have come to a party: Derek and Kate and Elaine, and Jocelyn with his wife,

214

and various authors and sales reps, and Robert, who comes over to Frances.

'What are you doing down there?' he asks, and bends to pick up the fallen matches.

'Nothing,' says Frances. 'Leave me alone.'

Somehow she gets to her feet. She pushes through the crowd of people towards Dora, who does not look at her, who is looking at everyone but her.

'Dora,' says Frances, 'Dora, please. I just want to talk to you – about us, about our friendship. Something happened between us . . .'

Then Dora turns to look at her, and in her face is everything Frances has ever feared she might one day see there: embarrassment, unease, retreat. Unequivocal retreat.

'Oh, no, Frances,' she says carefully, and suddenly looks very tired. 'Something happened to you.'

'Well – yes,' says Frances. 'Yes, of course that's true, you're right, of course, I didn't mean . . . But even so. But please. But Dora, please . . .'

But Dora has turned away again; she will not meet her eyes. Frances goes slowly back to her desk; she sits there staring at her piles of paper, hearing people talking to each other with interest and animation. Every time she looks up she sees Dora in conversation with someone different: she is receptive, revealing; she is looking at each of them but somehow never at Frances; her eyes are everywhere, she can take in everyone, but somehow Frances has become invisible.

The people thin out, the door of the office keeps opening to let them go; Frances sits watching them all, absolutely still, waiting for the moment when the last of them will have gone, and she can try again. But Dora goes out talking to another woman; she does not even flick a glance towards the corner, and Frances slowly picks up the pieces of paper on her desk, and rips them into shreds.

She woke in the darkness, in tears. Beside her, Oliver was deeply asleep, turned away from her, next to the wall, long heavy limbs

215

stretched out beneath the covers. The room was quiet, the house was quiet; a thin line of blueish light from the village street lamps came through the cracks in the shutters. I shall go back to sleep, thought Frances, as the church clock struck one, and find another dream. I shall go back to sleep and forget about this one, which is, after all, only a dream, and will never happen.

She turned over, wiping her eyes, tugging her pillow down into her arms, and lay looking at the cracks of light coming through the shutters at the other, smaller window at the side of the room, overlooking the garden. She tried to find Dora, the Dora she knew – but who did not, of course, know Frances, or the truth about her and her feelings. I have deceived her, thought Frances; I have implicitly lied to her throughout our friendship, and if she were to react like that I should only be paying the price. But I certainly could not bear it.

Her fingers dug into the pillow; she closed her eyes and tried to breathe deeply, steadily, to sink into sleep again, taking Dora with her. But an unapproachable Dora was waiting, and Frances, giving up, on the edge of tears again, softly pushed back the covers and crept from the room, closing the door behind her.

The corridor was lit by the moon, shining through the window on the landing which overlooked the peach tree. Silver squares of light, patterned with the shadows of leaves, fell on to the faded green carpet, an echo of the brilliant sun which lay here in the afternoons, when they all climbed the stairs to rest. She walked on bare feet over the creaking floorboards towards those shining squares, and down the wooden stairs which lay beyond them. She went into the sitting-room, so large, so open, and across to the desk in the corner, and she knelt down, quietly tugging open the bottom drawer, feeling inside for her writing case at the back. She drew it out, unzipped it, took out the letter; she zipped the case up again, replaced it, carefully closed the drawer. Then she slowly got to her feet, wondering what to do.

She could tear the letter to pieces, but what should she do with the pieces? Even a scrap, discovered, might betray her.

Then what? She could take it into the kitchen, which smelt of gas, and burn it at the little leaky cooker. Or she could do more than that. *I shall come down at night, when everyone is asleep, and seal up every crack* . . . That had been when Oliver was raging. He wasn't raging now. Besides.

Besides, it has not come to that, not yet, thought Frances, pacing the room. That is for when Dora – if Dora – is ever to be as she has been in my dream tonight. But she will never be, for I shall destroy this letter, and shall never write another.

On the table in the middle of the room where they left all their books and sunglasses, she had left her cigarettes and lighter. She picked up the lighter, and opened the terrace doors.

It was cool, and the sky was full of stars. A breeze stirred the leaves of the fruit trees and rustled the vines on the far side of the garden. The moon had risen high above the mountains beyond, where Oliver had gone walking; where wolves, or almost wolves prowled through the pines.

Frances shivered, holding her letter, holding the cigarette lighter tight. The moon climbed higher, and was taken by moving clouds. She stood in the darkness, afraid, and then suddenly a swooping streak of light shot through the starry sky beyond the mountains, and fell to earth. It happened so quickly, so silently, that she almost doubted she'd seen it at all, but she knew that she had: a shooting star, a moment's blazing arc, a star outshining all the others, rare and beautiful, and then it was gone.

Dora, said Frances, searching the sky for another, knowing it was unlikely that there would be another, I really did adore you, you know. I looked at you across that room, and everyone else disappeared.

Then she flicked on the lighter, and by its steady flame began to burn her letter, starting at the corner of the envelope, watching the edges begin to curl. Soon it was burning quickly, and she had to drop it on to the tiles, where she watched the flame consume it all, until only dark papery ash remained, which the breeze soon carried away.

The moon came out again from behind the clouds, and disappeared again, and Frances went on standing there. Unwillingly, she saw herself: a woman up in the night alone, out in the darkness unknown to anyone, destroying a letter she should never have written, estranged from her husband, thinking of death, and she thought: you are close to the edge.

She saw herself as Dora, who knew only a reserved but competent and collected person, would see her now, and she knew that she would be shocked and shaken, that to reveal even a hint of the person she was tonight would be unthinkable; and knowing all this was as if she were standing on one side of a great and impassable divide, between what she had longed for and dreamed of and what was real.

She saw herself returning to London, climbing the stairs to the office, smiling, greeting, lying; trapped between what she felt and what she must not show. She felt the kitchen, with its faint but pervasive smell of gas, await her like a friend, once more offering oblivion, and standing there on the empty terrace with these thoughts the whole of her life seemed to rear up behind her, to hit her in the back: this end was what had always been waiting for her, it had always been only a matter of time.

Well, then. Do it, then.

The moon came out again; the breeze rustled the vines on the far side of the garden. There was another sound, behind her, and Frances, realising that she was not alone at all, perhaps had been followed all the time, and watched all the time, turned round with goose-flesh rising all over her to see Tom, his eyes like blank and staring stones, making his way across the moonlit tiles towards her.

'Oh, Jesus Christ Almighty.' She never swore, but she swore now, half out of her skin with fright. Tom came nearer, walking slowly, somehow feeling his way; she crouched down so that she was at his height, and held out her arms. No, be careful, no, don't wake him, keep it steady and calm, holding him close might wake him, like last time, and frighten him to death. She was frightened to death, even though she had seen it before; it was different in London, in the flat, with everything familiar around them, and Oliver to call on, and work in the morning. And Dora in the morning. No.

He drew closer; carefully she put her hands on his shoulders to stop him, and he stopped.

They stayed there, and it felt as though those moments went on for ever: she searching his broad pale face, he, behind those hard blank eyes, miles away, locked away.

It was cold. Now it was really cold. Unbidden, scraps of a conversation held on a cold evening out here with the others came floating up now, like distant voices:

'. . . but I do believe in sin . . . Screwing up people's lives, I suppose . . . Do you love me . . . do I love you . . .'

Dora, said Frances, feeling herself reach out for comfort, for human warmth, have I entered the territory of sin? Do you believe in such things?

Slowly she rose, her knees trembling, and slowly she turned Tom round, and took his hand. She led him back across the terrace, and carefully over the step; hand in hand they crossed the huge open space of the sitting-room floor, past Jessica's room and up the stairs to where the moon fell in brilliant silver squares on the landing. Hand in hand they moved over the rag runner along the creaking corridor and into the bedroom where Jack lay sleeping.

She picked Tom up, so heavy and still – how was it possible that he had not woken through such a journey? – and laid him down on the bed, pulling up the covers, tucking them in very tight. And then, shaking, she sank to the floor by the bed, leaning against it, her head between her knees.

After a while, she got up, terribly cold, colder than she had ever been in her life, and went all the way down again to close the terrace doors. She went to the kitchen and heated some milk on a flickering blue ring of gas, no longer thinking of death, or indeed of anything now except how to get warm. She climbed the stairs again with her milk, she climbed into bed beside Oliver and drank it, and then she lay down close to him, wrapped herself round him, her face pressing into his neck.

'I'm cold,' she whispered. 'Hold me, hold me.'

But Oliver had walked for twenty miles, and he did not hear her.

The church clock struck four times at who knew what hour. Frances thought: I have laid it all to rest. Tomorrow I shall be different; everything will be different.

8

Jessica sat on the swing-seat, shelling peas. The pods lay on a sheet of newspaper beside her, some of them green and fresh, some wrinkled and yellow and tired-looking. Claire had said not to worry, it was almost the end of the season and they were the best she could find in the market yesterday, only throw out the really duff ones. She didn't worry: why should she, what did a few peas matter? She had washed up breakfast and brushed her hair and she sat out here being helpful, feeling nervous and excited as she waited for him to come out and join her.

The cicadas down in the garden went on and on, it was lovely and warm. She swung to and fro, and her finger and thumb pressed on the sides of one of the fresh young pods and popped it open; she stripped the peas into the white china bowl on her lap: they made a satisfying little ping as they landed and rolled around on the bottom. She picked up another pod: pop, strip, ping, ping, ping. It was nice.

Clicking noises came up the steps; Tom stood watching her.

'Can I do that?'

'No. Sorry.'

'Why not?'

Oh God.

'Why not?' He came over, and stood beside her, breathing heavily, watching. 'Please can I?'

Oh, *God*. 'Go on, then.'

He picked up one of the older pods, and squeezed it; nothing happened. 'What do you do?'

She sighed, and showed him; he tried again.

'Where's Jack?'

'I don't know,' she said, watching him mangle the pod between his fingers and crush the peas. 'Why don't you go and look for him?'

He shook his head.

'Don't you want to find him?'

'No.'

'Why did you ask where he was, then?'

He didn't answer, and she stopped shelling the peas and looked at him. He had dark circles under his eyes, as if he never got enough sleep, and he was breathing as if he'd got a cold, and even trying to concentrate on the peas, trying to shell them properly, which he couldn't, he was restless and twitchy and moving about.

'Tom?'

He didn't answer; he had that funny, far-away look in his eyes, and suddenly he dropped the pod he was making such a mess of, and just stood there.

'Hey,' said Jessica. 'You've dropped it, pick it up.'

But Tom didn't pick it up, he went on standing there with the funny grey look on his face, and then footsteps came across the sitting-room floor. It was him, it was him! She jumped, and the peas in the china bowl fell from her lap and on to the tiles, all scattered everywhere, rolling about, squashed and flattened by Tom's great flat sandalled feet, treading all over them as he came back to normal – where had he been? – and went wandering vaguely off again, back down the steps to the garden. So that Oliver, coming out through the tall white doors, instead of finding her all grown-up and sensibly occupied, not at all showing him how nervous and excited she was, found her flushed and cross and flustered, down on her knees trying to pick up all the peas, the white china bowl beside her, miraculously unbroken, rolling noisily round and round on the orange tiles like a spinning top. And though of course he was kind, bending down to help her, setting the bowl to rights, she couldn't possibly tell him *now*.

Frances woke to an empty room. The shutters were still closed, but the windows were open: it was warm, but not as it felt up here in the afternoons, heavy and still. It was fresh and airy, and she lay beneath the covers listening to the start of the day, to people calling to each other down in the village street, to the gate of the threshing barn swinging open, sackfuls of maize being dragged across the yard and up the steps, and after a little while the steady thud thud as the long dry stalks were beaten.

221

Every now and then sounds of activity drifted up through the house itself: Jack running indoors calling for Claire, and running out again; footsteps crossing the sitting-room floor; taps turned on and the pipes banging; Robert's voice, mildly exasperated, as he searched for the foot pump. She could smell coffee; she turned to look at her watch on the table beside her. Half-past nine.

Half-past nine, and everyone up and about, getting on with things. I could lie here for ever, she thought, but she knew that she must not, that on holiday with other people you must do your bit, and that she, on a holiday which was almost over, had done far too little. She pushed back the bedclothes and sat on the edge of the bed, shocked by how utterly drained she felt: as if she had been ill and were trying to go back to work too soon. And then, as she stood up, thinking: Today is going to be different, the events of the night, kept at bay by these pleasurably ordinary domestic noises, came flooding back with such power that she sank down and pulled up the covers again, and turned her face to the pillow.

Footsteps along the corridor, heavy and flat; funny noises, a knock at the door. She did not answer, her face pressed down, down, willing him to go away. The handle was turned and the door was opened, cautiously.

'Frances? Mum?'

Not now – please, not now. Later I'll come down, later I'll be all the things I should be.

'Mum?'

'What?'

'What are you doing?'

'Resting.'

Silence, a shifting of feet.

'When are you coming downstairs?'

'Soon. I've got a bit of a headache.'

He came closer, breathing heavily.

'Why've you got a headache?'

'Tom,' she said, hating herself, 'please go away. Please. I'll be down in just a little while.'

Silence. More breathing.

I should be taking him in my arms. I should be bringing him into bed with me, reading to him, talking about the day ahead. Or I

222

should be up and about, playing, doing things with him, making him happy. Instead I cannot even bear to look at his face: it's too much. Just at the moment it's too much.

'Please,' she said again. 'Go on.'

And he went, trailing off, she could feel he was trailing, leaving the door wide open.

'Close the *door!*' she snapped, and he came back and closed it, walking slowly away.

They left her a note to say they'd be back for lunch; they put it under a stone on the marble table, and they all went down to the river, taking the dinghy. Claire and Jack walked holding hands, swinging their arms up and down and laughing at elephant jokes; Robert and Tom made a detour to look at the pig, and Jessica carried the dinghy with Oliver, he in front and she behind, keeping in step with him, watching him, willing him to stop and say he was tired after yesterday, and perhaps they should have a rest and a talk, just the two of them.

'Oliver?'

'Mmm?'

'My arms are aching.' Well, they were.

'Dear, dear. Must be all that pea-shelling.' He slowed down, and turned to look over his shoulder, raising an eyebrow, and she laughed.

'What's so funny?'

'You.'

'I'm funny?'

'Yes.' It was just like before, they were happy and easy together, it was *lovely*. And the others were almost out of the way, Robert and Tom well behind them, safe with the smelly pig, Claire and Jack striding ahead, going along the nice soft path beneath the vines. There. She would tell him there. She'd wait until those two were well into the maize field, and then she and Oliver would stand in that lovely romantic place, and . . . And Robert and Tom might catch them up and interrupt and ruin it all. Out on the river. That was much better, no chance of anyone catching them up, or seeing, they'd be out of reach of all of them.

'Come on,' he was saying, turning round again, following

223

Claire. The dinghy bumped against her side and the nylon rope in her hand was beginning to rub; she changed hands for a moment, and wiped all the sweat off on her shorts, and he had to stop to let her do that, and waited, raising an eyebrow again, and he looked so wonderful she almost told him then, almost blurted it out, feeling the words well up inside her, but she wouldn't, she wouldn't, she'd wait like a grown-up, until the right moment had come.

'He's a funny old thing,' said Robert, getting to his feet. He brushed dirt and a few bits of straw from his knees, which hurt after being down there on the step. 'Okay, then? Shall we go?' It was much too hot already, especially after yesterday, spent in the car and the town, and his head was swimming a bit from standing up too quickly. He wanted to get to the river: he'd missed it, and now there were only two or three days left to enjoy it, with much of day three, no doubt, spent packing and loading the car. 'Come on, Tom.'

Tom didn't answer, still crouched on the step, still peering. Robert was about to start laying down the law when he saw Guida, coming out of the house with a basket, on her way round to the shop.

'*Bom dia*!'

'*Bom dia*, Guida. *Como estás*?'

'*Bem, obrigado. Eo senhor*?'

'Hot,' he said, gesturing at the sky, wiping his forehead. He imitated a wilting plant, and she laughed. Nice girl, easy to talk to. Well, not talk to exactly, but get along with. And they stood there, getting along in the sunshine, while Tom, shifting along on the worn stone step, sent messages in to the pig.

'I've got a lid in my head,' he told it, speaking in animal language. 'Have you got a lid?'

Did pigs have lids? Did other animals? He knew that people did – well, they must do, mustn't they, otherwise he wouldn't have one, would he, and he was a person. But animals. He wasn't sure. Did they have the same kind of feelings? Did they sort of come and go?

The pale wet nose was moving along the gap, the two dark holes in it opening and closing. All those bristles. Yes, it had a lid, the pig was saying, in animal language, pig language. What was it like? Well, it was a great big pink thing, bony but pink, and when it lifted, which it did very slowly, inside you could see . . . Ugh. Ugh. He didn't want to go on with this, animal lids were even worse, it was making him feel sick. And he got to his feet, and even just doing that made him feel funny.

'Tom?'

He wanted to answer, but he couldn't, not yet. In a minute, just a minute.

'Tom? You okay?'

He nodded.

'You look a bit . . .' Robert got down in front of him and put his hands on his shoulders. He had that grey look, beneath the suntan; he looked a bit under the weather. 'Not going to be sick, are you?' he asked.

'No.' Tom gave a little shiver. 'I'm all right. I just felt funny, that's all.'

'Probably the heat, and getting up too quickly – I go like that sometimes.'

'Do you?' They walked down the street hand in hand.

'Sometimes. I did just now, when I got up. All the blood goes to your head, and then if you stand up suddenly it makes your head swim.'

'Oh.' Oh. So that's what it was. Blood. Blood in your head. He hadn't known it was *that*. 'I thought it was a – ' he began, and then he stopped. Everyone must have one, but no one he knew had ever talked about theirs, and perhaps you weren't supposed to. Or perhaps when you grew up it went away – that would be nice. He hoped his would go away, he was getting fed up with it, feeling so odd all the time. He tried to imagine a time when he was much older, and could look back on now and heave a great sigh of relief that it had gone. But even that made him feel funny, imagining going back and forth like that.

'What did you think?' Robert asked kindly, and Tom almost told him about it anyway, but then he remembered that Robert and Frances were . . . Well. He took his hand away. He didn't know what it was about them together which didn't feel right, but it didn't, and how could he have forgotten? He couldn't possibly tell *him*.

In the end, Jack came out on the river with them. She was furious. Furious.

'Oh, come on, Jess,' said Claire, making ready to push them off from the bank. 'Don't look so grumpy. Why shouldn't he come too?'

'I'm not grumpy.'

'You look pretty grumpy to me,' said Oliver, and she made herself smile. 'That's better. Good – thank you, Claire.'

Claire, leaning over, gave a shove, and he dug one of the paddles into the soft grey sand to give them leverage. Then they were off, moving slowly out of the shallows, and Jessica leaned back against the rounded rim and tried to enjoy the swish of the paddles through the water, the silvery fall of it as he raised them, rowing so smoothly, so well, but it wasn't the same.

'Move up,' she said to Jack, getting squashed. 'Move *up*.'

'I can't move up any further, it's your great big bottom that's taking up all the room.'

'Shut up!' How dare he, how *dare* he?

'Children, children,' said Oliver, and she flushed, looking away, gazing intently at the cliff face and then the yellow hay-field, with its loosely made stacks piled up around long poles like witches' hats; she tried to detach herself, to rise above Jack and his horrible babyish teasing.

'Why do you think they make them like that?' she asked, because that kind of conversation seemed to interest Oliver, when the other grown-ups were around. 'The haystacks.'

'Stooks,' said Jack, making himself comfortable. 'Dad said they were stooks, not stacks.'

'I meant stooks.'

'I don't know if there's any particular reason.' Oliver rested on the paddles and looked across the water. 'It probably dries the hay quite effectively, but I expect it's just a tradition.'

'Oh.' Who cared, anyway?

They drifted for a little while then, watching the fish pop up.

'You know those dogs,' Jack said, as they moved on again,

226

slowly passing the trees at the water's edge, leaving the hayfields behind. 'The ones you met in the mountains.'

'I do.'

'Well, are you sure they weren't wolves?'

'Pretty sure.'

'How could you tell? I mean, if it all sort of happened at once, like you said, and you were very frightened, I mean they might've been wolves, really, but you just weren't sure.'

What was he on about? She didn't want him discussing it, it was *her* story, it was for her to discuss with Oliver later. And anyway –

'He wasn't frightened,' she said,

'Oh, but I was,' Oliver said seriously. 'I can assure you I was more afraid than I've ever been in my life.'

And she didn't know what to say to that. Of course, she'd known he must have been, but he'd made such light of it, calling it an adventure, and anyway, it was his being so quick-thinking, so, well, so fearless, that was the word, that was the kind of word which was used about heroes in books, which she realised now she'd been thinking of. To think of him frightened, to actually hear him *say* he was frightened – well, it felt odd.

They were rounding the bend; she turned, hearing splashing, to see Tom and her parents entering the water, all making a fuss, she could see, about how cold it was. Well, at least Tom wasn't out here with them, that was something. God, he was peculiar, how could Oliver possibly have had a child like him? When she grew up, she'd have – what would she have? She closed her eyes, turning back again, letting Jack go wittering on about wolves, and how amazing it would have been if they actually *had* been wolves, all hairy and grey, and allowed herself, just once, to imagine a future where Frances and Tom had somehow disappeared, and Oliver was waiting for her.

'Come on, Tom, that's it, well done, that's very good.'

Between them, Tom was swimming hard, churning through the water, panting, his eyes fixed on the rocks ahead.

'Almost there, we're almost there . . . good boy!'

They had made it, right across the river. Above them rose the face of the cliff, so high that they could not see the top of it;

227

breathing hard, they clasped the smooth round sunbathing rocks, whose roots sank deep into the water.

'Well done,' Claire said again, and with one hand wiped the water from her face. 'You're a really strong swimmer now, aren't you?'

Tom nodded. 'I think so.' He tried to haul himself up on to the sloping, sun-warmed surface of the rock he was holding on to, to use his feet as a lever against it, under the water. Claire watched him: under the water these rocks were covered in smooth brown weed and algae, they became slippery and treacherous, and seeing a flicker of panic cross his face as he tried to rise and sank back again, she put her hand on his shoulder.

'Careful.'

'I can't get out.'

'Yes you can, it's all right, we'll help you.'

'There's a lower bit over there,' said Robert, from the other side, nodding towards it, and they edged round.

This was the trickiest part, clambering out: you could slip, you could bang your knee quite painfully, as Robert had done once last year, bruising it badly. And once you were out it was too hot, really, to stay there for long: the rocks were completely exposed, the pines which grew up the slope behind set too far back to give any shade. You lay there and you baked, and although that suited the rest of the family it did not suit Robert; nor, he could see, would it really suit Tom, who every now and then seemed to find the heat a bit much. Nonetheless, there was always a feeling of satisfaction at having made the crossing, and he felt it now, particularly for Tom, as they finally heaved themselves out of the water and climbed up to a good place to sit, settling down on the smooth grey surface to drip and dry off and survey the river.

The others were out of sight in the dinghy. Later, perhaps, the village teenagers and older children would appear for a swim; sometimes an ancient tractor and trailer bumped along the stony path between the low wall and the field, chugging blue smoke through a rusting funnel, carrying fallen branches from the trees, or heaps of maize to be taken back to the drying huts. This morning there were no children, there was no tractor, and the river, now they were out, was smooth and undisturbed again, moving slowly, gleaming.

'I wish we could see another kingfisher,' said Tom, beside Robert.

'So do I. It was good that time with Jack, wasn't it?' Robert turned to look at him. 'Better now we're out? Pleased you've done it?'

He nodded. 'When's Frances coming?'

'Soon, I expect. You'll be able to tell her how far you can swim now, won't you?'

'Mmm.' He was running a little stone along a groove in the rock, up and down, up and down, thoughtful and slow. It was the kind of movement Robert associated more with Jack, who could concentrate, and be still. Tom, with his noises and his animals, his restlessness, his sudden withdrawals, was never still, though he did look a bit fresher now, his skin a better colour: the swim, and the achievement, had probably done him good. But where was Frances?

Robert shaded his eyes and looked out across the river to the sloping sandbank on the other side and the yellow fields beyond, searching for a slight fair figure coming slowly along, lost in a dream, miles away from any of them. Where did she go? The maize fields were empty, and no one came walking along past the low stone wall.

'What time do you think she'll be here?'

'Soon.' But it had been after eleven when he took off his watch on the other side of the river: where was she? What was she doing, up there at the house?

'We'll see her at lunchtime, anyway,' said Claire, soaking up the sun. 'Don't worry, Tom.' She was watching the dragonflies above the mossy rocks in the shallows, listening to the steady drone of an aeroplane, far above them, flying north.

Only another few days. The river, after a day spent away from it, was more beautiful than ever; everything, after a day spent away from it, felt calmer now, the night of the power cut and its terrors something so nightmarish it was hard to believe it had ever happened. Certainly all the foreboding she had felt then seemed now simply the stuff of the small hours, the kind of thing which anyone might be excused for dwelling on at a time of crisis but which, thankfully, dissolved like mist on a lake as the sun rose.

'Here they come,' said Robert, and she propped herself up and looked round. Oliver and the children were rounding the bend, he with his back to them, wearing his old straw hat, rowing slowly, looking relaxed, Jack with his shirt off, waving. Jessica was sitting hunched up with her arms round her knees, much as Robert was sitting now, gazing out over the water.

'Had a good time?' called Claire, as they drew near, and Oliver brought the dinghy up close beneath them.

'Very good, thanks.' He lowered the paddles, and Jack came scrambling out and up over the rocks towards her. Very deliberately, he put himself between Claire and Tom, moving about so that Tom had to edge right away from him, and put his arms round her neck and kissed her.

'Steady,' said Robert, almost pushed off the edge as Tom moved clumsily up against him. 'Steady on.' He got to his feet. Already, to do so felt uncomfortably hot, his soles burning on the rocks. 'Ouch.' He lifted one foot and then the other, and beneath him Jessica laughed, stopping herself quickly.

'Sorry, Dad.'

Well, it was quite funny, he supposed, but still. It would be nice just for once to feel more than a figure of fun. God, it was hot; even out on the river might be too much, they'd have to keep in the shade. 'Right then – who's for a row?'

'Me,' said Claire.

'Me,' said Jack.

'Tom?'

Say yes, prayed Jessica, down in the dinghy, scooping a humbug beetle out of a pool of water at the bottom. She put it on the rim, and watched to see if it would come to life again. Say yes, and then Oliver and I . . .

Above them, Jack was scowling. 'Why can't it just be *us*?'

'Jack . . .'

'That's fair enough,' said Oliver, looking up at them all. 'Tom, you come down and I'll take you back to the other side. It's cooler over there.'

No! No, no, no. *Why* did he have to say that, surely he . . . She flicked the humbug beetle hard, and watched it fly through the air, landing invisibly.

'You realise, Oliver,' Claire was saying, 'that he swam all the way out here with us? Isn't that good?'

'Very good. Do you want to swim back again, Tom?'

Tom sat on the burning rock and looked out across the water. Could he do it again? From right up here the grey sandy bank on the other side seemed such a long way away. The river sparkled, the river was dazzling him; he screwed up his eyes and saw lights behind them. Well, that often happened when you'd been looking at brightness, like a light bulb or something. It was only water, it was only sun on water.

'Tom?'

It wasn't just swimming all that way back, it was climbing down over the rocks again, that was part of the problem. He didn't like the way they were underneath the surface, the slippery brown stuff, and the way they went so far down, like teeth. They had long deep roots at the bottom and they stuck up like teeth. Ugh. This was a sort of a lid feeling: he waited. Nothing happened, it didn't lift up at all, but he knew he couldn't climb down there again. He was stuck.

'Tom!'

Robert was shaking his shoulder, gently, but he didn't like it. He opened his eyes and all that light and water danced up and down again, flicker flicker flicker.

'What on earth is the matter with you now?'

That was Oliver, all the way down there in the dinghy, which once had up-ended and tipped them all out.

'Where's Frances?' he whispered, and cleared his throat. 'Where's Frances?'

'I don't *know* where she is.' All the way down there in the dinghy Oliver was reaching impatiently up to him, holding out his hand as it rocked. 'She'll be here soon, I expect, don't fuss. Now are you coming across or aren't you? Everyone's waiting – the day doesn't revolve just round you, you know.'

Revolve meant going round. And round and round and round all spinning away into nothing. He stood up, and the sun went dark.

'Tom . . .'

He was going to fall he was going to fall –

Somebody caught him.

'He's white as a sheet . . .'

'Not enough breakfast – '

'Too much sun – '

'Too much swimming – it was too far . . .'

'Come on, Tom, put your head between your knees, that's it, down you go, good boy, you're okay . . .'

No lid no lid, just swimming and spinning and now he was down here he was coming back again quite quickly, going all warm, feeling better with blood in his head. He looked up, carefully, slowly.

'That's more like it . . .'

'Colour coming back now . . .'

Where had it gone?

'All right?'

'Better now?'

He nodded. 'I want a drink.'

'I'm sure you do. The Thermos is over the other side, lots of ice . . . come on . . .'

They led him down over the rocks, carefully, carefully, into the dinghy, which rocked.

'Come on, Jess, out you get.'

She scrambled out quickly, banging her knee. 'Ouch.' Nobody took any notice.

Oliver and Claire ferried him back to the shore, and Claire unscrewed the flask quickly, pouring a stream of cold water into the cup. Out came the ice cubes, clink clink clink. That was a – no. The lid stayed shut and he drank and drank.

'Sure you're all right now?' Oliver stood over him. Tom looked up, seeing his shape enormous against the sun. Almost as big as down in the cellar. He looked away again.

'Yes, thanks.'

'Good. Well, then . . .' He turned to Claire. 'What shall we do?'

'I'll stay here with Tom,' she said, kneeling up in the sand, still holding the flask. 'Then I think we'd better go up to the house, it's nearly lunchtime anyway. But if you want to stay here – '

Oliver squatted down to Tom's level, the sun behind him. 'I'll stay with you, shall I?'

Because his back was against the sun, he couldn't really see him properly, he was sort of in darkness, in shadow, and though he was speaking kindly, now, he still didn't like him being so close. He looked down into the plastic cup, where the ice cubes sat at the bottom, three of them, melting a bit, getting smaller. Soon they would change into water and disappear and he would swallow the lot.

'It's all right,' he said, tilting the cup from side to side, watching the cubes slide about.

'Wouldn't you like me to?'

He ought to like him to. He ought to. He tilted the cup from side to side and the ice cubes went sliding across, going wherever he wanted.

'No,' he said flatly. 'No, thanks.'

Oliver got to his feet. 'All right,' he said, from all the way up there, so enormous and so far away. 'I'll go and see about the others.' He walked over the sand to the dinghy and got into it, pushing himself off with a paddle, rowing fast.

There was a sort of a silence.

'Tom? Want another drink?'

'It's all right,' he said. 'I haven't finished this one yet.' He picked up an ice cube and crunched it between his teeth. He found he was suddenly wanting to cry, suddenly thinking all sorts of sad things, but he wouldn't cry now, he'd go back to the house and find Frances and tell her everything and if she wouldn't listen he'd kill her too.

'Please,' said Jessica, on the other side of the river. 'I don't want to go back yet.'

'Aren't you hungry?' Robert asked, offering a hand as they moved down over the rocks to where Oliver was waiting in the dinghy.

'No,' she said, ignoring the hand.

'But you've just *been* on the river with Oliver,' said Jack. 'What d'you want to go again for?'

She ignored that, too, reaching the lowest rock, standing there looking down at him as he waited for them, willing him to understand, to explain to the others, to make it easy. But he didn't say anything helpful at all, he was looking cross and upset, and all because of Tom again. Honestly. Just because he'd been out in the sun. They'd all been out in the sun, why should Tom have to go all funny, there must be something wrong with him.

'Please,' she said to Oliver, trying to make it sound all nice between them again, as it had this morning, carrying the dinghy together through the field. 'Please can we go?'

He did smile. 'Surely you've had enough.'

'No, no honestly I haven't. It's almost the end of the holiday, and it's so nice out on the water. Please.'

He was going to say yes, he was going to.

'Oh, all right then, if it'll make you happy.'

He'd said it!

'So long as it's okay with you and Claire,' he went on to Robert, holding Jack's hand, as he came down beside her.

Of course it was okay with them, why on earth shouldn't it be? You didn't have to *ask*, just to go for a row.

'Fine,' said Robert, helping Jack in. 'I'd better just check with Claire.'

She raised her eyes to the heavens, she couldn't help it. Luckily nobody saw except Jack, and she put out her tongue at him, and drew it in quickly.

'Why're you sticking your tongue out?' he asked, in his high deliberate way.

But she refused to answer, to be drawn into childish games, and climbed carefully into the dinghy, which really did rock now, with all of them in, and they rowed across again, and the others got out and Robert went over to Tom, who looked perfectly okay now, Oliver was right, he did make a fuss, and then they had to go through the whole rigmarole all over again with Claire, and was she sure she wanted to, and what about lunch, and at *last* they left them, and rowed away.

She leaned back on the warm blue rim and trailed her hands in the water, watched by the others, who must be jealous as they followed the steady rise and fall of the paddles, the gentle plash, until they had rounded the bend past the island of fallen branches, and were out of their sight at last.

Oliver rowed slowly, thoughtfully, leaving the loosely piled

234

stooks in the hayfield behind, approaching the meadow on the other side, fringed with tall, still reeds. Jack had been chattering away about wolves at this point, earlier on; now, with Jessica, leaning quietly back, not looking at him, just enjoying the scenery and the rippling water alongside the little boat, Oliver was able to reflect again on that walk. You can, he thought, make any number of decisions when you're alone. You can say to yourself, I have learned, I have made my discovery, and tomorrow everything will be different. Tomorrow everything will be in that longed-for and elusive state: all right. He had come down the mountainside filled with hope and expectation; within days, even within hours, he had discovered that he could not, quite so easily, be this or be that, and rowing now past the tall reeds on the riverbank, with the flowery meadow beyond, he felt as far away from Frances and Tom as he had ever been.

'Oliver?'

'Yes?'

She had turned away from the trees; she looked at him and then down at the rippling water.

'Yes?' he said again.

You can make all sorts of decisions when you're alone. You can say to yourself: I shall be this, and I shall be that, and from now on everything will be . . . Thus Frances, rising at last in an empty house, with the night's dreams and events and decisions all making war within her.

When Tom had gone she lay waiting until she could no longer hear his footsteps. She waited until the whole house had gone quiet and she knew they were all outside, that Oliver would have told the others to leave her, she must be tired. She guessed that no one, anyway, cared very much whether or not she joined them, that they were, on the whole, probably rather relieved to have her out of the way. From right on the other side of the house, down in the garden, she heard them all talking and laughing, Jack and Jessica happy again now that their parents were with them; she heard them go out through the big lower gate, taking the cobbled path down to the village, their voices retreating, fading, gone.

Frances closed her eyes, and in the unaccustomed silence began to relax, drifting off to sleep again, sleeping well; and if she dreamed she did not, when she woke, remember her dream, but lay a little longer in the shuttered room, hearing, from down in the threshing barn, the women still beating the grains from the maize. Then she got up, and went slowly down the stairs.

To have the whole house to herself . . . Airy and cool and quiet. She went past the door to the cellar and into the greenery-shaded bathroom with its black and white tiles and worn flooring, and waiting for the bath to fill wandered out again, into the sitting-room.

Sun poured through the open terrace doors, the bare wooden floorboards were warm. She stood in the middle of the room, letting the warmth soak into her, recalling the cold and darkness of the night, the journey she had made with Tom through the moonlight, taking him back to his bed, and she thought of the miserable moments she'd given him, earlier on, upstairs. From now on she was going to be generous and kind and pleasant company, with Dora banished, torn out by the roots and cast away, those moments upstairs with Tom to be forgotten, obliterated, a veil drawn over them.

The bath was full. She lay in the greenish cooling water, sank back beneath it and let her hair float out around her; she sat up again, gasping, and wiped the water out of her eyes. An immersion, a cleansing: I shall restore myself to myself, and I shall be – what shall I be?

She washed her hair, climbed out, dried herself, and went upstairs to dress with the towel wrapped round her.

The landing was warm, too, and Guida had left the ironing-board up, with the iron up-ended upon it, the frayed flex trailing: automatically she stopped to check that it wasn't plugged in. It wasn't, and she had no need to linger, but she lingered, looking at the thick cotton cover on the ironing-board, with its scorch marks here and there and its deep, pleasing air of ordered domesticity. Guida probably did not see it like that; it probably was not like that – ironing, after all, could be as much of a drudge as any domestic task.

Nonetheless, to stand on this sunlit landing, to look from the ironing-board to the peach tree at the window, with its glossy

236

leaves and ripening fruit, and back again at the smoothness of that thick cotton cover; to run her hand slowly along it; after last night to be here now, peaceful and undisturbed, felt more than pleasingly domestic, it felt still and profound.

It is Susan in *The Waves*, Frances thought, recalling long-ago hours in the library in Bristol, and Claire, coming up to tap her on the shoulder and invite her for coffee, to lunch, to a party. Had she really felt so much for Claire, all those years ago? She had, she had, and then it had faded away. Could you call that love?

She must go and get dressed, she must go down to the river and join the others. But she went on standing there, trying to hold on to this visionary moment: a vision of profound contentment, of love and fulfilment, of being so deeply in harmony with the everyday that it became more than the everyday, was transformed, shining, exalted: love at its deepest, love at its best, creating, re-creating, making whole.

The moment faded: how could such intensity last?

She thought, it was Susan, wasn't it? Such a long time ago: was that, really, how she had been? Frances turned from the window at last, away from the everyday ironing-board, and walked along the corridor, bending to straighten the rucked-up rag runner, faded pink and blue and green, remembering, as she passed the other bedroom doors and reached her own, a more recent encounter with Virginia, in moments which had felt as they more usually felt, restless and distracted: everyone out on the darkening terrace and she inside, in the sitting-room, turning the pages of a *Life* taken down from the shelves.

Virginia had not loved Vita, not in that way. Sitting there in the dim light from the parchment lamp, hearing the voices from the terrace, Frances had tried to summon Dora to her side, but Dora had refused to join her. And Dora had been right not to join her, as she had been right when she spoke in that terrible dream: something had happened to Frances, not to her.

Frances went into the bedroom and dressed in a long cotton skirt, grey T-shirt and a string of yellow beads. She brushed her hair, made the bed, and opened the shutters wide, and then she went out and down the stairs again, into the kitchen for coffee.

She stood with the door to the steps and the water tank open, fresh air filling the room, and no smell of gas, not even faintly, lingered and hung in the air. She put on the kettle, and sliced the maize bread, and when the half-starved cat appeared, creeping uneasily through the door, she gave it some scraps of potato and milk and stood on the step watching it lap them all up, feeling her hair drying, feeling pretty, as Jessica had done, down in the cellar, when they took down the shepherd's cloak on its stand. She carried a tray through to the sitting-room, thinking: did I really come down here last night and think of the gas in the kitchen with longing? How could I have done, how could it have been possible?

Even as she thought it, crossing the wooden floor with her tray, thinking that the room, with its tall windows and loose cotton curtains, was one of the most beautiful rooms she had ever seen anywhere, she knew exactly how it was possible. She thought of the one crucial thing about Virginia, the one thing everyone knew, that she had drowned herself; and she discovered all over again exactly how it might be possible to feel like that, because there was only one person to whom she might ever want to try to describe that moment upstairs, only one person she felt might acknowledge and understand it in quite the same way, and that was Dora.

Dora knew about things, she knew what was what. It sounded so simple, and it went so deep. She engaged in the world; she needed moments of stillness. For years she had been, for Frances, the heart of that vision – love at its deepest, love at its best – and she seemed, now, to be waiting for her, sitting over there on the sofa, looking gravely up from her book and then putting it aside: I'm here. Come and talk to me.

Frances put the tray on the table. She walked slowly across the room and sank down, sitting on the floor at Dora's feet, and said aloud: 'But I love you, I love you, you must understand that. There's no one who looks at the world as you do; I cannot bear to lose you.' She began to cry, and every resolution, every decision deserted her, flying away like ash in the wind, unimportant, impossible.

So that instead of greeting the others, when they arrived, with a warm smile and an easy manner, opening her arms to Tom and kissing him, making everything all right, she heard their footsteps and leapt to her feet, flying across the room, weeping and frantic.

238

And Robert, coming in from the terrace hot and concerned, saw Tom run towards her and his broad pale face fall in dismay and disappointment, and he suddenly lost his temper and made for her, grabbing her arm and swinging her round to face him, demanding: 'What the fuck is the matter with you?'

'Stop it,' said Frances, recoiling, trying to wrench back her arm.

Behind them, Claire was saying in consternation: 'Robert – for God's sake . . .'

Robert ignored her. 'Well?' he demanded again of Frances. 'What is it? What's going on in that head? Are you going to go on sitting about being sensitive for ever? Are we supposed to disappear just so that you can think your thoughts?'

'Stop it!'

Her voice was rising. Over his shoulder she saw Claire shepherding the children outside again, out to the terrace and down to the garden, her sensible competent manner belied by the way her voice shook as she said to them: 'Come on, let's go and let the hens out, poor things, we forgot all about them . . .'

'Let go of me,' said Frances to Robert. 'Let go of me! Leave me alone!' Her voice rose higher, she heard herself screaming – '*Leave me alone!*'

He dropped her arm, and with tears pouring down her face she turned and leaned up against the wall, by the place where the shepherd's cloak used to stand, sobbing and sobbing.

'I'm sorry, I'm sorry . . . please go away . . .'

'No,' said Robert. 'I want to talk to you.'

She washed her face, and he reheated the coffee and found her cigarettes. He left her sitting at the desk, a cigarette in the ashtray beside her, and went out to look for Claire and the boys.

The hens were out, and Claire and the boys were sitting at the table on the upper path, eating grapes in the shade of the vines.

'Mum's feeling better,' he said to Tom. 'Sorry if I got a bit cross just now.'

Tom didn't look at him.

'I thought I'd take her out for a breather,' he said to Claire. 'Just to calm things down a bit.'

She didn't look at him either.

239

'Is that okay?'

'Fine.'

'Look at me.'

She looked; he kissed her. 'I shan't be long.'

'Where are you going?' asked Jack, pulling bits of grape skin out of his mouth.

'Just for a walk.'

'With Frances?'

'Yes.'

'Why?'

'That's enough questions now,' he said. 'Look after Mummy and mind your own beeswax.'

'Mum doesn't need looking after.'

He looked at her, ready to make a joke of it, an easy parental exchange of eyes raised to the heavens, but she was tugging black grapes off a stalk, and there was no exchange.

'Right, then,' he said. 'I'll see you all later. I expect Jess and Oliver will be back any minute,' and he left them, sitting in silence, and went back down to the house.

They climbed the steps to the iron gate, where the water poured into the green-tiled tank, and they walked a little way up the road, and then they turned off it, down among the pine and eucalyptus trees. Their feet crunched over the carpet of needles and cones; from a long way away came the sound of sawing.

'So,' said Robert, and waited.

Frances said nothing, her hands in the pockets of her skirt. At last, looking straight ahead:

'I'm in love with another woman, and it's killing me.'

'Ah,' said Robert, and there was a pause. 'Ah. So that's what it is. Well, well.'

They walked on; twigs snapped beneath them.

'You mean you're having an affair . . .'

'Absolutely not. She knows nothing about how I feel.'

'I see.' He thought about it, and the events of the holiday, and everything he had wondered about all began to fall into place, click, click, click.

'Do you mind if I ask – does Claire know?'

240

'Yes.'

'Everything?'

'You should never tell anyone everything.'

'I'm not sure if that's true. What about Oliver?'

'Don't ask too many questions.'

'Well,' he said carefully. 'Do you want to go on? I'm listening.'

'I'm tired,' she said. 'I'm exhausted. I was up half the night and I banished her. This morning I thought I was better. I'm not. As you saw.'

'Tell me about her.'

'It feels like betrayal when I talk about her.'

'All right then – tell me about you. You're in a dream, you're miles away. What are you thinking of? Her?'

'All the time.'

'When you say all the time . . .'

'I mean all the time.' They were walking slowly; she said slowly: 'I mean from the moment I wake till the moment I sleep, and then I dream of her. She is with me every moment of the day, she's in my bloodstream. I am infected with her – with the way she looks, the way she thinks and talks, with everything about her.'

'Then you are obsessed,' said Robert, and he stopped walking.

'In love.'

'Obsessed. You are on the brink of madness.'

'You're saying that because it's another woman.'

'No,' he said gently, and put out his hand to stop her moving away. 'I should say just the same if it were a man. No one should take you over in this way.'

'It was a man, once. It is just how I felt about Oliver.'

'Dear me.'

She was looking at the ground.

'Don't cry again.'

She stopped, and covered her face.

'Go on, then, cry if you want to – why not? I'm sorry.'

'It's all right.' She shook her head; she pulled her cigarettes out of her pocket and lit one, blowing smoke away from him.

'Those bloody cigarettes.'

'I'm allowed to smoke,' she said, with the ghost of a smile. 'I am allowed to do that.'

241

A car climbed the mountain road and slowly rounded the bend. When it was gone it felt quieter than ever, walking in the midday heat and stillness amongst the trees.

If he made noises they heard him, so he didn't make any, he really tried hard; he just opened the door very slowly and went in, hardly breathing at all. He closed it behind him: click. Then down the steep wooden stairs, with no need to turn on the switch: he knew his way now, and anyway, the grimy window let in light, and you soon got used to it. He stood at the bottom, trying to breathe properly again, because sometimes just holding your breath made you go funny, but he couldn't breathe properly, not till he'd got past the shape. It was bigger than ever, and under the hat its eyes watched every single movement. He wanted to make a dash for it, but his knees were trembling too hard; he pressed back against the wall and skirted all the way round, not looking at it once.

He'd done it, he'd made it. He was down in the passage, out of sight, opening the cupboard door. He went inside and leaned against the cobwebby wall, and his breath came fast now, panting, and though the wall was cool he was sweating all over, all down the back of his shirt.

He waited; he felt better. He wanted to close the cupboard door behind him, but then it would be completely dark, like it was for the pig, all shut away down there poor thing, with no one to talk to, and its horrible bony pink lid. One day someone would go and open the door to it, and then it would be all right. Now he was going to open the door of his house, and see if the people were dead yet.

He undid the catch at the side, and the front of the house swung towards him. He waited, but nothing happened: no lid, no lifting, no blank feeling. Nothing. He was getting better! Even feeling funny in the sun this morning, it hadn't lifted once – perhaps it really was going away, shrinking or something. Perhaps by the time they went home it would have gone completely.

Now then. He looked inside. How were they all getting on?

He'd left them downstairs, all lying down round the empty table. Big one, middle one, little one. Someone had moved them, someone had stirred them all up and done things to them; they were scattered all over the floor. Who had interfered? He knew. He picked up the other big one, the one he'd made a few days ago. It had seemed so friendly and nice, but it wasn't. It touched her, it sought her out. It swore and it shouted, and made her cry. He picked her up, so he had one in each hand; he banged them up and down on the floor, facing each other.

Bang bang bang. Bang bang you're dead, fifty bullets in your head: who was going to die? Along came the little one: stop it stop it stop it. What could the little one do? Along came the big one, the really great big one, he picked up the middle one and threw her down the stairs. Goosey goosey gander, whither shall you wander, upstairs and downstairs and in my lady's chamber . . . Here comes a candle to light you to bed, and here comes a chopper –

'I wish you were *dead!*' He was shouting now, he could hear himself, picking up all the pieces and snapping them in little bits, throwing them everywhere, banging the door of the house. He hated all of them, the big one the middle one the little one the little one was peculiar the little one was the worst of the lot if it wasn't for the little one everything would be all right –

'Tom! Tom, what on earth are you doing?'

Claire was coming quickly across the cellar towards him. He'd upset her too, he was sorry, she was so nice.

'Here you are,' she said. 'I've been looking for you for ages, it's lunchtime.' Making everything ordinary again, making it all better. 'Goodness, you've found a doll's house – I never knew that was here, let's have a look.'

'No,' he said, backing out of the cupboard. 'It's private.'

She looked at him, sweating and pale; she took his hand. 'Okay. Come and have some lunch now with me and Jack, all right?'

She led him across the floor, past the shape, which did nothing, and up the stairs. She had switched the light on, everything looked ordinary and everyday, as it was meant to look.

'Where's Frances?'

'She's gone for a walk, remember? She'll be back soon.'

'Where's Oliver?'

'Down on the river with Jess, still. I expect they're getting hungry, they'll be on their way back for lunch, I should think.'

*

243

'If anything happened to you I'd die.'

There. She'd said it. It had taken her almost the whole journey, all the way up past the meadows and round the next bend in the river: field and mountain, field and mountain, so beautiful, so peaceful, rowing almost all the time in silence, but a nice silence, it felt just right, and she could see that he liked it as well. And now, as they came slowly home again, towards the island of fallen branches, she said it, and went on looking at him.

He shook his head in amusement. 'Come, come.'

'I mean it. I mean – yesterday. The wolves.'

'Almost wolves.'

'Almost wolves. You might've got killed.'

'I might have, but I didn't.'

'But if you had – if anything had happened to you – I couldn't bear it. . .'

'Jessica . . .'

The way he said her name. It felt – oh, how did it feel? She'd never known there were feelings like this in her life.

And then she told him. 'I love you,' she said, trembling, because it sounded so extraordinary, after all this time, actually to say it at last. As if everything else had disappeared, as if the only thing in the whole world was the two of them, drifting along on the water, with field and mountain falling away, everything falling away, because nothing else mattered at all. 'I really love you,' she said again, and waited.

'Jessica . . .'

No one ever said her name like that. It felt as if he were giving it to her.

'Do you love me?' she asked him, because she couldn't bear to wait any longer, she had to hear him say it too.

He didn't answer.

'You do love me, don't you?'

'Jessica . . . You don't know what you're talking about.' He was speaking slowly, as if he was trying to be kind. He did love her, didn't he, she couldn't have imagined it all?

'What do you mean?' she asked him, suddenly feeling all cold.

'I mean . . . you're a child. I'm fond of you as a child, do you understand? As a – well, as a daughter.'

'But . . .'

She couldn't bear to look at him.

'But nothing.'

'But I thought . . . We have such nice times together . . . I thought . . .' She began to cry.

'I had no idea,' he said. 'And I am sorry. Very sorry.'

She cried and cried. All out there in the middle of the river, which didn't feel at all now as if it was a special, enchanted place, their place, where nothing else mattered so long as they were together. It just felt like a river.

'Please,' he said. 'Please don't cry any more.' He dug in the pocket of his lovely old trousers and passed her a handkerchief. She blew and blew. 'Good girl, well done. And now I think we'd better forget all about this, don't you? Come on, dry your eyes, that's it, be brave. We're friends, good friends, aren't we?'

He was being nicer than he had ever been, she couldn't bear it, and she gave him back his handkerchief willing him to say it was all a mistake, that of course he loved her really, but he didn't, he just picked up the paddles again, and began to row. She sat, red-eyed and miserable, listening to the smooth rise and fall of the water; she leaned over the side and splashed her face, because if anyone saw her like this she'd die.

'Look,' he said suddenly. 'Look, quick!'

She raised her head and saw it – a bright, beautiful flash of blue, racing away downriver, brilliant, rare. Then it was gone.

'Well,' he said, smiling at her, 'I think we're the only ones who've seen two kingfishers on this holiday, don't you?'

'Three,' she corrected him. 'It was two last time, wasn't it?'

'So it was, you're quite right. Well done.' He smiled again, with affection, and she smiled back at him, trying to be brave. It was nice being friends, but it wasn't the same.

'Isn't all love obsessive?' said Frances, addressing the air.

'I don't think so. Not in my experience.' He paused, remembering a browse along the bookshelves the morning after Tom had gone sleepwalking and knocked over the shepherd's cloak. ' "True love wants what's best for the other person," ' he said. ' "Romantic love wants the other person." I give you that

245

courtesy of the Reader's Digest – rather good, isn't it?'

'Not bad.' She drew on her cigarette. 'Except that most of us want both, don't we? To give and to have.'

'Yes. Well – I suppose it's unlikely that the secret of life might be found in the Reader's Digest.'

'Most unlikely. Still, you never know.' She liked Robert: it was impossible not to like him, even if, not an hour ago, she had briefly hated him. Like Claire, generously taking over whenever it was necessary, he had qualities which in the face of her own emotional turbulence felt like rocks to rest on: he was fair, he was honest, he was kind. A good person, she thought, as they went on walking. Simply that.

'You said you believed in sin,' she said, smoking again. 'What made you say that?'

'Did I? When?'

'You know you did – surely you must remember. That evening out on the terrace . . .'

'There have been many evenings out on the terrace.'

'Yes, but you remember. When we were all talking – about God, and what we believed in. You said you believed in sin.'

'Must have had too much to drink.' He smiled. 'It's all right, I do remember now.' He bent down to pick up a fir cone, fiddling absently with it as they walked. 'The last person who had too much to drink on this holiday was Oliver, if I remember rightly. Another troubled soul. Do you want to talk to me about Oliver?'

'No.'

'Frances. He knows. Doesn't he? He knows something, anyway.'

'Of course he knows something. If he didn't know something he'd be a fool, and Oliver is anything but that.' She dropped her cigarette to the ground and stubbed it out with her heel.

'And you still – '

'Still what?' She gave another ghost of a smile, with a quizzical expression which reminded him of no one so much as Oliver. 'Still love him? Yes. Does that surprise you? I was asking you about sin – does all this sound selfish and wicked? Wanting two people?'

'Is that what you want?'

'I'm afraid it is.'

'When you say "want" – '

'I mean want in my life. Does that equal sin, in your book?'

He was twisting dry petals off the fir cone, flicking them on to the ground as they walked. 'It seems to me that sin is not so much a Milton word as an Alice word. It means just what you want it to mean, depending on what is troubling you at the time.'

'What about the absolutes? You said you tried to live by some kind of absolutes.'

'Mmm. I did have a lot to drink. I seem to recall you saying that there's always an "And yet". Isn't there? It seems to me a miracle that any marriage endures without some kind of – what shall we say? Venturing forth? Glances in other directions?'

'Have you and Claire ventured forth?'

'Don't ask too many questions. No, not yet. Not as far as I know, anyway. If we did, I hope we should survive it, that's all. Without making too many people unhappy. I think love is supposed to make things better, not worse. Is this woman you dream about all the time making things better? Why were you crying when we came back?'

'Because I miss her – why do you think?' she asked. 'Because I cannot bear to think of having to live without her. I can't tell you how lovely she is, how much I want to be with her. I want to talk to her about everything, for everything to be open between us, and it can't be. Not in the way I want. She has a family; I have a family. I want more; I know she doesn't. It's hard, that's all.'

They were walking up the slope again; a bullock cart creaked on the road above them.

'You can't make somebody love you,' said Robert.

'I don't want to make her love me. I just want to tell her, and for her to accept it. She might not be able to, she might be appalled.'

'It does sound a fairly modest requirement.'

'Try living with it.'

He shook his head. 'Has this ever happened to you before?' he asked after a while.

She didn't look at him. 'Once or twice. Twice, if you must know, but not for a very long time. I never did anything about it, if that's what you want to know.'

'But you wanted to.'

'Not like this. I'm grown up now, it's different.'

'And you're sure,' he said. 'You're sure she doesn't feel as you do.'

'Certain.'

'Then that saves you, doesn't it? From having to decide.'

'What do you mean?'

'I'm not quite convinced you really want more, that's all. If you were to tell her, and she were to turn round and tell you she felt the same – do you really want what you think you want?'

'Does anyone really want what they think they want?'

'Frances. Don't play games, don't try and be clever. This is serious, isn't it?'

'Yes,' she said, thinking of the night's events and the morning's upheaval; thinking of the past five years. 'It's serious.'

'Well, then. Answer me. You're saying that you've wanted a love affair – yes? With all that that implies – yes?'

Frances was looking at the ground again, at the grey drifts of pine cones, the dense brown carpet of needles, warm in the sun.

'It's the expression of everything, isn't it?' she said at last.

'Can be.'

They walked on in silence.

'So. Is that what you want?'

'I don't know.' Another pause. 'I think I do, but if it came to it – possibly not. Probably not. Certainly not with anyone else, I can tell you that. If it were anyone else I'd be ill.'

'This is the end of the twentieth century,' said Robert, 'as you are probably aware. There has been a social revolution, and men are out of fashion. All this seems to have passed you by. I cannot believe that in the last however many years you could not have found what you wanted if you really wanted it. Mmm?'

'Mmm.' She lit another cigarette. 'Sometimes I feel as if I don't belong anywhere, sometimes as if there is the possibility of access to everything. It's one thing to see other people's liberation, and quite another to liberate yourself. Anyway, I'm not ruthless enough.'

'Do you want to know what I think?'

She looked at him, and smiled. 'Yes,' she said, 'I do.'

'I think what you want is some kind of substitute for religion, a kind of dreamy worshipping of someone who will never make real demands of you. And that's one of the reasons I dislike religion so much – when it comes down to it, it's easier to love God than another person. Don't you think? Much easier to be the bride of Christ than the bride of a real man. Much easier to love at a distance than live with someone.'

'Actually,' said Frances, 'I think that the way to God, if there is a God, is immensely stony and difficult and full of sacrifice. And reached by loving other people. As for loving at a distance – well, perhaps you're right, but how dull. Loving at a distance can be inspirational.'

'You said it was killing you.'

She fell silent.

They had come to the top of the slope; they were out on the road again, where the sun beat down.

'So,' said Robert. 'Here you are. Agonising over what you might or might not want, or might or might not be able to have. You dream of this woman and you banish her. She has her own life. She may not want to be dreamed of – '

'I'm sure she doesn't.'

'She may not want to be banished, either. Doesn't she have something to say? If she is as nice as you believe, at the very least she deserves honesty. Don't you think?'

'I – yes.'

They crossed to the shady side, and walked slowly downhill towards the house.

'And meanwhile – '

'I know. I know. Is that what you meant when you spoke about sin?'

'An Alice word,' he said again. 'It means whatever you choose it to mean, neither more nor less.' He raised his arm and threw the fir cone across the road: it bounced on the verge and rolled away down the hill. 'Like God, now I come to think of it.'

'Like love.'

'I'm not quite so sure about that.'

*

Claire, after lunch with the boys, made sure that Tom was asleep before she left them, Jack still slowly turning pages as she got up from the yellow chair in the corner of the bedroom and went to open the shutters a little, to let out a fly.

'Go on, shoo, off you go.' It soared away on a current of air, out above the floor of the threshing yard, and she quietly closed the shutters. It was cooler, just a bit. Where was Robert? Why hadn't he come home?

'Mum?'

'Yes?'

He put down the book and stretched his arms, yawning.

'Hug?'

She hugged him, smoothing his straight dark hair.

'Where's Dad?'

'Coming back any minute. Go on, go to sleep now, I'll see you at teatime.' She disentangled herself and put his book down on the bedside chair; she went to the open door and blew him a kiss, and then, hearing noises, she went downstairs. The noises came from the back of the house: she went to the sitting-room.

Footsteps up from the garden; Jessica in from the terrace.

'You must be starving,' said Claire, 'you've been gone for ages.'

Jessica walked straight past her and into her room.

'Jess . . . where's Oliver?'

'Putting the dinghy away.' The door of the bedroom swung to, and was closed with a click. From beneath the terrace Claire could indeed hear the dinghy being dragged across the stone flags and put in its corner, the paddles propped up against the wall. Footsteps up from the garden: Oliver came through the tall white doors.

'I'm sorry we're so terribly late – I hope you've eaten.'

'Yes,' said Claire. 'I've eaten, so have the boys. They're both asleep.'

'Thank you, you're very kind.' He was putting his swimming bag down in the corner, carefully out of the way. An orderly approach to things, like Frances; not like her. 'Where are the others?' He straightened up again.

'They've gone for a walk.' She stood in the middle of the broad and open room which not two hours ago had felt as though it were going to explode with the sound of weeping and shouting and children's footsteps, running away. She felt as though she were going to explode.

'Is Frances all right?' he asked.

She wanted to say to him: No, she isn't, and neither am I. I am not quite myself today. She wanted to say to him: What is the matter with Jessica? She couldn't say anything, standing in the middle of the room with a man she knew she was a little afraid of, whom she didn't begin to understand, didn't know how to talk to, had never known how to talk to. Except in the ordinary run of things it was a very long time since she'd talked to any man except Robert, and where was Robert? Who cared for the ordinary run of things?

'Claire? Has something happened?'

'I wouldn't know,' she said coldly. 'You tell me. What is the matter with Jessica?'

He looked at her.

'She's been crying – '

'Yes.'

'Why?'

'Because – '

'What have you done to her?'

'I – nothing.'

'Are you sure?'

'Claire. Please. Please don't think – '

'I don't know what to think. About anything. Why was she crying?'

'Because,' he said slowly, 'because, as they say, I was blind.'

And so was I, she thought, seeing, like holiday snaps in an album, Jess and Oliver swimming together, playing endless games of chess together, talking, laughing, seeking each other out, rowing away down the river together, round past the island of fallen branches, and out of sight. What have I been thinking of, all this time? I've been thinking of Frances. I've been thinking of Tom. What about my own child?

They stood stock-still in the middle of the room in silence.

'Go on,' she said.

'I thought of her as a daughterly companion, and she . . . I'm afraid I have hurt her. But not in the way you might think. Claire? I do assure you. I give you my word.'

They looked at each other: two people with little, when it came down to it, to say to each other at all. Except now. Except over this.

'I give you my word,' he said again. 'You must believe me. For her sake as much as anyone's. Please.'

'All right,' she said at last. 'I believe you. I had to ask.'

'Of course.'

Noises came from the side of the house: the kitchen door opening, footsteps, Robert and Frances, talking –

'I except they're all resting,' said Frances.

'Probably.' Robert was opening the fridge. 'Let's have something to eat. I'm starving.'

'So am I,' said Oliver, hearing them. 'I'll go and join them, if I may. Can I get you anything? Or did you say you had eaten?'

'I said I had eaten. I don't want anything, thank you.'

Plates and glasses were clattering in the kitchen; she turned towards Jessica's room as he left her, and knocked at the door.

'Jess?'

No answer.

'Jess?' She turned the handle and went inside. The shutters were closed, and Jessica lay on the bed, on her tummy, her head buried in the pillows.

'Are you all right?' Claire asked. 'Do you want to talk?'

'No, go away.' Her voice was thick. 'Leave me alone.'

Claire went, closing the door behind her. Voices came from the kitchen, polite but friendly. She waited to see if Robert would come to look for her, but he didn't, and she climbed the stairs again, slowly slowly, walking across the brilliant sunny landing, stopping to fold up the ironing-board in case, God forbid, Tom should go sleepwalking again and bang into it. She walked along to the bedroom, bending to straighten the rucked-up rag runner, and she thought: I have been thinking of Frances and Tom. What about Jessica? What about me?

'Frances?'

'Yes.'

'Come and sit down.'

'In a minute.'

'Now?'

She stood at the door of the dining-room with the trayful of things from their lunch, about to follow Robert, who had gone to the kitchen to make them all coffee. She nodded down at the blue and white plates piled up, the half-finished bowl of salad.

'I'll just – '

'Leave it. Please.'

She came back, and put the tray on the sideboard. The shutters were half open, and a fly buzzed between them and the window-pane; outside, a ripe peach fell to the ground with a thump. Frances pulled out her chair and sat down, taking her cigarettes out of her pocket. The seersucker tablecloth was covered in crumbs; Oliver ran a fork up and down, up and down, over the bubbles of check.

'Claire?'

He closed the door behind him, and pulled off his shoes. The shutters were closed and the bedroom was shadowy and warm. Sunbeams fell here and there on the scatter of T-shirts and summer shoes, on the chaos on top of the chest of drawers, on the paperback books and on Claire, who did not answer.

'You asleep?'

She was turned away from him, her face, turned to the shuttered balcony window, hidden by thick dark hair. He went across to the low double bed and lay down behind her, kissing her neck through the hair.

'Sure you're asleep?'

He could feel her smiling. No, no he couldn't.

'What's up?'

'Nothing.'

'Doesn't feel quite like nothing.' He propped himself up, and leaned over, looking down into her face, eyes closed, suntanned, faintly lined. Quite a few lines. 'Mmm?'

Her eyes stayed shut. 'Where are the others?'

'Sitting in silence in the dining-room, with coffee I made for them, quietly tiptoeing out again.'

She smiled.

'That's better. Look at me.'

253

She looked. He rolled her towards him, on to her back. His hand moved under her black and white skirt; he touched her, in just the right place. She began to cry.

'Not more tears, surely. Surely there've been enough tears for one day.'

'It's my turn.'

'Yes. What is it, then? Why are you crying, my own true darling?'

She held him and held him; his shirt was soaked.

'If anything happened to us, I'd die – '

'Sssh,' he said, rocking her, holding her close. 'Nothing's going to happen.'

Across the landing the door was opened; one of the boys came out.

'I love you, I love you – '

'I know,' he said simply. 'I love you, too. We are built upon a rock.'

'What are we to do?'

'I don't know.' She sipped at her coffee, blacker than black, much too strong. What had Robert done to it? She tapped ash into a saucer; old china, green and white, English, brought out by the owners of the house, probably with a cup, once. The sort of thing Dora might like. Who were they, these owners? She pictured a woman out on the terrace in the early morning, drinking her coffee, watching the mist clear, watching the village wake up. She pictured Dora doing these things, standing by the parapet with her back to the doors as Frances came out of them, hearing a cock crow, starting the day.

Not love, but obsession . . . You are on the brink of madness . . .

'What are you *thinking* about?'

'Nothing. No, sorry. That isn't true.'

'I know it's not true. Look at me. Look at me!'

She looked. 'Please don't be angry.'

Footsteps, the bathroom door closing.

'I'm trying,' he said. 'I really am trying.'

'I know. I know you are. It's my fault.'

'Well, then. Talk to me. Please.'

She put down the cigarette; it burned and burned. Dora, in long grey skirt, turned from the parapet, holding her coffee cup, calmly regarding her, smiling.

Frances said slowly: 'I cannot relinquish a dream.'

'What?'

Water flowed in the bathroom; the door was opened; more footsteps.

Do you really want what you think you want?

Does anyone?

'One day I'll try to. Not yet. I can't.'

'What are you talking about?'

At the very least she deserves honesty . . .

I shall tell her, I shall tell her –

'Frances!'

He deserves honesty, too. I can't. I can't.

'*Frances!*'

The door swung open.

'Mum?'

In unison they turned on him.

'Just a minute – '

'Please! Not now!'

He fled.

Early evening, a little cooler.

'Jessie?' Claire knocked on the door. No answer. 'May I come in?' No answer.

She turned the handle and looked inside. Just before dusk, the sitting-room, with its tall casement windows and doors wide open, was filled with shadows, but there was still light enough to see by. In here, with the dense green bushes and creeper outside, the room was almost in darkness.

'Jess? May I put the light on?'

She was lying on her back with her eyes shut, wearing the Walkman; her fingers moved slowly up and down on the quilt. Claire went over and gently touched her. Jessica jumped, and frowned. Claire made gestures; she removed one side of the Walkman.

'What?'

'I said may I put the light on?'

'No.'

Claire sat down on the edge of the bed, hearing Frank Sinatra through the headphones. Her tape. Never mind. She took Jess's hand.

'Please turn it down. Or off. Just for a minute.'

Jessica looked at her, and then away.

'Please.' Claire made to remove the headset herself; Jessica took it off, her beautiful hair trailing after it, clinging with static to the earpiece. Sinatra sang into the crumpled quilt; muffled strangers wondered what chance they had. Jessica switched them off.

'What is it?'

'Just – ' Claire hesitated, wanting to get it right. 'Just that I'm here, that's all. And I'm sorry you're sad.'

Jessica looked at the window.

'Do you want to talk to me? Mmm? I won't tell a soul, I promise.'

She shut her eyes, and tears rolled on to the pillow.

'Poor little Jess. I'm so sorry.'

'Oh, Mummy – '

She cried and cried; Claire rocked her, holding her close.

'It *hurts*.'

'I know. I know.'

'What did he tell you?'

'Not very much. Just that you . . . well, had a crush . . .'

'A *crush*?' Jessica raised her head in fury. 'Is that what he called it?'

'No, no, I don't think so, not exactly – '

'Don't you *dare* call it a crush!' She was weeping all over again. 'How *can* you?'

'I'm sorry,' said Claire, drawing her back into her arms, stroking wet hair off her face. 'You're right, I'm sorry.'

And after all, she thought, as Jessica, at last, had no more tears left and got up to look for a hankie, what is the difference? Everyone talks of a crush when they mean you've built up something from nothing, idealised it, made someone something they're not. Well. Perhaps she saw things in him none of us saw. It doesn't mean they weren't there.

She got up and kissed her.

'May I suggest,' she said, 'that you have a bath before supper? They do help, for some reason.'

'Okay.' Jessica had found a handkerchief in the top drawer; she blew her nose and switched on the light.

'And when we get back to London I'll buy you something nice.'

'I don't want anything.'

'Well.' Claire opened the door. 'We'll see.'

'Okay. thanks.'

When she had gone, Jessica looked in the mirror, propped on the chest of drawers. Her eyes were sore with crying, her skin had patches of red all over it. Awful. She picked up her hairbrush from the midst of the little boxes and necklaces and suntan creams, and brushed her hair, over and over; she put on her nightshirt, and bundled her hair through a sweatband, rolling it tight. Then she picked up her sponge bag and quietly opened the door.

There was no one in the sitting-room, and no had one switched on the lamps; the last of the light came in through the windows and voices came in from the terrace. They were all out there, drinking and talking and eating crisps. Were they talking about her? Had everyone guessed? She went softly along to the bathroom and turned on the taps, she brushed her teeth and washed her face, and went out again, yawning, waiting for the bath to fill, and along to the sitting-room again. She stood in the half-light, listening to them all: they were talking about the weather. The weather!

In the corner of the room where the books were, she could see the chess set where she had left it on the desk, all ready and waiting, all set up on the board. All those pieces, all those lovely games. She went over. For a moment she felt like sweeping the lot off, watching them fall and roll about on the floorboards, but she didn't. She stood for a moment; she picked up the black queen, tapping it against her lips. Then she cleared everything off, but carefully, on to the desk; she turned the board over, so it was a box again, and she put in all the pieces, one by one: the brave little pawn, the swooping bishop, mighty castle and prancing knight, the lonely king, the omnipotent queen. She put every piece in the box, and then she closed it, fastening the catch at the side, hearing the bath fill, turning on the lamp.

Evening, a little cooler. They all remarked on it, deciding to eat in the dining-room because of it, lighting candles, seeing through the window the stars come out, pale at first, then bright as frost in a dark sky.

The children had eaten already; they hovered.

'Can we stay up?' asked the boys.

'You can,' Claire said to Jess.

She shook her head. 'I don't want to.'

They hugged each other; she went to her room, saying a general goodnight to the air.

'She all right?' Robert asked Claire, as the bedroom door closed.

'I'll tell you later.'

He shook his head, pouring more drinks for himself and Oliver as the women went to the kitchen. 'Now what?' he said aloud, and then, recalling how very subdued Jess had been all evening, and how quiet Oliver seemed now, said to himself: Oh, Christ. Now what?

Jack and Tom were beside him, pestering.

'Can we stay up? Please?'

'No.' He looked at them, as if from some distance. Tom, always better after food, still seemed a bit –

'You okay?' he asked him. Was no one okay in this household?

Tom nodded. 'I just feel a bit – '

'Time he was in bed,' said Oliver, sipping his drink at the table.

'Yes. You, too,' Robert told Jack. 'Go on, both of you, up you go.'

The boys went up, and the women came back. Claire had made a casserole from a piece of pork bought when the butcher was open, and frozen since. She served it with rice and the peas Jess had shelled in the morning, and they ate it appreciatively, hot food for once, making conversation, now they were all together, about nothing very much, thinking of separate conversations held earlier in the day, about everything.

Early morning, cool. Dark grey skeins of cloud dissolving above the mountains, the light growing paler, paler. Tom, deeply asleep,

258

got out of bed, and went walking.

Dawn came into the house through the cracks in the shutters; down in the village the first shutters were being opened and pushed back, the first kettles filled. Dogs got up from the steps and shook themselves, old men spat, a cock crowed. Tom went slowly downstairs.

It grew lighter. Down in the village Guida's father and uncle sat at the table in the corner of the kitchen, drinking from chipped mugs of coffee, dunking their maize bread, taking their time.

Tom reached the bottom of the stairs. He stopped, and went on again, into the kitchen, with its faint smell of gas. He crossed it, bare feet sticking on the worn brown lino; he came to the door, and went bump. Outside, sleeping beneath the steps to the garden, the dull-furred cat heard the sound and woke. She came up the steps to the door and miaowed, rustily. Tom heard her, a little less deeply asleep; he tugged at the catch, and the door swung open. From the threshold, the cat looked up at him. The air was cool and fresh. He went out, and past her, to the edge of the steps she had climbed, with their sheer drop down to the garden. His foot went forward, on to air; it came back again; he stopped, and went on again, turning aside, climbing the long flight of steps ahead, beneath the vines to the water tank and the upper path. It grew lighter; the cock crowed again.

Guida's father and uncle picked up their things and came out of the house, and down the steps at the side. They went round to the front and walked down the hill, three or four paces to the old plank door set beneath the house. They pushed at it, shifting dark sodden piles of straw, and went inside. There was a grunting, a food bowl was rattled. One of them brought in a bucket. One of them brought in a knife.

Tom bumped into the white iron table, and stopped; he walked on, brushing the tendrils of the vines, reaching the end of the path. He came to the bottom of the short flight of steps to the pool, and stopped; he climbed them; the cock crowed again. It grew lighter. The air above the pool was cooler: he sensed it. He woke.

How had he got there? What was he doing out here in the open? Right by the pool, where he might have fallen. He drew back,

259

looking at the greenish water, and away. Far across the valley stood the mountains. It was still very early, but they were growing lighter, and greener, and the sky went paler and paler as the sun began to rise. It was nice: a beautiful morning. What was he doing out here?

From down in the village came noises: doors opening, greetings, mats being shaken. And then something else. They heard it up in the house, too, and stirred in their sleep.

A hideous noise came up from the village: a squealing, an agonised squealing, and shouts. Stop it stop it stop it. More squealing, louder, and higher, desperate. A shriek.

And at that sound the lid in his head yawned open so widely, so horribly, that he couldn't possibly close it, no one could – wider wider help help the whole of him was opening no no no he reached out clutching for something to hold but there was only air and air couldn't hold you help and then he was gripped in a vice and he fell –

into the water help help and then nothing and down down down.

Oliver, who always woke early, had woken, and heard it again. He got up and went to the window, opening the shutters.

Dawn. An animal in agony. A splash.

He frowned. He went to the boys' room.

He ran.

Along the corridor, down the stairs, through the kitchen, the open door, a terrified cat leaping out of the way, up the steps and along the path and up the steps to the pool. Where he saw him, twitching and jerking and thrashing and flailing, and dived in, shouting, and hauled him in to the side. He heaved him out, and put him on his stomach, he pumped and pumped. Tom's face was blue, and the thrashing had stopped; his teeth were clamped tight and he did not move. Oliver went on pumping and sobbing and shouting; up in the house doors were flung open, and people flew down the stairs.

Tom lay still. Except for the ordinary, everyday noises, everything down in the village was quiet.

9

Footsteps, racing along the path.

Up the steps, stopping dead, seeing him lie there no no no –
'No! No!'

'He's alive.' Oliver was shaking from head to foot. 'He's alive.'
She flung herself down beside him.

Tom's face was blue, and his teeth were clamped shut, but he
was breathing, just. There was foam on his lips, flecked faintly
with blood, but no water came up and Oliver had stopped
pumping, turning him over, pressing his ear to his heart, which
was beating, just.

He stirred, the beating grew stronger. The vice on his teeth
unlocked abruptly: his jaw went slack and a little more blood and a
lot of saliva came out, on to the concrete. Oliver saw a swollen
tongue, frilled all round the edges.

He stirred again. Oliver and Frances gripped each other's
hands. Behind them, Robert and Claire and the children crowded
on the steps, still and silent, waiting. Tom's feet moved a little on
the concrete; his head moved a little; his eyelids fluttered, and
opened, and closed again.

'Tom – darling, darling – '

He tried to speak. He tried again. He opened his eyes and said:
'Mum – ' and pee went everywhere.

They carried him down to the house. They dried him and put
him in Jessica's bed, the nearest room, cool and dark.

'He went walking,' said Frances, white-faced, covering him up.
'He heard the pig and went walking – or the other way round . . .
He slipped and fell . . .'

'Much more than that,' said Oliver.

She looked at him. 'What do you mean?'

Robert ran down to the village and knocked on Guida's door. It
was half-past seven: she came to the door in concern, pointing

to her digital watch. She never came up to the house before eight.

'No,' he said, panting, thumbing the dictionary. 'Doctor – we need a doctor.'

She looked at the little worn book and led him down through the village. They passed her uncle's house, where the door set beneath was half open. Blood was running away down the cobbles from a bucket tipped up on its side; Robert, glancing, saw two men in shirtsleeves bending over something. He looked away.

They came, on the other side of the village, to a small house with a paved garden, a fig tree, a sleeping cat. They woke up the doctor, a small man, who spoke a little English. He came, bringing his bag, and his own dictionary, larger, with medical terms. He covered three villages, he told them, making conversation as they hurried back to the house; he had learned his English in Lisbon. Robert nodded, barely listening.

In the house, the doctor looked at Tom, who was sleeping; he listened to Oliver's description. They sat in the broad airy sitting-room and he turned the pages of his dictionary. Childish convulsion – fit, if you liked. Possibly the heat, possibly a high temperature. He had been running a fever? Nobody thought that he had. Possibly more than that. Perhaps to do with the sleepwalking, perhaps not. Had they noticed any . . . He went through the pages. Any absences? Times when he seemed to –

Yes, said Claire, there were often –

He dropped things, said Jessica. He dropped things and stood there.

There was something in the family? No history? No . . . epilepsy. The word, in his thick foreign accent, hung in the air. It was possible, yes. They must take him to a specialist in London.

They saw him off; he would come back, later, when Tom had woken. They sat in the dining-room in silence, drinking the coffee Guida had made them, heavily laced with brandy.

Tom slept and slept.

Claire and Jack and Jessica sat on the swing-seat. Peaches dropped to the garden below with a thump: one, two. Jack ran to pick them up.

'We can have them for lunch,' he said, bringing them up the

262

steps. 'Tom can have this one.' He tried the other: it was tasteless, and hard as a rock. He spat it out, grimacing, throwing it over the parapet. 'Ugh.'

'Never mind,' said Claire. 'It was a kind thought.'

He wandered over to the doors, looking inside. 'When's he going to wake up?'

'In a bit. He might have a headache, the doctor said.'

'He was nice, the doctor.'

'Yes.'

He came back, and sat down beside her. They rocked to and fro.

'When are we going home?'

'On Saturday.'

'When's Saturday?'

'The day after tomorrow. We're going to drive back across Spain, remember?'

'Mmm.'

They went on rocking.

'What's going to happen to him?' asked Jess.

'He'll go to a doctor in England.' Claire looked at her. 'Are you all right now? Getting over it?'

Jess shook her head. 'It was horrible.'

'Yes. Don't cry again.'

'I can't help it.'

Claire's arm went round her.

'I still don't understand it,' said Jack. 'I can't work it out.' His sandals scuffed on the tiles; he looked down, frowning.

The swing-seat creaked as it went back and forth, shadows from the leaves of the lemon trees played on the canopy. Robert appeared at the door, and saw them.

'How are we all?'

'Not very good,' said Claire.

Frances sat on a low chair in the corner of the room, watching him. He was breathing steadily now, not stirring or twitching, his face pale but his limbs deeply relaxed. The sleep of the dead – her stomach turned over: wake up wake up. She went to him, bending down, her hand hovering above his thatch of hair, dark-circled eyes, lips closed on the bruised and bitten tongue. Tom's chest rose and fell. She kissed him, and went back to her chair.

A cup of coffee, undrunk, gone cold, sat on the floor, with her cigarettes beside it, but although, while waiting for the doctor, and while he was here, she had smoked all the time, it hadn't crossed her mind to do so now: she had brought them in without thinking. The sash window was open at top and bottom; tendrils of dense creeper stirred. She leaned against the long-backed chair and shut her eyes. *Dora*, she wrote, *Tom has nearly died –*

Footsteps along the wooden corridor.

'Frances?'

She opened her eyes. He stood in the doorway, nodding towards the bed.

'I think he's all right. I've just checked him.'

Oliver went over, bent over as she had done. He sat on the chair by the bed; he took Tom's hand, and held it, quiet and still. He looked at her.

'Come here.'

Dora, I –

She got up from her own chair and went over. He held out his other hand, and she took it, and kissed it, and sat on his lap. His arm went round her, she rested her head on his shoulder. Footsteps came across the sitting-room. Robert appeared in the doorway, looking round.

'Oh. There you are.' He smiled. 'I think we'll push off for a bit, if that's all right with you. The children need a break . . . Or do you want us around?'

'No,' said Oliver, 'we'll be fine, we'll wait for the doctor.'

'Right, then. See you about five, I should think. We're just going to go for a drive, find somewhere for lunch . . .'

'Have a nice time,' said Frances. 'Thank you for all you've done.'

They looked at each other, and smiled.

'Give Tom our love when he wakes up.'

'We will.'

He went out again. Oliver swung the door to with his foot.

Frances and he sat kissing and kissing, hearing the others leave,

264

the car doors slam and the house go quiet; waiting for Tom to wake.

He sat on the edge of the bed, and the doctor asked him to do things. To follow a finger, as it moved past his eyes and away. To reach out and touch other fingers, each hand in turn, to wiggle his toes. His knee was tapped with a nice little hammer: his leg flew into the air. The doctor seemed to think that was good, but it was nothing to do with him, it just did it. The doctor looked into his eyes with a little bright light: could he see the lid in there? He had to shut his eyes, and touch his own nose with a finger – well of course he could do that, if you couldn't touch your own nose there must be something wrong with you. Very good, very good, said the doctor, and had he got a headache. He had got a headache, but it was his tongue that bothered him: it hurt and felt funny all round it. He stuck it out, and touched it; he slid off the bed.

'Tom – '

He went to the chest of drawers and tried to look into the mirror; he pulled it towards him, moving a jumble of boxes and bottles, Jessica's things, and stuck it out again. Ugh. How had it got like *that*?

'Tom, it'll soon be better – '

It reminded him of something, it made him think of something horrible. He frowned, prodding it. Ugh. *Ugh*.

'Leave it, darling, leave it – '

He leaned forward, right up to the mirror, sticking it out as far as it would go, seeing that funny dangling thing at the back of his throat get bigger. His elbow nudged something; one of Jessica's boxes, a little brass box with a hinge, fell to the floor and flew open, scattering beads –

He knew what it was, his tongue. The pig had had a lid, and when it opened, which it did very slowly, inside you could see –

something had happened to the pig –

stop it stop it stop it

He picked up the box and he threw it –

'Tom . . . Tom . . .'

Nobody shouting. Everyone being nice. They held him and held him. He cried and cried.

They drove to the cathedral town and parked in a side-street on the outskirts, near a funfair they remembered from last year.

'Can we go to it?' asked Jack. 'Can we go now?'

It was very hot. Petrol fumes made airy rainbows in and out of whirling spaceships.

'Later?' said Robert.

'Now? Please.'

'I think this morning they can have pretty much what they like,' said Claire. She shaded her eyes beneath the sunhat, and took out her sunglasses.

'True. Okay, then, who wants to do what?'

'Everything,' said Jack. 'Let's do them all.'

Shrieks came from thirty feet up: the roller-coaster rattled and swooped, and slowed down.

'That one. That one!'

It came to a halt, the engine whirring. Only two people per car.

'Want to come with me?' Robert asked Jess, digging escudos out of his pocket.

She looked away.

'You don't have to.'

'It's okay.' She climbed in with him, Claire and Jack behind. Jack bounced up and down.

'Wick-ed.'

'Hold on to the rail – '

They were off. Slowly, slowly, whoosh.

'Wheeee!'

'Heeelp!'

Faster faster faster. Their stomachs were left on the ground.

Jessica buried her head in Robert's shoulder; his arm went round her.

'Heeee-eeelp!'

It was brilliant, it was like flying, it was fast fast fast.

'You all right?' A bellow.

Her face pressed into him: she nodded, just.

They slowed, they were slowing, they stopped. He hugged her, she hugged him back. It was nice, but it wasn't the same.

'Phew.'

'Help me.' Claire was staggering, weak with relief.

'Wick-ed! Can we go again?'

'No.'

He helped Jessica out; she was laughing. They went across to the carousel. Snorting horses rose and fell, golden and white, with different-coloured reins and lovely music.

'Which one are you going to have?' Robert asked her when it stopped.

'This one.' He had silver and emerald reins; he looked distant and proud.

'Very good.'

She clambered on and smiled down at him. It wasn't the same, but it was okay.

They didn't do everything, but they did quite a bit. They went on the spaceships twice, the great wheel, and the children three times on the helter-skelter, Robert and Claire waiting at the bottom. Jack went on a little train roundabout, just for fun, and Jessica caught a floating fish and won a pink and green plastic necklace. She put it on. Against the white T-shirt it looked quite good.

'Okay, that's enough. Lunch?'

'I'm *starving*.'

They bought cans of Coke and drank as they walked across baking dusty ground to the wire fence, and out and up the steep street towards the centre. A tawny-coated bullock stood tethered to a lamppost, its eyes crawling with flies, a long line of drool swaying in the sun above an empty aluminium dish.

'If Tom saw that – ' said Jessica.

'He's right,' said Claire.

They looked for a tap.

'He can have some of my Coke,' said Jack.

'I don't think he'd like it.'

But there wasn't a tap, so he poured it in. The bullock slurped, and his sides heaved.

'Poor thing.'

They walked to the top of the hill, and found tables set out in a shady square. They ordered four different dishes so they could share them: rabbit and chicken and duck and –

267

'I think I'll have salad,' said Jess.

'We'll have salad anyway. With it.'

She shook her head. 'I don't feel like meat.'

They had more drinks while they waited, buying a bottle of mineral water for the bullock later, and Robert ate so much bread from the basket that he was almost full by the time lunch came. Well, that was what he said. He still managed to put away the whole plateful.

And ice cream. They had four different flavours, dipping in and out of each other's glass dishes.

'Yum-my.'

And coffee. And then they could hardly move. They sat watching other tourists, not many, but a few, and well-heeled Portuguese, sitting at other tables, talking and reading the papers. Scaffolding clanged on distant sites, motor bikes scorched down the main street. After a while, they pulled themselves together and made for the cathedral, the children groaning.

'There are shops all round it,' said Claire. 'We can buy presents. And it's cool inside.'

The narrow streets were heavy with shade; they looked into dark chemists with wonderful bottles of coloured water.

'You never see them at home any more. Such a shame.'

'Come *on*.'

The shops round the cathedral sold ceramics, brass picture frames and woven rugs. They bought things for Granny in Maidenhead and Granny and Grandpa in Derbyshire, and Jess bought a nice little box for her best friend at school.

'And something for Geoffrey and Linda,' said Claire.

Robert yawned. 'And then that's it.'

'And something for Tom,' said Jack.

'There's a thought. Is there anything here that he'd like?'

They searched and searched.

'I know! He'd like one of these.' He held up a tiny china cat, grey and white, curled up.

'Do you think?' Claire asked Robert.

They all thought he'd like it. The girl at the till wrapped everything in coarse brownish tissue paper and the bill came to four times the lunch.

'Never mind. It isn't as though we've been extravagant.'

'Isn't it?' Robert put a thin wallet back in his jacket, wiping sweat away. 'I've got to sit down.'

Pigeons crowded the cathedral steps; the carved doors were held back with enormous hooks. Inside it smelt of wood and polish and the pews were almost black. The children wandered, looking around; sun fell in from the door to the cloisters, and they went out, wandering through them.

'It's nice.'

'Don't you remember it? I told you it would be.' Claire sank into a pew with Robert. They sat watching old women in black get to their feet with difficulty, and a young guide take round a party. It was blessedly cool.

She put her head on his shoulder. A priest came out of a small side-door. She said: 'Robert?'

'Mmm?'

'When Tom – when we were waiting for him to come round . . .'

'Mmm?'

'Did you pray?'

'Oh, yes,' said Robert. 'I prayed.' His hand stroked her hair. 'I prayed like hell, didn't you?'

'Yes.'

Voices murmured in the aisle, dust danced on shafts of sunlight, as always.

One more day.

The weather was changing. Not much, nothing dramatic, but they could feel it, cooler today than yesterday, the morning breeze a little stronger. It was pleasant and refreshing: they all breathed a sigh of relief.

In the morning, Robert and Oliver went down to the cellar, to bring up the shepherd's cloak. The children followed, and Frances and Claire came after them.

It stood in the corner, where they had left it, dark and enormous beneath the cobwebby window. Everything had happened since they brought it down here, and everyone was different from then. Jessica did not prance about and sing, and when Oliver carefully

269

lifted the hat off and made, smiling, to put it on her head, she moved away.

'No, thanks.'

Frances and Claire took the cloak off, but Robert no longer thought about handmaidens, and two women together, in quite the same way, and he looked at them, smiling at each other as one took the shoulders and dangling sleeves and the other the great fall of cloak itself, and he wondered. He found himself wondering.

Jack did not make for the box of toys and race all the cars up and down. He stood watching Tom, who was standing in the far corner. The doctor had given Tom some medicine, Claire told him, to – well, to calm him, and help his head. He looked sort of sleepy and out of it. He'd liked the cat, though, he could tell.

'Are you feeling better?' asked Jack.

'What?' He stood in the corner, and watched them, taking it all to bits. Its face had gone: under the hat there was nothing, only that long thin neck with a knob on. How could you hide your own face? Somehow it hid it, and only put it back when the hat was on. They were up-ending the whole thing now, turning its body on its side: it groaned. Good.

'Jessica?' said Frances. 'Just keep an eye, will you, while we take it upstairs?' She nodded towards Tom; Jessica nodded back.

'Right,' said Robert to Oliver.

'Right.'

They lifted it, they began to climb the stairs. The wooden stand bumped and scraped; behind them the straw went rustle rustle rustle.

Jack went up after them.

Tom went to say goodbye to the house.

Jessica followed him.

The door was still open, from last time. He stood there looking at it, breathing – how? His breathing was different today, he could feel it. Slower. He felt slower. He looked at the people, all broken up, and something behind him moved. He jumped. Because everything was slow it wasn't an ordinary jump, it was all sort of heavy and thick inside him.

'Sorry,' said Jessica. 'I didn't mean to frighten you.' She was being kind, too. 'Is this your house, Tom? It's nice.'

'A lot of people died in it,' he said.

'What?'

'They were all very wicked,' he said, 'and I had to punish them.' He picked up all the broken bones and showed her. 'See? I left them to starve, that was their punishment, and then, when they still weren't sorry, I had to chop their legs off, and their arms. I don't know if they had lids, but I know the pig had one, and that's dead, too, isn't it? They don't protect you from anything, do they?'

Why was she looking at him like that?

'It's all right,' he said, as he swung the front of the house to, and fastened the catch. 'You don't have to worry about them now, they're dead. Nothing can get you once you're dead.'

Time to pack up. It seemed to take for ever.

'Surely we didn't bring all this stuff?'

'We need some clean things for Spain . . .'

Up at the water tank, beneath dark trails of ivy, Guida washed and washed, and hung everything up in the sun. Bulging cases were dragged down the stairs and heaved into the boot, paperbacks stuffed into corners, a litter of tapes in between the front seats.

Upstairs, Frances folded everything neatly, and zipped up her case. Tom sat in the corner, watching. The little grey cat was curled up in his pocket, sleeping well. She liked the afternoons. Frances put her case down, next to Oliver's, and went through all the drawers, just in case. Nothing.

'Right, then,' she said to Tom. 'Your things now.' She held out her hand; they went along the landing to his room, stopping to straighten the runner.

'It'll only ruck up again,' he said.

'I know.'

Claire had packed all Jack's things, and gone downstairs with his case. There was nobody up here now. The shutters of the bedroom were open, since no one was resting today and the weather had changed; the room, with its twin cotton bedspreads, bare floorboards, old chest of drawers and yellow chair, was sunny and warm. Frances began to pull open drawers; Tom went to the

271

window. Children were running about down in the threshing yard, pushing the cart up and down. He called and waved; they waved back, and went on playing. Far beyond, the mountains were hazy; above them, an aeroplane circled and climbed.

Frances was packing shorts and shirts and swimming trunks.

'You've grown out of almost all this, haven't you? Time for some new clothes when we get back.' He didn't answer. 'Tom?'

'Yes?'

'Feeling all right?' She came up beside him, and he rested his head against her. Their arms went round each other; they stood looking out at the view. The river wound on and on through the maize fields: the deepest yellow, the palest blue, on and on, round the bend and away out of sight, going on for ever and ever.

In the late afternoon, they all went down to the village. They sat beneath the awning of vines outside the little café, sipping tea and lemonade, watching, for the last time, their corner of the world go by.

Oliver leaned back in his chair, his hands behind his head. Jessica looked at him, and then away. He said: 'One last walk. Just a short one. Anyone interested?'

'Where?'

'Not sure, don't mind.' He leaned forward again, and his hand rested on Tom's. 'How about you? Would you like to come for a walk?'

He turned the little cat over and over; he brought her out to sit on the table, joining in.

Would you like to come? he asked her.

She said she would. So did Frances. Good.

'I tell you what,' said Robert. 'I could go and get the car and drive you three up to a place we used to go last year. Claire? That path that comes back from the next village?' He pointed up the road, towards the market town. 'It isn't very far, maybe a mile. And you come back past the frog place. Remember?' They remembered. 'Tom? Do you think you could manage a mile?'

'How far is a mile?'

'Good question.'

Robert went back to the house, and got the car. He drove them, because two miles there and back was too far for Tom at the moment, everyone knew that, up to a village with brown shiny tiles on the walls and bright flowery curtains. He pointed out the mountain path, and said he would see them back at the house in an hour, or send out a party.

'Thanks.'

They watched the car winding away down the hill.

Then they entered the mouth of the path, lined with bushes at first, which thinned out as they climbed through the trees, until they were walking on a clear and open piece of land which sloped gently down towards their own village. Below they could see the flowery meadow, the path leading past the ruined house, the damp little fields criss-crossed with ditches. Unharnessed bullocks were moving slowly through one of them; as they drew near they could hear the tinkling bells, the sound of them grazing, moving slowly through the long grass, swish swish swish.

'It's lovely,' said Tom.

'Isn't it?'

He was walking between them, a hand each. They could see, across the other side of the path from the oxen, the houses in their small flagged gardens, with fern and moss and ivy growing, and one or two people pottering about. Tom frowned.

'I've been here before.'

'Yes. We all have. Look, we all had our picnic there – see? That's where you and Jack caught the frog, remember?'

He remembered.

'Tom. Things are a bit better now. Yes?'

He turned the little cat over and over. 'Mmm.'

They walked on; he wandered ahead, showing things to her, telling her about everything: she was a good listener. Oliver and Frances watched him, walking with their arms round each other.

'Things are a bit better?' he asked.

'Yes.'

'Want to tell me anything?'

'One day.'

Ahead, Tom was walking slowly, murmuring things, making noises. Not quite so many noises.

'What about you?' she asked.

273

'A few thoughts.'

'Do you want to tell me?'

'One day.'

The sun was slipping towards the mountains; the air grew cooler, cooler. She thought of the long conversation she'd had with Robert, walking through the pine woods in the heat of the day. Such a little while ago. She thought of how it had ended:

An Alice word. It means whatever you choose it to mean, neither more nor less. Like God, now I come to think of it . . .

'Oliver? When – when it happened – when you found him – did you think it was an act of God? That you got there in time?'

'Difficult not to. But no, not when I thought about it later.'

'Why?'

'Too many people don't get there in time,' he said. 'Why should we be spared?' He paused. 'Not that I wasn't grateful.'

She was silent.

'But did you pray?'

'Oh yes,' he said. 'I prayed. Wouldn't anyone?'

They walked on, slowly, hearing the bell on the church clock chime four arbitrary strokes.

The last morning. Everything in a muddle.

Tom, Jack and Frances went to say goodbye to the hens. Jessica helped Claire clear out the fridge and make a leftovers picnic for the journey. Robert stuffed a wedge of escudos into an envelope and went to look for Guida.

She was upstairs, stripping the beds. They were just going to do that, no need for her –

'Guida?'

He stood on the landing. A pile of sheets fell softly to the floor in the boys' room; she came out in her denim skirt and flip-flops.

'I – ' He held out the envelope; she came over and took it.

'*Obrigado*,' he said. 'You've been wonderful. *Marvilhoso*. *Obrigado*.'

She shook her head, smiling. '*Marvilhosa*,' she said. '*Obrigada*.'

'What?'

'*Obrigada* – for the woman, yes?'

'Ah, yes,' he said. 'For the woman. Quite right.'

They stood on the sunlit landing, smiling at each other.

Leaves stirred in the peach tree outside the window; another peach fell to the ground.

'Well,' he said.

She kissed him on the cheek and fled.

Well well well.

The car was packed; Oliver's, Frances's and Tom's suitcases all stood up by the gate on the mountain road, waiting for the taxi. The weather had changed: definitely cooler. A few dry leaves blew on to the terrace and danced across the tiles. Everyone was out there, saying goodbye.

'Thank you for everything – '

'Thank you for coming – '

'Don't say that. I'm sorry – '

'He's all right. I hope so, anyway. That's the main thing – '

'Yes. We're phoning the doctor as soon as we get home.'

'Phone us, let us know – '

'We will.'

They shook hands, they hugged and kissed.

Oliver went over to Jessica. 'Goodbye, Jessica.'

'Goodbye. I'm glad Tom – '

'Thank you.' He put his hand on her arm; he kissed her cheek. She looked at him quickly and then away.

Tom stood on the threshold of the tall white doors, looking in to the sitting-room. Sun fell on to the floorboards and on to the shepherd's cloak. The straw looked yellow and warm. The hat was tilted forward a bit, as if it was asleep.

'Tom? Can I have a kiss?' That was Claire. He let her. He let all of them. What a fuss.

The taxi hooted up at the gate: they ran.

The driver was small and fat with a medallion at his neck. A photograph of his son in a plastic envelope was sellotaped to the dashboard; the Virgin Mary swung from a little piece of string. He helped them to put all the cases in the boot; they all climbed in; doors banged.

'Goodbye, goodbye . . .'

They waved and waved.

Everyone was waiting, out in the car. Claire made one last check on the house, going round all the empty rooms. It was quiet, it felt hushed, even. She'd never had it all to herself before. Outside, up at the water tank, Guida was washing all their sheets and pillowcases, using a huge bar of yellow soap. The water, as always, poured and poured.

Well. That was it. She checked all the bedrooms, she went slowly down the stairs, and into the airy sitting-room. The tall white doors to the terrace were open, a few more leaves skittered across the tiles.

Everything had happened in this house. Someone, on this holiday, had nearly died.

But he hadn't died, he had been saved. And nothing, in the end, had been taken away from her; nor did she feel that her life was over. She stood there, all by herself, and she felt like offering up a prayer. But then the car horn sounded, two impatient notes, and she crossed to the doors and closed them carefully. She went out, along the wooden corridor, through the kitchen, leaving a small dish of scraps for the cat, saying goodbye to Guida and going down through the garden, and out to the car.

'What have you been *doing*?'

She got in next to Robert; they drove away. Slowly through the village, then gaining speed.

'Let's have some music,' he said.

'Sinatra.'

Everyone groaned. 'Not *again*.'

She took no notice, slotting the tape in, pressing the button. The car was filled with Sinatra: they all began to sing.

After a while, Jessica stopped. She sat with her head pressed up to the window, looking out over the blue-green mountainside, the valley and the winding river, getting smaller, smaller, as they climbed.

And then I have to spoil it all
by saying something stupid, like I love you . . .

She shut her eyes, and the music floated through her, and out through the open window as they drove away.

*

Tom sat between them, waiting for lunch. Behind them, the trolley rattled and shook, coming along the aisle, but the plane was flying smoothly, and the little cat liked it. She sat on the plastic tray in front of him, waiting for her lunch, too.

Frances and Oliver looked at each other, over his head.

'He seems fine.'

'Yes. You okay?'

He nodded, and looked at his watch, returned to his book while he waited.

Frances looked out of the window. They were flying above the clouds: a thick, sunlit landscape of white, of such apparent substance and solidity that it was hard to believe it would not break your fall. If you opened the door of the plane and stepped out – surely you could walk upon those hills and along those valleys, surely you would be safe.

The plane flew steadily on. Far below them, far beneath the cloud, the mountains of Portugal were growing smaller and smaller, miles away. She saw before her the house, the garden, the darkness of the night, a cool breeze stirring the vines as she burned her letter, and Tom, coming up behind her, blindly seeking her out.

I shall be this and I shall be that, and tomorrow everything will be –

She saw him, lying as still as death at the side of the pool, his face blue and his teeth clamped shut; moving, twitching, trying to say her name.

Dora knew about things, she knew what was what. It sounded so simple, and it went so deep –

Dora, wrote Frances, leaning back, closing her eyes, seeing before her once again that oh, so lovely face, *beloved Dora, help me to make it right*.

KEEPING SECRETS

Sue Gee

'In *Keeping Secrets*, Sue Gee presents a relationship fraught with old scores.

Alice, the younger girl, was a tearaway but has settled into a happy marriage – until Hilda announces she is pregnant by a married man.

The story of the sisters' rivalry – plus the lonely alcoholism of the married man's wife – makes a compelling read.' *Today*

A Century Hardback

MY LIFE AS A WHALE

Dyan Sheldon

'Astonishing wit, brio . . . outrageously funny' *New York Times Book Review*

'At the summer of 1986, some stockbroker in the Village and I were the only two fully operational, healthy, solvent, heterosexual males within, shall we say, a twenty-mile radius of New York city, whose sell-by date had not yet expired.'

At thirty-four and single, Michael Householder finds he is acquiring the notoriety and appeal reserved for rock stars and serial killers. He finds himself as hunted as the finback whale – especially after his lover, Marissa Alzunco, packs her bags.

'A talent to amuse' *Sunday Times*

DORA

Polly Devlin

Can marriage work, with affection and effort, can it age without decaying?

Searching through her Dublin girlhood and glossy Bloomsbury twenties, through the dark, rich, complicated patterns of life with husband and children in the rooms and gardens of Keep Hall in Suffolk, and in a strange revisited Ireland, Dora attempts to discover what it is that binds us – wives, husbands, lovers and children – to each other.

'Tart and funny . . a celebration of that unsung virtue – the ability to forget the unforgettable, forgive the unforgivable, and invisibly mend the broken heart.' *Observer*

THE INFERNO CORRIDOR

Emma Cave

Together four young women – beautiful, promiscuous Ruth, ambitious Janet, mysterious Castalia and romantic Sally – walk down the 'Inferno Corridor' on their first night at Oxford.

Fifteen years later, the bonds of love, hate, malice and rivalry that unite them have survived marriages, careers, affairs. Each of them has walked her own 'Inferno Corridor' of hopeless love, stifling marriages, dark alleys and burning cages.

But which of them will commit a dreadful crime and which will take a truly infernal revenge?

TELLING ONLY LIES
Jessica Mann

An accidental remark on a television programme lands novelist Anne Medlicott in a potentially very damaging libel suit. The programme is about Nazi sympathisers in England during the last war. The other two guests are Professor Sir Hans Halm, an exile from Germany and the painter, Perdita Whitchurch.

Anne has known both people since childhood, or has she? Forced out of the comfortable cocoon which she has woven around her life, Anne faces truths which are considerably harsher, more painful – and more healing – than she had ever imagined.

DOMESTIC PLEASURES
Beth Gutcheon

When Raymond, Martha's ex-husband, dies in a plane crash, Martha never expected that he would leave his estate to their sixteen-year-old son – but then she never expected to fall in love with conventional three-piece-suited Charlie, her husband's executor, either. And after twenty years of failed marriages, rupture and pain, not to mention the excess baggage of their own children, Martha and Charlie find it hard to begin all over again.

THE MOUNTAIN IS YOUNG

Han Suyin

Abandoning her passionless marriage to colonial civil servant, John Ford, Ann journeys to Kathmandu, land of gods, temples and snow peaks in a voyage of self-discovery and spiritual awakening.

Against the erotic and deeply mystical backdrop of Kathmandu she learns the reality of love, with its pain and sacrifice. Here she meets the majestic Unni Mennon, worshipped by his own people, resented by the Europeans. And as they struggle against the rigid morality of European colonial standards and the man-made perversion of racial discrimination, their remarkable story – and the story of Kathmandu – unfolds.

A MANY-SPLENDOURED THING

Han Suyin

A love story which transcends the cultural and political gulf between East and West. Han Suyin's autobiographical exploration of love is a magnificent memorial to a romance plagued by adversity which ends in tragedy.

Beautiful Eurasian doctor Han Suyin's sympathies lie with China, on the brink of communist revolution. In the cosmopolitan setting of Hong Kong, she meets and falls in love with Mark Elliott, an English journalist steeped in the Western tradition. But as their love triumphs over racial discrimination, political upheaval and their conflicting intellectual heritages, the shadow of Korea looms . . .

QUEEN OF THE WITCHES

Jessica Berens

'Genuinely bewitching' Stephen Fry

Sheenah is High Priestess of the Divine Order of Isis and Director of the Witches' Liberation League. She lives in Shepherd's Bush with her huge feline familiar, Carry, an animal whose vile mood swings are controlled by lithium.

Sheenah is keen to be elected to the prestigious post of Queen of the Witches.

But Sheenah has a rival – Myra, her arch enemy and nemesis, Clan Mistress and Wiccan Mother of the South London Sisters Of Diana.

Myra, dark, soignee, green-eyed, five years younger than Sheenah, had been responsible for the break-up of her marriage to the Great Haroldo, and now Myra is prepared to resort to the dark arts to get what she wants.

Soon to be published

DANGEROUS DANCING

Julie Welch

As founder member Millie Francis dies after a mysterious car crash in 1989, the novel looks back over two decades in the lives of the dancers who have made up the changing cast: sexy, businesslike Tina and vulnerable, ethereal Collette, pious Juliet and ratty, resilient Alexa; Janey and Lily and machiavellian Joanna-Mary; Manon who was a junior javelin champion; and half-orphaned Florence from the wild Atlantic coast of France, whose dream was to dance with those English girls.

Celebrating their friendships and enmities, their hopes and longings, *Dangerous Dancing* conjures up every brash detail of their lives – the humour and bitchiness, the men, disastrous or gorgeous, the seedy provincial tours, their moments of glory.

OTHER ARROW TITLES